KEW HOUSE SCHOOL LI

R03455F505

FOU

are to be returned on or before

...below.

A Football Murder Mystery

Will J Robson

Foul

Copyright © 2014 by Will J Robson

ISBN: 978-1499315042

All rights reserved. No part of this publication may be reproduced, stored in a retrieval system, or transmitted, in any form or in any means – by electronic, mechanical, photocopying, recording or otherwise – without prior written permission.

This is a work of fiction. Names, characters, businesses, places, events and incidents are either the products of the author's imagination or used in a fictitious manner. Any resemblance to actual persons, living or dead, or actual events is purely coincidental.

Cover Design Copyright © 2014 by Josie Robson

Book design and production by Josie Robson, www.josiebrainfroth.wordpress.com

For Josie

Foreword by ghost-writer Will J Robson

When Brian first approached me to be the ghost-writer for this book, I have to admit I thought I was going to refuse him. I'd heard about what had happened through the papers, on the news, but to me it was no more than trashy tabloid gossip. As soon as I heard him tell his side of the story, I knew I was going to help him to write it.

Let's be clear, football is not my thing. Footballers even less so. While I'd written footballers' autobiographies before, it had always been for the money. Brian told me up front that he had no money. He also told me that the book he needed people to read was going to be very different to the formulaic pulp most footballers released just in time for the Christmas rush. This had to be 'a whole different kennel of fish', he insisted.

In that first meeting, as he described to me what he'd achieved in football and the type of life he led off the pitch, I realised that he'd literally had the world at his feet. From a deprived part of the country, he'd become one of the wealthiest and well-known people in the UK, if not the planet. All because he could kick a ball well.

At 26 he'd won every trophy on offer at club level and had 48 England caps, 9 of those as captain. He was revered by everyone. Away from the pitch, he'd never had anyone to tell him what he could or couldn't do. After all, by the age of 16 he was pulling in more money in a month than most people do in a year.

As I thought about the type of reality he must have known, it was obvious what an insane, out-of-touch life he'd led. And I could tell he'd been just as self-serving and loathsome as most of the other people in football I'd met. But the thing about Brian was that he'd been at the top. Then he'd fallen. Hard.

1

On the 30th August 2010, he was arrested and charged for the murder of Stevie Hurst, his supposed best friend. His teammate at both club and national level. It was game over. The press went wild. Within a matter of days he'd lost everything: his club contract, his international captaincy, his sponsorship deals. He was disowned by his wife, kids, parents – his whole family. The backlash was as vicious as it was entire.

I remember being disgusted that he'd been found not guilty at the court case. Putting it down to the rich and powerful being able to make their own rules. Not really appreciating that the verdict was only delivered after he'd spent seven months in prison awaiting trial. A prison stretch that had changed him.

When he first came to see me, Brian didn't know who had set him up. He was close, but he wasn't sure how the story was going to play out; the closer he got the more he wanted to start getting the story down on paper as soon as possible. Which is where I came in. And as well as getting me to write it down so he didn't forget what had happened, he also wanted a type of insurance policy. A way of safeguarding the evidence he was gathering.

After weeks of interviews with Brian and months of writing, Foul is now ready. It's a book that looks at the life of a footballer at the top of his profession in the 21st century and it does so without pulling its punches or sugar-coating anything. It looks at the fame, the games, the highs, the lows, the wins, the losses. But more than that, it looks at mankind's enduring obsession with life, death and most importantly football, through the incredible journey of one man. Or something like that.

Chapter 1

The morning I found out about Stevie I was training. As always. For some reason I remember training quite well that day. I mean I like training. I always have. And all my coaches, right from back when I was a lad, are going to tell you that. But when you're doing the same things every day, after a while it all blurs into one.

But that morning I've got a much clearer memory of training than normal. Perhaps because of what happened after, perhaps because I was on fire and banging in goals left, right and centre - as a few of my teammates have been quoted as saying. Either way, when I think back to that session, rifling shot after shot into the back of the net, I can see it as clear as day.

It was either a Monday or a Tuesday. We'd played a match on either the Saturday or Sunday – now that they keep changing fixtures for the TV it's hard to keep track. We'd won and we'd won well although I hadn't netted again. Counting last season that made it ten games in a row and not scoring was getting to me a little.

That day, the Gaffer just got us playing five-a-side. With all the money that had come into the club that summer there'd been changes all over United. From board level, to the team. We'd brought about seven first-team guys in, with more rumoured to be on the way, and we'd picked up about eight younger lads, who were expected to start in the reserves. When new faces come in, it can take time to get to know each other and build up that trust you need to really play well on the park. So that's why the Gaffer just wanted us to have a laugh. Everyone loves a bit of five-a-side. It's a good way to show what you can do on the ball and the manager just wants you to take it easy.

I had a stormer. The tackles I put in were all thumpers. On the pitch I sometimes got a bit of stick for going into tackles too hard. The thing is that's what I'd always done, even in training. I can't help it. That's me, I give everything my all. I got stuck into a couple of the new boys, catching them a bit late. But I managed to laugh it off. That's one of the things I've learnt from playing international matches and in Europe – how to calm people down even if you don't speak their language. And anyway, that's all part and parcel of welcoming a new signing, isn't it? Letting them know they're in England now with a nice strong welcome. I smashed in a volley into the top-corner. Sweet as you like. I ran away in mock celebration - two thumbs up and my tongue out which is my trademark. I turned from saluting my made-up fans and a few of the guys were shaking their heads. They know what I'm like. A bit of nutter I suppose. I looked at Shags.

"Great goal, Bri," he said giving me a thumbs up, "but go easy on the new lads, eh? They're on our side, remember? Shit 'em up, course you should, but not too much."

Shags is just like me really. A great bloke, even though he is a bit older. He looked after me when I joined United.

The manager pulled me off. He does it a lot. I could tell he was angry. Because of his age, he's got all these wrinkles that make him look like he's always grumpy and his red cheeks make him look drunk. When he thinks I'm messing around he lets me know, but I'm sure he's always had a soft-spot for me.

"What the f*ck are you messing around for you daft c*nt?"

I almost laughed. I bowed my head.

"Stupid pr*ck aren't you? So you score a nice volley, well done, have a gold star, a lollypop and go home and s*ck your teddy-bear's c*ck like

4

when you were a b*stard kid, because if you're not doing the business on the f*cking pitch when it matters you've got no right to prance around like a wet-a*sed f*cking school girl, have you? Sort your f*cking head out, you stupid f*cking brain-dead little tw*t-faced-pr*ck of a c*nt."

Normally I would have been annoyed. Possibly even argued back. Though having a go at the Gaffer and the coaches was something I'd been trying to cut down on. I guess it's because I'm so passionate, like I've said. Anyway, I was about to say something when I felt my mobile go.

I know what you're thinking. Mobile? On the training ground? Well, I know I shouldn't really have had it and the Gaffer had banned them, but I was captain of the country and time was ripe for me to cash in.

In terms of sponsors and deals it's a competitive place out there. There's a pool of about twenty who get offered the high-end work. After I lost out on a really, really important gig – it was for me to be the face of a brand of that disgusting raw fish stuff in Japan – I realised I had to be able to get to a phone at all times. I can't say which player told me about it, but there's a way of sewing a pocket into your training top just under your armpit. It keeps it well-hidden and it's easy to feel when it vibrates. I know it probably sounds stupid but if you've ever missed out on a million quid or more because you can't take a call, you'll understand when I say that asking your wife, your girlfriend or Nana to do some sewing isn't necessarily a big deal.

Turning away from the Gaffer and pretending to sort out my shoe-lace I checked to see who was calling. It was May, Stevie's girlfriend. Well, wife actually, I kept forgetting they'd got married. I was best man.

I was a bit angry she was calling me at training; in case Stevie had been with me. Then I realised I hadn't even seen him that morning. Sometimes the 'keepers go off and train together but I hadn't seen him at all.

I was just about to answer her, tell her not to risk calling me at training, when I felt a cold, strong hand round my neck.

"Brian, I can't f*cking understand you sometimes. Do you think I don't f*cking know you keep that b*stard phone in your bloody arm-pit? Do I look like your Mother's tw*t? Do you think I've got cows ars*hole for eyes? That's a fine. No argument. Shut it down and get out on the pitch."

A fine was £1,000 to a charity of his choice. I swore. At least he hadn't stopped me playing. Smiling as I ran onto the pitch I went straight into the back of one of the new boys and the Gaffer hauled me off and fined me again. I won't repeat what he said but I took it in good humour.

It was when we were leaving the training pitches to shower that I first thought something big might be happening with Stevie. The front gates were full of press and camera-crews. I said that it must be about Stevie to Shags. That he must have signed for someone.

"Nah," Shags said, "They're here about something else."

"How do you know?" I asked, curious, as I knew Stevie and Shags had the same agent, Tony Gibbs.

"Stevie's a 'keeper, nobody gives a shit about 'keepers. Look how many of them there are. Maybe if you got bought by someone this many people would give a f*ck, maybe…and f*ck knows why seeing as you're no f*ckin' good, just lucky," I laughed at Shags' joke and reckoned he must be right. "Nah," he continued, "No way this is about Stevie moving clubs."

"Have you heard anything then, about Stevie moving…from Tony?"

"Tony? Jesus, the man won't f*ckin' shut up about it. It's all he's been talking about for a while but I spoke to him this morning, he would have said if there'd finally been a breakthrough. He's so desperate for it to happen..."

"Desperate?"

"Let's just say the money Tony would get from Stevie being sold would go a long way to helping him settle with his ex-wife. He needs some readies sharpish..."

As I was about to go into the gym I stopped for a moment and looked at the press. There were more than when we were at the World Cup. It crossed my mind that I had been sold. When I'd met the new owner there'd been something funny about the way he looked at me. Some of the papers had been saying he only wanted the club's money and as one of their biggest assets, he might cash in on me. I wondered how much I might have gone for. People say it can weigh on your mind if you get sold for too much money. When I got bought by United for 20 million I just thought it was cool.

I could even hear a helicopter. I knew I was probably on camera, possibly being shown live on TV. They were shouting at me, almost like they were angry. In general, before what happened, I'd always had an ok relationship with the press. You have to keep them on side; that was one of the most important lessons I'd learnt in football. But even though they knew I wasn't allowed to give interviews during training sessions, that morning they were really pushing for me to come over. I almost did, simply because there was something so unusual about the way they were asking. I couldn't put my finger on it.

When the gym door was kicked open, it made such a loud noise I thought it was the Gaffer coming to have a go. It was Shags. He grabbed me by the arm and pulled me inside and pushed me into the meeting room. It was full. No-one was talking. They were glued to the plasma screens.

Chapter 2

The first day I actually met Stevie he had a nightmare. That night I had one about him. It was strange really, silly. At the time you don't know any better, do you? Although my Mum still says I don't know any better. Still, what does she know? I guess I'm just good at not taking myself seriously. You absolutely have to be like that as a professional footballer.

Let me explain. It was a 5-a-side tournament for youth teams. Stevie was playing for United, I turned out for Town and we met in the final. I was up front and even back then I liked to check out the goalie I was going to be facing. I felt nervous. Not loads, but the right amount.

As I was jumping up and down ready to go, I watched as Stevie – who a few of my coaches had said was the best goalie in the country for his age – strolled into his net. He looked so relaxed that I remember feeling unsettled. Who was this guy? He was meant to be so good, but he looked like he didn't have a care in the world.

Seeing him like that made me angry. We murdered them and I absolutely killed Stevie. I got four goals as we won 6-1. My finishing was really, really good and I gave him no chance. And Stevie? This big, bright hope? I was ecstatic at first at what I'd done to him. I'd made this guy look ordinary when he was meant to be the best. So it should have been me who went home to eat microwave pizza and microwave chips (still my favourite treat), play computers with my brothers and cousins and enjoy the win.

The thing was, almost as soon as the match was over, he was laughing. At the final whistle you could tell his team were gutted. A couple were even crying. But not Stevie. When I shook his hand, he had this big grin on his face. There wasn't the slightest hint of defeat, or shame or anger. It killed my good mood.

'Does he not know how important it is?' I asked myself over and over again as I collected my North East Academies Under 10s 5-a-side medal.

You see at that age there was nothing I wanted to do except play football. I wasn't very good at school because it just didn't interest me. Around the estate I didn't know one person who enjoyed their job, if they had one, apart from my Auntie Cathie. I don't know what she did though. To me, the only good thing in life was football.

As I had my picture taken for scoring the most goals in the tournament, out of the corner of my eye all I could see was Stevie and his family playing with their dog in the car-park. I knew if I'd lost 6-1, I would have felt terrible for ages. Not to mention how angry my Dad would have been.

Obviously when I lost I was gutted, but knowing my Dad would be in a bad mood was sometimes worse. I don't blame my Dad. He just wanted the best for me, but he made sure I knew when he thought I'd let myself down. As a kid he'd had trials for Town but his Dad, my Granddad, was a bit of a drinker and wouldn't always bother making sure my Dad got to the sessions on time. After a couple of months he was asked not to come back. He was Town mad, always had been, and I think it hit him hard not to make it.

9

That's why my Dad gave everything to get me to the top. Even when he did have a job, he made sure someone could get me to training. When he was unemployed he took me himself - in the car if it was working, on the bus otherwise (which was most of the time seeing as he never had much luck with cars until I bought him his BMW). On the way to training my Dad would invent situations for me to go through.

"You're one-on-one with a keeper, 10 yards from the box, pretty central, the goalie's rushing out and is already past the penalty spot, in your ear you can hear the big central defender who's got a good slide tackle a couple of paces behind you, and to your left is the full-back who's decided to try and get to the goal-line in case you get a shot off....what do you do?"

"One touch, feint right, then chip the 'keeper over his left shoulder."

"One bounce and in? Could work, son, could work, got to weight it right though, got to make sure."

So with all that in my head, I guess, I just couldn't understand how someone could seem so carefree after losing.

As Stevie got into his family car, Dad and me were at the bus-stop waiting to get home. Stevie saw me and gave me this big, toothy grin, "See ya," he said.

I didn't know what to say. His big smile stayed in my head as my Dad chatted excitedly about how to be even better next time. Despite the win, I felt empty and confused and all the time I could see that big smile even though he'd lost! It was so bad I didn't finish my three mini pizzas even though Mum had put extra cheese and ketchup on because I'd won.

And then, that night, I had a nightmare. It was of Stevie laughing, grinning and not stopping. I begged, pleaded, shouted, got violent, told

10

jokes, did some football tricks, all the stuff I normally did to get what I wanted, but he just kept grinning.

The whole house was awake by the time I woke up. My Mum was by my bed telling me it was all right, my Dad kept asking me what it had been about. I didn't say. At the time, apart from feeling a bit silly about being scared by another lad smiling, I didn't know what to make of it. I just did what I'd always done when I was worried. Played football.

After that tournament I went from strength to strength and the next time I saw Stevie it was when we first got our international call-ups together. As we were the youngest we were put in the same room together and from that time on were best mates. When I moved to United we got even closer.

And it wasn't really until that morning when Shags showed me into the meeting room, that I even thought about that nightmare again. In fact, it was the first thing that entered my head when I heard the news about Stevie, despite what the prosecuting lawyers said.

In the meeting room the news was on. The sports news as usual. Half the TV was showing footage of our training ground, and in fact the pictures were of me literally just going inside the gym a minute before. The other half of the screen was of an overturned black 4x4 at the side of a road. Underneath was a headline: 'Footballer's Car Found Crashed'.

I instantly recognised it as Stevie's car. As I studied the picture more I realised I'd driven down that same road that very morning; going from his house into town.

Then a picture of Stevie flashed up. Even though it was a recent one – actually from his wedding – the grin was exactly the same as the one that had haunted me in my nightmare when I was a boy.

I thought he was dead.

"F*ck," I shouted.

People turned.

"It's ok," Shags said, "Maybe. They don't know anything for sure yet."

"Ok?" I said, my hands trembling, my stomach feeling like I was going to be sick, "How can it be ok?"

"They haven't found him...he's missing....look..."

Shags was right, I hadn't read the screen properly. It was his car, it was in a bad way and it looked like it had been a bad crash, but there was no body. No-one knew where Stevie was.

Chapter 3

Feeling dizzy, I wanted to get out of the room, to find some space.

"Look, lads," our assistant manager Ray said, "It's almost 12, let's call it a day. This stuff with Stevie isn't good but he'll turn up. Keep your minds on the game tomorrow night. Watch your DVDs at home and make sure you know what you're going to have to do. We'll be in touch if anything changes, and let's hope Stevie's ok, we're told there's no blood in the car so he must be alright...."

Everyone else was rooted to the spot, watching the news. My mind was racing. I decided the best way to leave was to pretend I had a phone call. I put my mobile to my ear and began to nod and talk as I left the room.

"Hello....Brian...." said a woman.

I swiveled. I was alone in the corridor. Where was she? My heart almost stopped before I realised it was coming from my phone. I must have accepted the call with the side of my new hair-band before it even had time to ring.

"Brian...? Brian?"

To compose myself I had to get in front of a mirror. I moved through to the changing rooms and took the hair-band out so I could shake my long, blond hair. I loved my new look. It helped calm me. Stevie was always, always on at me for looking like a p*ff; I put it down to jealously every time. Out of the two of us, I was the ladies' man. He knew that.

"Brian, are you there? Brian! For god's sake! Talk to me!"

"Babe. Hi."

"I need to see you."

The changing room door went. A couple of the new lads came in. They were both Argentinean; actually the one's who'd given me the idea to get my hair extensions. Trying not to be seen, I slipped out the back entrance.

"Did you hear me?"

"Course I did..."

Out the corner of my eye I saw a flash. A photographer on a TV van roof was looking at me. I hurried round the building out of sight. I came to rest by the new building our chairman had had built for himself so he could watch training and do whatever business the businesses he had needed doing. It had deliberately been positioned out of sight from any public access. I was safe there.

"Brian! What the hell is wrong with you? You're ruining my charkas that I just neutralised with my crystals!"

"What?"

"We need to meet. Where's Yvonne?"

I felt sick, like my stomach had jumped into my throat.

I'd thought I was speaking to Yvonne.

I held my mobile away from me to double-check. May's photo was on my screen. I swore. That was the problem with being with two sisters. I'd been promising myself for a long-time to sort the whole, messy situation out.

To be honest I hadn't been able to. Whoever said I was perfect?

There's obviously been a lot written about May, Yvonne and me. Stevie too, I suppose, seeing as May was his wife. I'm not going to dwell on the whys, the hows, the ins, the outs.

I suppose what I found attractive about May was that she was so alike Yvonne, but so different, and you know what they say about 'when in Rome a holiday is a change'? Well it felt like that. Obviously being May's sister, they looked the same but I really I started liking May after she got into all that hippy stuff; you know wearing beads and flowers in her hair, really deep stuff.

Most of the girls I'd known all dressed the same. May had this makeover and suddenly seemed so exotic. Having her hair down, in jeans not track-suits all the time, wearing these long, frilly skirts. Like any man I like skirts as short as possible, but she was offering something I'd never had.

I remember being blown away one night when she came out wearing a coat. I'd never really seen that. I looked at my Yvonne who was shivering away and swaying with her bottle of alco-pops and then back at May standing there all elegant, drinking from a bottle of wine. She was in this massive, and I mean massive, fur white coat and I felt like I'd never seen anyone so sophisticated.

Stevie was off at the bar getting nailed and I just moved in.

When I found out later that the fur was the only thing she'd been wearing all night (and because she was so tanned the white looked great on her orangey skin). I could not resist. I felt like I was in a film or something, like she was the queen.

At the time I truly hoped no-one would never find out. It was like May and I couldn't help it: it just kept happening. And when it did just happen, we made sure we were in hotel rooms, or Stevie was out; always going the extra mile to make sure no-one would see us and get upset. So it wasn't like I didn't care about Stevie or Yvonne's feelings.

Still, I can stand up now and say it wasn't right. I'm man enough to admit that and not offer any excuses.

In my defence though, it wasn't just my fault. Once I was arrested the journalists seized on every mistake I'd ever made. In the papers, I was the one painted as this nasty love rat. But that's not fair seeing as all four of us had been unfaithful, not just me: it came out later that Stevie had been with someone else for quite a while, May was sleeping with me and Yvonne had cheated on me the year before (I'm sure you remember the headlines – YVONNE'S BEEN GIVEN ONE/ PARR-TNER SWAP/ PARR'S BIRD BANGS UNKNOWN BLOKE IN CLUB – WE'VE GOT PICS!!!).

So, if that's the case, how can I be the only one at fault?

"I don't know, May. I don't know," I paused, trying to buy some time, but she was rushing me, "Look, we can't meet, of course we can't..."

"Why not, Brian, why the hell...?"

"Because people are going to be all over your place, surely they are already? It's mental here."

"Yeah, there are some paps here, but we've dealt with this before."

"Look, not now. Stevie's my best mate, he's in trouble..."

"Stevie's my husband, and he's fine..."

"What? How do you know?"

"I can sense it. It's my angels."

"Did you hear from him this morning?" I asked.

"No, I fell asleep after you left..."

"So he didn't call? Or come home?"

"You know what he's like, he was out drinking. I heard his car arrive about ten minutes after you left. Sometimes I think he must be waiting for you to go..."

I clenched my fist, I'd thought that a few times too.

"..I heard some rattling about downstairs and then him swearing, which I presume from the mess in the kitchen is because he broke a wine bottle and a couple of my best glasses..."

"Anything else?"

"Well, apart from some blood in Carly's room..."

"Blood?" I said, shocked.

"Yes, blood...from the glass. When he drinks he's sad, when he's sad he likes to come home and watch the kids when they're asleep because I don't let him see them when he's pissed. So I presume he went upstairs, did his sad-b*stard thing in Carly's room and then went off to try and get it together for training. Jesus, Brian, what's got into you?"

"He's missing, don't you get it? Are you sure he was just drunk?"

"I'm looking at the drive-way, right now. The gravel's everywhere, he must have sped off, hammered and on his way to that Doctor you put him in touch with so he could try and pass himself off as sober at training. He must have come off the road, then....rather than hang around and get done for drink driving, again, he ran off...he's probably at that Doctor's in fact, he's always singing his praises to everyone..."

16

At that I said goodbye and hung up. As I leaned back against the wall I tried to think things through. I'd known Stevie had been drinking a lot. His Dad dying had hit him hard and I knew he wasn't getting along with May. But I thought it would pass.

He'd come to pre-season training still a bit pissed once and I'd seen that the Gaffer was on to him. That kind of thing wasn't massively unusual in the old days, but times had changed. When we'd lost the league the season before, some people had said it was down to the drinking culture we had. So I knew that this season the Gaffer wanted it to look like he was running a tight ship seeing as all the papers were saying the new owner wasn't going to shy away from getting rid of people.

As soon as the sale had gone through the Gaffer had called a meeting. He told us he wouldn't stand for any of us getting into trouble again. No scoops, no photos in nightclubs, nothing but football. Stevie was a big player for us, but considering these new rules, I'd hooked him up with this private doctor I knew who did a little bit of 'cleansing' on the side.

His name was Dr Malone and he had all sorts of supplements and drugs and techniques to make it look like you were clean. It was dodgy. It was expensive. It worked.

He'd approached me in a casino. I was hammered, celebrating a new contract with a footwear company. We were playing poker together. He's a big fan of United and knew I was meant to be playing the following evening. So he told me, on the quiet, that he might be able to help out. He said he was a high-flying doctor and had access to all the latest, most exclusive techniques. I put my hands up. I did use him a few times, but only ever to hide my drinking.

When I saw the Gaffer start noticing Stevie, I thought introducing him to Dr Malone might help him get over a rough patch. At first Dr Malone had been a bit pissed off that I'd told anyone about him. He obviously had his job to protect. But I think the amount Stevie started to use him, and therefore pay him, acted as a pretty good sweetener.

After that I'd kind of put Stevie's drinking out of my mind. When we went out for beers he was fine. But I guess, in my heart of hearts I knew that while I was only breaking curfew and club drinking rules occasionally, Stevie was doing it every night. May had said a few things, but we didn't like to talk about him too much. I guess the fact that he was out drinking made it easier for us to get together.

It also worried me about Carly, May and Stevie's youngest. She was one and a half. May sometimes let slip that she might be mine. I loved my two lads but I'd always wanted a girl. Yvonne kept saying she didn't want any more kids because it would get in the way of her TV stuff just as she was finally breaking into it. So in a way, I'd always seen myself as more than a godfather to Carly. I didn't like thinking about a wrecked Stevie hurting her.

Outside the chairman's office it began to rain. I couldn't work out what to do. Go to Dr Malone's and see if Stevie was there? Or go home to Yvonne, seeing as I'd had to pretend I was at a charity gig the night before when I was really with May?

Just as I was about to leave, I heard a voice from inside the office. A voice I recognised.

"So it's done," he said, "We did it?"

Chapter 4

Because I was pressed against the wall, to try and keep out of the rain, I was already out of sight of the window. I tried to hold my breath. I wasn't doing anything wrong; I just thought it would look a bit strange to be around the back of the building. And I didn't want to look weird in front of the person whose voice I'd heard.

It was my boss. Not the Gaffer, but United's new owner. Mr Repinov was Russian. An actual oligarch. They'd been around a while, mostly buying into London clubs, but now United had one too.

There were months of rumours about him buying the club before it actually happened. The day the deal was finalised, things had started to change quickly. One of the things they did was revamp the training facilities, including building the office I was pressed against. It went up fast and was then filled by a team of guys in suits who were always around the stadium and training ground. None of us really knew what they did, but I presumed it was all about money. Let's be honest, nowadays money's a big part of the game.

Some people say that's a shame. I think it would be, if the only reason people got into football was the money. I've never played because of money and I can truly say I would play for free. Although, obviously, I wouldn't get to play as much because I'd have to have a job. Like in the olden days when they were all milkmen and miners and stuff.

So even though we get a lot of flak about being paid too much, we play because we love playing first and foremost. However, if you think about it, if people are going to pay you to play, you'd be st   to let them. And as my agents say, it'd be stupid not to   much as possible. A milkman wouldn't turn down a m

19

milk-round if he was offered more cash, would he?

When I found out he'd bought the club, I really hoped Mr Repinov was doing it for love, not money. He said he was a fan of ours, but he'd said that he was a fan of a couple of other clubs he looked at buying too. Which is a bit suspect, changing your allegiance like that. I mean, I know I did that when I moved from Town to United but the contract they put on the table just showed how much they wanted me to join them. It made me feel really special how much they would pay me which helped me make that difficult decision.

Through a reflection in the window I could just about make Repinov out. He was a short guy, a bit overweight and balding. But the fact he was so rich meant he just about managed to look ok. Well, maybe not, but the girls he hung about with were really fit anyway, so it didn't matter he looked ugly.

"It's done."

I didn't recognise the other voice. It was an English accent.

"Are you sure?" Repinov asked.

"I'm sure. You'll see soon enough, everything is in place."

I heard the chink of some glasses, a drink being poured.

I wanted to move but now I knew I couldn't risk being found. It would look suspicious now that I'd obviously been there for a while and my Dad had warned me to keep on the right side of Mr Repinov.

Despite the fact I was really grown-up now, Dad was constantly calling to give me advice. He hated it when I was in the papers for what he called 'the wrong reasons'. I was surprised he hadn't called about Stevie yet that morning. For a long time my Dad had said Stevie could be the death of my career if I carried on drinking with him. I put it down to the fact that Dad was just jealous that Stevie's family was

20

middle-class.

"Thank you, it's good to know that that...problem has gone," Repinov told the other man.

What were they talking about? Was it to do with Stevie? I knew I was listening to a businessman with a lot of businesses so it could have been a thousand different businessy things. At the end of the day it certainly didn't sound like it was about football, but because Stevie was top of my mind something told me I should listen carefully.

"You've seen the news already?" the English voice asked.

"It looks terrible, terrible..."

"Doesn't it?"

"It's hard to believe that he wasn't hurt...."

"It looks like he was very lucky. Let's see what the news is now."

I felt relief, taking this to mean that Stevie hadn't been the problem they'd been talking about at the start. That I'd probably been right telling myself it wasn't even to do with football.

I waited anxiously as they turned on the sports news. I pressed myself nearer the window. Had they found him yet? No. My heart fell as I heard the presenter say he was still missing. I knew I hadn't been a good mate at all recently. The fact that I'd been having s*x with May for so long didn't feel good either.

"And when do we move on the other target?" asked Mr Repinov, "We need to have it sorted soon."

Hearing this I realised they might have been talking about football after all. The transfer deadline was in four days. I wanted to know who we might be buying. I leant further in, as the TV was making it hard to hear.

"On .....do you mean?" the Englishman asked.

21

I'd missed the name because of the TV.

"Of course, of course..."

"If everything goes to plan, we'll have the deal wrapped up by tomorrow night."

I missed a couple of sentences again because of the adverts; I'd always hated the way they were louder than the main program.

"He's one of my favourite players, you know, a testament to the people of my country!"

"I know. After the match we'll be able to enjoy it."

"And, Blake, thanks for doing everything so, so...efficiently and quietly. I have the future of this club, my club, to look after...we can't let human emotion get in the way..."

Suddenly I slipped. My boots sliding on the wet concrete. I froze

"What was that?" Mr Repinov shouted.

"Outside," Blake said, "There's someone outside the window."

I heard the office door slam open, saw the window begin to open and started to run.

Chapter 5

One of the few things I learnt from school, or more accurately from playing football while I was meant to be at school, was that when you're running away from someone – a teacher, a Wannabe WAG's actual boyfriend, an oligarch's bodyguard – is that it's as important not to be spotted as it is to not actually be caught. If they see who you are, they'll only get you later.

The closest door was into the changing room, which I knew would now be full of my teammates. There'd know something was up if I ran in and I didn't want anyone to know I'd been by the window. The next door after that was round a corner and about 20 metres on. It led into the changing room the Gaffer and coaches used. I pressed forward, using a burst of pace to get me there.

I shut the door quietly behind me and looked around. The room was empty. Jackpot. Rubbing my hands in victory I realised I needed the toilet, unfortunately for a number 2. It didn't take me long, presumably because of my scare, but as I was about to flush I heard the door open. I jumped up, pulled up my trousers and sneaked out of the cubicle. In the far-corner the body-guard came out of the showers.

With his back to me I had to take my chance. I crept over to the door and got back outside. I'd been stupid to have a p*o but at least I felt lighter. My best chance now was the kit-room. As I was sprinting towards it I instinctively, suddenly, came to a halt. Just like dummying the last defender, I'd stopped before I'd even thought about stopping. To my right, through a window, the bodyguard was hurtling down the corridor. If I hadn't stopped, he would have seen me.

I stayed where I was until I he was out of sight. After I'd double-checked things were clear in front of me, I jogged towards the kit-room door. It was open. I entered slowly and was pleased to find it empty, then disaster struck.

There was shouting, in what had to be Russian, from behind the building where I'd just been. I could hear people running. I swore: there were now even more of them after me. Shutting the door behind me I saw at least two running round the corner I'd just come from. Had they seen me? Were they coming in?

Scrambling for the door at the other end of the room I slipped on a towel. I swore again. I had to get out, but at the door I heard a bodyguard speaking into a walkie-talkie in the corridor.

Spinning round, sweating under the pressure, I spotted my next best move. There was an alcove covered by a rail of the bathrobes we all wore in the steam-rooms and physio rooms. I ducked under a few towels. The door opened. Why hadn't I locked it behind me?

I wasn't completely hidden, but I was out of sight. I held my breath. Someone entered. To be safe I had to get behind the robes. I was in my boots still: if I moved they'd hear me.

The other door opened too. They were coming at me from both sides. They started talking, I couldn't understand a word. To my left was a basket of clean hand-towels. I grabbed two and wrapped one around each boot. The two bodyguards had stopped talking. I felt sick. As carefully as possible I edged my feet forward, one after another like I was sliding on snow, the towels making sure the boots didn't rake over the tiles as I moved further into the sea of laundry. Behind me one of the doors shut. I froze. Had they left?

For a moment I thought they had, but then, in an instant, I heard towels and robes being ripped from their hangers and rails. They wasn't messing around.

I made it to the last rail and slipped behind the robes without making a sound. As soon as I was there I realised I might have made a bad choice. I had nowhere to turn. Like when you think you can make it into the box on your own but once you get there you're in a cul-de-sac; you're shepherded into the corner by a couple of defenders and the best you can hope for is for a push, a dive, a penalty, maybe they'll get a straight red and you'll bang the ball in from the spot.

At that moment I didn't fancy my chances of being saved by a whistle.

24

I could hear him breathing heavily. I tried to think of an excuse. Was there anything I could say?

"Hi, I like the smell of freshly washed men's robes."

I mean I always have done, but I didn't think he'd buy it.

His walkie-talkie went. My eyes bulged with hope. I thought of my first manager telling me it was better to be lucky than good and then my Dad telling me that was a load of rubbish and to train as hard as possible.

I heard him step back as he said something into the walkie-talkie. Was I saved?

No, the next moment he stepped forward, stretched his hand out and dragged all the robes off the rail.

Desperately I launched myself into a shoulder barge. I grabbed the last robe and threw it over his face as I burst past him so he didn't see me.

I gave him a little dig to his knee and knocked him over into the towels. I feinted towards the back door then decided that it was safest for me to be inside where I was meant to be. I gritted my teeth as I pushed open the door into the corridor. It was clear. The guy was still on the floor. I shut the door behind me and I was away.

I got a couple of funny looks in the changing room, which I put down to the fact I wasn't showering and the fact people knew I was close to Stevie.

"Hey, Brian, you cool?"

I turned to Edi. He was a new signing, a Nigerian kid who I thought was going to be a great player for us at right back. He'd come out with Stevie and me when he'd first arrived.

"Yeah, Edi, I'm cool," I replied, because I felt it.

Chapter 6

While I was driving home, I tried to work out why Mr Repinov had got so angry at someone listening to his conversation. He always had good security, so was it just normal? Obviously I knew that in Russia there's lots of spy stuff going on which could have explained it, but was it just that?

I stopped thinking about it when I got to the top of our drive and saw Yvonne getting into her car. I'd forgotten she was going out to do her TV presenting work and it annoyed me. I wanted a quiet night in with her. I had nothing else to do. And the fact she was wearing a matching tracksuit, her tattoos were showing and she looked dead classy because she'd just been to the tanning salon made me horny.

Which is proof - despite what many of the papers have said – that I still felt something for her. Cheating isn't a good thing, and I've apologised for that, but I can honestly say I never stopped thinking she was fit.

"Why the hell have you got towels round your boots?" she said after I'd parked up and walked over.

"Oh," I said, "Erm....the car, to stop it getting muddy."

"Most people take their boots off."

"Do they?"

"Yes, Bri, course they f*cking do, what's wrong with you?"

I looked at her.

"Oh, is it, Stevie? Look, babe, I mean, he'll be ok, probably just hiding from all the bl*ody media..." she said.

"Do you have to go out tonight?" I asked her.

"Why wouldn't I?"

"I want to see you, I'm worried about Stevie."

26

"You, worried? That's new. Look, I've got to go. Etienne's got the boys' dinner; I'll see you at the match tomorrow."

I nodded. I hated her doing the poker TV show. It went on all night which meant I was normally on my way to training before she got back. And because it was a bit sleazy, a lot of the lads made jokes about her doing it.

Etienne was our nanny. He was gay and we'd got him after Yvonne got paranoid that I was sleeping with the old nanny, even though I told her I hadn't slept with Julie like the papers said. Because I had slept with Julie, I had to give in to her.

I wasn't really happy with my two lads being looked after by a gay guy but it was better than the thought of a straight guy being in the house with Yvonne while I was playing away.

Actually Etienne was a great bloke really. He knew his football which was half-surprising, half-not in that he was gay, but he was the nephew of Pierre Raquin; United's first ever French player to win the FA Cup.

I went and got the lads and sat with them while I watched the DVDs to prepare for the game the next day. Etienne put the lads to bed at 7, brought me dinner, and then left me to it.

For the rest of the evening I didn't see or speak to anyone else except one person. Much has been made of the fact that I originally said I hadn't seen anyone at all. But I was trying to protect someone who trusted me, not trying to protect myself.

At about ten o clock the gate-buzzer went. I know it was 10 because it interrupted me thinking about the fact that in 24 hours' time I would have played the match and I'd know if I'd managed to score or not. I went to the CCTV and saw it was Dr Malone. I buzzed him in once I'd turned the CCTV off: that's what I always did when he came over as we both felt it was safest there was no record we ever met. After we'd talked, I forgot to turn the CCTV back on because I was so wound up about Stevie. That's why there's no CCTV of the following days, not because I was trying to hide things.

As soon as Dr Malone got to the house, I could tell he'd been drinking.

"Where the f*ck is he, Brian? Where is he?"

I invited him in.

"No, no way, I'm not staying, I just need to know," he said, his eyes looking at me like he was mad.

"Know what?"

"That he'll keep his mouth shut!"

"Look, come in, let's talk about this."

"What is there to talk about? I'm finished, I'm done for!"

It was hard to control him or work out what to do.

"What are you talking about?"

"You should never have told him about me. I hear he goes around telling everyone that he's got a Doctor who makes sure he can drink and take coke all the time..."

"Coke? All the time?"

"He's been caning it and while he has, he's been out there, bragging about this famous doctor, his saviour. I warned him, told him to shut up before he got us both done, but he was too out of it to care most of the time and do you know what he said, Brian, do you, Brian...?"

"What?" I said, anxious he might wake the lads which would mean me having to call Etienne.

"He said to me that it was ok because he using a nickname for me...said no-one would ever know, said he was telling everyone that his mate Dr Bugsy was his ticket to freedom..."

"Bugsy?"

"I know! It doesn't take a genius to work it out that it's me, does it?"

"Like the Bunny?" I asked.

"The Bunny? God no, I'm Malone, aren't I?"

"Sure," I said, confused, "Look, has Stevie called you today? I think he was drinking before he crashed, I thought he might have left the car to see you..."

"Drinking? Coke and Ketamine don't you mean?"

"Ketamine?"

I didn't like the way the list of stuff Stevie was taking was getting longer and longer.

"He came to me late last night, about midnight, he was coked off his face and he wanted something to calm down. All I had was Ket, so I gave him that and then the stuff he'd need to wash it all out before training....problem is the idiot crashed, didn't he? And now he's going to have to say how he's been so full of drugs with no-one knowing about it. He'll ruin me, everything I worked for....."

He stood still, tired out by his anger.

"Well..." I said, searching for words and definitely not trying to hide anything, "I...I haven't seen him…"

"Fine, but when you do, tell him I won't lose everything because of some f*cked up footballer..."

I watched as he bombed away down the drive. I went back to the TV. The headlines told me Stevie was still missing which started up a familiar feeling of sickness.

Chapter 7

A home match at United is something else. Obviously it was special when I was at Town because they were my home-town club. At the time I didn't believe it could get any better, running out onto the pitch in front of the same fans I'd been standing amongst a few years earlier. When I moved to United I discovered I was wrong. Running out into that stadium, in front of over 60,000 fans made the hair on my back stand up. It didn't matter that I wasn't their hometown buy, because when there's that many people cheering and chanting for you, you just get carried away. I suppose it was partly because the fans at United were something else. At Town people liked me, but it is a smaller club. At United, the fans are crazy. I was stalked by people who did nothing else but follow my life. They were that mad about me. It was nuts and it all added to the atmosphere of playing for United.

That evening we were playing a league match against one of the newly-promoted teams and even though I'd watched the DVDs about them, and my Dad had been on at me about them, I didn't really know much about the guys we were playing except we were expected to win. Easily.

On the pitch the game started slowly. The crowd were restless. Partly because everyone there expected a win, partly because Stevie wasn't playing. He was a fan's favourite because he'd come up from the academy and because he was so good.

There'd been a press conference earlier that day, where the Gaffer had been grilled over whether we should still be playing the game with Stevie missing. He said Stevie wasn't the first player to go AWOL and he was sure he'd be found sooner rather than later. When asked if he thought the team would lose focus, he'd said that he was sure that we'd be as professional as always and if anything we'd be trying harder, out of respect for Stevie.

About ten minutes in things weren't really happening. The couple of the times I'd got the ball I'd lost it. Granted, they'd put in a couple of good tackles but I just wasn't really feeling right.

Then something happened.

Our reserve keeper, Sebastian Falco – a good goalie actually but always an understudy to Stevie – kicked it long, Shags got a head to it and I got it under control. I span back to create some space. To my left was our new Argentinean winger, Rodrigo (who I'd nick-named Rodders which he didn't like but I'd made sure it stuck). He'd started the season really well with three goals already – one of which I'd set-up – but as I was about to pass to him, I decided not to. I'm not sure why.

I heard the crowd shouting at me. I backed away. There were two guys around me. I was about to give it to Rodders a second time when the ball was gone. Their centre-back had been quicker than me. I stood there. Why had I not passed? It had to be Stevie. I swore at him.

The Gaffer was having a go at me. One of those moments when you can feel the camera doing a close-up on your face. Except all of a sudden there was something more important to watch.

The centre-back had played a ball down the right. Their winger skinned Edi who was making his first start for us, nipped into the box and calm as you like smashed it into the back of the net.

1-0 down. We couldn't lose. Not tonight.

From that moment on, playing became a struggle. Our timing was out and we were always second to the ball. I've played so many matches and I've lost many times – although luckily I've won far more than I've lost or drawn – but one of the worst things is when you lose control of how you're playing as a team. Losing in the final minute to a wonder goal is painful, but if you've played ok until then, you get over it quicker. But there are moments when you just can't get a grip of the game. Everything goes out the window, all your confidence, all your skills, all your tactics just get washed away by a tide far too strong to stop.

That night, as soon as they scored we dropped. I was running all over the place to try to change things. I was hustling their defenders, working hard. But instead of well-timed tackles I was fouling every time. I picked up a booking. I couldn't believe how the game was turning out. No-one was getting the ball to us upfront and when it did come to me I was as bad as everyone else.

I can't even remember their second goal but I can remember the Gaffer in the changing room at half-time.

"Brian, you're off..." he said as I came through the door.

"I am not," I told him.

"I want you f*cking out of your kit and off."

"Do you want to f*cking win this?" I asked him.

"Course I f*cking do."

"Well, we won't if you take me off, you know it."

I stared at him. Standing up to him like that was a risk. But as soon as I'd got off the pitch I'd felt calmer. We were 2-0 down, but there were 45 minutes to go. I knew the night was set up for me.

The changing room was quiet.

"That's what I wanted to hear! If you wouldn't fight for your place I wouldn't want you fighting for this f*cking team. Sit down. Right you wh*re's douche-bags, listen up..."

We came out after the break with fire in our stomachs. The Gaffer's words worked. That was when he was good. That was when he made us play. Not in front of the cameras at a press conference, but in the changing room, behind closed doors. He'd been the manager for almost ten years; he'd played as centre-back for the team from the age of 16 to 33. He was United through and through and would do anything for us to win.

Within a couple minutes Shags played me through and I feinted one way, turning my marker and then reversed a through-ball to Rodders. He hit it first time. I was about to cheer when it smashed the post. I knew we couldn't get down-hearted and for the next ten minutes we bossed the game. The crowd started getting back on side.

The ball was played to me. I laid it off to Edi and sprinted forward, looking for space. Seeing a channel between the centre-back and right-back I screamed for it. He played me in. I got a touch then felt a hand on me. I was in the box. I went down. The whistle went. Foul or dive? Penalty. They were screaming, calling me a diver. Shags jogged up and helped me up with a wink. The defender touched me. That wasn't my fault. I could have carried on but I might have stumbled. I did the best thing for my team.

I stepped up. I knew I was going to score and I did. The first of the season; the first in too long. I grabbed the ball from the back of the net and five minutes later it got even better and there was nothing they could argue about. I was 30 yards out. The defender was right behind me, his hand on my shirt. The ball came to me on the bounce. I turned my foot down and to an angle, making it as soft as possible. With a cushioned flick I sent the ball round the defender to his left. With a kick I span the other way and met the ball behind him, completely taking him out the game. The ball was still on the bounce. No need to think. I struck it as sweetly as I could remember. 2-2. Top corner. I raced to the flag and slid towards my cheering fans.

From a corner three minutes later I headed in my hat-trick goal. 3-2. What a come-back! What a night! My smile was cheek to cheek, my ears throbbing with all the noise from the stadium. That was what it was all about. I was still buzzing as we started to play keep ball. With about five minutes to go I went in for a challenge. I got the ball. I was sure.

And then football was football.

I heard the whistle go. When I turned to see the ref running towards me with a yellow card I couldn't believe it. My second card of the match. As he took out my third card I stood with my head in my hands. It was so unfair, such a bad decision. I've shouted at refs before over much less, but that night I just shrugged and walked away.

As I went down the tunnel I told myself that at least I'd got a hat-trick, at least we were winning. And then I heard a collective moan. The bottom fell out of my stomach as I realised what had happened. They'd scored direct from the free kick. A peach. I couldn't believe it. I turned back. Not thinking, just acting, and ran back to shout at the ref.

Chapter 8

After a result like that, when there's still unfinished business, I get a feeling inside of me that I can't shift. Like an itch you can't scratch. Just when I think I've forgotten about it, it comes back, or I get a text from my Dad about what I did wrong and I feel angry again that I can't do anything to change what's happened. I guess the problem is feeling weak and unable to do anything about something so important. In football, once the game's over, that's it. That's why you have to give everything you have during the game.

In the club-bar I was chatting to a few of the lads when Rico, my agent, came over. I almost shuddered when I saw his slicked back hair and perma-tan because I didn't really want to talk to him. Rico was ok. He made me money. I just got bored that that was all he was into.

But at least he was nice to me. The only time he'd ever got really cross was when he'd organised a competition for fans to design a T-shirt, with one lucky winner getting the chance to meet me. The idea was for me to meet a kid. Make his dreams come true. But we did the judging live in some shopping centre. And I chose the only entry from a grown-up. When I picked out his T-shirt this guy ran up to shouting 'I'm Malcolm Malcolm! Your number one fan and that's official!'

Rico hadn't been too happy. Instead of a photo with me and the happiest kid ever we had to have me and a 50 year old who was a bit mental. Eventually Rico persuaded the nutter to bring his own kid into the photo so it didn't look weird, but this kid looked angry the whole time and said he didn't even like football!

I'd always liked the club-bar; its rich wood colours and classy lighting always made me feel important when I was in there. Talking the game through with the lads was good too and it was important to hear them agree I shouldn't have been sent off. But I had no choice; I had to chat to Rico. When he was at the games, it was because we could make a lot of money.

"Well played tonight, Brian."

35

"I should never have got that second yellow."

"It's the goals people will remember, isn't it? Your reputation can handle a few reds; just don't get known for it, we don't want people to think you're a thug."

I shrugged.

"I have an offer for tomorrow," Rico said.

"What is it?"

"It's big. You need to take it. A photo-shoot for three hours. You're free."

"Fine," I said, happy to keep it simple.

"There is one thing, though."

"What?"

"It was meant to be someone else...."

"Stevie?"

He nodded, "With this tax increase you've got to take all you can get. If you don't take his place, someone else will."

Like I said, I trusted Rico when it came to making me money. But taking Stevie's gig? The fact he was still missing was really starting to get to me. Too many people were putting it down to a bender. I knew that something wasn't right. He'd never been away this long before.

"Well?" Rico asked.

It felt wrong, "Is it a lot of money?"

"Too much to refuse."

I nodded. He stood up with a smile, shook my hand and at the same time took out his phone. I sat back into the leather sofa. Thinking about Stevie had ruined my mood again.

I jumped as I felt a hand on my shoulder.

I turned to see Shags. He was with his agent too, Tony, who looked

36

nowhere near as rich as Rico. Then again, seeing as Tony was Stevie's agent, I could understand why he'd be worried.

"Calm down, mate," Shags grinned, "Tony just wants a word, alright?" I nodded.

"Have you heard from him?" Tony asked, sitting down while Shags went to the bar.

I shook my head. Close-up, Tony looked even worse. Shags had told me a few times Tony was having a bad time with his ex-wife and wasn't exactly flush. This stuff with Stevie wasn't likely to help. Did he know I'd just done a deal to replace his client? Stevie had to get back soon or he'd start missing out on things. Companies wouldn't want to be associated with someone dodgy. Rico had taught me that you have to be squeaky clean - or appear to be - to make the big money.

"Have you?" I asked.

"No, no," he snapped.

"You must be worried."

"More like hassled. I've got the club, companies, his Mum, his wife all ringing me every hour of the day. It's a nightmare...and to top it all off, this b*tch Kiki is threatening to go to the papers again."

"Hold up, who's Kiki?"

"Kiki, you must know her, he's been with her a long time...." He saw I was clueless, "Shags knows her; he bloody introduced them. May certainly knows about her and soon, if he doesn't turn up, the whole world will know about her and the bloody kid..."

Tony was really worked up; beads of sweat were on his forehead and I was beginning to feel as stressed as he was. "A baby? Stevie?"

"You're meant to be his best mate, how do you not know? She's a dancer at that club him and Shags go to, they're always there, stupid b*stards the pair of them...."

"And May knows...?"

May had told me that Stevie had the odd one-night stand which was ok by her because that's what karma was and she was sleeping with me, but she also said she'd never forgive him for anything long-term.

"May found out ages ago, and do you know what she did? She called me and said she didn't mind as long as it didn't get into the papers. She's clever, she knows how much the adverts with their whole happy family are worth...well we're screwed now. Kiki says she's going to the press, she says he promised her cash for the baby and now he's gone she thinks the best way is selling the story...."

I was reeling. While I'd been with May, Stevie had been living a double life. I felt betrayed. By him and May. And Shags; when had they been such good mates?

I told Tony I'd go and look for him that night.

"Guys, guys," the Gaffer suddenly said, "Our owner, Mr Repinov would like to say a few words."

I hadn't even seen him come in, but he was already right by the bar with his entourage.

He began talking but I was too busy trying to avoid eye-contact with his bodyguards to listen. I was fairly sure they hadn't seen me, but I figured it was best to keep a low profile.

"...now as you all know, I've given the club funds to get new players for a bigger and better squad that can go on and do great, great things. And to show you I will keep investing, I would like you to meet our latest signing...."

At this I heard the Gaffer, who was behind me, breath in, like he was shocked.

38

"We have kept it quiet so as not to excite the press before it was finalised and following the unfortunate events surrounding our usual goalkeeper, Mr Hurst, it couldn't be better timed, please say hello to the goalkeeper of my own national team, Nickolas Ivankov..."

There was stunned silence, broken by Mr Repinov clapping and everyone else slowly doing the same. I turned to the Gaffer. I was sure he was doing his best to hide something. Surprise? Anger?

Was this the target I'd heard them talking about or had they got someone in as cover after yesterday? Either way, Stevie was already being replaced. I had to find him.

Chapter 9

As soon as I went for my car I knew I was going to have a hard time. There were loads of press waiting. I'd hoped they'd already left but how often does the England captain score a hat-trick and get sent off in the same game (that had actually been the third time I'd done that but I'd like to say I'd never deserved any of the red cards)?

Getting into my ride, I couldn't work out what was going on with us signing Stevie's replacement so soon. How long had the deal been on the cards? It crossed my mind that Stevie had known and that was why he'd gone on a massive session: out of all the goalies in the world, Ivan was the one closest to being as good as Stevie.

But if Stevie had known then surely Tony would have too? After the announcement Tony had looked gutted. I was sure it had been news to him.

So perhaps they'd done the deal quickly after Stevie went missing?

They were new to football, maybe they didn't know that sometimes we needed to let off steam. In the industries they were used to, people didn't have to perform in front of the entire country every time they worked, did they? It's not a pressure many people understand. So maybe they freaked out? Maybe they thought him disappearing meant he was gone forever and so signed another player?

On the other hand, it could have been part of their plan all along. Before Stevie left, they could have been aware of his lifestyle – I was beginning to realise I didn't know all that much at all - and decided to make sure we had good back-up before it was too late?

The only thing that was clear was that I had to save my mate.

Driving out of the gates I was glad I had tinted windows and a modified SUV engine. The camera flashes started, the shouting of my name began. I indicated right, waited for a second and then sped off left. I checked my mirror. Two cars had set off behind me. I took the T-junction at the top of the road far too fast. My tires skidded, wheel locked, I slammed on the brakes and just got control back and pressed the accelerator down flat. This was when being able to pay to practice in F1 cars came in handy.

In the mirror I saw one car pull over realising they were never going to keep up. One to go. The light turned to amber, I gambled. I looked back. They'd gone through a red. I knew that now I could legally say I had the right to drive dangerously because they'd broken the law when following me – at least that was what I'd said last time I'd been to court.

I quickly threw a left. Down a smaller road and I was heading towards a one-way road. Going the opposite way to the one I was. It didn't take long for me to decide I couldn't spend all night being chased by some tw*t from the tabloids. As the road narrowed I saw that luck was with me. A car was about to come down the one-way section. I gritted my teeth and darted in. My tires screamed, I hit the curb, my steering-wheel kicked round, their horn sounded, but I made it.

I laughed as I came out onto a main road and saw in my wing-mirror that the two cars I'd left behind had come to a stop head-to-head in the middle of the one-way bit.

Then I saw a flash. Another pap? No, a speed-camera. I swore. Every time it cost me more to get off. It was so unfair.

Shags had given me the names of a couple of places that Kiki had said Stevie had taken her to before. He said they were discreet members clubs which was a good thing as I wanted to keep this search out of the papers. The bad thing, was that they were in a sh*t part of town and when I arrived at the first one I couldn't believe there was no car park or valet.

Eventually I built up enough courage to leave the car on the street and found the club. You had to walk down behind some railings and below street level to get in. I wasn't a member so I paid to join. It was a couple of hundred but I needed to find him. I figured it would be a small price to pay to see him safe. As normal, I used a fake name to keep a low profile. I always used Alan Robson after my favourite players.

Inside it was full of candle-lights and booths. There was some music on, I can't remember what but it was quite chilled out. It was like out of an old gangster movie, the waitresses were all dressed up and I'll admit most were very attractive. I could smell drugs. In one booth I could see a line of drugs being sniffed. In truth, I had been to places like this before, as a young lad, but not since I'd been an England

41

player really.

I wanted to get in and out as quickly as possible. I got a drink and went for a walk around. Very cleverly pretending to be searching for somewhere to sit when actually I was looking for Stevie. Some people got annoyed by me which wasn't fair because I was trying to be cool and calm like James Bond. Stevie wasn't there.

Sitting at the bar I spotted a well-dressed older woman sitting at the end of it.

"Excuse me," I asked, "Can I ask you a quick question?"

I moved over, telling myself to keep everything on the down-low. The story of Brian Parr being in a place like this looking for his mate was not one I wanted to read about in the papers.

"I'm looking for a friend."

"Been stood up?"

"Erm, no, but it's kind of sensitive," I said.

She raised her eyebrows. It was time to tell her the truth. My power and influence normally worked.

"Look, I suppose you know who I am, and who I'm looking for?"

"Never seen you before down here, have I?"

"No...but..."

"So why should I know you?"

I was getting irritated, "Ok, well, my friend, Stevie Hurst..."

"Oh, someone else looking for Stevie?"

"What do you mean?"

"Are you from his bookies or his dealer?"

"Erm..."

"You look too straight for drugs."

"Look, when did these people come looking for Stevie...?"

"About every night for the past week."

"And he hasn't been here?"

"Not for a week or so..."

"Erm....look will you let me know when he comes back?"

"No," she said blankly.

"Please?"

"Look, darling, people come here because it's a private club and it's staying that way."

I left. There was a whole world of Stevie's I had no idea about. And by the sounds of it, he was in a lot of trouble in every part. No wonder he was hiding. I had one more bar to check. I nodded goodnight to the doorman and stopped in my tracks. My car had been replaced by broken glass.

Chapter 10

I'd left my phone in the car so I had no way of getting in touch with anyone. By the time I got home I was still raging, but it had been numbed by my exhaustion.

In the kitchen I got a smoothie out and tried to fight the temptation to put some rum in it. Once I'd fetched the Havana Club I had enough energy to read a note Yvonne had left for me. She was angry that she'd gone to the match but I'd left before she'd finished an interview about what it was like to be one of the best WAGs in the world.

Despite my tiredness I knew I wouldn't sleep. The red-card, the hat-trick, the draw with a team we should have thrashed, the car chase, the speed-camera, the news that Stevie was in trouble with gambling and possibly drugs, the car being nicked – it was all too much.

In a faint hope he might have turned up I switched on the sports news. People were talking about my performance. Every time I watched the second booking it got me angry again, especially when some of the people on TV said I deserved it.

I decided to go for a swim. I fixed another drink. I stripped down and jumped in the water– when I'm at home I don't bother with my trunks. My body seemed to scream, it was so cold. I jumped straight out, angry. I'd told Etienne to leave the heating on at all times. I knew he thought it was un-green though. I do understand looking after the planet, but no-one wants to live on a planet where they can't have a hot indoor pool whenever they want, do they? I couldn't find my robe so I decided to just go into the basement to turn the heating on.

I sipped my drink as I went. I remember finishing it on the stairs. I remember turning on the light as soon as I got down into the basement and feeling something sticky and thinking it was pool-water. After I flicked the heater on, I was about to head up stairs when I looked down. My feet were bright red, covered in blood. All at once everything seemed to collapse.

Stevie's body was lying at the far end of the room, also covered in blood.

I didn't scream, I was far too frightened for that. I shat myself. Literally. Something which shows just how shocked I was on seeing him like that. I had no idea how he could have got there, or what had happened. Who'd done it? Himself? If not, who? And why was he there? In my house?

I ran to him, to see if I could help him. I slipped and fell. I knew he was dead, I knew he was, but I tried to wake him, to shake him, to get

44

some life into him.

I couldn't believe it. Stevie was dead.

Chapter 11

Holding the body of the guy I'd thought of as my best friend, I lost track of time. Nothing else in the room existed apart from Stevie and me.

By the time I went back up the stairs there was steam coming off the pool. The winter before, Shags had got his brother's company to give all the United players deals on installing these amazing new pool-heaters and the whole thing can be hot in twenty minutes, so it was at least that long.

I stopped in front of the wall mirrors. I was naked. I was somehow still carrying my glass. Stevie's blood was everywhere. Some had even pooled in the creases of my 6-pack. I fought the urge to be sick.

The kitchen door opened. I sprung to attention. Not because I was guilty of anything, simply because I didn't want it to be seen by one of my lads. Chesney was 4 and Baggio was 5, imagine seeing your Dad covered in blood at that age? So to protect them, I tip-toed behind one of the pillars.

"Bri? Bri? What are you doing?" Yvonne called.

My words caught in my throat, what was I going to say? I closed my eyes, maybe she wouldn't see me.

"What the h*ll are you hiding for? I can see you even if you have got your eyes shut. What's this on the floor? Have you been playing in the garden again?"

I stepped out from behind the pillar, wishing I wasn't naked. This was a really serious situation and it didn't seem right to have to tell her about Stevie when I wasn't wearing anything.

She screamed as soon as she saw me. She went nuts, hysterical.

"What have you done!?" she wailed, "What have you done?"

"I...I...." I stuttered, "I haven't....it wasn't me!"

"It's blood! Oh my God, Brian!"

"I didn't kill..."

"Look at you! Look at you!"

The tension got the better of me. The glass cracked as my fist clenched. I moved towards her, wanting to calm her down.

"No, please, not me, not me," she said, her eyes widening, scrambling away

"Yvonne, Yvonne, listen to me, I haven't...."

Her hands clenched like she was ready to hurt me if I approached her. Her face looked so intense, so angry, I hardly recognised her. I'd only seen her like that once before, the first time she'd thought I'd cheated on her.

But this time she was much worse. It made me think about her Dad, and that she was his daughter. I didn't know much about him, except he was a criminal. Some people said he was a gangster and a really bad one. I'd met him a couple of times. He seemed ok, but one time he got angry at May – Stevie and her were there too – which wasn't nice because his face seemed to change in an instant. From a nice old man, to someone who could hurt you. He'd been sent to prison for loads of things a few seasons before which had got me some bad press. Yvonne said she'd been brought up with him so she was used the sudden changes in mood and anger.

I wasn't. And I wasn't used to Yvonne looking at me like she was ready to attack me. I could see why it maybe looked bad that I'd found Stevie. But didn't she know me?

"Brian, get away from me..." Her voice was trembling with anger, "If you come near me I'll make you pay. Put down the weapon..."

"Of course, I'd never hurt you..."

I dropped the glass. It splintered everywhere. I felt some nick into my leg. Yvonne screamed louder than I'd ever heard. Even louder than when she was in the Zombie Strippers film with some other totty from the lads' mags: Yvonne had been the first lap-dancer who'd been bitten and got to infect the rest of them which she'd been really pleased about. Some of the glass had hit her in the face. Only slightly, but there was some blood. She was silent as she checked the cut with the palm of her hand.

"Babe, I'm sorry..." I said bending down to hug her.

She kicked out. A quick hit that knocked me off balance. Glass cut into my back. I roared in pain. Shrieking, Yvonne got to her feet and ran. I was hurting but I knew I had to get to her to see I hadn't done anything.

"Yvonne!" I shouted as I burst into the kitchen. I stopped for a second, my heart loud in my head, as I tried to figure out which of the three exits she would have taken. Through one of the doors I spotted her running up the second staircase towards our bedroom. I gave chase.

"Daddy?" I heard Baggio say. Both boys were standing in the doors of their bedrooms. They started giggling as I ran up to them.

"He's all red. Messy boy."

"I can see his tiddler."

"Hello, lads," I tried to say nicely as Yvonne slammed the bedroom

47

door, "...back to bed, yeah?"

I got my tone wrong, or maybe it was the look in my eyes, because in a second they were both screaming. I had to get Yvonne.

As soon as I was in the bedroom I realised I was too late. There was no way I could get to her; I'd made sure of that myself. The season before a few players had their houses robbed when they were playing away. Shags' brother had started doing a line in panic rooms so I'd got involved. The walk-in wardrobe, with all her jewelry and designer dressers, had been the obvious place to make secure. It wasn't completed yet, but he'd already replaced the doors, saying never mind a hammer you'd need a Hummer to break in.

I did have a Hummer. Of course. But I didn't fancy my chances of getting it up the stairs, despite all the modifications I'd had done.

"Yvonne!" I shouted, "Yvonne! I haven't hurt anyone. I swear. I found him like that!"

"Who is it, Brian, who?" she said, her voice still.

"Stevie."

I heard her gasp, it sounded like she'd fallen to the floor.

Suddenly I remembered that Stevie was dead. I felt sick as it sank in. I had to call the Police.

Chapter 12

I had my hand on the house phone when I stopped myself. Yvonne had made a mistake. The equivalent of a striker making a break without any team mates and by the time you do look for help you're on

48

your own with nowhere to go and the other team can take control.

Making breaks like that was something that had been drilled out of me. At that moment Yvonne could have benefited from having had that training, but she hadn't because she couldn't even kick a ball properly. Which had been embarrassing when I'd got her some trials with United's women's team after she'd seen a film about girls playing and thought it would look cool.

You see the previous weekend I'd got a text from Shags' brother apologising that he still hadn't installed a phone and internet in the panic room. And as for her mobile, it was on her bedside table charging. So there was no way she could call anyone and tell them what she thought I'd done. Result. Not because I was glad she was trapped, it just meant I had some time to work out my tactics without someone else calling the shots.

The thing was, if the person I was engaged to had instantly thought I was the one who'd hurt Stevie what would everyone else think? I had to do things properly. I had to call the Police. I had to shower and get dressed. But which to do first? What if they thought I'd showered to cover something up? Could I let them in when I was naked? I was the England captain!

Could I get Yvonne to see sense? I doubted it. It sometimes took an hour to say sorry when I hadn't noticed another new haircut. How long was it going to take to convince her that even though I'd hidden from her, approached her with some broken glass and then chased her around the house covered in blood, I hadn't done anything wrong? Two hours? One and a half if I promised to get her something? By then it would have been ages since I'd found Stevie.

My mind was racing. I had no idea what to do.

In the following months people spent a lot of time examining what I did next. I kept arguing that when people are upset they act without thinking properly, and that's what I did. But the prosecution people kept pointing out how I was on the pitch to disprove that. They said I was famous for always being able to deal with intense pressure - despite the odd red card for being over eager. It would have been flattering if they weren't saying it to get me locked up forever.

The fact is people have always commented on my extra special ability to take my time on the pitch. As if I know what's going to happen before it does. The modern game is so fast, so ferocious and yet even when I'm surrounded I never rush. I stay in control.

To be honest I don't fully know how I have so much composure on the ball compared to everyone else - it's just something I've always been able to do. In interviews, I normally just say it's like things are in slow-motion. That, though, isn't it really it. I only say that because normal people seem to understand it easier, maybe because they slow football down on TV so much.

Really, it's the opposite of slow-motion. When I'm playing my mind races ahead of what's happening and then I can decide what's best to do. It's like I fast-forward a couple of options – like pass to the guy on my right, or dribble past one defender and then shoot – and once I've seen both I go for the one which works out best.

I suppose a lot of it is instinct, but a lot of it is preparation. To be able to fast forward and work out properly how doing one thing will play-out you need to know everything about who you're playing with and against. So if it's between passing or taking a defender on, I'll really quickly need to know how fast my team mate is and whether he'll want a pass to his feet or his head. And I'll also need to know if the defender is weak on his left or right side and if he's good at slide-tackling. All of this plays out in my head like it's the most natural thing in the world and at the same time I also have to keep focused on the ball and running and everything else.

Off the pitch though, surprisingly perhaps, it can be a different matter. I don't have this ability. Which is why it wasn't fair of them to try to use the way I am on the pitch as evidence that I knew exactly what I was doing that night. They said every step had been thought out. From the moment I forced Yvonne into the only room with no phone, to everything that followed.

That's not true. I admit I'm not the most intellectual guy on the planet. I'm not thick but in real life, I can be rash and I do make mistakes. And in that situation how can it be my fault that I didn't make all the right choices? Imagine facing something like that yourself? What would you do?

I was there on my own and I had nothing that had prepared me for being in a situation like that. I was scared. I simply tried to do what I thought was right. And as you read on, you'll see that there was a reason for every choice I made.

The blood was drying. I could hear Yvonne crying. From the sounds of it the lads had started having a kick-about on the landing, which they weren't allowed to do at the best of times, let alone at 3 in the morning in the middle of what was essentially a crime scene.

I considered calling Etienne to get them to stop but I decided they would benefit from the extra practice. Both of them had pretty poor ball control.

First things first, I needed clothes. I looked around our bedroom. There was nothing. We'd gone through a lot of cleaners before we found one who wouldn't nick my things to sell and who could keep things as tidy as my Mum. The one we'd ended up with was good. Because she was, actually, my Mum. But that was bad because it meant all of my clothes were in the wardrobe with Yvonne. The only thing I could see was one of Yvonne's Japanese dressing gown things.

I'd been man enough to wear pink since it became manly and cool, but in Yvonne's gown I wasn't so sure the colour was right on me, or the flowers; especially next to the blood that was crusting up from my ankles to my blonde extensions. And it really didn't help that it was far too small either - I could only just tie it round my abs. All in all it was a bad look, one my stylist would have screamed at. I'd go so far to say I looked mental, straight out of a scary film.

What I did next, though, I did because it was the exact opposite to what they do in those films. If they find something bad they never call the Police or anyone, do they? Instead they try to deal with it themselves, which always, always gets them in more trouble.

I resolved not to do that. I picked up the phone. I called 999 and told them I'd found the body of Stevie Hurst and gave them my name and address. As I put the phone down I thought I'd heard the 999 person say something, but I didn't hear what. I figured they would be on their way over anyway.

I then decided, finally, not to have a shower. When they first saw me, I knew they'd see the blood and think it was weird, but they'd work out that I was bound to be covered in it if I found him. Washing would only seem like I was hiding something.

Instead I decided to try and see if I could get through to Yvonne. When the Police came it would look better if she wasn't mad at me.

I banged on the wardrobe door. I banged louder.

The phone rang.

I went over to it and picked it up.

"Hello, hello?"

There was no-one on the other end of the phone and the ringing was still going. I realised it was a mobile that was ringing. Mine was in the kitchen next to the rum. Yvonne's?

Her phone had stopped ringing by the time I picked it up. There was a photo of a guy, a foreign name. I didn't recognise him and was going to take a closer look when another phone rang.

It seemed really loud and was coming from the window-sill. Whose phone was that?

The ringing was still going. It was all getting too much.

I dropped Yvonne's phone, checked out of the front window for any sign of the Police, remembered I'd need to open the gates, heard one of the boys start crying, stubbed my toe, noticed the wardrobe door handle move slightly, and then, to stop the ringing, picked the mobile up. It turned out to be one of the most important calls of my life.

"Brian Parr! You're being set-up!" a man's voice said.

"What? Is this a joke? What are you...?"

"Brian, I don't know how exactly, but people are trying to get you in trouble!"

"About Stevie? Because he's dead?"

"What?"

"Stevie. I just found his body...I called the Police."

"F*ck! I didn't know they were going to go so far!"

"What do you mean?"

"Look, Brian, listen to me. You're being set up. They must want people to think you killed him..."

"I didn't!"

"Exactly. Look, leave now. The only way out of this is for me to prove you're being set-up. That you didn't do it."

"I didn't!"

"I know that. J*sus I thought they were talking sh*t when they said you were..." I couldn't hear him but I think he swore about me.

"Look," I said, "I don't need..."

"What you need is to listen to me. Stevie's in your house. People want you to take the blame...I need time...you have to leave now, or you'll have no chance."

"Who are you?"

"They'll do you for murder. I'll call this mobile in an hour. Get somewhere safe until then."

"Why should I do what you say? How do...?"

"Right now, it looks like you did it, doesn't it?"

"Ye-s," I said, thinking about how Yvonne had reacted.

"So you need to get away before everyone just assumes it's you and you get trapped. The cops, the papers, the public will condemn you," he told me, and something in his voice made me believe him, "I can help. I just need you to get stay safe for an hour. After that, if you don't like it then you can go to the Police and say you were chasing someone from the house who you saw and thought it could be the killer."

"I don't know..."

"Trust me, if you stay, it's all over."

Chapter 13

The phone went silent in my hand.

I turned and looked at myself in the mirror for a moment. Some of the flowers on the gown were already blood-stained.

Racing downstairs, I didn't even look at the lads, but they started laughing, presumably at the sight of their Dad in a girl's gown. From the bedroom, I heard Yvonne screaming at the boys to come to her in the wardrobe. Their laughter turned into crying. The bedroom door was slammed shut behind them.

In the garage I went to the safe where I kept the keys. Which car should I take? Normally I would've taken my SUV, but it was gone. I cursed my luck and surveyed what I had left, from the Lamborghini nearest to me, to the two Porsches down at the end. There were eight remaining cars. They were all great motors, but the problem was some of them were too flashy, too awesome for what I needed to do - I know what you're saying, how can a car be too flashy? But please, reader, think about it, I had to lie low. It was important I had the right car to do that in.

That night, in the garage, I had two cars in luminous greens, my Hummer which I'd had done like it was Spiderman, a very pink Audi, and an Aston Martin done with polka dots like a Dalmatian – that one made the papers the first time I drove it and people had said it was the ugliest thing that had ever existed bar none. But I'd actually copied the design from one of the WAGs of a team we'd played on a tour of Russia, so their claim was a lie and I'd looked into suing.

The painted ones were too brilliant to try and be secret in, which left me three to choose from. Not wanting to waste any more time, I grabbed a set of keys and typed in the code to open the garage door.

I was three quarters of the way down the drive-way when it hit me that I might have made a big mistake. I slammed on the brakes, skidding a little, but managing to keep control.

The Ferrari F430 Spider I was in was mine, but it officially belonged to Stevie. A couple of weeks before, one of the last nights we'd had out on the town together, we'd finished off at his house playing a football tournament on the Xbox.

As we played the stakes got bigger. It had come down to Stevie and me. Nearly everyone else had given up and gone. Only Shags was left. But he was crashed. We were both playing as United. In the final it went to penalties. He had to score. He was playing as me. I was in goal as him. He sent me the wrong way, but he blazed it over. I won. The prize was any of his cars.

In court Shags testified that he remembered us playing the game for big bets, but couldn't say for sure whether I'd won the car off Stevie. That was awkward because the prosecution were saying Stevie had driven it to my house the night he died.

But, stopped in the middle of the drive-way that night I didn't know how much trouble taking that car would be. When I saw a blue flashing light coming down the road the only choice I had was to hit the accelerator. I guessed that they'd be coming from the city, so I went the other way. Looking in my rear-view mirror as I turned off the main road onto a smaller one by the church, I saw a couple of cars turn at speed into my drive-way. I floored the Ferrari and felt it roar.

Did I feel relieved? Of course I did. Although I didn't really know what I was running from, something in the man's honesty, and how serious he was, had made me leave. A seriousness matched by what had happened to Stevie. Because that's what I was really running from. Someone had killed him. Then they'd put him in my basement. Why? When? How? If they'd done that, what else were they capable of?

Suddenly a horrible thought hit me. What if the murderer was still in the house? With Yvonne and the lads. What if it hadn't been planned, it hadn't been a set-up? It was the people who'd been robbing everyone and they'd got Stevie as he was coming to chat to me after the match?

I almost span the car round there and then. Until I started thinking straight. I was driving away from the house was because the Police were there. If the Police were there, then the lads were safe, weren't they? No-one was going to mess with the Police, were they?

I pressed on to get away from them.

By the time I'd put enough distance between myself and home to slow down, it had been ten minutes since the call. That meant I had 50 minutes left. 50 minutes. I told myself to think of it like picking up a booking early in the first half; you've still got to give it absolutely everything, but one mistake and its game over. Early bath. Not allowed to take part in the next few matches.

So how was I going to ride the 50 minutes out? Keep driving so I was as far away as possible? Or pull off the road and hide?

I checked how much petrol I had left. That made up my mind for me. I was almost out.

Chapter 14

I'd first come across dogging one night when I was waiting to see May in a lay-by. I'd turned on the radio to see if anyone was talking about our next match. I liked the local stations and their football phone-ins. Obviously I enjoyed it more when I was doing well, because I'd always loved hearing people talk about how great I was playing. When they called up to give me abuse it was less good fun.

The night I was waiting for May, the phone-in had nothing to do with football. I was about to turn it off when I heard the word 's*x'. I decided to give the show a chance. People were calling in to say they liked to go dogging. I gradually started to understand what it meant, but what I couldn't understand was why they were calling in to tell the world about it. Or at least the people listening to the local radio at half eleven on a Friday.

"If they're happy to make l*ve in front of other people, I'm sure they're not going to feel shy about making a phone-call, are they?" May had said, once she was in the car.

Apparently I was one of the last people to know about dogging. May said it was all over the papers, and everyone was doing it. I told her straight-up that footballers weren't and none of us had even heard of it - imagine the papers if they found out that the England team were out having s*x on their car bonnets each week!

She'd smiled that knowing smile of hers. The one she normally did just before she made me pick some of those weird card things so she could tell me what was going to happen in the future; I hardly ever listened unless she said I was going to score in the next match. As I drove on she started pointing out all the dogging spots she knew about in the area. And then, the very next week, an ex-Scottish player was caught in a layby having a romp.

We'd all had a massive laugh over that during training and May had texted me saying she was sure her predictions were getting better all the time. I pointed out that she'd said I was going to get a hat-trick and I hadn't even had a shot on goal. We'd never talked about dogging again, but whenever I drove those roads I liked to look at the places she said were the local hotspots.

With the petrol running low, as I approached one of the dogging places I decided to turn off and park up. It being late, I reckoned the place would be empty. The perfect place to wait for the man to call.

Despite the time, I was still on red-alert as I entered the clearing. I kept remembering May saying that there were lots of rules about dogging. The way you flashed your lights, how much you opened your windows, whether your doors were locked or not - they all told others what you wanted to do. The problem was I had no idea what meant what. I shut my windows and locked all the doors, hoping that the message would be clear that I was no-go if people did decide to show.

The main problem was the lights. I wanted to be discreet, so my instinct was to turn them off. But what if that was the biggest come-on? What if that meant anything goes, whereas full beam means you just wanted to watch – it makes sense that lights on means you want to watch, right?

I had to be careful. I had an image of suddenly being surrounded by loads of naked weirdos all wanting to have s*x on what would probably be the best car they'd ever seen.

I switched to side-lights, deciding it was best to play it safe. I thanked my lucky stars that there didn't seem to be anyone else there. Knowing as much as I did about making hasty exits - from the press, husbands, Yvonne - I turned the car around so I could get out fast, then turned off the car to save petrol.

I checked the mobile I'd found on the window-sill. How had he got it there? I told myself to remember to ask him when I called. And who he was. And how he knew about Stevie. The list was endless.

On my own, in the dark clearing, I didn't feel quite right. I felt vulnerable.

I'd put my own phone on the passenger seat. I had 30 missed calls. As I tried to see who they were from it started vibrating. Incoming call. I was going to cancel it, but for some reason I decided to tackle things head-on. Typical Brian Parr.

"Brian Parr? This is DCI..." in my confusion I didn't hear her surname, "We need to know where you are. We have your wife, she's very upset. Brian, are you there?"

I was frozen. I couldn't say a word.

"Brian, it would be better for everyone if you came back, help us clear things up..."

In the background it sounded like all hell had broken loose at home. What had I thought was going to happen? That they'd quietly clean everything away so I could slip into bed beside Yvonne at dawn, calm her down with one of my usual excuses then go to training and bang in some goals as normal?

I was covered in sweat, completely unsure about whether it was a good call to be where I was right now: on the run from the police in the area's number one dogging spot.

Then, in the middle of all the noise on the other end of the line I heard someone say a sentence. A sentence I'd heard a million times before said by someone I truly respected. I knew I'd made the right choice to leave home: *This is Jock Fountain, reporting for Live Sports News, from Brian Parr's house...*

I hung-up. Panicking.

I scrambled to turn the radio on. I needed air. I wound the window down a little; it wasn't enough so I unlocked the door and opened it.

It didn't take me long to find the sports radio - annoyingly, if I'd chosen my other cars I could have watched Jock's report as they all had digital TV (Stevie had never realised how important it was to take your cars seriously).

The radio show was looking back at the evening matches. They mentioned my sending off and said I deserved it. I swore hard at them.

"I'm going to have to stop you there, we've got some news about Stevie Hurst..." My heart leapt, "Reports are coming through that there is a huge police presence at... Brian Parr's home."

Devastated I put my head onto the steering wheel.

"We're hearing that there are already a lot of press on site, and as soon as we can get through to a reporter, we'll be telling you people at home everything....there are reports, unconfirmed, that ambulances are there too...."

I clenched my fist and head-butted the wheel. The horn sounded. I head-butted it again. And again. It began to hurt and in a funny way it made me feel better.

Then I felt the whole car move.

Terrified I looked up.

"Hello, darlin', we've been waiting for you to ask us over..."

Right by my face, in the open window, was a p*nis, "Lovely wheels, like this, we didn't want to miss out!"

61

"Oh, look at him, he's dressed up and all..."

"I love a man in a silk gown, you look very pretty darlin'..."

All around me were smiling faces. But they weren't nice smiles. I saw bits of everything. A man and women were already b*nking on the bonnet. Three or four people, in various states of being naked and turned-on were peering in. A light flashed over me.

"Oh, he's ripped, he is ripped, and on his own too. Need anyone to help you out?"

"With a car like this you can take your pick."

I held up my hand to shield my eyes from the torch.

"He's dark too, look at him...?"

"Come on love, you might not look it but I get the feeling you're straight so wanna play," said a women, with huge t*ts but a bit too much of everything else too."Hang on! That's not skin....it's not brown, it's blood!"

There was a scream. Everyone got off the car. I was still frozen.

Then I heard a sound. From the sky there was a bright spotlight. A helicopter!

Chapter 15

The searchlight circled the ground. All the people scattered to the trees. Once again I was the only one in the middle of the clearing.

I couldn't hear much over the noise of the blades, but I thought I could make out someone shouting my name from somewhere. I slammed the car-door shut, turned the key in the ignition and revved the Ferrari's engine.

Flooring it, I caned a wheel spin before speeding forward. In the headlights I saw a tree-stump directly ahead. I pulled down on the wheel hard, felt the car bottom out on uneven ground, heard the metal grind on wood and then took back full control as I hurtled down the track.

The road was empty. I took a sharp left, presuming that anyone trying to find me would be coming from my house. I had thirty minutes to stay ahead of them. That was all. Hold out for the last third of the game. I knew how to do that, didn't I?

After that, well, who knew? That was up to the man.

More pressing was the matter of the fuel gauge. I was going to struggle to keep going at this speed until the man called but I had no choice but to keep going as I neared the ring-road. My mobile rang. Rico. I had a sudden urge to speak to someone who I could trust. Well, someone who would want to make sure I carried on being the country's most popular football player anyway.

"Brian!" he shouted.

"Rico."

"What the h*ll are you doing?"

"Rico, calm down..."

"Calm down! My number one client's all over the TV being chased by the police! Just come in now so we can sort this out."

"That's what I want to do but I'm not sure..."

"Sure! Well, be sure that Yvonne is saying some very bad things and your house looks like an episode of CSI. The longer you hide the more you become the only suspect."

"So what do you think I should do?"

"We need your spin on it. You see," he said, hushing his voice, "...it's your word against hers. The sooner you start talking, we can pin it on her."

"Pin what on her?"

"Stevie..." Rico said seriously, "Look, with me behind you there's no way anyone will believe her over you! By the time it comes to court no-one will ever be able to imagine you doing what you....did..."

"I didn't!" I shouted, taking a corner to quickly, instantly grateful for the Ferrari's formula one-grade traction and carbon brakes.

"That's exactly how I need you to say it."

"But you think I did that to Stevie, and you don't care?"

"Tony's clients are his clients, Bri. And to be honest, even if Hurst had come over to my stable I'd still have to back you over him in this. For one, goalkeepers are only ever remembered for their f*ck-ups so their earning potential is limited, and two, he's now dead...."

"Rico. I didn't do it."

"Sure, sure."

"I can't believe you don't mind," I paused as I hit the slip-road at speed, "...I mean, you think..." luckily the ring-road was clear, meaning I could pull out without slowing down, "...I killed him....and you don't care!" I said feeling sick.

"I'm an agent. Your agent. And," he said in the way I knew he was running his hands through his head, "...you've just said you didn't do it."

"I didn't. It's a set-up."

"No, don't go saying that. Crazy talk, conspiracies, people being framed does not work with sponsors, the public. Do not go there, Brian."

"Rico, this is madness."

64

"The set-up excuse is. Look, come in, we'll do a straight-up case between you and her. Easy."

"This is Yvonne, the girl I'm going to marry!"

"And thank god that's the case. If you'd already married her, it could be a lot messier. This way we can cut her off starting yesterday; there's no way she'll be able to hire the right people to fight us."

As I powered along the ring-road I was about to ease off to save on the petrol when I caught a glimpse of the helicopter's light in the corner of my eye.

"That's settled then. Come back, let them arrest you and then let me get the PR guys and lawyers working over-time. But you have to do it now. If they catch you d*cking around in your car and force you to stop, it'll be like OJ Simpson all over again – we might get you off, but you're not going to be worth a penny to anyone because they'll assume you were guilty and trying to run.

"Come back here and it looks like you've realised that with the police there, the murdering bitch can't hurt you, comprendre? You'll be out in no-time, and Yvonne will take your place. Happy?"

Chapter 16

I hung-up. I was very far from happy.

That Rico had no qualms about me killing someone and blaming the mother of my kids didn't surprise me; he loved having money, and I made it for him. With a World Cup coming up, at which I was going to be captain, he was in line to make even more. So of course he was going to do anything to make sure I was still bringing in the cash.

In a brutal way Rico had made perfect sense. He'd put forward a scenario that would mean I wouldn't get in trouble for Stevie's murder. Which meant I'd get to carry on playing football.

It occurred to me that they might ask why hadn't I taken the lads if I was afraid of Yvonne being a killer? But firstly the F430 only had two seats and secondly, I could just say she was only after me. And Stevie of course.

And then, actually, how did I know Yvonne hadn't done it? He was in our house which only we had keys to – apart from Etienne and the cleaner and a few others. And she'd never liked the way he treated May. And it had certainly been someone, so why not her? She could go mental quickly, something I'd seen that night.

Driving along, I realised that Rico's plan seemed the best move. The other choice was trusting a man I'd never met who'd said he was going to call me, but I had no idea whether he would or what he'd say. Yet I still had a feeling that the man on the phone had wanted to help for the right reasons.

I decided to hedge bets. If after the call my instincts about the man were wrong, what was stopping me going back home and doing what Rico said? Rico had been insistent that I couldn't get caught trying to run away, and I was sure I could manage that. I knew these roads and if they caught me on my way home I could just launch into what Rico had said. Blame Yvonne. Blame fear and wait for him to save me.

It made sense to park up again. Especially if I wanted to have enough left in the tank to make it home. I made a list of all the hidden places in the area. Not for dogging this time, but places I took the lads to put them through their paces at football. Even though we had a big garden, if I wanted to really coach them, I had to take them away from home.

66

Otherwise Yvonne would tell me to stop being too harsh or they'd cry and want to watch cartoons. I decided to go to a place actually on a road that circled back towards my village. It was perfect.

To try and relax, as I headed off the ring-road, I turned the radio back on.

"So what you're saying," the radio presenter was asking, "is an ambulance has pulled away, but not at any speed?"

"That's righ'," came a crackly voice, "A few villagers said they did see a stretcher, like, go in, but I sleep with plugs in and a mask on. I'm tough to wake."

"For all you listeners who've just joined us, this is the situation at Brian Parr's house, where there's been an incident possibly involving missing player Stevie Hurst..."

"Yeah, it's crazy...they've done a road block and everythin' right outside my house, do you know it? By the Red Lion. I hope it's not there long, I've got work..."

"Can't say I do know it, thanks for calling," the radio presenter cut in.

The road into the village by the pub was the one that I'd planned to take if I did take Rico's advice. I'd have to be careful in case they'd put any more blocks up. If I was going to hand myself in, doing it at a road-block wasn't so bad. But if possible I wanted Rico there to fight my corner and I didn't want any press. Nothing ends golden handcuff sponsorship deals like a pair of real handcuffs – something Rico had drummed into me a thousand times.

"On to our next caller...Linda, are you there...?"

"I've always said he's a bad 'un...and this proves it, he is..."

"Whoah, there Linda, let's not jump to any conclusions now..."

"But it's all around, that that mate of his is dead, and he did it...."

"That's a pretty big accusation there, what's it based on?"

"What everyone's saying down by his house, and you can tell he had it in him, he's always had it in him, you'll see. It'll all come out..."

Linda hung-up just as I swung the car off the road, into the deserted clearing and turned the engine off. Without thinking I'd picked up my mobile and dialled the radio show. I wasn't going to be bad-mouthed like this. I'd heard of one player who'd called in to a phone-in when people had said he was a terrible brother because his brother had killed himself over drugs. He'd given them a rant about how people should stop judging when they didn't know the facts. He got a lot of respect for doing that, it showed he had balls.

I was automatically put on hold. As I sat there drumming my fingers, it came to me that if I was set-up the best thing to do was get it out in the open. That way they'd have to take it seriously rather than just hushing it up. There'd once been a Brazilian player who'd got caught up in betting. They kidnapped his wife and told him they'd kill her if he didn't throw a match, but instead of doing it he told the press. Once it was public the fix was never going to work so his wife was released. He was shot in a bar a month later, but the thing was by getting the press on side he'd started a proper investigation. That's what I needed to do.

There were about 10 minutes left to wait. The machine said I was seventh in line to speak.

"...and now I'm told we've got a very exciting caller, with a live update, it's....Dave?"

"Dave, that's right, I'm Dave. D-A-V-..."

"..E, Dave?" the presenter interrupted.

"That's right."

"Well glad we've got that sorted," the presenter said, "...I heard you've got an update on this Brian Parr situation?"

"I have."

"Could you tell us what it is then, Dave?

"I'm not meant to."

"Oh come on," I said, talking to the radio like I do the TV when the football's on. Here was some idiot who didn't know anything calling in to talk about me, while I had to wait in line: I knew much more about me than he did.

"You're not meant to? Why not?"

"The police told me not to. But I don't like them."

"The police? Ha! And I take it you don't mean the band?"

"What? Look, I'm a farmer, and I just saw Brian Parr drive past going towards his village."

I couldn't believe it, was he lying?

"You sure it was him?"

"He was in one of them Ferraris he's always driving around when I get up to tend to my cows."

"And you called the Police?"

"I did. And then thought I'd tell you. It's fun listening to it on the radio, isn't it? Like a game."

"Amazing, well, let's hope it helps the police....thanks for the call, Dave."

He must have seen me after I'd left the ring-road if he knew I was heading home. So I knew I was half-way between his farm and the village. If people were looking for me, they'd follow this road.

I had to move. But petrol was low. There were 5 minutes to go. I was fifth next to go onto the radio show.

Revving the engine, I looked around and sh*t a brick when over the trees the helicopter suddenly loomed large. How had it got so close? The radio was on so loud! To the left and right were flashing lights, sirens. I had to get out of sight or Rico's game was up.

Chapter 17

Grabbing both phones I opened the door and legged it into the woods. My legs were still heavy from the match but fear drove me on. It was dark and I was running through trees but there was enough light to help me see a metre or two in front of me.

Once I'd got far enough I glanced over my shoulder. The helicopter light was on the Ferrari, people had surrounded it. I could say I was so low on petrol I'd left it there and had to jog home. It would be best to call Rico and let him know. The man on the phone didn't seem a very stable shout anymore. I wished I'd turned back when Rico had told me to. What had I been thinking?

There was a ringing. The same ringing as in the bedroom.

The man was calling.

Having lost my concentration slightly to check the mobile, I lost my footing. My ankle twisted, I felt a sharp pain. Crashed to the ground, spilling both phones as I tried to break my fall.

For a second I felt light-headed, dizzying flecks blurring my vision. I'd snapped a ligament before so I knew how bad things could be. Luckily, this was a sprain; with the right treatment you can be doing light-jogging within days, kicking a football in a week, a two week lay-off at most. In terms of what it meant there and then, I knew it'd hurt, but I'd make it home. First though I had to get the phone.

"Brian, hello, hello...?" I could hear the man saying. It was covered in mud but it wasn't my phone so as long as it worked I didn't mind.

I held it to my face, took a deep breath, and was just about to say hello when he hung up.

I couldn't believe it. I'd driven for an hour, risking everything, and I missed the call? The phone was old and after a minute of thinking it was a touch-screen, I tried the buttons. F*cking antiques! I managed to work it out in the end and found the call log: number unknown. I couldn't call him back!

There was no time to think about that though because just then I heard a sound I didn't want to hear. Dogs, and the helicopter coming closer.

I grabbed both mobiles and pulled myself up with the help of the tree. Biting my lip I put some weight on my ankle. It hurt, but I knew that if this was an important match I wouldn't be signalling over to the bench just yet. Some players would throw in the towel as soon as they felt a twinge. It was pathetic and I was proud of the British Bulldog in me that kept me going whatever it was, something I thought that every England captain should have.

For the next five minutes I made good progress. It seemed that I'd won a bit of luck too because through the trees the helicopters searchlight seemed to be veering off to the right away from me. I could only hear them and they seemed to be further away too.

Once I was out the woods onto the field going was a lot easier. To forget the pain, I started to sing. In fact it was more of a chant, like they do in the army, which I sometimes did in training. I know it sounds a bit self-obsessed, but I liked to sing one of the chants the fans sung about me to the tune of *Yellow Submarine*. Even though some people think fans are they're all stupid, the fact is they can be very poetic:

United is the team I love,
And there's a man who plays for us
Every match he scores a goal,
I love it when he scores a goal.
We all like Brian Parr to play for us,
Cos he really is the nuts,
He really is the nuts!
We all like Brian Parr to play for us
Cos he is the dogs b*llocks
He is the dogs b*llocks!

I was caught up in my singing when I realised the mobile was ringing.

"Brian?" the man's voice said

"Yes, it's Brian, it's me! I'm so glad you got through to me," I said, through heavy breath.

"Are you ok?"

"I had to leave the car, I'm hurt, but not badly."

"Where are you going? Are people following?"

"I'm in a field, there's a helicopter looking for me, it's about a mile away..."

"Good. You can't be caught, that's what they want."

"Who? Who?"

"Look, just focus on not getting caught, you need to be careful."

"Of course I need to. They're trying to get to me for killing Stevie!

"That's why I told you to leave your house."

"I did leave the house. It *was* a set-up!"

"I know you did, I know you did, look, just try to calm down."

"Don't tell me what to do, you don't want know what it's like!"

"Do you want some help?"

"Yes," I admitted, desperate for everything to be ok again.

"Well, Brian, the thing is there's quite a lot behind what's going on tonight. The way you've been acting hasn't been great has it?"

"What's that supposed to mean? Who are you?"

"I'm someone who cares. We need to work together to stop the people trying to ruin you."

"F*ckers! I hate them."

"Well, quite, but you've got to listen. Promise?"

"Promise," I said, feeling like a kid. I'd got to the top of the hill.

"What I'm about to say is going to come as a shock. The sooner you can understand it, the better, because then I can tell you exactly how to get yourself out of this. Firstly, whatever happens, do not trust Rico he's..."

"I never have trusted him."

"Good," he said, "and don't start now."

"Sure thing."

"He won't like it, he'll try to convince you to do things his way..."

"Well, it's his own fault really, isn't it?"

I turned round, to double-check I was still in the clear. My heart jumped up into my throat, my eyes popped out.

The helicopter was heading straight for me. From out of the woodland I could see torches, could hear the dogs. A 4x4's headlights were fast approaching from the field to my left. Without thinking I started running.

At the time of that phone-call I'd forgotten that in the car I'd called the radio show on my own mobile. And not hung-up. Sometime during my struggle across the field I'd been put through to the presenter. It was in my hand as I started singing about myself. People listening thought I'd lost it.

The presenter had tried to get through to me but obviously, not knowing I was connected, I'd just carried on singing.

Someone at the radio called the Police and they tuned in just as I started talking to the man. The problem was, while I was talking to the man, people listening to the radio thought I'd started talking to the presenter at last. That's how the Police knew where I was and a lot of what else they heard didn't help me out later either:

"Brian?" the radio presenter asks one last time, "Is that you Brian, it may be time for me to hang up if you don't..."

"Yes, it's Brian, it's me! I'm so glad you got through to me," I say, through heavy breath.

"Are you ok?"

"I had to leave the car, I'm hurt, but not badly."

"Where are you, Brian?"

"I'm in a field, there's a helicopter looking for me, it's about a mile away...."

"Ok, well, you're live on SportNight radio, talking to Barry Day."

"Who? Who?"

"Maybe I'm not important, if you've called, you must need to say something?"

"Of course I need to. They're trying to get to me for killing Stevie!

"Really? We had heard reports that you'd left your house?"

74

"I did leave the house. It was a set-up!"

"Was it Brian? Well perhaps it's best to let the police help you?"

"Don't tell me what to do, you don't want know what it's like!"

"Do you mean to kill someone?"

"Yes," I say, sounding like an angry teenager – possibly the worst way I could have sounded given the question and circumstances.

"Wow, you heard it here first folks live on SportNight. Brian, that's quite a statement to make live on-air..."

"What's that supposed to mean? Who are you?"

"Like I said, I'm Barry Day, are you ok, Brian? Do you want to tell me where you are so I can let the police know?"

"F*ckers! I hate them."

"Er, ok, Brian, sure. I can see how you might think that. "

"Promise."

"Promise? Sure...if you'd like me to. Sure, I can see why you might not like the boys in blue right now. But if you could just tell me, why you did it, Brian, why you've done this to Stevie?"

"I've never trusted him."

"Trust, so you had a disagreement?"

"Sure thing."

"You sound pretty nonchalant about that, Brian?"

"Well, it's his own fault really, isn't it?"

"You really don't sound very remorseful Brian, I mean this is a man's life? Brian? Brian?"

And then you hear me fall over and the line goes dead.

As I ran from the helicopter my bad ankle gave way. The kimono ripped under my foot and came undone as I fell hard. My own mobile was underneath me and stabbed painfully into my stomach. Ending the radio phone call without me ever knowing it had happened.

I was focused on trying to hold onto the mobile I'd found in the bedroom.

"Brian!" the man shouted.

"What shall I do? Who's set me up who's done this to me?"

"Listen, all you need to do..."

At that moment a police dog reached me. I struggled to get up, holding my hands up. It leapt, its fangs bared. I ducked, it flew past only hitting my hand. The hand I was holding the phone in. Or had been holding it in, because my palm was now empty. I screamed. And then so did Yvonne.

Chapter 18

I don't think I'll ever forget what happened next. Somebody said it was the most memorable football moment there'd ever been even though it wasn't on the pitch; bigger than the Hand of God, bigger than the 'They think it's all over...it is now' moment, which for me, it seemed, it was.

All of the photos show me with my legs splayed, on a field, trapped in a spotlight. Watched over by police-men and their dogs. That would have been bad enough if I was fully clothed and clean. I wasn't.

The photo's all show that year's highest earner in world football wearing a ripped, pink, flowery kimono and some feathery slippers. Nothing else. The way I'd fallen meant my d*ck and b*lls are very much saying cheese to the camera. To accessorise with my cross-dressing and full-frontal flashing, I was also smeared with a lot of blood, some mud, and cowpat.

From that moment on the story of Stevie dying, of me fleeing the house, being chased, being caught and being arrested, provided a sales boost for every single national newspaper in the UK. It was the kind of coverage I'd always dreamt of, but it wasn't the right kind.

In the past I'd taken flak for red cards, missed penalties, own goals, 'accidental' elbows, pushing refs, swearing at fans, I'd done the lot. I'd survived the lot. This made all of them look like a match report on a friendly - this was like I'd deliberately lost the World Cup final for England and then laughed about it.

A few people initially took my side. They were angry that the press had been allowed such a free reign to follow and film my arrest and then put it out for everyone to see so everyone thought I was guilty. Not many others agreed. They brought up the amount of money I'd made from photo shoots of the biggest moments of my life – passing my driving test, the exclusive about my first sports car write-off, buying the house with Yvonne, the lads' births, our re-done kitchen, our second kitchen renovation. They said if I was happy to let people see those moments, shouldn't the public who'd bought into me, get to see my arrest? Didn't they deserve to see my down-times too, warts and all (thankfully at the time of the photo I was free of all STDs and my d*ck looks ok considering)?

That moment in the field was the most intimidating experience of my life. I've played in front of over 70,000 fans, with millions watching on TV waiting and counting on my every move. I've caused riots in Asia by stepping out of a taxi. I've met world leaders. I've joined a rock band on stage and sung – despite the fact I can't sing– in front of the whole world to help stop something bad that was happening. Yet that

77

evening I was more out of my depth than I'd ever been. And on camera it showed. Which I think is why so many people lost faith in me that

Honestly, having seen the footage, what else could you believe? I don't blame even my most loyal fans for thinking the worst of me. Who was going to take my side when my fiancé was metres away screaming at me, shouting I'd done Stevie and then tried to kill her?

"Yvonne?" I managed, trying to get myself to my feet, "Why are you being like this. I wasn't going to..."

"Stay right there!" a stern voice told me.

I couldn't see who'd said it, I was blinded by the spotlights on me. I could hear the helicopter touching down behind me.

"Look," I tried, holding my hands up as I limped to my feet, "This isn't...I mean..."

"Stay where you are!"

"Please, you've got to understand," I said, words failing me, "Please, listen, I beg you..."

"No. You've got to listen to me. Do not move."

I'd had a lot of media training in my time. When I was playing well, and being interviewed a lot, I often found myself talking to my mates like I was on camera:

"You know your missus, Bri? Any good in bed?"

"She's professional, Shags. She gets her head down and she does a job, I can't ask for any more than that."

"Brian, do you think we should complain to the school? Baggio's a clever boy but every test he takes he does badly."

"I hate to blame it on the marking, Yvonne, but sometimes you've got to question whether these people have trained hard enough to tick the

78

right boxes when push comes to shove."

In the field that night, however, I was lost for words. None of my usual phrases sounded right. How can you talk about a game of two halves when you're half-naked and covered in blood?

"Look, please, everyone, this has nothing to do with me."

"What doesn't, Brian? What doesn't?"

This time it wasn't a policeman who was asking, it was a journalist. In the background, I could hear Yvonne telling people I'd killed Stevie and threatened her. Over and over again she was saying it. It looked like she was being interviewed. All I wanted to do was get to her. Find out why she was so against me all of a sudden. But the journalists kept shouting, kept pressing.

I couldn't deal with them all. Look at the video. You can see me sweating, my eyes bulging, my fists clenching.

"What has nothing to do with you, Brian? We've all been involved in a manhunt for you!"

"Yes, but it's not true."

"Why did you try to run?"

"I didn't!"

"You were in a Ferrari!"

"I know. But no. You see, this...with Stevie. I found..." I tried before being submerged with questions – there seemed to be more press in the barricade around me than police.

"Why were you trying to escape, Brian?"

"When you said on the radio just now that you knew what it was like to kill did you mean Stevie?"

"Radio?" I said, not knowing at that point about the mix-up, "I haven't been on the radio."

"See he's lying."

"I'm not!" I protested.

One of the reporters played me some of the radio interview from his Dictaphone, I was too confused to work out what had happened.

"But that's not me!" I shouted.

"It sounds like you..."

"You say your name!" someone said.

"You say you're in a field!" another added.

"You say you've hurt your ankle!"

"No, listen, please. I'm Brian Parr. I'm England captain!"

A silence descended. In the crowd I saw Rico next to Yvonne. Our eyes met. He shook his head. He knew what I was going to say. He'd already worked out how to save himself, but he couldn't help shaking his head to stop me.

"I didn't kill Stevie. It's a set-up, I'm being framed. I don't know who by or why, but it's true. And I'm vowing from this day that I'm going to find out who's done this to me and I need you all to help me…and help find who killed Stevie Hurst."

Silence.

Frantically I glanced around for a reaction. Was it too much to expect a 'Bobby Moore' and for people to see I was a hero and hoist me on their shoulders like the time I'd won the cup with two goals – one toe-poke, one off the knee?

Or maybe it was all a big joke? Yes, one of those TV prank shows! One of mine and Stevie's England colleagues had done his own version and it was great. Maybe Stevie was about to come out of the helicopter and wipe all the make-up off?

"Hang on. I'm not stupid. Is this a joke for a TV show?" I asked.

"Save him," a policeman ordered.

The press erupted. The police kicked into action, cordoning me off and pushing the cameras and reporters away. I was hand-cuffed and read my rights as they arrested me on suspicion of murder.

Chapter 19

"I've always been a Town fan."

"He has."

"He's always been United though."

"I have."

"His kids have got your posters on their walls."

"They do."

"Which one of you is the good cop?" I said speaking for the first time in a long time, "Because at the moment you both look like you're really bad at this job."

My line worked like I'd hoped it would work, apart from the fact my lawyer spat out his coffee all over me and looked at me like I was crazy. To be fair, I didn't care about the coffee. They weren't my clothes it had gone on. I was in a sweatshirt they'd given me, and a pair of cords. I know, the Parrster, the face of Italian fashion houses for the past few years, in cords! And they were green! What was going on? Well, once they'd booked me at the station, they told me I had to choose between the geeky cords or the kimono.

The good cop, bad cop line was Shags'. It had the exactly the effect he'd said it would. It took them both by surprise, their stern, frowning faces crumpling as the Town supporter rocked back in his chair and the

81

United one sat down. Both shutting up. Shags had told me it after I'd once been arrested (after some Town fans had started on me in a nightclub) and I was telling Shags how much I hated being interviewed by the police. Even though I wasn't at fault (my five punches and six kicks had come after one of them had pushed me first) I'd had a tough time in the interview room so Shags took it upon himself to give me a few pointers:

"You've got to remember one thing about policeman, Bri" he'd told me.

"What's that?"

"They're some of the most hated people in the country, after Town supporters of course, especially your pikey family..."

I laughed, punching him on the shoulder, he loved taking the mick out of my family and how much they were Town through and through.

"And the thing about us, Bri..." he carried on, "...is that we're the most popular people in the country. Fact. So when they get us inside that room, they're in heaven. They get to have a couple of hours of power over us - so you have to get it back, here's how..."

In the interview room that night I was too worried at first to even remember Shags' line, let alone use it. Compared to my other times in the police station, there was one big difference. I didn't feel like I was going to be leaving any time soon. Before, United or Rico flexed their cash or power and got me out with a caution and a 'good luck on Saturday'. This time I was on my own. At the mercy of the two cops.

They'd been hard on me. Asking me over and over again what had happened that night and since Stevie's disappearance. I told them virtually everything I've written in this book so far except things I didn't think were connected to his death.

Until they'd talked about United and Town I hadn't been able to think

82

straight. But the football chat cleared my head somehow. Suddenly I realised that this wasn't easy for them either. They'd both expected an easy ride. Having seen me in that field they thought I was definitely guilty. They'd said there was so much proof against me both of them had told me the confession was all that was missing in the case against me. But they hadn't got it yet and while I looked bad, they didn't look too pretty either. There were sweat patches under their armpits. Their eyes were red. They looked like they'd never even thought about buying their own tanning bed, let alone having five to choose from at home.

I was sure they knew that all the other police people were outside waiting for them to close the case any minute. The longer they were in the room, the faster their reputations were dissolving and the less respect they were going to command.

If I could keep them waiting I'd get more and more power back, just like Shags had told me to do.

"I'd like to talk to my lawyer," I told them.

"Really?" my lawyer said, nervously.

I looked at him, irritated, "Yes! Excuse me officers, but it is very late and you might have heard I played a match a few hours ago and scored a hat-trick..."

"And got sent off..." the Town supporter smiled.

"I am entitled to breaks," I carried on, "...by law, so if you'd kindly let us have a moment of privacy, I'd be most grateful."

They looked at each other. I'd got it right. They were dreading leaving without a result. The thought of having to face their work-mates even for a minute in the knowledge they weren't living up to expectation was stressing them out.

"Don't you forget, Mr Parr," the Town supporter said, "You've been arrested on suspicion of murder..."

I turned to my lawyer. Signalling for his help. Instead he looked like he was going to sh*t himself. Not for the first time that night I felt let down by Rico; he'd said my normal lawyer couldn't be contacted but assured me that the lawyer he'd get sent along by the same firm was a new hot-shot on the scene. He'd lied.

The guy's name was Laurence something. He was a lanky, looked like Harry Potter, with glasses and unadventurous hair and had probably never kicked a football in his life. He was so nervous he kept burying himself in his notebook. I'd actually have preferred to have Harry Potter, even if he didn't know much about law, I bet his wand could have come in handy.

"Erm, yes, that's...I believe that is correct. My client is correct."

"See, now please officers, let me have some time with my lawyer?"

"You're going to be having a lot of time with your lawyers if you carry on lying to us," the Town supporter said nastily.

"I'm not lying."

"We've gone over this already. We have you at the scene, covered in his blood..."

"Because I found him."

"We have you trying to attack the first person who found you, your own fiancée, with a broken bottle!"

"I was trying to hug her."

"We have you leaving the crime scene, in the victim's own car!"

"I won it on the Xbox!"

"We have you evading arrest until your petrol ran out."

"I was trying to take a phone-call! Someone told me it was a set-up.

84

Which it is. That's why we're here now! Someone wants it to look like I did it!"

"It really does look like it was you, we believe that," the United supporter said taking up the reins, "especially seeing as live on radio you as good as confessed it! If anyone's setting you up, it's yourself. Which is why I can't believe you're sat here denying it when you've already told the whole f*ckin' world."

"I didn't do it!"

"Why don't you just tell the truth?" the Town fan shouted, banging his fist on the table, "It'll make it easier. On you, on your fiancée, on your kids..."

"On your club, your fans...?" the United supporter said, "Look, Brian, I've worked in this job a long time. I've never seen a case where it's so obvious we'll get a 'Guilty' in court. If it goes all that way, it'll be all over the papers for months, do you want to put your family through that? Tell us you did it and it'll be made easier. We'll see if we can get you a better prison, your own cell..."

"Look, my friend is dead, my best friend. I found him! Dead! Do you know what that's like?" I breathed in, I had to get rid of the red mist and think, "Look, you two have seen Stevie and me. On the pitch, in the papers, we're best mates. Our partners are sisters, I'm so close to his kids I treat them as my own....why would I do it, why would I kill him?"

"You're right. Motive's the one thing we don't have, good point," the United supported accepted.

"Thanks," I said.

"But you tell us, what motivation did the person who set you up have? Who and how?"

"The press are all over this," the other added, "The public want to see a murderer brought to justice. When we have all this evidence why would we spend time looking for someone we don't believe exists? If you can tell us something concrete, maybe we could look into it?"

The events of the past few days spun through my head.

"I...I...."

"Your fiancée has told us you must have done it. It's out of our hands unless you can tell us something."

Chapter 20

When we were alone, Laurence turned to me, "You're doing very well, Mr Parr."

"Brian."

"Yes, sorry, Mr Brian."

"No, I'm Brian Parr. Do you not know who I am?"

"You're my client?"

I nodded. Was I cleverer than him or something? I couldn't believe it.

"Look, I'm sorry, I have no time for football, but I hear you're very good."

"What are you doing here?" I asked.

"Me? I'm a trainee lawyer. I normally do commercial law but I expressed an interest in doing criminal law about a week ago and then this evening I got a call asking me to come here. I'm sorry if I haven't been very good. I've never been in this situation before."

I swore at Rico. What game was he playing?

"So, ok," I said, trying to cut him some slack, like I did whenever some of the youth team players got the chance to play alongside me,"...what do you mean I'm doing well?"

"I've been making notes. You've not once changed your story. And the two of them have been trying to make you."

"That's because it's the truth!"

He nodded.

"The problem is..." he ventured.

"Yes."

"Is that although you're sticking to the same...truth...a lot of it, well, it doesn't seem like it is the truth, perhaps..."

"Like what!"

"Erm," he was visibly trembling, "Well mostly, you fled a crime scene because of this man on the phone. But we don't know who he is, and neither is there a phone...."

"The dog took it when I was arrested, I told them that."

"But you heard them...the dog-handlers say the dog hasn't got it and it's not been found yet."

"That's what happened though!"

"Yes, but in law, all law, you need proof...and from what these two are saying there seems to be lots of evidence to show you.....did it....and none to say you didn't..."

I nodded. I wanted to run through everything again, to work out what would be the killer ball to unlock the defence and help me prove my innocence. I just felt so tired.

"So what do you think they'll do?"

"You're not going to confess?"

"I'm innocent! You really don't believe me, do you?"

"From hearing you, looking at you, I believe you. But looking at the case and its facts...they are pretty insurmountable."

"In-sur-what? Don't use legal talk with me, pal," I told him, "Look, either way, my mate told me they can't keep me in for more than 24 hours, can they?"

"They can actually, as it's a serious charge, but I don't think they will."

"Really, so they'll let me go?" I asked happily.

"No, Brian, I'm afraid not. Even without a confession, they have enough to charge you."

"Charge me? But you just saw me break those d*cks, I was in charge, not being charged! They want me to tell them something concrete."

"And can you?"

"I just need some time."

And with that the door burst open.

I looked up, startled at who it was, and then angry, "Rico!"

He strode in, his hair looking slightly messy, which was unusual for him, but his eyes were all business as usual. He was holding a piece of paper.

"Do you know what this is?" he said, sharply as he sat down in front of me.

"Rico! What's going on? I need help in here, why is Laurence here, not a proper lawyer? No offence."

"None taken," Laurence nodded.

"Except there is an offence, and it's ruined your career," Rico snapped, "You can kick a ball but you've f*cked up this time."

"Hey!" I said, shocked; I was used to being sworn at by Shags and the Gaffer, but not my agent.

"Why didn't you listen to me? We had a great story to tell you and me. We had a murder in your home, an arrest, and then if you'd done what we said we could have had the vindication when we proved you were innocent, the moment you got back on the pitch. It would have been wonderful, the perfect CMS!"

"What?"

"Client Meltdown Simulations. It's my own invention and I'm great at them. As soon I got the call about Stevie's body I was working out how to pull off the biggest PR resurrection ever. Think about it, you were about to be married to a bullying murderess – probably due to post-natal depression or something – but you managed to live to tell the story. It would have made you the hottest thing on the planet, Bri, and I would have made us both more in a month than we've ever made..."

He was speaking with such passion, it was impossible to not believe him; but it was also horrible, the idea of making so much lovely cash from Stevie's death.

"...but you thought you knew better and now you're going to be crucified."

"Look, Rico, I..."

"No, it's too late. This exists now," he said holding up the piece of paper, "Which means you're finished. Entirely finished."

"What is it?"

"Your charge sheet. For murder. I threw you a lifeline, you went against me, and now this piece of paper is your death sentence."

"Rico how can you be so...nasty."

"Nasty! Jesus, you really are a child, aren't you?"

"I'm not," I replied, stamping my foot in anger, then screaming as I hurt my ankle again, "This isn't fair! I didn't do it!"

"They said you were saying that. Still crying set-up...I warned you

89

against that. Chr*st you have no idea how badly you're going to get ripped apart, do you? With the headlines that are going to surface today and over the next week I'd feel sorry for your agent and PR team if you still had one."

"What? But you're my..."

"No. That was terminated the moment you hung up on me. We no longer represent you!"

"Rico. How can you be this cold? This is my life you're talking about..."

"What about Stevie's life?"

"I..." I floundered, the memory of Stevie's lifeless body knocking me off track.

"Now, I've been allowed in here to try and make you see sense and get you to plead guilty at your plea-hearing."

"What's that?"

Rico looked at me, his eyes ruthless as he shook his head, "If you were to plead guilty it would be beneficial to the police, and my newest and biggest client."

"Who's that?

"Yvonne."

"Yvonne!" I said, "But you've never taken her on before! She's begged for ages for you to help her with her TV stuff and you've always said no."

"I don't work with two-bit presenters. But the only person in the world who had to live with the world's richest, most popular murderer is an entirely different proposition. Which is why I'm really here - to offer you a deal. If you let her have everything she wants – the house, the cars, the dogs...she'll let you keep the money you have in the bank...deal?"

"What about the lads?"

"I don't think she mentioned them, but for the photo-shoots they're obviously important....anyhow, what she wants, she gets. Once you've signed you won't owe her a thing. It's a clean break. It's best for both of you...she gets the stuff which you won't need in here, and you get the cash, because you'll need it if you want to get out. I'll draw up the contract. You can sign next time I see you."

"Why should I?" I knew I had to protect myself because Shags always said his ex had robbed him of loads of cash. He even joked that every time he got a goal bonus he had to give her some, which was why he never scored.

"Because if you do make things difficult, some of the things she says are going to be very bad for you."

"Like what...the...girls?"

"No. The girls will all be cashing in themselves...there are other things that only she would know about you."

"Like what?"

"Well, the details are sordid, but who will people believe? The murderer or the poor, pretty single mum of two?"

"You're lying. She wouldn't do this to me. She loves me. Why are you...?"

Rico flicked his phone out. He pressed a couple of buttons and then held up a recording of Yvonne:

"Brian," she said, "everything Rico says is true. All those wh*res you've f*cked, all the times you've lied to me about where you are, and now Stevie? It's too much and it's time for us to move on. Sign the paper. Give me what you owe me. Or regret it."

The recording stopped.

My face said it all.

"Thanks, Brian," Rico said, getting up, "Like I said, you'll get the cash in the bank. It's better than most footballers get when the WAG has enough of all the cheating. And also, plead guilty, for your sake. You'll be out in ten years....you'll have saved your money, you could live well...

"I didn't do it!"

"Think about it. Because if it goes to trial, the bill will be huge. And you'll still go down. By the time you get out, you'll have nothing left in the bank at all."

"Rico, why are you being like this?"

He looked at me and shook his head.

"Because as well as being Yvonne's new agent, I'm also – keep this quiet though, we'll do an exclusive spread in a couple of weeks – her new fiancé. We're going to make a great team."

"This is..." I shouted, "How've you done this, it's only been a few hours!"

"CMS, Bri, CMS. Once you closed the door on me I had to open another one, didn't I? You said it yourself, she's begged me to help her for years. This is mutually best for both of us, she saw that and went along with my plan.

"Now, Laurence, you were retained by me, for Mr Parr, which I had to do until I could personally inform him our arrangement was over. Seeing as that's done, I'd be grateful if you would come with me..."

Laurence, looked at me. I nodded; there was nothing I could do.

"Happy reading, Brian."

Rico threw the piece of paper at me and left. Followed by Laurence. I

92

tore the piece of paper up. I noticed that Laurence had left his notebook. I slid it to where I could see it properly. There was my story, everything I'd said to the police, but he'd also noted down some of his own questions. As I bent down to read them properly the door opened.

The two policemen walked in. They confirmed I was being charged with the murder of Stevie Hurst. I'm sure I had feelings. Those emotion things. But all I can remember is numbness. I had to go to court the following day. Seeing as I'd lost my lawyer they asked if I needed to make a call, or if I wanted the one you got for free. I said I didn't care. All I wanted to do was sleep. It had been the worst day of my life.

Chapter 21

The moment I woke up there was none of that 'It was all a dream' stuff you see in films for girls. It was real.

I sat up on the cold, hard mattress. Something wasn't right. I felt dizzy, weak, my breathing almost hurting.

I vomited, my sick hitting the wall about a metre in front of me. It was disgusting, but I couldn't stop puking until my throat burnt and there was nothing left to come up. The policewoman who opened the cell wouldn't come in and said she'd get me a doctor. All I could do was lie down and wait. I started crying. I tried to stop, tried to live up to my reputation; as a brilliant hard-man footballer. When I realised that my name was probably as ruined as I felt, I only cried even harder.

I was helped into a different cell to lie down and wait for a doctor.

"It's probably stress, Mr Parr," a serious voice told me, half-waking me up, "You have got yourself in a very stressful situation."

I felt a needle stab into my fore-arm. I felt woozy. I was still lying on the single bed. I tried to open my eyes, but they kept shutting, my head and my body felt really heavy; I remember thinking it was like in P.E. when they used to make you wear pyjamas in the swimming pool. The only lesson I'd always enjoyed.

"Don't try to move. I'm just taking a blood sample. You've done this before....we've done this before."

Something inside of me kicked into gear as I recognised the voice. His voice. Dr Malone's. What the hell was he doing there?

I forced my eyes open and tried to get up off the bed. His hand shot to my neck. His grip strong and hard.

"Sit down, Brian!"

I had to sit back, his fingers so tight I couldn't fight him.

"What's....what's going on?"

"You needed a doctor."

"But why you, Dr Malone? You're not a...prison doctor are you?"

He smiled at me and came over and sat in front of me on a chair, "No, Brian, I'm not a prison doctor. But neither is my name Malone."

I looked at him astonished. Compared to the last time I'd seen him, raging drunk and threatening Stevie and me, he seemed like a completely different person.

"What do you mean? I've known you for..."

"You've known what I've told you; so did your waste-of-space friend."

"Hey, don't..."

"Look," he said, holding up an ID card. The name on it wasn't Malone. "I've always used a fake name for you as a means of protection, and

94

this is another fake name I've used because I needed to speak to you."

"This doesn't make sense," I said, "How did you get in here? Are you a doctor at all?" I said, rubbing the arm he'd just taken blood from.

"Of course. You've seen what I can do. Not just anyone can do that," he smiled, "Which is why I tried to stop Stevie and you bandying the name Malone around….not because it would lead directly to me, but because if anyone chose to believe you and did some digging, it wouldn't take too long to go through the doctors in this city with the required skills….that's not something I can afford to happen."

The way he was speaking was scary. He'd always been a great bloke in the past; either really caned when I met him on nights out, or nice and professional when I needed him to make it look like I hadn't been drinking. Things were very different now. And somehow he'd managed to break into prison – I was sure that wasn't meant to happen.

"Don't bother saying anything about this to anyone, Brian. People will only say you're delirious - you already keep saying you've been set-up. Now, I'm not here to harm you, I just need a chat..."

"How do you know what I've been saying?"

"I know some important people. How else do you think I'm in here? How else do you think I know about Stevie's post mortem?"

"What's that?"

"The post mortem?"

"Yes. Is it a letter?" I said, thinking fast, before getting the answer, "Oh, is it his will?"

"Will? No, it says how he died."

"Oh," I said flatly.

He paused and watched me, "That's good Brian, that's really convincing. If I didn't know better I'd have believed you don't know

95

how he was killed."

"I don't, I found him like that," I said angrily.

He held his hands up in defence; like people do when they've fouled someone, and know it, but they want to make the ref think they haven't. "Fine, fine, look, I'm not here to talk to you about Stevie's death," he said.

"Really?"

"Sure, that's between you and the police. What I'm here for is to make sure you don't talk to anyone about the work, I've done for you...and Stevie."

"I haven't."

"And I want it to stay that way. Or else."

"Or else what?" I asked.

He looked awkward for a second, then leant in, whispering, "It's not just me telling you this. There are other people who want you to shut up too."

"Who?"

"Let's just say they have a financial interest in what I do. They're like my managers. I do what they say, and they are very serious people who need our business to stay secret. They were getting ready to act on the fact Stevie was talking about me until last night..."

"Is that what you meant the other day when you said you'd warned Stevie?"

He paused for a second, and then nodded.

"Well, it could be them then, his killers! We need to tell..."

"No, Brian, it wasn't them," he said forcefully, "Stevie was in debt to me, and them, and before doing anything physical they would have gone for his money first. This isn't their style and they've sent me here is to ensure you don't say anything that might get anyone sniffing around."

"How do you know they didn't do it? We have to get help."

Dr Malone, or whatever he was called, began to roll up his sleeves. He had burn marks, up his wrists. I winced when I saw them. I couldn't imagine the amount of pain he would have gone through.

"I was thinking like you after he went missing. Then they made me see sense. Have you noticed? I'm a lot calmer, it's because they've told me what to do. And I'm doing it," he said, hiding his arms again, "This type of killing isn't their style. It's all about business and he was worth more alive to them then dead. As long as he shut up about me, and started paying me, he would have been fine with us and Stevie knew that. He knew that because I told him that just before he crashed the car that night."

In a rush I realised something, "You're the last person to see him alive."

"The important word there is 'alive'. Look, Brian, forget my backers, the post mortem has no reports of Stevie being beaten or hurt. He was killed with a knife, the kind of wounds you find in a crime of passion."

"A what?"

"It's when someone kills someone because of anger, not for money. This isn't gangster work, this is someone who knows him, who killed him in a struggle. It sounds more like it was you if I'm honest. When he came to me in a state, he did sometimes rant about you..."

"Did he? About what?"

"His wife and you. So maybe he brought it up, you two fought, you won."

Hearing that hit me hard. I didn't know what to say.

"I see that's given you something to think about. But like I say, we don't care about that. What we care is you not talking about me."

"Why shouldn't I?" I spat, feeling annoyed at him for talking at me like I was nothing.

"There would be the small matter of me helping you take tests illegally…we both know it was only alcohol you wanted out of your system, but if you do the dirty on me….who's to say I haven't got evidence that suggests you were taking things?"

"You wouldn't?"

"You'd lose a lot of the medals you've won. You wouldn't want that would you?"

I shook my head. I couldn't take his word for it that these people hadn't hurt Stevie, but at that moment I had nowhere to turn. As he packed up, I knew he was getting away with something, but as Laurence had said, it's all about proof and I had none. I swore as I realised I'd got rid of evidence myself. When Dr Malone had come round to mine the night Stevie had gone missing, I'd turned the CCTV off – as I always did. I had nothing to prove he'd come round. I didn't think I could prove anything about what we'd done together. I always paid cash. I always went alone.

"Good luck, Brian," he said smugly, knocking on the door, "And remember, my managers will hear if you start talking about me. So don't. It's not just you they'd hurt to protect themselves."

"What do you mean by that?"

I wasn't certain, but I was fairly sure he put his hand down by his side and stretched his hand out flat; as if signalling a child, as if they might hurt the lads. I kicked the bed I was laid on. What could I do? Here I was, under arrest, charged with murder, and being threatened by someone working for people I didn't even know? It was crazy! I felt like my brain was being boiled in my head as I tried to work things out! What could I do to get out of there? And help Stevie? And speak to Yvonne? And protect the lads? What could I do?

Chapter 22

My first ever memories, and United fans might hate to hear me say this, are of Town. Dad's always said Town's in his blood and it's in mine. When the offer to go to United came it was a wrench, a real wrench, because until I left Town they really were my life. They were the first thing I thought of in the morning, and as I fell asleep each night I did so with posters of my favourite players watching over me as I lay there in my Town Y-fronts. As soon as I understood what playing football was I wanted to play football. And I wanted to do it for Town.

When I was about twelve, I'd been on their books for a while and although every year other boys were let go and told not to come back, Dad and I just seemed to know that I was going to make it.

That season I had a blinder. I scored 54 goals in 28 matches. I thought I was good enough to play for the first team. And I was desperate to because that season was the worst in their history. They were awful. And they couldn't score.

While I led my youth team to our own championship, it was hard to celebrate when the club as a whole was doing so badly. From about Christmas onwards everyone was saying we were going to get relegated. It was terrible. Whenever we lost, which was a lot, I felt like someone had died. Dad and me would talk about it all the time, trying to find ways out of it. Desperate to think of ways we could stop losing.

It was all we could think about. If my school work could have got worse, it would have done, but it was my mood that was most affected. I'd always been a cheeky kid playing pranks on people; giving them dead-arms, kicking a football at their face. That season, that stopped. I was too worried. I went right off my mini-pizzas. That threat, of going down, was like nothing I'd ever faced. It was unthinkable, it was a nightmare, life wouldn't be worth living.

As the end of the season got nearer and there were fewer and fewer matches left. Every time we played, even though the odds were against us, I'd have this sudden surge of hope. An inbuilt feeling of self-confidence that it was going to be ok. Then we'd lose. And that bit of hope made the loss hurt even more.

The matches - the life-lines - came and went. 'It's ok, there's still five games left', became 'it's ok, still four to play for'. Still, I thought about it all the time. Still, I hoped. Still, it made me want to cry even though I didn't cry because I was Brian Parr even when I was young.

I'll never forget that feeling of hopelessness. Of wanting something so much, with every part of my brain and body, and yet not being able to do anything at all about it. But what got me through, when I look back, was my Dad. For two reasons. Firstly, because his own unbreakable belief it would be ok made me think it would be. And secondly, because it meant that I had someone to share it all with - share the sadness, the hope and the faith it would be ok – which just made it all feel easier to face because I wasn't alone.

Having my Dad alongside me got me through that horrible season. It taught me the importance of being in a team.

Unfortunately, as soon I was charged with Stevie's murder I found myself being dropped by everyone. One by one, just as that season each game came and went without us winning, the people I hoped would help me, didn't.

Rico was true to his word. He came back the next day with contracts. I was about to sign them when I thought of something. Rico had always told me he was amazing at getting people to sign things to get what he wanted, not what they wanted. Up until then we'd always been on the same side, but what if he was trying to get one over on me? I cleverly checked the contract a bit longer. He was sat there opposite me. Texting. It seemed simple enough. Yvonne got our things and I got all the bank accounts. I most liked the bit where it said she could never get any more money off me ever. Losing the cars made me most sad, but I knew I could buy more once I got out. Then I remembered the lads.

"What about the lads?" I asked.

He sat up, "What about them?"

"It says here I can never see them. Shags still gets to see his kids..."

"You're in here, Bri..."

"Not for long. And when I get out I want to see them. Or I'm not signing!"

"Ok, ok," Rico said, holding his hands up, "Yvonne wanted you to never see them, but I thought that was harsh. I know how much you love them, don't you?"

"I really do," I nodded.

"Which is why," he said, making his voice quieter, "Without Yvonne knowing I brought another contract. In this one, it says once you are free you can talk to Yvonne about seeing them. So it's not a ban like she wanted...look, read it..."

He took out another contract and showed it to me. He was right

"The rest is all the same, all the same," he told me, "Check it. All it means is that if you get out, you could see them. I think, as their Dad, you have that right."

I tried not to smile that I'd beaten him. I signed straight away. That's how Brian Parr does business.

Rico left without saying a word.

That afternoon I got a call from my Dad: the next person to drop me.

"Dad?" I asked, turning away from the policewoman who'd led me to the phone, "I'm so glad you called. This is really bad isn't it?"

"Brian, it's what you deserve."

"What?"

"You heard me."

"Dad? Where are you? It'll all be sorted soon, but it'd be good to see you."

"I'm in Spain, son. I'm not coming back except for Town games."

"Spain? What are you doing there? I need you, Dad, I need help."

"I said that for a long time, Brian, you ignored me."

"Dad!" I said, not believing what I was hearing, "It's a mistake. Someone else killed Stevie. We have to find out who did it!"

"He deserves it too."

"Dad?"

"He does. I've always said that about him, United through and through and every bit as bad. I told you not to join..."

"Stop it!" I shouted.

"Mr Parr, you have to..." said the policewoman, stepping forward, her hand signalling me to keep the noise down.

"Dad, please, please," I half-whispered, "I didn't do it. You know me, I

102

couldn't kill anyone, you have to believe me."

"I do."

"So why are you being so mean? Why have you left? Come and help me."

"Man-up, Brian, for god's sake. You bought me the flat here so I wouldn't cramp your style. Well, look where your money and your partying has got you now...."

"Dad, I need to see you, don't be like this, I need to see you."

"Not me, you've got all that money, you can pay the right people to help. The time that I could help was over a long time ago, I just didn't see that. I tried to cling on. Not any more, Brian, not any more..."

"This isn't fair..." I pleaded.

I recognised his tone, though, it was the same way he used to talk to me after matches. Normally ones I'd lost; he meant what he was saying and he was sticking to it.

"Fair? Life's not, Brian...and yet out of everyone you were blessed weren't you? You got born with a gift and a family who gave everything to help you get it - but instead of devoting yourself to the game that took you and all of us out of that horrible estate, you had your head turned. By him. And look at the pair of you now..."

"Dad, why have you called? Just to tell me you were right?" All I wanted was for him to tell me everything would be ok, and we could put things right next match.

"Yes. I deserve that, after everything I put into you. We had a good run, son, I just wish you'd carried on listening to your old man. "

I did wonder, even at that moment, how he'd managed to get to Spain so quickly. He must have literally flown as soon as he'd heard the news. But at that moment, all I could focus on was that he'd left me.

And maybe that some of what he'd said was right; maybe Stevie and I had lost our way. Last season we'd won a cup, but neither of us had really been on the top of our game if we were honest; there'd been a lot going on off the pitch.

I was left with a dialling tone. I handed the phone back to the policewoman.

The news from Dad hit me hard. I felt really, really sad in my cell as I waited for the plea-hearing. I didn't cry though and soon I had another phone-call to make. A guard slipped a note to me from a lawyer who'd asked me to call and said he was on his way as soon as I'd picked up the phone and told him my name.

"Who are you?" I'd asked when I was brought through to the interview room.

"I'm the only person glad you're in here, Brian!" the guy said with a smile.

Naturally, I tried to hit him.

Despite the fact Rico was one of the people I was most angry at, because this lawyer – Mr Nathan Lyle - reminded me of Rico, I trusted him. I was so used to having Rico sort everything out that paying someone else with the same slick smile to help me felt right. He had gelled, short hair and wore snazzy black suits like Rico. He had a small, fit, gym body like Rico and the same orangey tan as Rico. It also helped that he was expensive like Rico. Which means things are good - like me at football.

Once he'd calmed me down, Nathan explained exactly why he was pleased I'd been arrested and he did it quite well by using my kind of language.

"If United were at the bottom of the league..." he'd begun.

"They wouldn't be..." I said angrily.

"But if they were..."

"But, we're really good, really good!"

"I know, Brian, but say, you were injured..."

"I wouldn't be, I've got a great track record..."

"I know, I know, please, just go with this....so United are doing badly, they might even get relegated..."

"Never!" I shouted, slamming my fist on the table.

"...but then you return from injury," he continued, "And because of you the team goes on and wins the league!"

"That's more like it!"

"And how would you feel if that happened?" he asked.

"Amazing," I told him.

"Because?"

"Because it's because of me, that's why because I would have been the one who won!"

"Exactly, and that's how I see myself when I look at your case. Right now, today, you're about to be relegated, but I'm here to make you the champion. And if I do, you're champion and everyone knows it's because of me."

After he said that I gave him the job. At the plea-hearing he asked me for the last time how I wanted to plead.

"Not guilty. I didn't do it," I said proudly.

He looked at me. He nodded, "You know if you're taken to trial, it could take months, maybe over a year....we'll represent you, but we're not cheap...you know I want to help you, but it has to be your choice to plead 'not guilty'..."

As he said this I could see a glint in his eye. Again it was something

I'd seen in Rico many times; being on the brink of cashing in big-time. "That's why I said yes to you. Because you want to fight for me. For the money, for me or for Stevie, as long as you do the best it doesn't matter."

To be honest the hearing went by in bit of a blur. A short trip in a van. A crowd of press the police kept me away from. A room full of people all looking at me. I said my name. I said 'not guilty'.

Then the judge adjourned everything until the pre-trial review. At the time I didn't know what that even was. It may sound silly, but a bit of me had half been expecting to be tried there and then. I didn't know anything about how the law courts worked really. Obviously I'd seen some films with courts in, but I always fell asleep during those bits. I preferred chases.

Seeing the judge hammer the bench, say my name, was another nail in my bubble of self-confidence. As I sat in the court I thought about the guy who'd tried to warn me. Where was he? And I also hadn't heard a thing from United (that was around the corner). Even though I knew people were watching me, I began to cry.

Back in my holding cell I sat on the bed and did more crying. As far as I can remember a couple of days went by, nothing much happened apart from my crying and clinging on to the last bits of hope. That didn't last forever.

"Visitor, Mr Parr," I was told early one morning.

In the room my visitor was sat waiting. I recognised him from the plea-hearing, but I didn't recognise him. It was a man, with thick, long, dark black hair, big brushy eyebrows, weird plastic glasses and a big fur coat.

"Hello?" I asked.

The guy stood up.

"F*cking hell, Brian, you've got yourself into a big, white, milky t*t of mess here, haven't you?"

"Gaffer?"

The Gaffer took off his wig, "There's that much press outside I had to do something even though I look like a tw*tting kiddy fiddler."

"Have you come to help? What's happening at the club? Mr Repinov?"

"Sit down, stop f*cking jumping up and down like there's a tongue up your ar*e."

I took my seat. So pleased to see him.

"How is everyone?"

He shook his head, slowly.

"Gaffer?" I asked.

"You want me to have answers, or good news, don't you?"

I didn't' really know what to say, "Why've you come?"

"Despite the fact you're a preening, prancing p*of most of the time, I almost like you..."

I smiled, I always knew he had.

"...I was there to see you plead guilty?" he asked, "How come, Bri? Are you saying someone else did it?"

He'd never called me 'Bri' before. If felt nice. "Of course someone else did if I didn't."

"Do you know who? Have you told these guys who?"

I shook my head.

"I mean do you have any idea?" he said harshly.

"Gaffer!" I said, surprised at his tone, "Look...I'm not..."

"You're not sure, are you, Parr?" he sat back as he said this, sounding

107

like the Town fan cop, "Someone said you'd been sniffing around the club on the day before, but you were probably just trying to find your f*cking' curlers."

"I use straighteners, Gaffer," I told him, "Why do you want to know so much?"

"Look, Brian, you've got tough times ahead. And you've always given me your all on the pitch. For me, that deserves a thank-you. You need to keep your chin-up."

"Thanks, I'll be ok, I hope...I think if more people stick by my like you..."

"Brian. I can't do that. The club won't let me do that. After today, that's it."

"What? Why? What do the club...?"

"That's not for me to say. I just wanted to say I respect how you are on the pitch."

He stood up.

"But Gaffer, I need help, I need people..."

"Brian, have you seen the f*cking photos in the paper from when they caught you? You're dressed like a homi-bloody-cidal Japanese p*ffter. This is it for you, boy, and the sooner you realise that the better. Shags says hello."

I tried to talk him into staying. He didn't.

After a few more days of being in the holding cell, with nothing but meetings with Mr Lyle - who still hadn't been allowed to give me a newspaper because the stories were so bad - my last hope died. Even if I'd been playing a match and found myself 10-0 down with a minute left (unlikely due to my skill) I'd still keep going, trying to make it 10-

1 at least. Or even 10-2. That's who I was. Who I am.

But even I struggled after the visit I had after the Gaffer had come.

Once again I didn't recognise the man who stood up to greet me. He was a big guy, had bushy white hair, black dark bushy eyebrows, and was wearing pin-stripe suit.

I did however recognise his voice. It was the one I'd heard when I was hiding against the wall outside Mr Repinov's office.

"Hello?" I asked.

"Brian Parr? Blake, Blake Baxter. Good to see you again."

I looked at him. My face blank. He didn't look familiar, something he picked up on.

"United's CEO. Mr Repinov gave me the promotion when he took over. Before that I was simply a contract executive. We met at the end of last season, to negotiate your three year extension, with your agent, Richard Smith."

I could remember Rico doing most of the talking that day. The end of season party had been the night before. I just sat there listening to figures, feeling safe in the knowledge that even though we hadn't won the title, I was the club's top-scorer and player of the year. There was no doubt I was going to get great terms so why would I spend my time thinking about the man in the suit who was desperate to keep me?

"Brian, I'm not going to beat around the bush here. I've spoken to your lawyer, Mr Lyle – we sail together actually – and he says you have no formal representation when it comes to your playing contract anymore?"

I nodded.

"Ok, so that's why no-one else is present for this."

"For what?"

109

"Brian, the club is terminating your contract. As of now."

"What? Why?"

"We've called a press conference to announce it in half an hour where we'll make the decision public."

"But I'm....I didn't do it! I haven't been found guilty....yes, you can't do this! Not until they find me guilty....which they won't...and then I can bang in goals, you know? 'Brian Parr, Brian Parr....Got caught banging a bird in car....he's a f*cking super star, Brian Parr, Brian Parr'. The fans love me, they won't stand for it..."

I ran out of steam.

"This has nothing to do with you being in here. Obviously we don't like the disrepute you being in here and doing what you did..."

"I didn't...!"

He raised an eyebrow and carried on, "...has done to the club, but until you're actually found guilty your contract would make it hard for us to cancel."

"Yes!" I said, unable to help myself.

"But the problem for you is that we have many other reasons why we're going to terminate your contract."

"Like what?"

He looked at me, "In one tabloid alone today, there are four stories, backed up with evidence, that are about you breaching club rules and the terms of your contract."

"What does that mean?" I said, irritated and running my fingers through my hair which made me realise that I was overdue having my extensions serviced.

"There are stories and picture of you drinking and gambling on nights before matches, breaking the club's curfew countless times. Quite frankly, you've broken so many rules we could probably take a civil action against you and get back some of the fan's money we've been giving you week after week."

"Mr, please...?" I said, trying to say something great like they do in the movies, using Mr to make it sound proper and stuff.

"Please, what?"

Words failed me, "Please, be....nicer?"

"Look, we just want this whole unfortunate business to be forgotten. As of now you are no longer a United player or our problem."

"Why are you being so nasty?"

"Nasty? I'm not being nasty, you're the one who's done these things."

"It is nasty."

"Is it nasty to beat a team 7-0 when you know that it means that team will be relegated? Or do you just do your job and win the game?"

"Well, at least I'm still England captain!" I shouted, "I'm still the captain, I'll get another team and beat yours! You can't throw away the England captain like this!"

He rolled his eyes. He didn't say another word.

Chapter 23

During the meetings I had with Brian to help me ghost-write his story, he expressed a reluctance to talk about his time in prison and refused to help me turn it into a section of his 'autobiography'. For the sake of being able to understand his mindset once he was released, I convinced him to let me interview him about his life in prison; on the understanding I'd then include the transcript of the interview in the main book.

This took place while we were still investigating Stevie's murder, about two weeks after we first met. We talked in my office and Brian spent most of the time pushing himself around the room on my wheeled desk chair.

What was prison like?

A nightmare. A bad one.

Ok, well, let's start at the beginning, what was the first thing that happened?

(eventually) I got put in a van. I was driven into the prison and processed. And I hated it. Why? Because they were treating everything like it was really funny, when it wasn't. And then to make things worse, the worst thing that could have happened happened.

What was that?

All of the guards had these smug smiles - like when someone gets you sent off for head-butting them. I lost my cool at this ginger minger one. I asked this guy if he knew who I was. He asked me who I was and I said 'England Captain'. He laughed in my face. From behind the counter he picked up a newspaper and showed me the front page. My heart sank. I'd been stripped of the captaincy.

Some might say it was stupid of me to even think I'd still be captain, but I'd expected them to tell me face-to-face. Underneath the headline the manager said he had no choice. I felt tears in my eyes and turned away from the ginger tw*t of a guard.

What was it like settling in?

Lyle had told me he'd managed to make sure I wasn't a category A prisoner. He said I was lucky because people were saying I was a psycho. I told him I'd f*ck up whoever had said that about me.

Lyle shook his head, and told me, "It took me a lot of time and resources to persuade them you're not a danger, thus if you fight, all my hard work is undone. As a category B you can wear your own clothes, see your own doctors, speak to me whenever you want, have more visitors, they can't force you to work. Any questions?"

"What does 'thus' mean?" I asked. He didn't tell me – in fact the first time I found out what 'thus' meant was a few months later and I've used it ever since to sound clever.

How did you cope with being inside? What was going through your mind?

I've always been told it's best to be yourself. I've found that especially true on the pitch. If you're doing something in front of thousands of people each week you've got to keep doing what you do, even if it goes wrong. Take a shot, miss. Shoot again, miss again. The crowd is shouting at you. Saying your girlfriend takes it up the you-know-where. What do you do? Well if you stop shooting, are you ever going to score?

So, that first night I decided that I should stay the way I was. The next day, I immediately knew I had to change. And quickly. Blonde hair extensions may look very, very good under the flood-lights on a night of European football, but in a prison they made me stand out. I won't repeat all the nasty things that people said to me that morning. I've taken corners in front of opposition fans, so I can take it from a lot of guys at the same time like the best of them, but this was something else.

How did you change?

Mr Lyle had said that as I was on remand I was allowed to see my private doctor and important people like that. So I asked for Sebastian my stylist to give me a new haircut and Toni the designer of my fashion label to come with some tracksuits. They refused both requests and once word got out to the other inmates who I'd asked for it made me want to change even more - I got my hair cut short and I asked for some prison clothes.

You were in there for 8 months, before we get to the work you did on your case, how did you pass the time?

There were quite a few people who, after their first nastiness, seemed excited to be able to talk to me. A story to tell their kids and grandkids when they got out – 'Grandson, sit on my knee, let me tell you about the time I was in prison...' That kind of thing.

Those people, and it was probably well over half of the people I met, helped me settle into life at prison. But some guys kept on trying to start a fight. It wasn't just name-calling, it was physical. I got into a few fights.

I suppose in their own way they just wanted a story too: 'Granddaughter, have a toffee, have I ever told you about the time I called the ex-England captain a c*nt when I was in the clink and then punched him...?'

Was there anything to do?

The first couple of days I used the gym every second I could. Back then I still allowed myself to wake up every morning and hope that I might get let out and if I did I wanted to be fit to walk back into United's first team. Or failing that another team in the division – or even Spain where lots of the other inmates seemed to talk about going to a lot.

With that in mind, I decided that I had to keep my ball skills up to scratch and started a kick-about with a few lads. Within a week, the gym was full of people wanting to play during exercise hour and soon we had a league - which some of the cleverer guys started taking bets on.

We had enough teams to play a league properly. I decided early on not to make it just about me. So I said I'd captain, manage and play for my own team - 'Parr's All Stars' - but let everyone else sort the rest out. I ended up with a group of five young guys who'd all played together since school and grown up in the roughest part of the city. They started off too cocky, trying to do tricks all the time. I felt like the Gaffer the way I sorted them out. But once they listened, we were unbeatable.

That sounds like it was fun?

It was, but it didn't last that long.

Why not?

(*awkwardly*) We'd been playing for about three weeks when during a warm down we were approached by a few guys. There were over a 1000 prisoners so I didn't know everyone, but I'd never even seen these ones before. They looked foreign, east European, and reminded me of Mr Repinov's bodyguards except a bit thinner.

They told me they'd been sent by two guys who worked for Mr Lewis. At first I had no idea who Mr Lewis was. Then I remembered.

Yvonne's Dad. And her sister's Dad, May's.

The day before the papers had broken the story about May and me. I already knew that stories about me and lots of girls were coming out. Girls I didn't recognise were saying I'd b*nked them, r*mped with them, sent picture of my w*lly to them. But knowing my affair with May was in the papers was far worse news for me to hear. As soon as they told me I felt sick. I wanted to get back to my cell and do some crying but the next thing I knew, one of them had a knife.

I stood, frozen, bricking it. This is it, I thought, their Dad is taking his revenge. If you're a gangster with a reputation, and the fact someone's been having s*x with both your daughters comes out in every newspaper, what else can you do? Luckily they didn't kill me dead. They said it was a warning and that if I ever tried to contact either May or Yvonne again, Mr Lewis would do me.

What did you do after that?

One of the All Stars had got the paper for me and I read it in my cell. The story had actually been broken by May and Yvonne! I couldn't believe it. They were both sat at my kitchen table – the one I'd paid thousands of pounds for – telling a reporter about what a b*stard I was. There was no mention of May being at fault. Yvonne had forgiven her. May and her were closer than ever. I was the one, they told the reporter, the paper and the whole nation of the UK, who was the bad guy.

Did you feel betrayed by them?

Of course, and then it got worse, didn't it? The following week I saw on the TV confirmation of what Rico had told me. Yvonne and him had got married. It hurt, especially because she looked fit in her wedding dress - everyone in the TV room said so. And I seeing my two lads dressed up as bridesboys was a killer too.

I also noticed, especially after what'd happened in the gym, that her Dad was there to walk her up the aisle. In all the hours and hours Yvonne had gone on at me about our wedding, she'd always said he wasn't coming because he was such a sh*t Dad. What had happened? Why were they friendly again? After that I stopped playing football. I

116

hardly left my cell, and things just got worse...Tony for instance.

How did you learn about Tony?

My Mum, god bless her, sent me a radio. Saying she still loved me and so did Dad even though he refused to visit. It was almost Christmas and after listening to United just scrape a draw against a pretty bad team, I heard the Gaffer being interviewed. I could tell that he was really p*ssed off about the match and that his job was being questioned. Then there was this pause, as he was told something, and then his voice lost its normal gruffness and he simply told the press that Tony had been found dead, hanged.

How did you feel?

I was really, really shocked and really, really sad. All the papers the next day said it was because since Stevie had died and Shags moved to Rico in October, his divorce and debts had got too much.

And was that when you felt really low?

Yes, because it was also around then Lyle said they'd matched the murder weapon to something found in my 4x4. I could tell in his voice he was beginning to be less convinced we'd win. He thought rather than proving I was innocent it was best to see if they could find a mistake in the police work and get the case thrown out. I no longer had the strength to say I wasn't guilty. On Christmas Eve I was put on suicide watch.

How did you turn things around?

Three things. The first was a date for my trial being set. The second thing was I ran out of money. The third thing was Miss Bewley, the most lovely looking woman, who didn't wear make-up. The fourth was that I met my biggest fan for the second time.

So four things?

117

Sure. *(after prompting)* Well, the first two came at once. Lyle demanded to see me, and gave me two bits of paper, documents. The first was the date for the trial. At the end of April. The business end of the season. When the title is decided. The second was an unpaid bill. I'd run out of cash in one bank, and had to sign something for him to get it from another. And he said I had enough to pay for him until the trial, but literally nothing else.

That must have been a blow?

At the end of the day, I like money but that doesn't mean I understood it. Rico had always sorted all of that out. On one afternoon when I was 15, I'd gone from having 3 pounds of pocket money a week to having to pay a man with a suit to sort out my money because I was earning so much. Now, I was going to be poor again.

What did you do?

When he left, I stayed in my chair. Trying to stop my lip wobbling. I looked around the room to see if anyone had noticed, when a woman caught my attention. She had a badge, which meant she worked in the prison. She was wearing a suit which wasn't something I'd really seen before apart from on boring women at weddings and strippers dressed up as gangsters. She was what my Dad called my Mum: an English rose. Except she was fitter than my Mum.

Who was she?

She was Miss Bewley. She did maths and reading lessons in the prison. She was the first fittie I'd seen in the prison and it stirred something inside me, something romantic.

Did you talk to her?

No, because then the fourth thing happened. As I was about to follow her, this guy tapped me on the shoulder. I turned round to do what any normal guy would do and whack whoever had done it to me, when I stopped because I was met with a big goofy smile and someone saying hello. He had big glasses and a horrible old United tracksuit.

And that was the first time you met Malcolm Malcolm?

Yeah, definitely. Well, no, actually. But at the time I didn't remember that I'd met him before. He was shaking me by the hand, he unzipped his top and got out a T-shirt with my face on it and he kept telling me he was my number one fan that he'd won this competition once to prove it.

That must have been strange. How did you cope?

I love it when people understand how great I am - and what was better, was that he told me his son was training in law and Malcolm wanted him to help me. After Lyle had been so down about the case, I thought why not?

So that's when you started working with Malcolm Malcolm and his son Neville?

Yeah, that was when I started to do a Brian Parr again.

To 'Brian Parr'?

To win. I'd always been taught to never let anybody stop me. That's what I was famous for. But that was on the pitch, not off it. In my life outside football everything was done for me; by Rico, the Club, Yvonne, May, my Mum and it had been that way since I signed my first forms with Town.

Not anymore. After those four things happened, I changed. I started to care about winning this case in my real life as much as I'd always cared about winning a trophy in football. I started working with Malcolm and Neville on the case. I started maths lessons to try and be able to understand my money and most importantly I started caring about my image again.

Your image?

When I was sad in jail I'd grown quite a long beard and I wanted to do something with it - everyone knows some Argentinian players have great beards.   My hairdresser Sebastian could have really helped me do something special but even though I asked every day the governor wouldn't let me see him. I mean, I literally went to the governor every single day to ask to see Sebastian, for months, and he still said no. How stubborn is that?

What work were you doing with Malcolm and Neville?

Malcolm and me had a great time talking about all my greatest moments. The best goals, the best comebacks, all of that. I'd always liked to talk about footie and about myself, but when I did I could sometimes see people not listening or trying to change the subject. All the girls did it, even my lads did it and they were tiny. With Malcolm Malcolm, both of us wanted to talk about the same things.

What about Neville, was he a fan too?

No, he'd hated football since he was a kid. He said his Dad was always at games, or watching games on TV, or memorizing football facts. Malcolm spent all his time on football it meant he never spent time with Neville so Neville decided he hated the sport.

A couple of years before, though, Malcolm had been banned from driving for speeding when he was late for a kick-off. This meant it was harder for him to see United all the time, so he was at home more and he started seeing Neville more. But instead of Neville going easier on the beautiful sport of football, he said having his Dad home more showed how much football had stolen from him! Which meant so he hated it now more than ever! I never trusted people who didn't like

120

football, but with Neville it actually helped.

Why did that help?

Because he hated football he'd made a point of knowing nothing about it; instead he'd filled his brain with something else. Like his Dad, Neville found it easy to remember stuff. They had photographic memories or something. I can't quite recall. It sounded like when I was playing football when I could look up and remember exactly where everyone was. Then I'd look at the ball and decide what to do with the 'photograph' of what I'd just seen to guide me.

Malcolm and Neville had that too but with words instead of football, and Nev had chosen to learn about the law. At first, I thought it was weird that while all his mates were playing football, Neville was reading about courts and stuff. And I told him that. Which was when he told me he was g*y. And that once the guys on the estate knew that they'd bullied him and so even if he'd wanted to play they wouldn't have let him.

How did that make you feel?

Malcolm Malcolm looked uncomfortable but what did I care? I've never minded people being g*y. S*x is amazing, why should anyone else get to choose who you do it to? Unless it's kids or dogs. So his being a p*ff didn't matter, all I cared about was that I was sitting down with someone who loved law and who wanted to help me for free. Funnily enough, he'd just been accepted on a training course at Lyle's company for the following season, but to get there he had some college sh*t to do first.

So what did he suggest?

Lyle was trying to get me off on a technicality, so we thought we'd let him do that while we tried a different angle and try to find out who did

121

it. Surely that was the best proof? Nev drew up a list and three times a week, he'd come and ask me questions.

You were narrowing down a list of suspects?

Sure. Thus we did.

And who was on it?

Take your pick. Blake and Repinov obviously. I wanted to take off May, Shags, my Dad, and actually also Yvonne and Rico, but Neville wouldn't let me. Then there was the Gaffer, and even Stevie.

How did it make you feel, having to think about your friends like that?

I found it hard try to work out if people I liked had anything to do with Stevie's murder. For each one I had to think why might they have wanted to kill Stevie and ruin me? Then I had to think how and when? What would they have been doing when Stevie was killed and things?

Was it easy?

No, especially when it was someone I liked. Like, Stevie for example. Nev thought Stevie might have killed himself, because of the drink and drugs and his dad dying; and he wanted to punish me for d*ing May.

Was anyone else difficult?

I remember Nev asking me about Ted Hooper. Ted Hooper? I said. Turns out it was the Gaffer's name, which I thought was 'Gaffer'. It felt weird thinking it might be him, he'd backed me up so many times in the past. He'd played me after all the scandals and things, but when Nev came up with the theory about him, I couldn't ignore it, could I?

A theory?

At first Malcolm and me said it wasn't him; the Gaffer was so honest he got angry if we got caught diving. But Nev pointed out that he'd come to see me in disguise and kept trying to find out if I knew who'd killed Stevie. Nev thought he might have been checking to see if I knew it was him!

Did you think that?

Not really, but it showed me that everyone could look guilty if we tried.

You mention Malcolm, what help was he?

Malcolm could remember everything about United and me. He knew about Blake, the take-over, the Gaffer, everything– without him Neville and I would be making things up but Malcolm knew the facts. And as Miss Bewley was telling me in my lesson, to get the right answer you can't just write ' a number' on your times table test sheet, you needed real facts.

And why the lessons, to improve your education?

It might sound soppy, but one reason was I was thinking about the teacher a lot when I was in bed and I wanted to see her. But it wasn't the only reason. As part of sorting myself out I'd called Lyle and told him I wanted to see all my money. You know, I wanted to see the photo of the room I had in the bank which had all my piles of money in it. I mean, I had to know how much I had, didn't I?

The problem was he said I didn't have a room like that and all Lyle did was send me a folder with loads of numbers on I didn't understand. I decided the best thing to do was learn about numbers with Miss Bewley's help. And once I started maths, she got me doing English too. Normally the longest thing I needed to read was the team list, but I didn't want to disappoint her.

I get the feeling you wanted more than just a teacher though?

(laughing) Every time I was there I used my best pout, one that I was taught on my first ever fashion job – a shoot for some Y-Fronts, nice pants. And every time I looked at her I knew I was falling for her, it

was dead romantic, my eyes were always hooked on her because she always wore these tops which didn't quite show anything, but nearly did.

Did you learn much when you were preparing your case for court?

I like to keep my football simple – bang in goals. But I'm clever enough to know that one of the biggest questions in football, is do you stick to the same tactics no matter who you play, or change your game depending on who you're facing? I'd always preferred having the b*lls to play your own way, not letting the opposition decide. It's not a surprise, is it that I've always wanted to play with my balls? At United I was always saying we should try to play open, s*xy football - like a Brazilian. A Brazilian with balls.

But like Neville said, that was football, this was the law. When I'd been arrested I'd been all balls. Thinking that if I told them over and over again they'd see I was talking with my balls and heart in my mouth and they'd have to see the truth.

Neville showed me the law couldn't be played like that; you couldn't batter its door down just with your balls. If I was going to go into that court and get the result I was going to have to put my balls away. No matter how much I felt I needed to release what was inside of them, I had to keep my balls in check.

I had to think and answer questions properly. Not get angry. Stop just saying 'it wasn't me' all the time. I had to be ready to sit back and defend myself, let them tire themselves out trying to attack me. They were going to expect me, Brian Parr, to shoot my balls off. They weren't going to be expecting me to be cautious, say clever things and even have some evidence to back myself up.

Did you have any breakthroughs?

One morning I was in my bed thinking of the last time I'd seen May and what we'd done. Which led me to think about the last time I'd spoken to her. She'd called me at training and we'd chatted about Stevie being missing before hearing Blake and Repinov.

Until that morning I'd mostly forgotten about May and focused on Blake and Repinov and what they were saying. But what May had told me was also very interesting. She'd told me that after I left her house, Stevie had turned up and she'd found broken glass in the kitchen, blood in the bedroom and tire marks in the gravel.

Later that day, when I told Nev this, he agreed it could be a lead as it showed how Stevie was on a bender before he crashed and that I had nothing to do with it. When we found out later that May had never told the police what she'd told me, Nev got even more excited, saying we could be onto something. Because why would she lie about it?

Did you find anything else?

Malcolm did good. He went around the bars and clubs and found out that Stevie had done a lot of gambling with a guy called Ryan Prince. He was part of a biker gang, who'd got rich with poker games and stuff. The rumour was, Stevie owed a him lot of cash. I asked a few guys in prison and everyone agreed Ryan Prince was a serious guy.

How did you use what you found?

I took it all to Lyle about three weeks before the trial. He was pressing ahead with the technicality defence and said he was hopeful on a couple of things, but I could tell he had nothing really. So I expected him to be pleased with our progress.

What did Lyle think?

That we were wasting our time. He even seemed to suggest if Nev carried on helping me he could cancel Nev's job, although Nev was sure it would never happen.

Why was that? Because you didn't have anything?

In the end we had nothing that was certain. We had found a taxi driver, one of Malcolm's friends, who had seen me walking along the road that night which could prove my car was stolen and that I hadn't dumped it to get rid of evidence. Which is what the prosecution were saying. But Lyle said because the taxi driver was an alcoholic and a member of my fan club he might not get listened to.

It must have been frustrating to work for months and not get anywhere?

Don't forget that I've been brought up to carry on doing what I have to do. You only get to the top in football if you slog away and keep fighting. So actually, working on the case was the only thing and the best thing I could do. Even though, Lyle said it might have worked against us...

What do you mean 'worked against' you?

By trying to make a fight of it, we'd got people worried and so the prosecution had worked really hard too. They didn't want to be known as the people who'd let off the most guilty man in the UK, so we'd stopped any chance of them relaxing making mistakes Lyle could use.

Tell me what it was like going to court. What do you remember about the first day?

Having read the papers I knew that most people thought that for justice to be done I had to be found guilty of murdering Stevie. I'd tried to hope that actually, once I got out of the van and people saw my face again, and my smile, and remembered how much they'd once liked me, then they might change their minds and hope I'd get off.

As soon as the doors opened a United shirt, with my name on, was

126

thrown at me. It had a p*o wrapped in it and only just missed me. After that I realised I was stupid to have hoped people might like me and everything was bad and sad for me.

I do remember seeing Stevie's mum in the court and it really hitting me that my best mate was dead. All this time I'd been trying to prove I hadn't killed him, I hadn't thought properly about what it meant that Stevie was dead. It began to sink in that he wasn't alive. He was un-alive. That's all I could think about as the trial began and I couldn't get rid of the image of his dead body out of my head.

What do you remember about the case?

That it looked hopeless. The prosecution were like a football team specialising in 1-0 wins. Doing exactly what was necessary, impossible to break-down. Lyle tried but they had so much evidence that made it look like I'd done it! It was so unfair.

It annoyed me that there was no coin tossing. The prosecution went first. That's how it was. So every time they got someone on the stand they made it seem like I'd definitely killed Stevie. And only then did Mr Lyle's team get to try to prove it wasn't me. Well, I don't know about most people, but I know that I tend to believe the first thing I'm told rather than the second. Unless it's obvious that the second thing is much more true than the first.

What was the evidence they used?

The prosecution people told the court that the murder had happened because Stevie had found out about me and May. And the fact that Carly was my daughter. You see in court DNA results proved she was mine (which was a great moment because I'd always liked her, a scary moment because it proved their motivation and a sad moment because I didn't think I'd ever get to see her if I was made to live in prison for my whole life).

They said that on that Monday night, the 26th, Stevie arrived home, realised I'd just left and went after me, but his car had crashed and I'd driven off leaving him there. I'd gone to training, thinking he was dead. Which was why, as many people from United said, I was so shocked when the news said he wasn't in the car.

Then they said the following night, on Tuesday 27th, Stevie had called me from outside the house. He'd driven there in the Ferrari I later tried to escape in. At that point I had turned off our CCTV and Stevie and me argued – the lads said they'd heard some shouting that night - and then I'd killed Stevie to keep the secret about May and I safe. The following night, Wednesday 28th, after the match I was trying to move his body when Yvonne found me.

So what happened in court, what turned it around?

First of all I fell apart. When I took the stand I forgot all the work I'd done. Everything looked lost, and I...well, essentially I tried scoring from my own half, with a bicycle kick, against 1000 'keepers.

What do you mean?

Well, I tried the impossible. You see as the prosecution took me apart I got angry. The lawyer was so smarmy and clever and I did the only thing a man could do - I stamped my feet and began to shout that it wasn't me and that it could have been Repinov who wanted us off his books, or the Gaffer who was angry at our partying, or someone else.

Then, as everyone else in the court watched me create a huge mess for myself, I said it could have been Dr Malone and the drugs and the gang who had threatened me. Then I said it could have been suicide. Then I said it could have been Tony who needed the money and who then killed himself because of the guilt.

These last two claims, didn't go down well at all. You probably saw the headlines. I was crucified.

Is that when Dr Malone visited you a second time?

The night after my shouting I had what I think they call a panic attack. I'd finally had my say and I'd finally put the final nail in my coffin. As I thought about it I started shaking, trembling, and shouting. The guard called for a doctor. I couldn't believe my eyes when the doctor who came in was Dr Malone. I was so scared that I snapped to and everything came clear. He was with someone else, dressed as a doctor, but who definitely wasn't one.

Which is when they threatened you?

They said that if I mentioned them again, and Stevie's drugs, they'd kill me.

How did you deal with that?

I didn't have time. Lyle came in and started shouting at me for what I'd done in court. I told him I kept picturing Stevie's dead body which was why I'd flipped. He got angry and threw down photos of the murder scene telling me I'd be picturing it for the rest of my life now. And that was it!

That was what?

When I saw it. The photos showed Stevie, dead. The same image that had been in my head all trial, apart from one thing. The tool-belt. When I'd seen Stevie, my tool-belt – which I'd got at photo shoot I'd once done for a calendar – was full. But in the photo, the leather-man knife wasn't there.

What did Lyle say?

At first he didn't get it. I explained about how when I played football I was able to take brain photos in my brain of the people around me to

129

work out what to do. I said that when I saw Stevie's body I took a photo – and in it, the leather-man knife was in the belt! And in the photo it wasn't!

Which was the murder weapon?

Yeah, Lyle went and got all the other photos and guess what? One of the earlier photos showed the knife had been in the belt that night – which meant after I had left the house, someone had stolen it.

How did you feel when Lyle took that evidence into court?

Lyle was great. Like me in the penalty box. He started off by agreeing with everything the prosecution said about Stevie being stabbed; it was done with a pen-knife like mine, probably during an argument and probably by someone Stevie knew. He also agreed it was my knife that was found in my 4x4 with Stevie's blood on it. And then, and this was the well brainy part seeing as it made the prosecution sh*t themselves, he showed them the photos. He proved that the knife had been moved after the police had arrived at the house. The court kicked-off...it went nuts!

Did you know then you'd be found not guilty?

Not 110%, because as Lyle said I could still have put the knife back in the belt after killing him, but the fact was it proved the prosecution was wrong. And then the second piece of evidence turned up.

Which is the video you're still trying to find out about?

Yes. The night after Lyle had told the court about the knife he was sent the video. It was footage of my house, taken from next door and it showed our garage. There was a man, dressed in a cap and a leather jacket, coming out the garage with what looks like Stevie's body. He gets about a metre out then goes back in. You never see his face.

Lyle played this in court, and again he played a blinder, because when

130

the prosecution said it could be me in the cap, Lyle pointed to the time and date. Then he showed what I was doing at that very moment – getting sent off in the match I played. When Lyle showed the footage of the match to prove I was on the pitch, not outside my garage, I couldn't believe how obvious it was I shouldn't have been sent-off: f*cking referees.

What happened next?

It was a whirlwind. The jury found me not guilty and that was it. I was free.

That must have felt amazing?

Kind of, but I was expecting the press to take my side, to call me a hero and get me back into the England team and into United. Instead they kept saying I was guilty, that I only got off because of my money. I told them they were stupid for thinking that and it just got worse and worse. No-one was pleased I was free, not one person.

Really? Not Lyle, not Malcolm and Nev – and didn't Shags meet you?

Lyle only cared about himself and how well he'd done. I asked him to help me find the killer now it definitely wasn't me but he said he was too busy taking on new clients to bother and that I should give up as the police would never help me. Mal and Nev were happy, obviously, and Shags – well, yeah, we did have a party, but even that went t*ts up. Literally.

How was it seeing Shags after all that time?

At the time, great. Now, weird. Why? Because at first he was all apologetic about not seeing me and how about he'd been warned by Rico not to visit me because it would damage his sponsorship. He went on about how everyone would think I was a d*ck for a while but he didn't care now I was out and I shouldn't either.

The problem was, he did care. At first he said I could stay at his place, but after two nights of partying some of the girls we'd been messing about with went to the papers. When the story hit, Rico arrived at the house and told Shags I had to leave or Shags would be tarred with the Brian Parr brush.

I thought Shags would fight for me. He didn't. That was when, even though I was free, I knew my life had changed forever. And not in a good way, in a really ungood way.

Chapter 24

I left Shags and Rico talking about work. I'd had a brief chat with Rico. He said the lads were good. I called him a c*nt for marrying Yvonne he just smiled and looked at Shags who asked me to leave before any press saw me still living at his.

Feeling sad in my face, I slipped out onto the road and decided to make a journey I'd done a thousand times before. Though normally in an amazing car. From Shags' house to mine.

It was really strange staring at the closed gates of my drive-way. That I had paid for. I hadn't been back since I'd raced away on the night I'd found Stevie. It took a bit of man-courage, but I buzzed the house and got Etienne. He sounded pleased to hear me and said that Yvonne was out.

I told him it was the lads I was after, but he said it would be breaking the law to let me in. The forms I'd signed meant I was only allowed to see the lads with Yvonne or Rico's permission. He let me say hello to them over the intercom. It only made me sadder. And angry, because

I had paid for the house I couldn't go into.

I was about to walk away when I realised that that was exactly what the old me would have done. Just walked away from my lads. Not anymore. These were my lads, I had to see them. So I waited. It was quite a nice day and it felt good and stuff to be out of prison.

Waiting was boring though. More than once I thought about giving up. But I stuck in. I was there twenty minutes. Just waiting. I was pleased with my new mental strength. It felt good to be doing it for my lads. And I wondered how their footie was coming along. It worried me that Rico wouldn't put them through their paces properly.

Then I started thinking about Carly. I was her Dad too. What did that mean? Would May let me see her? Was I going to have to pay for her too?

"What the f*ck are you doing here?"

I looked up to see Yvonne looking really angry as she slammed her pink Jeep – that I got her – up to the gates and got out of the car.

"Yvonne, hi...I..."

"Get the f*ck away from me!" she spat,"You have no right being here!"

"I got found not guilty!"

"Get away from me before I call the police."

"Hey, don't, why would you do that...? I want to see the lads..."

She was getting out her phone, "I don't want you around here ever again. It's over."

"Yvonne, I get that we're over...but the lads..."

"Brian! I warned you. I'm calling the police," she said, typing in the number with her big bright pink nails, "Don't forget you tried to attack me that night, you had glass in your hand."

"I wasn't..."

"I've never been so scared in my life, I have nightmares."

"Scared? You were angry!"

"Of course I was scared. You tried to attack me....'Hello, Police, please'..."

"Yvonne, please, I want to see the lads."

"Yes, it's my ex he's..."

I put my hands up.

"Ok, you win. I'll go. But I've changed, Yvonne."

She hung up.

"Changed? Not from what I read in the f*cking papers today. More sl*gs! Already?"

I almost grinned, but it wasn't the time to boast, "No, I mean I'm not going to give up just because something's hard. I never did it on the pitch, and now I see my whole life as a pitch."

"What are you talking about you daft w*nker? Come near us and I'm going straight to the police."

"What's this about, Yvonne? You've got Rico, the house. Why are you taking the lads too? Is it May?"

"What?" she said.

"You know, is it about me and May? I thought, from the papers, you two were friends again?"

She sighed, "Yes, Bri, me and May we are ok. But that doesn't make me and you ok. You treated us like sh*t, that's why I don't hate her or Carly, because you kept cheating on both of us..."

"Your Dad wasn't happy either."

"Dad? What's he...?" she said, unsure of herself for the first time.

"He sent some guys to tell me not to ever try to see you again."

134

"Did he? Good. I'm f*cking glad he did."

"Yvonne, why can't we just put this behind us?"

"Brian. Leave us alone or I'll call the police and my Dad and see who gets to you first."

With that she got back into the car and drove into the house.

I flicked open my mobile and went through my contacts to see if anyone could help. I called everyone. The Gaffer, people at the club, players. No-one wanted to know. They said I was toxic.

I didn't know what 'toxic' meant but I knew from that the fact they hung up really quickly after saying it that it wasn't good. My Mum and Dad were in Spain. As were all the members of the rest of my family, like my cousins, who I'd helped buy flats and houses for out there.

I have to admit, after that I had a cry on the village bench. I felt alone. Almost as bad as when I'd been in the clink. At least then I'd been fighting for something. I realised my only option was to call the people who'd been on my side in prison. One day, I'd read Miss Bewley's organising book, when she wasn't looking and written her number down.

"Hello?" she said, answering straight away – my luck was in.

"Hi, darling, this is your lucky day, it's me calling..." it was a line I'd used a lot on girls before and it had always worked.

"Who is this?" she said as if she was telling me off.

"Calm, down, it's me, Brian Parr."

"Brian, what are you doing? How did you get my number?"

"Don't you worry about that, why don't I come over. I'm not in prison now, how about I teach you a few things for a change?"

She hung up. I didn't really understand why. That's the way I'd been successful in the past.

I called a few more times. It took a while but she got through.

"Brian, is this still you?"

"Course it is, look I'm sorry, I just thought I could say thanks. I really liked you...I think you liked me too...go on, admit it."

"I did like you, yes...but you were a..."

"I'm out now...I thought about you a lot in prison, if you know what I mean, at night in my cell..."

"Brian!"

"...and I think I fell for you...I think if we meet if could be the start of something really serious. I'd like it to be. I have a new start and..."

There was a pause, I knew I sounded great guns.

"I saw the papers today...Brian. Please don't call again. You're sweet but you haven't changed...and I don't want a man like that."

"I f*cking have changed!"

She hung up.

I swore and kicked the park bench a lot until I started getting looks from people. I was free, but I had nothing. Except Malcolm Malcolm's number.

As soon as I saw Malcolm Malcolm's place I knew I didn't want to stay there long. I was grateful he'd invited me round, but his house was a sh*t-hole. It was exactly the same type of council house I'd lived in as a kid. Back then I'd managed to stop living like a poor person. Now I had to do that again, and soon.

Something inside me told me I had to get back everything I had before it was taken from me and Stevie died. There was only one way of doing it - proving I was innocent by finding the killer.

As soon as I sat down in his tiny, tiny living room in front of Malcolm

Malcolm's 54 inch TV plasma I asked Nev and him for help. Before Nev could even speak Malcolm had signed them up.

Repinov was our biggest suspect. Why? Because he was rich and had power. Because of what I'd heard at the window and how quickly they'd replaced Stevie. Because of how Blake had spoken to me. And yes, because he was a Russian oligarch and that's what they did!

The problem was getting proof.

Nev went to college and came back and Malcolm and I still hadn't worked out how we could find out their secrets. So we changed tactics. We decided to focus on the film Lyle had been sent. It was possibly from the same person who'd tried to help me on the night of the murder. If they wanted to help me so much that they got a phone into my house and sent a film to the court, they would hopefully want to carry on helping now.

But how to find them?

Malcolm Malcolm was quick out of the blocks with our first lead. He'd recognised the view of my garden straight away when the film was played in court. Because he'd once spent a night on the roof trying to get a glimpse of me.

A couple of years before, he'd met a fellow United fan, a guy called Roy, who'd bought the house next to mine. He was a computer geek who owned a multi-million pound IT company; which surprised me as I thought all really obsessive fans didn't have jobs, like my Dad and Malcolm.

One night at their fan club meeting they'd joked about setting a camera up on the roof of his house to film me. The next time they met, he had a clip of me practicing my keepy-uppys in the garden. Malcolm had instantly asked for a copy and to come over and watch me.

Malcolm had stayed for a week without one sighting – but while he'd felt gutted then, it all seemed worthwhile now because it meant he knew exactly where the footage was from. The evening after he'd seen the footage in court he'd called Roy and asked if he'd sent the tape. He said no and that all the tapes he made were all in his library as normal. Apparently when Roy had gone to check, he'd been astonished to find one tape actually was missing even though there were no signs of a break-in.

As soon as Malcolm had told me this, I was up off my seat. To get to Roy's place I asked Nev if I could borrow his scooter. He said he was going to use it and refused. It felt strange, him saying 'no'. Even when I got Malcolm involved Nev wouldn't budge. He said it was because even though he'd help, now I was free his priorities had changed. He had a course to do, a job at Lyle's to start and he needed his scooter to do that.

So once again I found myself walking. Roy's eyes almost popped out when I knocked on his door but he chilled out when I said I was here for help, not to bust him for filming me.

As I signed a few of his tops, he told me only four people knew about the filming. Including himself and Malcolm. One was a fan in Hong Kong who paid Roy to send DVDs of what he recorded (I was too busy to think how weird that was at the time) and the other was a man called Greg Neal, another mega-fan.

"So it could be one of those two?" I said.

"Well, I didn't send the guy in Hong Kong DVDs of that part of the night, because there was nothing of you on it. In fact, Brian, I owe you an apology."

"For the weird filming?"

"Erm, yes, but I meant for not spotting that guy had a body!"

"H*ll's bells, Roy! You mean you saw that guy and didn't say anything?"

 "Kind of. I watch the films on fast-forward and if it's not you in the footage I don't stop. I knew that you were playing football at 9.30 on that night so I didn't pay attention when I saw the guy and didn't see what he was doing! If I had seen it, it would have been me who got to help you out in court, not whoever broke in here and took my tape!"

Roy said he'd take me to Greg Neal as a way of saying sorry. On the way there I remembered I'd seen the name Greg Neal before. In my head an image flashed up from pre-season training. Playing 11-a-side. I had the ball at my feet but still a lot of defenders to beat as well as Stevie who was in goal – so I'd taken one of my mental photos to work out what to do. In Roy's car I couldn't remember if I'd gone on to score - probably did - but I could remember that in the background of my brain photo was the building work for Repinov's HQ. The building was half built and on the scaffolding was a sign: 'Greg Neal – Building Innovators.' Which told me that Greg Neal was a builder. I wasn't sure about the 'innovator' bit though or what that meant.

"The thing is, Bri, that from day one, I've known Repinov is not what he seems."

"What do you mean?" I asked, as Greg led me into his study.

Greg was a bit like a successful Malcolm. He had big glasses, a beer belly and he was pasty faced and a bit short, but he also had expensive clothes and designer glasses.

"Now, I'm not crazy. You get a lot of fans who are, who let everything become a fantasy, but I've seen Repinov first hand. And Blake bl*ody Baxter too. I've seen how they operate.... that's why I started this!"

"Started what?" I said.

He pointed to a poster on his wall, "The United Army!"

The poster was the colour of United and in the middle was the club badge. Over the badge was Repinov's face with a red cross over the middle. I wasn't quite sure what they were getting at.

"The United Army," Greg said again, "We're dedicated to saving United. We've been around for a while, making sure that the club isn't treated badly by money-grabbers and stuff. But since Repinov came along we've had real problems. I mean look what he did to you," Greg carried on, "We can't let that happen again, can we, Brian?"

"No, of course not....but what do you mean when you say what he did to me?

"He killed Stevie and set you up. And I have proof.

I felt an excitement rise up inside me. I was finally with someone who said they had the answers.

Chapter 25

"This, Bri," Greg said, "Is where it all happens."

I couldn't look because I'd been blindfolded.

As we'd driven in his van, Greg had insisted that I tied a United scarf round my eyes. This had taken me a bit of time. I'd never been good at knots which is why I'd got my boot-makers to design some Velcro boots for me. Rico made sure they named them Velcro Parr when they hit the shops and I'd told Yvonne that I thought Velcro would be a good name for our next boy.

"Do you know how I know you're my favourite ever United player,

140

Bri?" Greg'd told me, "Well, let me tell you. I've got fifteen tattoos. Do you know what they're of? That's right, United.

"Not any woman or any of my kids. They're all of United. The badge, the flag, the dates of our biggest successes. Do you know why they're of United? Because United is the only thing in the world I guarantee I'll always love.

"Now, take my missus. You've been hanging round with that Malcolm Malcolm, ain't you? Well, my bird is actually his ex-wife..."

"Nev's mum?" I said, surprised.

"Yeah. Now, for her age she's pretty tidy but that doesn't mean that she won't get fat, or cheat on me and I'll get rid. If I had a tat done for her, well - what the f*ck? And as for your kids, well they could turn out to be nasty little greedy b*stards, like mine. Or hers, for that matter."

"D'you mean, Nev?"

"Yeah, imagine getting a tattoo for him on your body, you'd be gutted!"

"He's...."

"He's a little creep, that's what he is! Always spying on me, creeping around on that piece-of-sh*t scooter of his," Greg spat, "Your team, though, Bri, are a constant. Your club is your club, till you die. Ain't it, Bri?"

I nodded.

"Course it is. Anyway, the way I know you're my best player is that you're the only player I've ever got close to having a tattoo of. I didn't actually get it, but at one point, I was on the seat, I was ready, I was going to get you with your hands on your hips and your shirt round your neck like after a game."

141

"What happened? Why didn't you get the tattoo of me done?" I asked, trying not to show how hurt I felt.

"I realised you might go to Europe to play for a bit. And I think that would be understandable, as a player deserves to try another league. But as I sat there in the tattoo parlour, I wondered what would happen if United had to play you in Europe? What would I do?"

"Tough call," I nodded.

"Unthinkable, ain't it? And I couldn't get that out of my head as I heard the needle go. So I didn't get you on my shoulder. But the fact is, I almost did."

After that Greg took of my blindfold.

"This, Bri," Greg said, "Is what we call the Fan Attic."

It took some time for my eyes to get used to the light, but we were certainly in an attic. You could see the roof-beams and only in the middle was there enough room to stand.

"Where are we?"

"The Fan Attic, Bri, I just said!"

I noticed that in the far corner there was someone else. A man. He was fat and had a big beard, glasses and was completely bald, with headphones on, staring at a small TV.

"I mean, where are we?"

"Well I blindfolded you so you wouldn't know. Just in case?"

"We're near the training ground, aren't we?" I asked, because I'd noticed we were heading that way as the blindfold had been put on and the journey was about ten minutes which was how long it took to get from the town centre to the training ground.

Greg looked at me, a bit annoyed I'd worked him out, "We're near. This is Tone's house. This fat guy is Tone."

"Hi, Tone!" I said.

"Shh, keep the noise down, his missus hates it when we're up here..."

Tone looked up, I could see his shock at seeing me, and how happy he was. He waved, kissing the badge of his United shirt.

In between a lot of the beams there were TVs. Greg crawled along the sides of the attic and turned them on. It didn't take me long to work out what I was looking at. Every screen showed a room from United's training complex.

I couldn't believe it. There was the changing room, the physio room, the gym, the pitch, even Mr Repinov's new office.

"I don't understand. They don't know, do they? How...?"

"Bri," Greg said with a smile, "Look, you know what I was saying earlier about being United till I die. The only thing I'll ever really love?"

I nodded.

"I meant every word of that and I'll do everything in my power to protect us. Now, you've been in prison but you must have heard about what's happening out there in the football world? A couple of clubs don't even exist anymore! Three have been relegated because they lost points when they went bankrupt, loads more are f*cked financially. People like me have loved these clubs their whole lives only to see them being ripped apart by gr*edy fat cats who want the cash and want the reputation of owning a team. The problem is these rich g*ts don't really want what's best for the club or the fans who spend their wages on the team every week, they just want what's best for them, know what I mean?"

"I think so."

"Now, you know United were family-run for all of my life until last summer?" he continued.

"I know, Mr Birkley. He was a great guy."

"Course he was. But he's ill, he had to sell, I get that. But what I don't get is who he sold it to. Sergei Repinov is as dodgy as they come and what's the first thing he does? Promote Blake Baxter to CEO - one of the shadiest local businessmen there is."

"Is he?"

"Trust me, I did my home-work," Greg told me, "Which is why, when I won the contract to build his new office, I made a call."

"To who?"

"No, I mean I made a decision. You see, for the past few years, Tone and me have done a bit of business filming DVDs of United training and stuff like that and selling them."

"Like Roy?"

"Yeah, he's got a great view of your place and there are some fans out there who'll pay a lot of money to see that stuff, so why not cash in?"

"Because it's an invasion of...piracy?" I said.

"You mean privacy? Well, the way I see it, you lot plaster yourself all over the magazines and billboards to make some money. What privacy do you have? Compared to what you put in the papers, us filming training is hardly that bad is it? It's not like we're selling them to rival teams."

I shrugged. He had a point.

"Once Repinov came in I knew I had to keep an eye on things. Anything illegal we'd be able to pick up on straight away and let the right people know: the police, the FA, the league, whoever."

"But how have you got cameras in here?" I asked.

"I made sure I won the contract to build Repinov's extension to the HQ

144

and as we worked over the summer put the equipment in. Not everywhere, but we do alright."

I looked at the screens, "So you just listen to them? To see if they say bad things?"

"Well, we haven't got mics with every camera, but yeah, it's a way for us to watch over United. And the nice thing is, because he was throwing money at us to get it done quickly, he paid for the kit!"

"And they don't know?"

"Course not. Now Repinov, being as dodgy as he is, does have tight security, but in the comfort of his own office he tends to relax a bit. Those guards of his do too. Which is why you managed to escape them that morning…I watched that, it was fun."

"Not for me…although I did beat them…" I said proudly.

"Yes, you did. Which is what we plan to do. I've got the contract to keep the place maintained so there's always a reason for us to go over and look after the cameras which will allow us to keep up the good work up here. The only thing that would get us caught is if they did a sweep for bugs, but even then they'd think it was a rival club trying to steal tactics. It would never be me who'd get blamed as long as no-one tells anyone."

"Thus the blindfold?" I said with a smile.

"Yeah. Thus!" Greg replied.

I thought about what Greg was doing. If I was still a player and I'd found out I was being filmed I would have been angry as f*ck. But being in the position I was in, trying to find out about Repinov, I was glad Greg and Tone were doing this. I believed him when he said he'd do anything to protect United.

"What have you found out? I have to find out who killed Stevie. I

145

think it was Repinov. Do you think he did it?"

I was in such a rush to find out, Greg had to slow me down.

"Yeah, he did it alright. Why else would I bring you here?"

"Really? What's he said?"

"Well, things have been quiet for a long time and then, since the day you were found innocent, the meetings haven't stopped."

"Meetings? Between who?"

"Greg!" Tone whispered, "They're here."

"Who?" I asked.

Greg handed me some headphones. We crawled over to Tone's screen to see.

"Great timing Bri, just like when you're on the pitch, Blake and Repinov have just walked in!"

I watched Blake's bushy white hair, and big lumbering figure, bowing his head to the fatter, smaller Mr Repinov who did not look happy. Blake was holding a briefcase

"Do you have everything?" Mr Repinov said, "Or have you f*cked up again? I mean FML when I found out about last time, I swear I thought you'd stopped caring about this!"

"Why's he talking like that?" I said, "What does FML stand for?

"I know. Sounds like a tw*t doesn't he?" Tone said, "My daughter says FML is 'f*ck my life' or something. They use it on that facebook sh*te."

Blake handed over the briefcase to Repinov, "It's here."

"Well, at last we have it Blake, do you know what I mean? I was beginning to think you like weren't bothered, or something...?"

"Of course not," Blake said, "It's in here."

"You better be right. Because I'm totally p*ssed over your total f*ck-

up with this!"

"It's the birds Repinov hangs out with," Greg whispered, "they're all young enough to be his daughter. And obviously, he's engaged to one now, Tammy Saunders..."

"Tammy? Yeah, I know Tammy."

Tammy was the last WAG I'd slept with apart from May. Actually as I stood looking at Repinov it dawned on me it had been in a club the night I'd won the Ferrari off Stevie. I'd had s*x with her in the VIP room while Stevie and Shags had waited for me.

"Well, he's been seeing her since before he bought United, and now he's started to speak a bit like her. F*cking embarrassment if you ask me."

Repinov keyed in a code and opened the briefcase.

"What is it, Tone? Do you think they're talking about evidence?" Greg asked.

Tone nodded. I couldn't believe my luck.

"And you're sure that this is like everything?" Mr Repinov asked.

"I collected everything myself."

"What do you think it is?" I asked.

"Yesterday they had a meeting, which we taped," Greg told me, "They started talking about you being released and then started going on about Blake getting back what they called the 'important things'."

"Which could be evidence, linking them to you, couldn't it?" Tone said.

"Could it?" I beamed, "I f*cking hope so!"

"Mmmm," Mr Repinov said, "It looks like I you have it."

"I got it out just in time," Blake said, "It would be obvious who it belonged to as soon as they saw it. See, it has their signature all over

it... and here are the photos too..."

"Wow, they've even got photos of, Brian!" Tone said excitedly.

"Of what?" I said.

"Can't you see?" Greg asked, insistent, "Someone killed Stevie...they probably paid someone to do it, Russians do that all the time...don't they, Tone?"

"Yup," said Tone who was now typing on a lap-top as he listened.

"And now we've caught them covering their tracks because you've been released," Greg told me.

"Are you sure?" I was excited, but Lyle had told me all the time to be careful about evidence.

"Very good, Blake, put them in the safe until we can move them totally securely..." Repinov ordered.

"Exactly, and this time I'll do it properly," Blake said. "Our best players are involved after all."

Greg tore my headphones off.

"You see, Bri! They're talking about you and Stevie! 'United's best players.' This is massive!"

He took Tone's laptop from him. He'd been writing down what they'd said.

"This is for the Fan-Attic site on the internet. Look at the proof we already have!"

At the top of the website were pictures of Tone and Greg. But it wasn't actually them! They'd disguised their faces with caps and sunglasses and put the heads onto bodies of two United players. It was upsetting they hadn't used my body because the players they had used had a worse fake tan than me.

Underneath the pictures, Tone had written down what we'd heard.

148

He'd made some sentences stand out by making the letters bigger. Blake and Repinov were **relieved** about **something involving big United players being found**. They said that if other **people had found** whatever it was **they'd work out what it was** and Blake and Repinov were **both very worried** about that happening. Tone had finished by saying he was convinced it was them talking about destroying evidence linking them to Stevie Hurst's murder.

My heart was pounding. It had happened so fast. Ok, I didn't know they'd killed Stevie, but I thought I'd just seen them with evidence linking them to it. That was surely enough to get the police to do something.

We had to be quick. I didn't know how long they'd both be there.

"If we nail them now, they'll have to sell up. The new owners could re-sign you, Brian. You're a free agent. You could be playing by the end of the season. That would be amazing, wouldn't it Tone?"

Tone agreed. So did I. And it was really possible! Of course if they got locked up they'd have to sell the club. Which new owner wouldn't want me? Once someone else had been done for the murder then surely then the papers and the public would start being nice to me again.

My first call was to Lyle. It took a while to get through. Eventually he answered.

"I take it you weren't going to stop calling until I answered?"

"Not today, it's too important."

"I have three minutes. What is it?"

I told him what I knew and what I was going to do. Greg had told me to not to blow his cover so I left that bit out.

"Brian, that's the stupidest idea I've ever heard. Now please listen.

149

The police called the other day. For some reason they think I'm still your lawyer, saying that I was to warn you not to cause any trouble trying to prove your theories. They are investigating…"

"Are they? How come I know this and they don't then?"

"Listen, Brian, it's not your job to go around trying to catch criminals. Stay out of it. If you put one foot wrong, they'll arrest you. Some policemen believe you're a murderer don't forget, they'd be happy to see you locked up on any charge. That's three minutes. Go home, stop this."

I'd hoped Lyle would provide me with back-up and show me exactly what kind of evidence I needed to find to prove that Blake and Repinov were guilty. Still, I put his nastiness down to the fact I hadn't been able to tell him about the Fan Attic. If I had told him about what we had on tape I presumed he would have taken me more seriously.

Nev and Mal were my next hope. They didn't pick up. I didn't have time to wait and the only other call I could make was the Police - after what Lyle said, it didn't sound like they'd take my side. With time ticking away I had to do it myself.

"Bri, it makes sense to do it on your own, this is your mission," Greg told me, "Your quest. They started it. You've got to end it! And we'll be here. Recording it so we can show the world that you're right and they're wrong. Yeah?"

"Yeah!" I said, making my mind up to finish things off for Stevie.

"Look, you have a bit of time," Tone said.

"How do you know?"

"Repinov's just put on a TV show. It's something he does every night before he leaves the office. To unwind, he says."

"I heard him tell Blake once he learnt English from watching episodes

150

of TV shows," Tone said.

"What's he watch?"

"Well, he records the shows during the day, and then watches them with a drink before he goes out. It's normally 'Murder She Wrote' or 'Diagnosis Murder'. He loves them. Laughs along to them and everything..."

Tone came up with the plan.

I was going into Mr Repinov's office. I'd surprise them both and tell them that the morning of Stevie's crash I was behind the window. Why? So I could plant a bug to hear what they were saying. Then I'd play them the recording of the conversation we'd just heard to prove we'd caught them. The reason that they wouldn't attack me, or get their guards to, was I was going to tell them I was filming everything and sending the footage to somewhere else. I'd then get the evidence and call the police.

"That's the beauty of it, Bri!" Greg smiled at me, "They haven't even heard of the United Army yet! They don't know we know everything about them and it's time for Brian Parr and the Fan Attic to get United back on track! You with me, Bri?"

I nodded, feeling like I'd just been given the best team talk of my life. That was when I had a brain-wave. One of the things Rico had taught me was that if I was going to do anything worthwhile, I should do it on TV. Or at least in a magazine. After I'd been filmed opening some school or something I'd once had s*x with a local news producer. And we'd met up a few times since to do the same thing. Not opening schools, though, but have s*x.

I gave her a call. She was a bit worried that I didn't know what evidence it was, but I persuaded her. What better way to prove to the

151

public I was really innocent, than doing it on TV?

Chapter 26

Cindy, a camera-man and someone with a furry pole, were right behind me as I walked towards Mr Repinov's office. Greg had used his keys to get us in. Tone was using cameras to watch for the bodyguards. The coast was clear and none of them knew Brian Parr was back in town. It was dead exciting and action-filmy.

I put my hand on the door-knob. One turn and I would be in the office. I looked at the camera. Cindy had told me not to do that. She'd said that they wanted it to look serious and that it wasn't set-up. I had to act as though the camera wasn't even there but I was enjoying myself so what the h*ll!

"J*sus Chr*st!" Blake said, standing up and as I barged in, "What the h*ll are you doing, Parr?"

They were alone in the room. Once Cindy's team was inside I locked the door.

Repinov stood up, glaring at me with silent anger. He paused the TV.

"Say hello to the public people, yeah?" I said, trying to be cool for the camera, but actually feeling a bit nervous.

"This is outrageous. You're way out of line," Blake said.

"I'm like, totally, calling the police," Mr Repinov said.

"I wouldn't do that if I was you," I said, "Because I'll be doing it for you in just a little bit."

It felt good to tell him that. Taking control and things, you know?

"Parr, have you gone mental? You can't just walk into people's offices" Blake said, "Cindy, why are you filming this?"

"What? How do you know, Cindy?" I said, before realising this was about me.

"Right. Look," I shouted calmly, "I'm here to prove who killed Stevie Hurst. And just like I was destroyed on TV, it's now going to happen to you on TV. Which is why Cindy's here, because this is live...."

"This is, like really, really the worst move I've ever heard of, Parr," Repinov said, with a nasty stare.

Without the tape recording in my pocket, I would have felt nervous. The only thing I could do was carry on so I ignored Cindy shaking her head and turned to the camera:

"To prove who did the murdering, without any more time being...gone, please listen to this members of the public... a conversation that I recorded today between these two men...."

As I pressed play, Repinov's guards started hammering the door. They weren't guys I wanted to mess with, but the door was locked and even if they did get in, would they risk beating me up on TV?

Without Greg and Tone getting so excited, the recording didn't sound quite as good. But the cameras were rolling, the evidence was close by in that safe, I had to focus. I imagined the Gaffer watching, barking instructions at me 'to keep f*cking concentrating you dumb b*stard'.

The recording ended, "So there you have it," I said, to camera, "Which now means, of course, that we need to look into the briefcase..."

"This is ridiculous," Blake said, "You're making a huge mistake, Parr."

"OMG. Just, let him," Repinov said, sitting down.

"Thank you, Mr Repinov, I'm glad you're seeing sense at last, it makes....sense" I said, sharing my triumph with the camera.

I knew that as I opened the safe the camera-man had to be able to film me. Rico had always been furious when I'd got in the wrong position when I posing and doing stuff for my image - you know, like blocking the sick kid's face from the camera when I did signatures in hospitals. I needed maximum impact to make sure I'd be playing for United in a week or so. It was going to be glorious. I was going to look amazing on TV.

I tried to shift my feet round so I could almost walk sideways over to the cupboard and still face Cindy. It felt awkward but I just kept smiling into the camera. Then things went t*ts up - with my feet walking sideways, I tripped over the foot of Mr Repinov's desk. I hit the deck hard.

Within seconds, Blake was on me. He was a big guy and I couldn't get free. Repinov went straight to unlock the door.

"Keep filming, keep filming," Cindy shouted.

As I struggled with Blake the room flooded with guards, "Cindy," I shouted, "Open the cupboard. Save the evidence!"

I couldn't believe I'd fallen over. I bet the people at home couldn't either. What had happened to the Parrster? Once known for his balance, for being able to stay on his feet, unless a dive was the best option, and now I'd messed up walking to a cupboard?

"Keep filming, keep filming, this is live! This is live! Police come and help us," I screamed, "Stop them from hiding the evidence! Police! 999! 999! Come here! 999! 999!" I shouted into the camera as I was hauled to my feet.

"Parr, will you shut-up!" Blake said, getting to his feet.

I carried on shouting. He slapped me. I shut up.

"Firstly, this is not live, stop pretending it is," he told me.

"What? Of course it is….."

"My god, you believe it don't you? Haven't you noticed, Parr, that all you have here is a camera man? To broadcast live you need a whole OB truck…"

"A what?"

"You must have seen them, the big trucks with satellites on to send the footage? Parked outside stadiums on match days? Do you see that here?"

"The deal I had with Cindy was that if I gave her the story, we'd do it live, wasn't it Cindy?" I told them but as when she looked at me and I knew she'd tricked me.

"My executive said there was no way we could go out live with this, but if we got a good story he'd run it when we got back."

"Cindy, it had to be live!"

"Jesus, Brian, my exec told me it would be rubbish and I'm beginning to think he's right…"

"Cindy! This is….we're about to prove…"

"WTF! You're about prove nothing," Repinov said from his seat.

He'd lit a cigar. I didn't like how relaxed he was. Even if this wasn't live I was still busting him.

"This, Brian, is what you heard us talking about, is it not?" Blake asked opening the safe and laying the briefcase on the desk before flipping it open.

I stepped forward to see what was inside.

"F*cking' h*ll, Brian," Cindy said stepping away from the briefcase, "Come on guys."

"Cindy, wait, what?" I asked leaning into see.

In the briefcase were some United shirts and team photos. Signed by

Shags and the Russians they'd brought in since I left.

"What the...? Where's the evidence?"

I tried to search the brief-case.

"Stop him!" Repinov ordered, "Mr Parr, please, Blake has only just got these back, I don't want them being ruined...."

"I don't understand! You were talking about getting rid of evidence!"

"No, Brian," Blake told me, "We were talking about these shirts. The team wore them at the centenary match and then they were auctioned for charity and bought by Mr Repinov's sister's husband...

"This man, by brother-in-law" Repinov explained, "is very important in my country - someone who you totally don't want to upset ..."

"But last week I almost sent them to someone else who'd been at the auction, I only just got them back," Blake added.

"It can't be true!" I shouted, stamping my foot.

They both looked at me, I could tell they thought I was mental which I knew I wasn't so I stamped my foot again.

"Look, Brian," Blake said, putting on a soft voice like my Mum used to when I got done for forcing my brothers to play football with me during the night, "You've just got out of prison, you're looking for someone to blame, aren't you?"

I nodded, I couldn't believe he was being so nice and I stopped stamping.

"I get that," Blake continued, "We get that, don't we Sergei?"

Repinov shrugged.

"But you can't go round accusing innocent people of things they haven't done."

"Or getting reporters to back you when all you have is sh*t," Cindy said from behind me.

"Now," Blake said, "We're going to keep this between us. United doesn't need any more bad press."

He nodded to the guard who was holding the tape and told him to break it. Cindy tried to save it, saying she could do a story to help Blake and show the world what a d*ck I was trying to blame them for Stevie. Blake refused and the guard snapped the tape.

I was grateful for that, even though at the same time I was already thinking he could still be guilty. Sure, this time he'd proved I had misheard a conversation, but that didn't mean 110% he hadn't killed Stevie, did it?

"If we ever see you round here again, or you try and investigate us again, we will call the police. Understood?"

I nodded.

"Hey, Brian," Repinov said, "Look, like totally try to relax, this sh*t takes time?"

"What do you mean?" I said.

"OMG, you know, finding murderers. Look, Angela Lansbury is like my total hero and in 'Murder She Wrote' she never finds anything out first time..." he said, "Her first lead is never going to be the real killer. Where's the story if she solves it half way through the episode?"

"I don't know. But isn't that TV. Couldn't I just solve it now and start a nicer story?"

"You serious?" Repinov asked, "F*ck! I thought from the way you played you were a proper man! Nicer! Look, get totally out of here and from now on stop thinking I'm not like bothered about who killed one of my players, yeah? United's having a well bad season because of it."

Chapter 27

After the disaster of what had happened, Cindy refused to give me a lift back to town. I had to walk back. Along the way I found a ten pound note. Lucky I suppose, though I didn't really feel it. I bought some alcohol. I drank it all very quickly.

I knew I'd also been really lucky that what had happened hadn't gone out on live TV. That would have been terrible. But that didn't mean I didn't still feel terrible. I thought I'd solved it and then found out I was wrong! I hadn't even narrowed the list of suspects down. You know, with the whole process of elimination that Nev had told me about in jail. Because even though Repinov had given me advice and told me it wasn't them, from what I'd seen I still thought it could be them.

All I'd succeeded in doing was make it even harder to get to them in the future and prove once again that my balls get me in trouble.

By the time I got back to Malcolm Malcolm's house I was really drunk. And I'm sad to say that I stayed that way for a few weeks. Every morning I thought about what Repinov had said about it taking time for me to find stuff out, but I found it hard to do anything. If some commentators had been watching me, they would've said I was lacking that bit of spark which a player needs when he's in a bad run of luck.

The only good thing about those weeks was that Malcolm's living

158

room was the perfect place to watch football. Of any kind. At any time of the day. It was weird actually. The rest of the house was a bit rubbish. He only had five rooms and one was apparently so dirty he wouldn't let me go inside. I quickly learnt not to even try to get in there because he got so upset if I went near it saying that he was so ashamed at the mess.

As for the other rooms, the kitchen was small and not that nice because everything looked a bit brown. Although I never really went in because Malcolm liked cooking mini-pizzas for me. The bathroom was tiny and didn't have room for a Jacuzzi even if he could have afforded it. The two bedrooms were small but at least they were both covered in football posters. Even Nev's because even though he didn't like football, Malcolm said he had too many great posters for one room and as it was his house Nev had to have them up. At first I thought that was harsh on Nev but then I grew to like it because soon Nev's room kind of became mine. You see he stayed with his Mum a lot so I got his bed – which was so nice of him and he didn't seem to mind me bumming around his house one bit.

But the house was all about the TV room. Malcolm lived for it. He'd designed the room so he had football *past* (hundreds of DVDs of old matches) *present* (his TV and computer had access to every league in the world) and *future* (he had a second TV that was always on the sports news in case anything happened while he was watching a game) whenever he wanted.

When I was a kid, we only had enough for a tiny TV and yet Malcolm, who I knew was on benefits, had all this great stuff. And he had a season ticket too which cost a lot and he tried to go to as many away games as possible. I knew that being a true fan cost a lot of cash, so how could he afford it?

I presumed he did some work on the sly like some people I knew but he denied it and said he was just clever with his benefits. How did I feel, having been someone who'd paid a sh*tload of tax for the past ten years when I saw how he spent his benefits? Well, I thought, fair play. At least it was United, and not drugs he was hooked on. Football's never done anyone any harm, has it?

One thing Malcolm did do was volunteer as a coach at the local football club. The first time I saw him in his sports-klt I laughed, thinking he'd got dressed up for watching a match on TV like I did sometimes. When he said he was off to do some coaching I stood up straight away. Even though I'd had a fair few beers I wanted to go too. I missed football and teaching kids would be good for my image. Malcolm was clever though. He pointed out that a Korean game was starting and I'd just opened a beer.

The next time he was about to go training, I got up again. This time I hadn't drunk anything all day. Except one beer which I'd opened to celebrate a great goal in a mid-table clash in the Australian League scored by a guy I'd played against when he was still good enough to play in England.

"I'll come this time, Mal," I said, "Look, no open beer."

"Better to watch TV though, Bri?" he said.

"Mal, what you talking about? It's me, Brian Parr. Your number one player, saying I'll come along with you to help coach the kids. How cool are you going to look? Parents love it when they see me going at it with their kids!"

"That's just it, Bri."

"That's just what?" I said, getting a bit irritated.

160

"They…they've told me not to bring you."

"Who?"

"The parents."

"Why? Why don't they f*cking want me to teach their b*stard kids?"

I felt anger growing inside me. I opened a can.

"Look...they just don't think you're the right kind of person to be teaching kids any more…"

"But that's…." I stuttered, my body getting sweaty, taking another swig "…that's not fair!"

I couldn't handle it. This city had once loved me and now they didn't. I told Malcolm I was going to leave.

"Don't, Bri, don't. I like having you here."

"Thanks mate, but I'll be gone when you get back. If lots of people find out I'm staying with you and lots of people hate me, I can't stay!"

"Bri, look, Nev says we should keep an eye on you and I agree. Stay here while you get your feet back, yeah…"

In the event I decided to finish my can and watch highlights of the first time I won the league with United. A lot of the footage was of me scoring and the team doing well. When Malcolm got back he did mini-pizzas with extra cheese and beans and it felt alright.

In truth though, those days weren't easy. Most of the time my family were in Spain. I'd had a couple of chats with my Mum but my Dad didn't want her to see me and wouldn't talk to me. My cousins and other people I spoke to said I should just give him time. I could tell, though, that a lot of my family thought I'd been lucky rather than innocent. I'd explained what had happened in court, but I could tell people thought I was bullsh*tting. One of my cousins told me that a lot of his mates thought that the guy who'd been filmed with Stevie's body must have been someone I'd paid to help me.

I knew it was the papers fault people hated me. They'd done such a job on me that people believed them, not the courts! I couldn't think about it without getting angry.

Then one day, something good almost happened. Before the press ruined it. Malcolm and I were watching a repeat of the latest United game - another loss which meant the papers went mad with rumours about the Gaffer being sacked - when someone knocked at the door.

It was an agent. I hadn't heard of him, which was a bad sign, but he looked like Rico, which was a good sign. His name was Gav Gleeson and he thought we could help each other.

"This time of the season is panic time for teams facing relegation and some clubs would do anything to stay up. And I mean anything."

"What do you mean by anything?" I asked.

"Well, I mean, sign you."

"But they should be grateful to have me, I'm brilliant at football!"

Gav loosened his collar, "Look, Brian, two of the clubs I'm talking to would be really grateful to have you but they're not sure how the fans would react..."

"The fans! They..." I was about to say they 'love' me, but I stopped.

"Look, what I'm proposing is to see if I can work out a deal. Let them sign you for the rest of the season, ten games max. If they stay up, the fans are hardly going to complain. And we can move on from there."

"How much are we talking? At United I was on..."

"This is a whole new ball game," Gav said, "These two clubs are down at the bottom for a reason, and you are seen as a risk. They don't think they could be seen giving you a big pay day...yet...but if you helped them not get relegated we could sort something better for you."

"So not much? What? 50 a week, 65?"

"50 grand?"

"Of course."

"The figures mentioned are between 5 and 10."

"Are you joking?"

"No."

"10 grand a week? They must mean a day, which would be...10, 20, 30...about 60 grand a week."

"Brian. 10. A week. Max."

"Gav, I am Brian Parr. Not Max. And Brian Parr should be paid more than that."

"That's what they said, Brian. They'd be taking a huge risk on you, the negative backlash in the press, it could threaten sponsorship deals ..."

"But 10 grand, I was on that ten years ago!"

"What are you on now?" he asked.

I sat back. It was time for thinking and being clever.

Rico once told me about the power the footballer has on the pitch. As a modern footballer you're bound to attract negative attention. Everyone's seen it in the press. It's gang-bangs and love-rats galore. But it doesn't matter that much if you get caught cheating in your private life. Because you can earn forgiveness on the pitch.

No matter how bad the stories are, no matter how many papers say you're nasty for cheating on your wife, or how many threats you get from sponsors to sort your act out or they'll stop paying you, if you go out and score next match, everything is forgiven. If you're playing well, it doesn't take long for fans to forget and the papers will follow.

"Look," Gav said, "Once you've played, showed people what you can do, then we can re-negotiate a deal. What do you reckon?"

"Let's do it."

Gav looked chuffed. We shook hands.

"Erm, excuse me," Malcolm said.

"Yes, Mal?"

"Aren't you forgetting something?" Malcolm said.

"What?" I asked, "...win bonuses?"

"No, Bri, what teams they are?"

"Oh, yeah. Gav?"

"Rovers and City."

"Fair play."

"Any preference?"

I shook my head. I just wanted to play. I didn't know what kind of flat or cars you could afford on 10 grand a week, when you still had to live and look like a footballer, but it would surely be an improvement on what I had!

Anyway, for the next day or so I felt excited and nervous at the same time. I cut down on the beers and looked at the phone a lot.

In the end I didn't have to wait for the phone to ring to get the news. Half way through a Chinese match, Malcolm suddenly turned the mute on the TV. I was about to kick off when I noticed he was watching the TV with the sports news on.

There were load of fans outside a ground. A headline read: *Brian Parr inside Rovers Ground Ready to Sign.* Then another came up: *Fans protest to stop move.*

Apart from the fact that some of it was actually untrue, I couldn't believe it.

"Why would anyone protest against me signing, Mal? I could f*cking

164

save them."

"I know you could."

"They can't do this, can they?"

He told me that the season before, a player hadn't had their contract renewed for making racist comments. When another club was about to sign him, their fan's had protested and the club pulled out. In the end he'd gone to Spain and was apparently fitting in.

That's when Gav rang. He was inside the ground not me. And he'd just been told that Rovers were pulling out, and when he'd called City they said the same.

"I have a few contacts in the..."

"In the what?"

"In the..."

"In the...Europe? Bit of sun, I wouldn't mind that? What do they pay?"

"No, in the ...lower leagues. Not the one's getting promoted, but respectable clubs."

I hung up. Yeah, I would get paid, but not much, and was anyone going to see me to start forgiving me if I wasn't in the top league?

Course not. No-one watched lower leagues. I asked Malcolm to do a deal with me - if I signed one of his shirts, would he buy me a bottle of rum?

Chapter 28

"Guess what I've got, Bri? Guess?"

"Beers? I thought you didn't have anything else to sign. Can I sign things twice?"

"No."

"What then?" I said, turning back to the TV.

"Tickets."

"I can't go anywhere near United..."

"It's not United. It's someone else."

"Why would I watch someone else? Town, maybe, but I'd get beaten sh*tless. Come on mate, your TV's great..."

"It's England," he said, almost whispering, "the qualifier. Two days' time. I won them in a quiz...if they win they go through to the World Cup."

"I've never been to an England match before."

For some reason Malcolm found this really funny and started laughing. So did I. Although inside I was sad because I should have been getting more international caps, not being a fan.

We got the bus down to London to get to the ground early. I didn't want to be recognised so I'd borrowed some sunglasses and a cap from Nev who Mal said was good at dressing up because he went to lots of parties dressed up. I read the papers on the way down, one with loads of football pictures, and I could feel the excitement growing.

Feeling like a kid on the bus was enough to make me feel better. But getting the tube train to the ground was even more eye-opening! I couldn't believe it. The whole platform was rammed. Everywhere I looked there were scarves and shirts and flags and painted faces. The best thing was that virtually everyone was supporting the same team.

At Town I always remember feeling a bit unsafe when we saw opposition fans. Dad used to do his best to hide me from it all, while

166

he had his turn swearing at the opposition fans, but sometimes it felt that the day wasn't about football, it was about whether people were going to end up fighting. It was great to see there was none of that tension at a home England game.

I knew what it was like to be in the dressing room before kick-off playing for England. At that moment it didn't feel half as exciting as being a fan. As a player when there's that level of expectation it can get stressful. I still loved playing football, but it had become something I could fail at. But not as a fan.

As a fan you love the team, you want them to win, but there's nothing you can do to change the result – and because of that, as I waited for the tube, I felt free. Nervous, yes, because it was football and it mattered, but there was nothing I could do about it for once.

When we got on the tube the feeling of just loving everything I was doing got even more ramped up. There were loads of blokes talking and laughing. I even heard one guy, only about a metre away, who said 'we would have already qualified if Brian Parr was still playing'. That made me smile, even though everyone else called him a 'f*cking c*nt' and then called me a 'f*cking c*nt' too.

People had carried on drinking, even though it was against the law on the tubes. They ignored the police and carried on singing and chanting as we left the station. It felt like the fans had all the power, they owned the streets for the day.

I noticed people who weren't going to the game looking at us like they wished they were going. And us lot, we all looked like a team that belonged together as we made our way to the huge ground. I never wanted to forget that feeling.

As for the game, I'm sure everyone remembers that we lost. So to get into the World Cup we'd have to go through the play-offs. It was disappointing, but we'd been unlucky with a few decisions and fallen asleep in defence at the wrong moments. But I loved it anyway because as a fan I sometimes liked to lose. Weird, eh?

You see when Town lost, Dad and me always had more to talk and think about. We spent ages trying to work out what had gone wrong. We were more desperate for the next game to come along to see if Town could get it right. If you win, it's great – course it is – but you say you're pleased and that's it. When we lost Dad and me had great chats about it.

On the bus on the way back we hit the beers big time, and by the time we got back home, I was pretty drunk. Malcolm wanted to go home but I decided I wanted to carry on being a fan and go to a pub with everyone else. He kindly lent me some money and off he went.

We carried on for a good few hours. I don't remember how, or who from, but I got a lift back to my old village. For a while I stood at the gates of my house. Pressing the buzzer. I got no answer.

After that I started walking.

I found myself in the middle of a field. I think I sobered up a bit when I realised it was the place I was arrested. I was back in the place where it had all come tumbling down.

That night, I did too.

The next day, with a splitting headache, I woke up under one of the trees. I stank. My hands were shaking and my head felt awful.

I leant against a tree and was sick. Then I was sick again. I looked down at what I'd thrown up and was about to kick some of the leaves and branches to cover it when I realised I was going to kick a bone. I stood back and saw that underneath the dirt and stuff there was a dead dog. Most of it was bones. There was some fur, but it was mostly a skeleton.

I felt a bit sick. I liked dogs. I was about to stand up when I noticed that between its teeth was something black. And long, and rectangle shaped. I couldn't believe it.

I couldn't believe it.

A mobile.

The phone I'd found in the bedroom.

I ran all the way back to Malcolm Malcolm's. My hangover cleared. I felt like a different person because of the experience at the England game and this bit of hope.

Nev was with his Dad and I got them to come back to the woods with me. At first Nev said he had work to do for his law course, but Malcolm sorted him out. We took photos of it, and then Mal called the Police and said he was a fan of mine and he'd heard me talk about a dog taking a phone and he thought he'd found it. Apparently at first the Police had treated Mal a bit weirdly, but once they'd seen it, they seemed to take it seriously.

"So what will they do?" I asked when Mal came back home and told us about it.

"Check who owns the phone....from...records?" Mal suggested.

"Yeah, but these records, they can be very hard to trace to protect people's privacy," Nev replied, "And that's even if it can be traced and has a registered owner."

"I've got it." I shouted.

"What?"

"Records!"

"I know, I've said that, Brian, but the police will do that" Nev told me.

"No, Nev! Records!" I shouted again.

"What you talking about, Bri?"

"Kiki," I said, "Stevie's girlfriend, she was pregnant, right?

They nodded.

"Well, she must have given birth by now…it takes some months doesn't it? As soon as the lads were born Yvonne and I were desperate to get the records done so we could get the certificate for the first exclusive baby pictures we were doing. We could get those records, and find Kiki….and see what she knows!"

Malcolm seemed excited. Nev was quiet, "What do you think, Nev?" I asked him," Will you help?"

"Brian. I can't at the moment. I have so much work to do. I'm sorry, I really am. I'm going to be late with some work I needed to hand in today because I came here!"

"Nev?" I asked, "What's wrong? Why don't you like me anymore?"

"I just have to work hard so I can qualify! G*d, why do you have to make everything about yourself?"

"What are you talking about, Nev, this is Brian Parr and this is my home!" Mal shouted.

"Well, Brian treats it like it's his! I'm glad we got him out of prison, but what has he done since then? Wake up, Dad, he's using you."

"He's not, he's got nowhere else to go..."

"Nowhere else? He's said himself that agent could have gotten him a club somewhere…"

"The lower leagues!" I said.

"It's still a job."

"They hardly pay you!" I replied.

"They pay you a lot more than most people get paid…for playing a

170

bl*ody game."

"Football is not a game!" I shouted, standing up.

Malcolm stood up too, but didn't really know what to say.

"Look, Brian, I'm sorry, I'm angry. But look what you're doing to my Dad. He's spending his money feeding you and buying you beer! You've done nothing for weeks and now you want us to drop everything? Until when? Something else bad happens? And you stop again? That's all it took when you came out! One thing went wrong and you gave up! But now you say you're back! You're either excited or sulking, you don't stick at anything..."

There was a stunned silence.

"Ok. I'm sorry," I told him, "I'm sorry. I have been...selfish. But now I'm certain I won't stop until I get the truth! And I need your help!"

"No, Brian."

"Please! Malcolm and me can't do it on our own. So hey," I said thinking of a clever way to get him to do what I wanted like Rico used to do, "Why not do it for your Dad, not me? You want to help your Dad, don't you?"

"Of course I want to help my Dad, and getting you out of the way is the best thing for that."

Nev left.

Malcolm looked like he'd seen a ghost.

I sat down. He made us some mini-pizzas.

"What you need, Bri," he said, wiping up his bean sauce with some pizza crust, "...is someone who can help you investigate. Someone who's job is investigating....not someone like Nev, he really does have to study, he is a good boy, but he's busy."

"Like who then?" I asked.

"What about the press? Journalists are meant to be good at investigating, ask one to help."

"You can't trust them."

"Why not?"

"Rico told me. The moment I went to a newspaper man, they'd go along with it and then break the story the moment I did something stupid."

"So someone else then, someone else who could make money from telling your story."

Chapter 29

When Brian first came to see me, I wasn't interested in going back into the footballer's world of the super-rich and super-vain. Not even for a large amount of money. As a young writer I'd taken footballers books on so I could make a living. Having done about ten I'd told myself I had to start doing something more meaningful.

In Brian's case it wasn't the money. He had none.

By the time I met him, Brian certainly didn't look like a stereotypical footballer. Well, actually he probably did, if it was the stereotypical look of a footballer who's fallen from grace and lost all his money. He was in a cheap tracksuit – navy with white stripes down the side – and white trainers. His face looked stretched and tired with bags under his eyes, he was covered in shaving cuts. Apparently he'd wanted to get rid of his beard to look more 'business' but his hairdresser Toni wouldn't see him for free so he'd had to do it himself. Still, he did look in good shape, despite the fact he said he needed a good pre-season to sort his

172

abs out.

What I liked about his story were the conspiracies and theories and the fact he believed all of them. Every time Brian talked about each suspect he convinced himself that person had done it. Then he'd move onto someone else and convince himself all over again. As a writer, I knew that that was exactly what you needed in a good murder mystery.

The one thing we were lacking, the one thing he obviously wanted but couldn't be sure about having, was an ending. Brian needed that to put the whole thing to rest. I needed it for any book I wrote.

The question I asked myself was would Brian be able to find his ending? Would he find the killer and who set him up? Were they even the same person?

I understood his argument for doing it on his own and not going to the police, but I was also wary of getting involved in anything illegal. As long as I wasn't involved in the actual groundwork I was beginning to think I would take on the job of writing his story. And when it came down to it, if things were to get hairy, it did seem like he could handle himself - either because he was lucky, good or both.

"So what's next?" I asked him.

"We have to find Kiki, she may have some information..." he said before stopping, "What? What is it? I know journalists and I know how they look when I've said something wrong."

"You said 'we' Brian, I haven't even said I'll write the book yet, and even if I had, that wouldn't mean I'd follow you around like your side-kick..."

"Side-kick? What's that?"

"Like Batman and Robin."

"Oh, from the team in Belgium?"

"Pardon?"

"Belgium have two players called that. Batman's the striker. He's scored 60 in 80 matches and 40 of them have been set-up by Robin, the left winger. They could be nicknames though..."

"Sounds like it. Anyway, Brian, the point is I've got a lot of writing to do. I can't follow you around."

"I'm sorry. I'm still getting used to doing everything on my own."

I looked at him. He looked like a kid with no sweets. James Bond after losing all his gadgets. In a tracksuit.

"I need to read all this information, interview you, transcribe all your interviews, and get up to speed. Once I've done that I might be able to help you work things out. But from here. Not by running around the city."

"Really? You could help from here."

"Yeah, you may have missed stuff. It's hard to be objective when it's your own story. So I'll keep my eyes out for any plausible leads or things you said at first and haven't remembered."

He was nodding.

"Ok, Brian?"

"I don't really know what you were saying. But it sounded good?"

I could see why people got annoyed with him. He could go from being quick and sharp to an idiot in a flash. And not for any lack of intelligence, just simple lack of education. I mean he had a photographic memory which was incredible, but he'd only ever been praised for using it when playing football. No-one had ever thought to say what an amazing brain he had and suggested he could use it in other walks of life. If he'd been taught to use his skills for things other than kicking a ball into a net, who knows what he could have done?

174

Maybe nothing, but the fact was he was in his mid-20s and he'd never even thought he could be good at something away from the pitch.

Before he left he signed a contract giving me the rights to write his story - whatever happened. The cynical side of me thought there could well be a book in Brian Parr simply f*cking up – something which seemed just as possible, if not more so, than him being able to actually solve the case.

Stepping out of the ghostwriter's office I felt a lot happier because I now had some tactics (Shags had told me about him when he'd done a book and said that though he looked qu*er, he wasn't, and though he didn't like football he was actually a good lad).

Some managers are all about getting players fired up. Motivators. You go out on the pitch ready to die to win. Sometimes it works, but if after thirty minutes things aren't going your way it's hard to know what to do. You start feeling insecure because the tactics aren't there. Other managers are all about the prep. The research. So when the game begins, you know everything about your opposition, which can help, unless you get too bogged down in questions and lose the passion.

Obviously the best managers combine both - bulldog spirit and brains – but it's funny how few can do it. The Gaffer was one. And now I felt like I was one, with the ghost-writer, Will. I felt like the team of me and him had both the brains and the bulldog. Which is what I needed.

First up was Kiki. I texted Shags. He replied even though it was training time – he was the one who told me about stitching it into your shirt!

He said he hadn't seen Kiki since Stevie had died. He knew Stevie had bought her a flat somewhere in the city but he had no idea where.

Malcolm Malcolm was coaching so I borrowed his bike and set off on my own. It wasn't quite my polka dot Bentley but it was good fun. Even the kids shouting 'Parr's a w*nker' and 'Murdering f*cking c*nt' didn't dampen my spirits.

When I got to the big building I'd registered Chesney and Baggio at, I was told I had to have an appointment. Which was annoying. I didn't want to have to stop that soon. I wanted to prove I could do it on my own to the writer, and to Nev – who I wasn't angry at, but who'd annoyed me a bit by being a bit nasty.

I racked my brains. Before, if I didn't understand something I asked Rico. He was the one who'd told Yvonne and me about the registry thing in the first place. And that's when I remembered Tony. If I'd ever bought a flat for my pregnant girlfriend, Rico would have sorted it. So Tony was bound to have helped Stevie, wasn't he?

Now I knew Tony had died. Which was sad. But surely he'd still have all the documents and his office was smack bang in the town centre. So I cycled there, put in the pincode to his office which Stevie had told me for when we wanted to take girls somewhere after a night out, and walked up the stairs. The office was as cool as always – with big sofas, wide-screens, glass rooms with desks in - as Tony had spent loads making the place look sweet to get the best players. But it felt a bit dirty and smelly too, I guess because it hadn't been used for a while.

Seeing Tony's face in a few photos on the wall made me sad for a moment. I'd been low enough to think about suicide, but I hadn't been serious. To get that bad, he must have been really, really sad.

I started to look around. I felt like one of those spies you see in the

176

movies. Though they seemed to know what they were doing a bit more. Because they always went to people's desks, that's what I did. I'd never really had a desk. I'd had a study built in the house because Yvonne said a man should have one but I'd only ever used it for my sticker books which I collected for fun, mostly for Baggio and Chesney really. Every season I bought a sticker book for each of us. Mine was always full first. I'd always been good at stickers.

I opened some drawers and did some reading and realised it wasn't Tony's desk. It was his secretary's who I'd always thought was hot. I found some photographs of her and Tony doing s*x things. He looked happy in them – she was a looker and the things they were doing would have made a dead man smile– so it made me feel better.

As soon as I went over to Tony's desk I couldn't believe my luck. There was a pile of papers on the desk. Lots of bills and things. But in one envelope, quite near the top of the pile, there was a birth certificate. Dated 12th December from the year before. Stevie was named as the dad and the mum was called Kathryn Kyle – using my alphabet learning with Miss Bewley I knew that had to be Kiki, didn't it?

The baby was a boy and it was called Stevie Jr Kyle. Why was it on Tony's desk? From what I could remember he'd killed himself a couple of days after.

"Can I help you?"

I almost shat a brick. I looked up and there was a woman in a big fur coat staring at me. She was older than me, a bit fat, but also had big breasts, blonde hair and big boots. So she was hot. She looked rich. I had the certificate in my hand and I put it in my track-suit pocket.

"Erm….I'm….I'm…."

"You're Brian Parr," she said.

I nodded.

"And why are you in my ex-dead-husband's office?"

It was Tony's wife! Ex-wife! I remembered when I'd spoken to him how desperate he was for money to give to her. She looked like was she doing alright with all the jewelry she had on.

"I'm just picking up some stuff of mine."

"Stuff? All of this belongs to me. Show me what you just stuffed into your pocket."

She started to walk towards me. I found her a bit scary and I sighed with relief when she stopped as she saw the photos of Tony and the secretary that I'd left out.

"Oh my," she said. "There he is in all his glory. If he'd kept that in his pants, he'd still be here, don't you think?"

Every time she spoke she was looking at me directly in the eye. I knew what normally happened after women did that to me. I sh*gged them and then had a new story to tell Shags and a new injunction to take out.

"I'm not sure....I didn't know Tony that well."

"Lucky you."

She strode over to me. I stepped back but tripped, the desk chair broke my fall. She let out a little laugh. I could smell wine on her breath. I liked how much lip-stick she had on. Her hand went into my trouser pocket and she took out the certificate.

"Brian, from everything I've read this isn't how you normally are with the women, is it?" she said, still bending over me, "By the looks of you, you do seem like a bit of broken man....how disappointing...although that six-pack I've seen so much off hasn't entirely gone, has it?"

Her hand went to my side, her fingers crept up my tummy.

"I'm not broken. Well, I'm fixing it."

"It?" she said, opening the certificate, "Ah, you're after her...so this is you playing at private eye? I heard what you said in court. Accusing everyone of killing Steven, including Tony..."

"I'm sorry about that, I was..."

"It's fine, I don't have any feelings other than hate for my ex-husband."

"Right...."

She lit a cigarette and leant against the desk.

"But he didn't do it. I mean why would he? It was always about money for Tony and with Steven dead he only lost out."

"Shags told me Tony needed money," I said, "He wanted Stevie to move to get a big cut of the transfer fee - I thought, well, that he might have got angry when Stevie said no?"

"The pr*ck did need money after I finally got proof he was f*cking everyone who worked for him," she agreed, "... and if Steven had moved clubs Tony would have had a big payday. But the truth is, if Steven had stayed for another season he would have had an even bigger payday from United. "

"What do you mean?"

"Last year when it came to renewing contracts they were negotiating with Blake, who was new at the time and had been told he had to keep hold of Steven no matter what. Tony knew this and got it written into Steven's contract that if he stayed at the club and made it to ten years as a first team player he'd get a massive loyalty bonus...like another signing-on fee, and we're talking millions. Tony had never been happier with a deal in his life..."

179

"I never knew that! Why didn't I get that?"

"You hadn't been there for ten years. And while the fans liked you, they loved Steven because he'd only ever played for United."

"Right....well, I guess you're right that Tony wouldn't hurt Stevie for the money then."

"It could be about money for someone else though," she said with a smile, her leg touching mine.

"Who?" I asked desperately.

"It's a theory, there are lots of people who could have done it."

"Tell me about it!" I said. "Who do you think it could be?"

"When Repinov took over, he told Blake the club had to be profitable in two years. Partly because of Repinov, partly because every club is going to have to be soon for the fair-play rules. Blake realised he was at fault for handing out huge contracts with huge bonuses and started trying to make up for it before Repinov found out. But with Steven and you still at the club, what could he do? Now both of you have left, so have your huge wages."

I let this sink in. Although I was also thinking about her foot that was now stroking my leg.

"You know a lot about it," I tell her.

"That's because I've made it my mission to get what's mine. I've fought Tony's partners for this place and United for every bit of money he was owed – and last week everything was finally agreed. I'm here to pick up some things before these offices go on the market."

There was silence for a moment. She stubbed out her cigarette.

"And your plan was to track Kiki down to...?"

"See if she knows about anyone who threatened Stevie."

"She may know. I need to speak to her too. That flat was bought in this company's name so no journalists would know Steven had a mistress. Which means, technically it's mine..."

"Do you know her?"

"Only about her....she caused Tony a lot of grief. Constantly saying she was going to the press, which he had to stop so Steven's image wasn't ruined. In the end, though, Tony was the one who was going to break the story...he was that desperate for some money he got the certificate from her and wanted to do a Boxing Day exclusive about the baby."

"What happened?"

"His suicide", she said looking at me as if that had been obvious, "It surprised me actually...I never thought he was a quitter."

"So he did... it was definitely suicide? Not like a fake one from on the TV?"

"I found the body myself. He'd never been so well hung before..."

"Oh, right."

She ran her boot up the inside of my leg.

"What about you, Brian?"

"What?"

"You don't quit, do you?"

"Do I look like I do?"

"In that nasty f*cking tracksuit, yes. But the fact that you're here tells me otherwise."

"D*mn right."

"Do you think you can find out who did it? A lot of people I know expect you to be an alcoholic within a year."

"I'll show them. I've promised. To myself, to Stevie. I'm not going to stop."

"And you're starting with Kiki? Well good luck with that."

"Thanks."

I could feel her staring at me. I stood up, deciding I needed to keep moving.

"Where are you going?"

"To Kiki's."

"Where's that?" she said, her tongue licked her lips slightly.

Oh yeah, I thought, I had no idea. I needed that certificate back, or some details of the flat.

"Can you tell me where she lives?"

She looked at me for a moment and took off her fur coat. Her top showed a lot of her big t*ts.

"We could always come to some arrangement."

"Like what?"

"You could take of that nasty tracksuit and make love to me on each and every sofa. And by the way, my name's Ruby."

Chapter 30

Brian sounded a bit flushed when he called me to say he'd found Kiki. He also started talking about Blake Baxter and how he thought that Stevie might have been killed because he had such a big contract. I told him to calm down and promised I'd look into Blake for him. Despite the fiasco in Repinov's office and how Blake had let Brian off quite lightly, it did seem like he might have some skeletons in his closet.

I'd already done some background research into Repinov. While there was nothing obviously wrong with him, there had been claims in the press from his own country that he'd made his fortune through corruption. Nothing had been proved though and the fact that he always had a large security detail wasn't exceptional either when you're that rich. But I could see why Brian had placed him near the top of the list of suspects.

As for Blake Baxter, he was a man with hands in a lot of pies. His Dad had been a local building contractor and using those contacts Blake had got into the local property market and made a lot of money in the late 80s and early 90s.

I learned from press archives he'd attracted a few complaints mostly surrounding building developments and contested planning permission – he'd always come out on top and he'd always kept his reputation intact, if not squeaky clean. One drug dealer who'd had three large bits of property seized had used Blake as his property broker – Blake was never charged with anything, claiming he'd taken on the business in good faith and never known the guy was a criminal.

He'd been a United supporter all his life and held a corporate box since 1993. He'd started pushing to join the executive arm in 1996 and since 2000 had worked in their commercial team. Initially he'd used his property expertise to get new training facilities and stadium extensions through and then he'd moved onto the United board and into players' contracts. The only surprising thing was how and why Repinov had made him CEO. There were more senior people who'd worked for the old chairman who would have been more obvious choices.

There was nowhere near enough evidence yet, and Brian hadn't exactly struck gold with his earlier attempt to catch them, but of all the *suspects, Repinov and Blake had the contacts, power and money to kill Stevie Hurst and try to frame Brian. Could Ruby have just given us a clue to their motive?*

I was, however, wary of focusing on them and overlooking other people. I started looking into the suspect I thought we knew the least about – Dr Malone. I wasn't surprised that he could cheat drugs tests, because I'd read about that, but how had he managed to get into Brian's cell? How had he managed to take a heavy with him? And who were the gang he talked about? Were they connected to Stevie's underworld problems in any other way?

After an hour with Ruby I felt a bit sore cycling. As well as Kiki's address Ruby had given me one of Tony's old suits he'd kept in the office – she said she hated the idea of someone she'd slept with walking around looking like they'd come out of council estate, even though I had. She'd also given me her address because I'd lived up to my '*6 romps in one **Parr**-ticulary **Bri**-lliant night*' billing.

Cycling around town in a dead man's suit whose wife I'd just sh*gged felt strange. I didn't feel like I'd let myself down, because actually it had been very good, but I was aware that I'd had s*x with her to get something for myself. It was normally the other way round. And she was much older than me. Which again, was normally the other way around.

I left the bike opposite Kiki's place. It was a really old building which, from the looks of it, had been turned into really plush flats. You could tell just by looking at the place it was going to be sweet inside. Typical Stevie, though, he'd gone for a place where there was only outside parking. Why had he never put his cars first?

"Brian Parr? Is that you?" Kiki said when I said 'hello' into the intercom machine.

"It is," I said, wondering if she was going to let me in.

As soon as I got into the huge penthouse I could see it had everything a bloke wanted - loads of TVs, stereos, fish tanks and a mistress. But as well as that, it also had all the girly things too like really expensive sofas and curtains and carpets and stuff. It was a flat perfect for magazine exclusives, but it had all been kept secret by two men who were now dead, Tony and Stevie.

Kiki came back into the room with a glass of water for me. I'd seen her on the topless, glamour model photo Tony had showed me that night after the game. She was just as pretty and classy up close. Her hair was raven black, she was thin, really tanned, and had lots of make-up on which made her lips look like a p*rn girl; she was what I called 'a walking shag'. More my style than Stevie's.

"I'm Brian."

"I know. Steven talked a lot about you," she said, looking into my eyes.

What was it with women calling him Steven and looking at me like I was a piece of s*x meat? If Kiki said she'd only tell me what I wanted to know if I did her, would I be able to? I mean I could - I'm Brian Parr – but would I and should I? I felt guilty about May now that people knew, would I still feel guilty about b*nking Stevie's woman now he was dead?

"What did he say?"

"That you were sleeping with his wife."

"Oh…"

"That you pretended to be his friend but you f*cked over everyone to

185

get what you wanted..."

"Erm..."

"And that he'd once loved you, but he'd watched you change and that made him ...sad. When he went out with you he hoped you'd be the old you, but you never were. He didn't care about May really, or the fact he thought Carly was probably yours, it was that you didn't mind lying to him and he hated that he'd lost a friend ....Here," she said, offering me a tissue, before leaving the room, "Sit down."

I hadn't noticed the tears running down my cheeks until she passed me the tissue. I'd sorted myself out when she came back with a baby in her arms. She was looking at me in the eyes again, but I'd worked out that it had nothing to do with s*x. It was because she had important stuff to say. The other reason people look you in the eye.

"Is this Stevie Junior?"

She passed him to me. I'd always been good with babies so it was fine with me that he started screaming when I bumped his head on my knee.

"I'm....I'm so sorry...about Stevie."

She smiled, taking back the baby.

"I didn't kill him."

"I know."

"Do you?"

Her eyes welled up, and I passed her a tissue.

"I love this flat."

"We chose it together."

"I can tell," I said, looking around, "You can tell this was his place...it still feels like it..."

It looked like a leather jacket of his was still hanging on the door. And

186

some boots on the shoe-rack – he'd always had a weird dress sense, Stevie. She saw me noticing, "I know, I know," she said. "It's been months, I should tidy his things away, but I can't make myself do it."

Despite how she'd looked, all s*xy and everything, she was actually a really lovely person. I could see why Stevie had fallen for her and I felt sad that Stevie had never spoken to me about her. I think because I'd only ever heard about Kiki from Tony, and he was complaining about her, it made me think she was trouble. She didn't seem like that to me. She said she'd played dirty with Tony because that's how Tony played.

Apparently he hadn't been happy for a long time, way before he found out about May and me. For a bit he'd done what I had, slept around, then he'd met Kiki and that had all changed. He'd been seeing her for a while when his Dad had died; after that he wanted to change.

Stevie told Tony he was going to leave May. Tony told May – not everything about Kiki, like the love, but that Stevie had got her pregnant and he was thinking of leaving her. May and Tony decided to put on a united front and both kicked off at Stevie. They both knew Stevie moving in with Kiki would mean a huge loss of income, a lot of bad press and an expensive divorce.

Stevie didn't care about the money for himself, but he didn't want his kids with May and the one with Kiki to suffer. So he agreed that he wouldn't leave May but he'd get a place for Kiki. May didn't know about that, but was happy for Stevie to stay and for them to keep making the money from being one of English football's first families.

The whole thing had kind of worked. Kiki said she was mostly ok with it as Stevie had seen her most days. She was happy to wait a few years until after his career and then he would leave May and just be with her.

But Stevie had hated it. He felt he was living a lie which was when he started drinking and stuff. Especially over the summer when there was no training. He was still nice to Kiki, but she hadn't been able to stop his destructive side. She hadn't known he'd been gambling until about a week before he died – when someone had approached him in a club and threatened him.

The problem was he was living two lives, in two homes. And with his money, it was pretty easy for him to go missing and mess himself up. With me not there, Shags had tried to help, as had Tony, but she said in the last couple of weeks Stevie was pretty much out of control.

"I could tell that," I told her, "I tried to help him, tried to cover his tracks....but I guess that wasn't what he needed?"

"No. He told me you'd done that. Put him in touch with some doctor."

"Yes, I did, I did," I said, happy he'd told her I'd done something nice for him.

"He hated that. He hated the fact you had a quick-fix for everything and thought it was disgusting you'd been using the doctor yourself."

"Why? What's wrong with that?"

"He was living a lie, and hated it. And then he saw you'd been living a lie for ages and didn't care. Since you'd left your old club?"

"Town. Yeah, Town."

"He said that when you changed clubs you started to always be lying or cheating. You were, the richest celebrity in the country, or close to it, but it was all false."

"Was he jealous?" I interrupted.

"No. Not jealous. All these people, these kids, looking up to you, spending their money on posters and computer games with you in them, wanting to be you and yet you were nothing like the image they

188

were sold. And you didn't care. When he told you about it, all you did was say it was fine!"

"Well it is," I said, trying to defend myself, "I didn't invent it, I just made the most out of it."

Kiki looked at me. She wasn't judging me, even though she was saying a lot of quite nasty stuff about me. She was just telling me what Stevie had said.

"I never knew," I agreed slowly," I never knew he hated it so much."

To be honest I never had. I wasn't sure he even did, really. You see Stevie thought I was great and he'd always been jealous of me - from what Kiki was saying, a part of me was thinking that it must have done his head in that I'd got May too! And that I was holding my life together and not too into drink and things. So maybe he was jealous just not saying so? I was going to tell Kiki this but decided not to, because I needed to find out what she knew.

"He was so angry by the end, drinking too much, doing c*ke quite a bit."

"Was he really bad in the last few days? I didn't notice in training."

"No, he managed to pull it together for training, but as soon as he finished, he was off..."

"Did you notice anything strange? Did anyone else try anything on with him, like in the club?"

"Two nights before, when he came here, he was drunk but he was terrified. He said he'd been chased. He thought it could be the police, or a fan, or people wanting money."

"But he'd got away?"

She nodded, "The horrible thing was, he kept saying he wished he'd been caught. He knew he was in trouble with loads of people, and he just wanted it to be over."

"What happened then?"

"He said he had to leave. He got all of his stuff from the flat, absolutely everything and just left...I asked him if I'd see him again, and he said yes, but he had to stop living two lives and then with all of his things he left..."

Suddenly, she was in floods of tears. I went to try and be nice to her but she walked over to the window.

"Was that the last time you saw him? Or did you see him after the crash, before I found him at my house?"

She shook her said, and told me she couldn't say anything.

"Why not?" I asked, "Why can't you tell me?"

Still she wouldn't tell me. In the end I'd had to leave her. I could tell she knew something, but I had no idea how I'd get her to say anything about it.

Chapter 31

Brian dropped off the Dictaphones I'd lent him as soon as he left Kiki. I told him to leave me to listen to the conversations with Ruby and Kiki and go home. He looked pleased, saying Malcolm and him were going to watch a 5-a-side tournament featuring ex-professionals. He giggled to himself and told me he loved seeing these old players with big bellies and balding heads but who were still really skillful.

I was astonished at what he'd found out. It was good work. What was it about him? Did the fact that he appeared to have no real intelligence mean they felt comfortable telling him things? His good looks?

190

Whatever it was, he'd made good progress and my mind was on overdrive as I listened to both women open up to him. The only thing I wished I hadn't heard was Ruby literally opening up to him.

The next morning, we chatted about his next move.

"There was something about Kiki," he said, wearing Tony's old suit - which was a bit big but better than his tracksuit, "the way she refused to talk to me at the end. I've seen it before, last year in the England camp during the Euros...."

"What do you mean?"

"Well, at the Euros there was loads of bad press about the manager...you must know..."

I shook my head.

"Well, basically, he was being a tw*t. The way he wanted us to play wasn't working. We all knew that – us players, the press and the fans - but it was like he didn't want to admit he was wrong and we were banned from talking about him. The press knew we wanted to say something, but we'd been told not to..."

"Go on."

"Well, that's how Kiki was. She wanted to talk but she thought she'd be in trouble if she said anything. I've been in that situation a million times"

"And how do you break that?"

"Well, it's obvious isn't it?" he told me, "You let the person think that you already know about what you want to know. If the journo says,' was there a fight in training?' you say 'no, course not, we're all pulling in the same direction'. Whereas if they say 'Brian, why did you kick Tazza in the face?', because you think they already know, you say more to them."

"Why?"

"Well, Tazza's got this really annoying smile when he does something good and..."

"No, why do you say more to someone if they pretend to know about it already?"

"Oh, well, you see, you've been wanting to talk about it anyway, and because they ask the question like they already know everything, you think what harm can it do now they know?"

"You think that works?"

"Course. Now, you might still only say something obvious like 'temperatures always run high in a tournament like this, it's good to see passion out there and any handbags is part and parcel of that...' But the fact is, it gets you talking and gives them evidence..."

"So what you're saying is we need to talk to Kiki as though we already know what she knows...?"

"Sure," he said smiling.

"What're you smiling about?"

"You said 'we' that's what 'we' need to do. We're a team now aren't we?"

I smiled too. His enthusiasm was infectious.

"Ok," I said, thinking, "Well, for that to work your journalist had to find out from someone that you kicked Tazza..."

"He hit me first!"

"Ok, but what I'm saying is that for your method to work we need to find something else out about Kiki."

"How?" Brian asked.

"That's what we need to work out."

The ghostwriter, Will, said he wanted to meet Mal and Nev because they knew about the case. My mission was to get them.

"Mal," I said on my mobile, "I need you to get Nev and come to Will's office."

"But there's a match on, Argentinean league, Juniors are 2-1 up."

"Who scored?"

"That young lad…"

"Dos what's-his-name…"

"Two lovely goals. Diving header and edge of the area volley…"

"Nice. Nice," I said, "Still though, Mal, can you record that and come here?"

"Have you got a team again? Is it United?"

"No, Mal, not yet. But it might be soon. Do you think Nev will come?"

"I don't know…he went out yesterday…to one of those places?"

"Do you mean a gay bar?"

I couldn't even hear Malcolm's voice, he hated talking about Nev being a p*ff. I was sure that I'd be ok if Baggio or Chesney were g*y, not that there was any chance of that happening. Ever. You could just tell by everything about them.

"Well, tell him I'd really appreciate it. Tell him I've found this guy who thinks Nev can help."

Will said he needed to work and that I wasn't allowed to play on his wheely desk chair so I spent the next two hours going from newsagent to newsagent looking at the pictures of girls. Once I'd been in for too long I'd get thrown out and have to change shops. As I headed back to Will's I was pleased to see Malcolm and Nev waiting outside

"Thanks, Nev, I appreciate this, I know you've given me so much of

193

your time."

"Brian, it's fine, of course I'll help if I have time...it'd be good to see what this guy thinks."

If it hadn't been such a serious thing we were going to be talking about I think I'd have actually enjoyed myself. I'm not a soppy bloke - I'm Brian Parr - but there I was in a room with three people who'd agreed to help me out. At a time when no-one else had. That meant a lot to me. I was part of a team again.

We were all in the office. Will was at his desk, Malcolm and Nev were on a sofa and I'd managed to grab the cool chair with wheels. Not that I was going to be wheeling around the office. This was serious.

"One thing we should remember," Will was saying, "Is that whoever murdered Stevie and whoever set-up Brian..."

"So you think it might be different people?" Nev interrupted.

"Possibly, yes..." Will said, "...as I was saying, whoever it was, they've had a long time to cover their tracks. Which is going to make it hard for us."

"What's your role in this?" Nev asked.

"Well, I'm," Will said, "Sorry, Bri, can you not do that? It's putting me off."

I'd got some pace up by the time he asked, but I slammed my feet down and stopped the chair after completing my fastest lap of the room.

"I'm writing Brian's story," he said, "I'm his autobiographer."

"Yeah, but they don't decide the story. They record it."

"We know that, Nev," I said, "Sh*t sorry, Malcolm," I added as I misjudged my speed and rammed the chair into his shins, "And I'm still the one in the hot seat, I've just asked Will for some tactics."

I pushed my chair back into position. They were all looking at me, I could sense some dressing room tension between Nev and Will.

"Ok, I think what we should do is something we used to do in training," I said, trying to show off a bit I suppose and take charge of things, "What we did was go over the opposition players and imagine what type of position they might play and what type of goals they might score....even if they're the goalkeeper, because goalkeepers can score, you know..."

"Do you mean go over the list of suspects?" Nev asked, "Like we've done before?"

"Well, that's not what we called it in training, but..."

"Did you really do that in training?" Malcolm asked.

"Well, no, I did it in my head...on the coach on the way to matches."

"Oh, right, but it works does it?" Malcolm said, "Because I could try it on the kids I coach. I could call it the Parr Method. Is that ok?"

"Yeah, Malcolm," I said chuffed, trying to keep my cool but feeling my voice waver, "That'd be great. Sh*t sorry," I told Will as I knocked over one of his lamps after I'd decided to see what it was like to go backwards in the chair.

"Having heard Brian's story, and read everything," Will said, having cleared up the broken lamp, "I think we have a number of suspects and I've put their names in a list."

Will had a teacher's board at the side of his office and he span it round and revealed the list.

"11 suspects, Bri!" Malcolm said, "Like a team."

"I know, great isn't it?" I said, not really listening, my mouth open, as I used my feet to get the chair closer to the board.

"No, Dad," Nev said, "There are 12 names there."

"Brian, could you....not use the chair like that anymore?" Will asked.

I wasn't listening to him either.

"Stevie? A suspect?" I asked, "Nev said that once too. Do you really think?"

"Ok, well I'd say that's one of the 'goalie scoring an overhead kick' ideas. Or whatever it is they do. Stevie killing himself is a long shot, but it could have happened," Will told us.

"Go on..." I said, deciding not to tell him a goalie would never be able to do that because I was glad he was using the Parr Method.

"The stuff Kiki was saying, about Stevie and how much he hated, well, disliked you means he could have had enough! On the evening he crashed he was really angry at you, at himself, and he was high and drunk. So he could have decided to kill himself and at the same time try to hurt you...."

"So that's why he did it my basement?" I asked.

"Well, maybe, but like I said, this is a long shot," Will nodded, "He could have gone to the basement to teach you a lesson, because it's not nice cleaning up a dead person, is it? Or, if he was being really calculating he could even have done it to set you up? He wanted to die but also to make it look like you'd killed him. Some kind of payback for May and Carly?

"I mean Kiki said Stevie was ok with you about the affair, but you never know."

"Do you really think he could have killed himself?"

"I know people who've had fewer problems and done it," Will replied.

"I thought that too," Nev said, "It has to be considered. Stevie has a lot of motive, that we can prove, that shows he hated you and that he might have wanted to bring you down. And on top of that he was in so much debt and addiction he could certainly be seen as a likely suicide case."

"I thought that too," Malcolm joined in.

"Really, Mal?" I asked.

"You wouldn't have seen it, Bri, playing up front, but when United were losing, or not playing well, that boy really threw in the towel sometimes...I've watched him be like that since he started playing for the reserves at 16. He could just give up if the mood took him."

"Well, it seems like a good case," I said, trying to work out if Stevie could have really done what Tony did, "Shall we tell the Police? Call some papers?"

"No, Brian! Don't jump the gun! We're just brainstorming."

"I have no idea what that is," I said.

"We're saying everything we think to try and work this out," Will told me, "Because while those things mean he might have done it, a lot of things might show he didn't"

"Like what?"

"Well as far as I see it," Will said, "Firstly the stab wounds. It's a strange way to kill yourself, though not impossible if he wanted to get you blamed; and then there's the man on the CCTV in the garage....what would he be doing there, if Stevie had killed himself?"

I thought about this.

"Brian!" Will screamed, "For f*ck's sake!"

I jumped off the chair which I'd just run over Will's foot with because I thought he was going to throw me off it.

"No harm done!" I said, putting my hands up in the air as I would have done to a ref to show I was innocent.

"Is there anyone else that you guys have thought of, that I haven't?"

Will asked after he'd put some ice from his little freezer on his foot.

I shook my head and looked at Malcolm and Nev. Mal copied me.

"I think you've got it pretty much covered," Nev said, "What does that mean by Repinov? Who's Tammy?"

"Tammy is Repinov's fiancé," Will replied, "A week before Stevie died, Brian had s*x with her in a club while Stevie waited. Didn't you, Brian?"

I nodded, feeling like I did every day at school when the class got told I hadn't done my homework.

"She wasn't engaged to Repinov at the time," Will carried on, "But it might be the case that Repinov heard about it and…took his revenge."

"Sh*t! But he was so nice to me, kind of, when I was in his office! Do you really think he knows about Tammy and me? Is he still after me?"

"Brian, it's just a theory."

"Right," I nodded.

"Look, Brian" Will said, "If you want to find out who did it, you'll need to look at all these people."

"But that'll take ages!" I said as I managed to stop myself launching the chair towards the fridge to see if Will had any fizzy pop.

"Maybe, but you did well with Kiki and Ruby. I mean, before that I had Tony up there too. But I was able to eliminate him after what you found out."

"Yes!" I said, "Back of the onion bag!"

"Exactly, so you need to keep doing that!" Will said.

"How?"

"Well, you know the case, I don't need to tell you what evidence you're missing again, do I?"

"I suppose not."

198

"And if someone tells you something, don't just treat it as fact."

"Ok. Definitely."

"Question why they might be saying things to you."

"Right."

"Do you know why you should do that?"

"No. Why?"

"Because if they're lying then we need to know why and find out what they're hiding. And if they're telling the truth it might point us to other people and other leads."

"Look," Nev said, "I'd love to sit hear listening to you teach Brian how to be a detective, but I think you guys have got this under control."

"I've got practice," Malcolm said.

"That's not until four."

"I have to write up notes on the Parr Method, Bri!"

"Great, nice one," I said with a smile. The Parr Method. Brilliant.

Chapter 32

The first name on Will's list that I thought I should deal with was my Dad. Could it have been him? As I thought about it, some things added up. My Dad had always hated Stevie and his influence over me. What if he'd found out about the drugs and stuff? Could he have snapped and killed Stevie who he blamed for getting me into that scene, and then set me up? Hoping I'd get off and then start playing football again without all the footballer's lifestyle I'd got addicted too? All of these things could be true, but to get to my Dad I had to speak to my Mum. Luckily for me, I knew where to find her.

People think I got my work ethic as a footballer from my Dad, but he'd never worked! Apart from football coaching. Not like my Mum, who worked like you wouldn't believe. If cleaners were like footballers she would have been the Brian Parr of cleaning. I'm not saying, she would have been renowned for seeing dust where other cleaners couldn't, or for elbowing other cleaners out of the way when it came to dealing with corners. What I'm saying is that she was known for putting her all into what she did.

As she worked so hard, my Mum was always busy. People could trust her. And as I went up in the world so did her clients. Which was good for her because her pay got better. From United, as well as being my cleaner she also did Shags' gaff, and the Gaffer's houses. Before I'd gone to prison I'd also set her up as Edi's cleaner too. Looking at the lists of other suspects it would have been handy if she'd been Repinov's cleaner.

Dad was spending virtually all his time in Spain, but my Mum liked working so much she wouldn't give it up. Having spoken to her on the phone occasionally when I was inside and once I was released, I knew she now spent weekends in Spain and came back to town to work during the week. Seeing as it was Wednesday I knew if she'd kept the same schedule she'd be at Edi's place around noon.

Edi's place was part of an old warehouse that had been turned into a block of flats. Not the one Kiki lived in, but similar. They looked like great places, lots of windows and balconies and I knew it had an underground car park. Which was good for any footballer.

That's where I headed, and when I found my Mum's car I looked at the parking space and saw Edi's was on floor 2. First though, I had to disguise myself as my plan was to talk to my Mum as if I was someone else and try to get her to talk about Dad. That way she might let slip some clues.

"I need a disguise!" I said to the lady in the first fancy dress shop I found, "Now!"

She pulled a face and pointed to the shop, "Take a look. That's how shopping works."

The problem was finding a costume that would allow me to ask Mum questions. The shop I was in was great. But I didn't think turning up as a pirate or a saucy maid was going to help. I tried them on anyway for fun, and I dressed up as a dragon, a nurse and a big penis too. After an hour I realised I had to hurry up.

Even though the lady said my beard was stuck on properly by the time I arrived at the glass door of the block I could see half of it was hanging off. If Mum asked I'd have to say I was going bald on my beard or something just as clever as that.

When I got to the second floor I had two doors to choose from. I rang one of the bells. I straightened out my beard, flexed my gloved hands and adjusted my dark sunglasses.

A little girl about Baggio's age came out and screamed.

"It's ok, it's ok!" I said, "I'm sorry. Wrong door."

She stood staring at my face. I had to check something.

"Why did you scream?" I said, worried, "Hang on, do you recognise me? Do you recognise me, little girl?"

Beginning to cry, she shook her head.

"Yes!" I said, happy that my disguise had worked before hiding round the corner from her mum. When the coast was clear I rang the other doorbell, "Hello, Mrs Parr, I'm from a company!"

"Oh?" she said.

I'd thought of that first line, and practised it while I waited. I was pleased with it too. I hadn't thought of a second one.

"Yes..."

"Yes?"

"Yes."

"Yes?"

"Yes we make sure that....that cleaners are working properly. We're from the government company. Can I ask you some questions?"

"Ok," she said, looking at me strangely.

For a moment I thought it was because she recognised me, but hardly any of my face was visible under the shoulder-length wig and sunglasses so I stayed calm.

"And you are?" she asked.

Sh*t, I hadn't thought of that either.

"I'm Mr Dis...guise...Smith. Mr D. Smith! Call me Mr D Smith."

Sat down on the sofa I felt better. Mum made tea which had exactly the right amount of sugar which was lucky for me.

"So, Mr D. Smith," she said, "How can I help?"

I was glad she was being nice.

"Well," I said, deciding to start with the keys, because that was more directly linked to cleaning, "I've decided to start with the keys, because it's more directly linked to cleaning."

"Oh...what do you mean?"

"Well, you know you have keys to people's houses?" I asked, she nodded, "Well, we at the government, like, need to know that keys are safe."

"What keys do you mean, B...I mean, Mr D. Smith."

"Well, let's take a house," I said, talking over her, "any house. Say, Brian Parr's house…the keys to that, are they always safe? I mean say, last year, in August, were they always safe, could anyone close to you, maybe Dad…Brian's Dad, could he have got them?"

She looked at me. Thinking hard. Taking me seriously. This was working. I was doing it.

"Brian, love," Mum said, "What are you doing?"

I couldn't believe it.

"My name's not Brian!" I shouted, standing, "My name is Disguise!"

I kept my cool. I stamped my foot.

My Mum stood up, she took my wig off, "Ever since you did dressing-up at school, you've never been good at it have you, love?"

She carried on taking off my facial hair, "I remember seeing you in the nativity play when you were four. You were the worst sheep I've ever seen. You kept saying moo."

"Hi Mum," I said, feeling stupid.

"Give me a hug."

And I did. And it was lovely. Ten minutes later I was eating Edi's mini-pizzas with some fizzy pop in a glass. We talked about Edi and it was good to hear he loved the place apart from he had problems with the people in the penthouse making noise late at night which made him tired for training.

"Your Dad did take the keys to your house," my Mum told me after we'd caught up a bit, "He said it was to check up on you."

"Why did he do that? I'm a bl*ody man now, Mum," I said.

"Oh Brian, don't' spill your pop, I've just cleaned that table."

As she cleaned, I tried to work out how to get clues out of her. I couldn't believe she'd seen through my disguise! She was sharp, like me I suppose. I had to be clever.

"Ok, Mum," I finally stated, "So you know the night that Stevie crashed, could Dad have had the keys that night? Could he have met Stevie there?"

"No."

"Are you sure?"

"We were in Spain, he flew back just before that match when you were sent off. "

"It was never a red card!"

"Look, Brian, your Dad does lose it sometimes, but of course he wouldn't do anything that bad!"

"Mum, it's just...look he's on a list of suspects!" I shouted.

"He's your father!"

"He doesn't act like it anymore. He says it's all my fault. "

"Well, son, perhaps it is."

Chapter 33

A couple of days later I was on my way to see Dr Malone. This time I wasn't alone. Which was good, because the last time I'd seen him his threats had properly sh*tted me up.

Will was with me. He was driving in fact.

Since I'd found out my Dad wasn't involved, I hadn't made any more progress. People were away, busy, or we didn't know where they were. I was impatient but I had to force myself to wait. Will was trying to work out how we could find Dr Malone and I waited for him to give me a call. Finally, he said he'd done it.

The place I normally met Dr Malone was a small but nice flat by the river. When we got there it was empty. We'd expected that, but seeing as Will had found out his real name and where he actually worked, we knew where to go next.

Will had shown me all the webpages he'd gone through to find someone who matched my description of Dr Malone. He was looking for a hot-shot doctor who had a private clinic and probably the contacts to get into the prison. The private clinic route got him nowhere so he had done some research into the local doctors who were assigned to prisons. And that's when he found him.

There'd been an incident, a month or so before, when a prison doctor had been attacked by an inmate. Not seriously, but he'd had to go to hospital himself. The doctor was called Dan Webb. Will had found a photo of this guy and it matched exactly what Dr Malone looked like.

The plan was to find out when Dr Webb was working and then follow him home in Will's car. Because I thought I'd be recognised, Will went to the reception to do some spy work. He looked red-faced and a bit nervous when he came back. He'd obviously found it difficult. I'd done loads of spy missions already, but as it was his first I let him off and only took the p*ss for twenty minutes or so. We were going to have to wait an hour or so. Dr Webb was still on duty.

Will moved to the back-seat to write while I listened to a match on the radio. It was Town in the cup which was good to listen to but made me feel restless. I had my head in my hands after an awful miss by the Town centre-forward, and almost missed Dr Malone, or Webb, come out of the building. He walked to the parking spaces outside the building and got into his car. Now I was used to seeing him in a BMW but he was in a sh*t old car that looked second hand! Still, he shot out of the car-park quick enough, and seeing as I was in the front seat and Will was in the back I jumped into the driver's seat and drove off.

It wasn't much of a car chase seeing I was such a great driver, but it was fun anyway. It was the first time I'd driven since the night I was arrested. We followed him straight to the place by the river. He parked in a space out front, got out and went into the building.

We thought that would be as good a place as any to talk to him. But before we could follow, he came out of the door, handed a package to someone on a motor-bike (which Will got a photo of because he'd brought his camera) and then got back in his car.

He drove out of town and then pulled into a new housing estate. Lots of family homes and all pretty boring. Was that his home? Why was he living in a place like that when I knew how much Stevie and I had paid him over the last year? It must have been a front. I knew Shags had tried to look poor for a bit by only having two houses before his divorce so he wouldn't lose lots of cash. Maybe Webb was doing that?

"You ready?" I asked.

Will nodded. To be honest, and I know he'll read this seeing as he's going to be the one actually writing this because that's his job, at the time I wasn't convinced Will had the b*lls for what we might have to do.

Still, it was better than doing it on my own.

We thought it would be best if Will knocked on the door. That way, he'd open up and then I could get in. I could feel my body pumping with tension. Like before a big game. The guy who the Dr had brought into the cell with me was at the forefront of my mind. Skin-head, eyes that wanted to kill, and then even worse what he'd actually said about killing me. If this went wrong, and the Dr went to the people he was working for, it could end really, really badly.

But it was something we had to do sooner or later, and I've always been a 'sooner' type of guy.

Will knocked and the door opened straightaway.

"Dr Dan Webb?"

"Yes, how can I help you?" I heard him say.

"Who is it, sweetheart?" came a man's voice from inside the house.

Sweetheart? A man? This threw me, and Will too. I saw him glance at me, and so did the Dr.

"What's wrong, who are you looking at?"

I knew instinctively that he was about to see me, so I made the first move.

"Brian!" Will cried.

"Brian?" the Dr shouted.

I grabbed him by the collar of his shirt and pushed his chubby body back into his house.

"Will," I ordered, "Shut the door!"

At the end of the day, I'm not a thug. Despite what people might say. And all those photos of me snarling at refs, and the odd fight I've had in clubs when the DJ won't play my favourite songs. Because I'm not a thug, I didn't really know exactly what I was doing. I just put my mean face on and hoped for the best.

At the end of the hallway, there was a door which I pushed him through. He was trying to free himself from my grip, but I was too strong. We went into the living room and I threw him down onto a chair. I looked about the room, exactly as I would if I had the ball and only had a second to look up and see what and who was around me.

He'd threatened me before, so I needed a weapon. What could I use? I saw a wine bottle? A pen? A slipper? His keys? His car-park fob? A newspaper? Could that hurt me? Could any of those things work?

I relaxed. Slightly. My heart was pumping but what I'd burst in on was more like a normal, home situation rather than an army of angry dealers.

I turned around and jumped when I saw a man lying on the sofa. Was he a threat? I looked at him, he was stroking the kind of small, furry dog that Yvonne used to get w*t over and drinking wine.

"Stay where you are!" I shouted.

He looked surprised, but he just nodded. Once.

"What do you think you're doing?" the Dr asked.

Will was behind me in the room, looking a bit scared. I looked at the person lying down. Properly this time. I knew him!

"You!" I said.

"Me!" he said with a girly wave and a bit of a smile.

"I know you!"

"Guilty as charged!" he said quite happily, like he was enjoying himself.

"Norman!" the Dr said, "Don't!"

"I don't get it," I said to Will.

"Course you don't," the Dr said dismissively, "Because you're bl*ody thick!"

"Oh, Daniel!" Norman said, "He's just confused. He's much more impressive than the last time we saw him, isn't he?"

"Don't get what, Brian?" Will asked.

"This guy," I said, pointing to Norman who gave another wave, "He's the one who came in with Dr Malone. It's him...but he doesn't look

208

like a nasty dealer, does he?"

"I'm an actor darling," he said, getting up and pushing the dog to the floor, "And I was rather pleased with my role that day, it was marvellous fun."

"So you're not a dealer?" I asked.

"Of course he's not, he's a nurse," the Dr said, going over to the bottle of wine and pouring himself a glass.

"What?" I said, "A nurse? But he's not a woman."

"I'm close!"

"He's a male nurse," the Dr said rolling his eyes at me before going and sitting down.

"A male nurse. You mean a Doctor?" I said.

"Look, Bri," Will said, "It's just a nurse. They can be men and women."

"Really? Wow!"

"May I?" Will said, pointing to the bottle.

"Go ahead, glasses in the kitchen!" Norman said cheerfully, "And get some nibbles."

I'd expected a fight, maybe some torture. Not wine and nibbles. I was a bit disappointed to be 110% honest because I'd got myself so ready to fight. Still, they were really good crisps.

"So you made it all up?" I asked, kind of angry, kind of relieved, "You don't work for any dealers?"

"Look, I, we, like to live the good life at times. Doing what I did for you and Stevie is a great way of paying for that. I can make a lot of money, doing very little, and what harm does it do? You're just footballers."

"Harm? If it wasn't for you, Stevie wouldn't have got so into drugs and he might still be..."

"Oh, don't be daft. He's an addict, that one. The drink, the drugs, the gambling. If I hadn't helped, someone would...and if not then the gambling would have done him, Ryan Prince from what I've heard."

"You know Ryan Prince?"

"No, thank goodness."

"So you're saying you're not connected to Stevie's dealers?" Will asked, "We've heard they're after him."

"No, look, my business is simple. I do it for people worried about getting caught dirty. Professionals, footballers, whoever. People who can't keep what I have at their homes, or on them. Which means I get to charge a lot, don't I, Brian?"

I nodded.

"So, with Norman's help, even though I'm just a lowly prison doctor I created a flash persona. I rented out that wonderful place on the river, put on an act for people – who tend to be f*cked anyway – and give them what they want. Normally it's fine. But, when he died, I thought you might bring me into it. After I went to your house, drunk, I saw how you didn't know anything and, I'm sorry, I thought the best way was to stay safe was to scare you away..."

"We did that right enough," Norman said happily, before mouthing 'sorry' at me.

"But all those things you said, about them hurting you, you showed me your wounds..."

"The attack in the papers," Will said, "You were injured, you just told Brian someone else had done it to you."

"Exactly," he said, "Look, Brian, I'm sorry."

I looked at him. I wanted to hit him quite a lot, but for some reason I couldn't.

"So, what are you going to do? Are you going to…'out' him?" Norman smiled.

"I could. Will took a photo earlier, of him selling stuff to someone."

"Now that was legitimate, that was a prescription for someone. I'm not a bad doctor, I just…well…"

"Look," Will said, "All we came here for was to find out what you really know about the night Stevie crashed."

"Ok," he said, holding his hands up, "That night, he called me, late. Me and Norman had just dropped off, hadn't we?"

"We had, Daniel, we had."

"I had to get up, go over to the river-front place. I met them and I gave him some downers so he could try to sort himself out for the morning…"

"Hang on," Will said, "You said 'them'. Brian never said you met two of them. Who else was with him that night?"

"That girl, he brought her occasionally…"

"…a black pony-tail, called Kiki?" I said.

"That's her. Beautiful girl," he nodded, "They normally seemed good together, that night though…they were shouting when I arrived and shouting when they drove off."

"What about?" I asked.

"I don't know," he said, "I just wanted to get back to bed."

"Did you hear anything though?" asked Norman, "Sorry, I'm just lapping up all this mystery!"

"She kept telling him she wanted to go home, he was shaking his head, all messed up…"

As we were standing by the door, I had another thought, "So all that stuff about dealers was rubbish, but you must know something about his actual dealers? Someone else, in a bar, said he was in trouble with them, that's why when you said it as well I believed you."

"Look, the amount he was taking the last few weeks, it wouldn't surprise me if they were after him. That's why I went with that story in the first place, but they have nothing to do with me."

Chapter 34

It was quite late, about ten, but I wanted things to move as quickly as possible. We had the secret information we needed to use on Kiki and I wanted to see her. We decided it was best that there weren't two of us knocking on her door. So Will stayed outside. I'd call if I needed help. That's if she was in.

She was. It seemed that she had been doing what Will and I had been doing - there was a bottle of that pink wine stuff open and some nibbles. I accepted a glass, pleased out how classy drinking wine made me feel. The I stuffed my face with some more crisps.

"Look, Kiki, I'm here for a reason."

She laughed at me.

"What?" I asked, "What's so funny?"

"Of course you're here for a reason. You should see your face. You're so serious. "

"Am I?"

"What is it? What do you want to know?"

I was surprised she was being so open about it. Last time she'd been upset. With my sensitive head on I knew it could have been the shock of meeting me bringing up memories of Stevie that had moved her. Or she could have been on the blob. Either way, she seemed calm now and I wasn't about to miss an open goal.

In the car I booted up my laptop and started going over the stuff Brian had pulled together since I met him. Now we'd cleared up the link between the Dr and any dealers – taking everything with a pinch of salt of course – depending on what Brian found out from Kiki, we had to work out the next move. Shags? Yvonne? May? Or focusing on finding Stevie's dealer?

They all needed to be looked into but before that I wanted to double-check everything new in case we'd missed anything. As I looked through what we'd put together I was impressed with how Brian was turning up better stuff day-by-day and the fact I was seeing some things first-hand could only mean that my writing about it would be better. The kind of solid journalist stuff I'd wanted to write before the ghost-writing.

I thought about calling my agent and telling him that I was definitely taking Brian's book on. After my initial call I got the feeling he thought I was probably being led up the garden path, but now I was certain I was onto a winner. No matter what happened. Seeing it was getting on, and my mobile battery was low. I decided I'd get down to my work instead.

"Dr Malone said we were arguing?" she asked, looking a little annoyed.

"Yeah, he said you were shouting the whole time, and Stevie was hammered."

She checked her watch again, "Yeah, he was. I hadn't seen him since the night he took his things."

213

"When was that again?"

"Two night before - which was a long time for us to be apart when he didn't have an away match."

"So what did you do?"

"Well, first, as you already know, I made him go to the Doctor's. He needed something to take the edge off whatever he was on. When we got what he needed, he decided he wanted to go home."

"This flat?"

"No," she said, "Not our home."

"Stevie took you to May's house?"

She poured herself another big glass of wine. I noticed her check her watch again. Now she was beginning to look nervous. I had to put her at ease, try to make her feel this was a chat, not an interview.

"Is this pink wine made from mixing white and red," I asked, feeling a bit silly, but thinking it was worth a go, "I think it's alright."

She didn't look impressed.

"I'm sorry," I told her, "Look, Kiki please help me. I'm trying to find out what happened to Stevie. No-one else is helping me, well there's one guy who's outside right now, but not the police, or United. I'm the only one trying to find out who killed Stevie."

She got up, looked at her watch again, took a big gulp of wine and nodded. She went over to the balcony doors and opened them, "Sorry, I feel hot…is this ok?"

"Of course."

"Ok, I'm not meant to say this, and I'll tell you why once I've said it."

"Ok, ok."

"I'm not sure what his plan was, but he was sure you'd been with May that night. He'd decided to tell her it was over and to prove she wasn't the only one cheating he was saying he was going to get me to meet her," Kiki told me, "I didn't want to do it, but I did want him to leave her, so I went along."

"I was with her that night."

"So, we drove to the house. He parked outside then told me to stay in the car and he disappeared."

"You'd never been there before?"

"Never," she said, "After a while I hadn't heard anything. So I decided - it was stupid I suppose - to see if he was alright. I found him at the kitchen table, crying. When he saw me, he said that even though he loved me it was going to be hard to leave. Then the lights came on, and..."

"May came in?"

She nodded.

"What did she do?"

"She went insane."

"May? But she's so...well, she likes yoga..." I said, but as soon as I did I pictured Yvonne going mental at me and realised it must be a family thing.

"She started throwing things, broke glasses, and Stevie got cut trying to stop her..."

"Did he say anything?"

She nodded, "Stevie lost it. He started shouting at her, swearing, telling her how he knew all about you and her and he was going to tell everyone what type of people you were..."

"And then?"

"We heard the babies crying upstairs, Stevie told me we were leaving, and he drove away as fast as he could..."

She was trembling. She drank some more wine as I remembered what May had said about finding blood and glass on the floor. May had lied to me, I told myself to tell Will that.

As I was re-reading the notes from Brian's meeting with Kiki a cold sweat ran through me. I'd missed something. At that very moment I looked up and saw a 4x4 pull up across the road. Five bikers got out. A tall guy with bleached hair seemed to give them their orders. Then they moved quickly and quietly into the building; the guy with the bleached hair had a key.

When Brian had noticed a man's coat and boots by the front door, Kiki said they were Stevie's. But later in the conversation she said that two nights before his crash he'd cleared the place out of everything he owned. With so much to take on board neither Brian, nor I, had thought anything of it. Until that moment.

I reached for my phone. Kiki must have called them as soon as he'd rung the buzzer. Brian had told me he'd felt sad seeing a leather jacket on the door, because it proved that even though Stevie was dead he still had a bad dress sense. Well, the five bikers in the 4x4 liked leather jackets, unlike Brian, and there was only one flat they were going to.

My phone's battery died before it even connected.

I sensed we were getting to the end of her story. Obviously, I knew Stevie had crashed as he drove away, but why? And how had he got away from the wreck?

I reckoned it was best to take my time. She'd said someone had told her not to talk about it, so I couldn't rush her.

216

By the time I realised the front door had burst open it was too late. I counted five of them in an instant. They were pros. I was surrounded. No gaps for me to burst through.

Kiki looked stressed, tense, but not surprised.

"Kiki! What are you doing?" I asked her as two of them ripped me off my seat.

"She's obeying orders, mate," one with bleached hair told me.

I tried to shake them off, but they were big, strong.

"Why? Why do you care about me?" I asked Mr Bleached-Hair.

"I don't f*cking care about you, I care about me!"

"But how have I...?"

"You're famous, you get headlines, I don't need that..."

"What is your business? Who are you?"

"I'm Ryan Prince? Heard of me? I loan people money, and if they don't pay me back I take it."

His eyes stared at me. They were really nasty eyes. From what I'd heard he wasn't someone to f*ck with, and I didn't want to find out if his reputation was deserved. I had to get away. Somehow.

"Kiki, you've got to help me..."

"Brian, these guys are looking after me, I have to think of Stevie..."

"Which one?"

"That's e-f*ckin-nough," Ryan said, "You don't talk like that in my gaff."

"This place is Stevie's."

"Not any f*cking more. Haven't you been listening?"

First up, I used one of Shags' fighting techniques. I relaxed. My whole body went loose. The two guys holding me thought I was giving in. Then in a flash, I smashed my elbows up. Catching one in the nose, the other in the chin. Then I was all limbs blazing. I kicked one in the balls. Landed a punch on the other's head. And I was loose.

I swung around. Searching for my next move. Exactly like I would when I played football. Balcony doors.

I jumped onto the couch then launched into mid-air. I was there. I was going to make it.

Just as I was about to land, as I was half out of the room, a pain exploded on my side. First a deep, heavy knock, then sharp pain as I was cut.

I didn't land, I crumpled. I was soaked. With blood? No, wine. The bottle they'd thrown had smashed all over me.

Ryan was standing over me. The guy with the broken nose went to sit down.

"Don't you dare get blood on my f*cking sofa," Ryan screamed, not even looking at him, "Gummo, give me your lighter."

Gummo did. Ryan got out a cigar.

"What are you going to do?" Kiki asked.

"Teach him a little lesson," Ryan said.

The cigar was lit.

I tried to get away, but Gummo held me.

"Wait!" I managed to say, "You can't. You can't."

"Why the f*ck not?" he said, baring his teeth like vampires do in those movies about vampires. With the hand not holding the cigar, he pulled up my sleeve, exposing my left arm.

"I'm Brian Parr..." I gasped, "I'm the England captain."

"He is Gov," Gummo said, "He is the England captain..."

Without blinking, Ryan b*tch-slapped Gummo hard. Then he turned to me. Grabbed my wrist, and put the cigar to my skin.

I howled. The pain! The smell! Ryan laughed as he left me on the floor. I clenched my fists, gritted my, taking deep breaths to get it under control.

"Ryan!" I heard Kiki say, "I thought you were only…"

"Shut it, b*tch," he said, pushing her to the sofa.

I'd done some bad things to girls, but I'd never hit them unless we were having s*x and they'd asked me to or I was pretty sure they wanted it. Kiki may have set me up, but could I blame her if they had a hold on her? Well, a bit, but I'd liked her, and Stevie had loved her, and I wasn't going to do nothing while she got knocked about.

"Hey, don't you…" I said, staggering to my feet.

"Lock him up," Ryan sneered.

I tried to fight, but three of them dragged me into a bedroom and locked me in. The pain was still killing me but I knew I had to do something.

I ran my hands over my suit. They hadn't taken my phone! Within a second I called Will. It went straight to answerphone. I tried again. If he didn't pick up this time, I'd call the police. I had to get help. Who knew what they'd do with me?

"F*ck," I said when Will didn't answer again, what was he doing?

I'd pressed in 999, but not the call button when the door opened. It was Gummo. He looked like he'd just been told off.

"I can't f*ckin' believe you didn't take his f*ckin' phone," Ryan shouted from the kitchen.

I didn't have time to react before he'd snatched my phone and pushed me onto the bed. The door locked behind him.

Brian had pointed out the penthouse balcony when we'd parked up, so

I knew where I had to get to.

I decided my best chance was to see if there were any fire escapes. It was an old building after all and as soon as I got round the side of the building I saw my luck was in.

Some metal fire escape stairs went all the way up the side of the building. The problem was, to stop people breaking in, the steps began above head level and you could only roll down the ladder from the stairs themselves.

I tried to jump. In less than a minute I was out of breath and getting further and further away from reaching the ladder. Even if I did get my hands on the lowest rung, would I have the strength to pull my entire body up? I'm a writer, not a footballer.

I needed something to stand on. Almost absentmindedly I started playing with my car keys, rolling them between my fingers to help me to think. After a minute of that I realised what an idiot I was and another minute later my car was parked under the ladder and I was swearing as I hauled myself from the car roof onto the steps.

At the top of the fire escape I began swearing again. There was a gap between the steps and the penthouse balcony. It was pretty big and it was a long way down to the ground. If I missed my jump I'd fall parallel to the fire escape, down the side of the wall and onto the pavement. Not even a bin to break my fall like in the movies. What choice did I have?

I made it. And I felt instantly proud. Then immediately stupid. I'd landed in front of the open doors. Metres away from where Kiki and the guy with bleached hair having an argument.

I hit the deck.

For a few torturous seconds I lay on the ground praying they hadn't seen me. My heart was all I could hear. Once I'd settled I began to tune into what was being said.

"...you swear you said nothing about us being on the road?"

"Of course I didn't..."

"You better not, you're a clever girl, you know what would've happened if we hadn't saved you from that car. Keep doin' what you've been doin' and I'll treat you right, just as I have been, ok?"

"Ok."

"That's it, that's my girl."

"Ryan?" she asked, "What are you going to do with him?"

"Dunno. It ain't good if he's digging around. F*ck knows who stabbed the guy, but I'm f*cked if I want people knowing we were there."

"You're not going to...you know..."

"Does anyone else know he's here? Did he say anything?"

"No," she said quietly, after a pause.

"Well then, I'm going to have to think. He's bad news, but so is getting involved in another murder. Fellas, let's play cards, Kiki, get me a drink...and shut the balcony doors, its freezin' in here..."

I did a quick check of the room. The only two ways out were through the locked door or through the window. The window was small, but the top half did open onto the balcony.

I had to try.

Was my body up to it? The bleeding on my side wasn't bad but it hurt. The burn on my skin made me sick to even look at. I'd been a part-time model for a long time. I wanted to do it again. I knew that even I would have trouble making burn marks trendy. But this wasn't the time to be sad about wearing long sleeves for future fashion shoots.

As quietly as I could I moved the table from the side of the bed and stood on it. I glanced towards the door. If someone checked on me, they'd need four steps before they got to me.

A few times I'd done army assault courses during pre-season and I knew it helped to work out what you were going to do before doing it. If you didn't you could get stuck or at least have to start again. Up close the top half of the window was really thin, but if I put one leg over first, and steadied my body with my hand on the window sill I reckoned I'd be able to slide out sideways. As for what I'd do when I was the other side I had no idea, but hopefully I'd land on something soft.

I took a deep breath. I had to do it right away, I had no idea how soon they'd come for me. I counted down to three and then opened the window.

Once they closed the doors and started cards I was thinking about moving when from above I heard something opening. A door I hadn't noticed? A window?

I closed my eyes and clenched my fists. Ready to be grabbed (yes, as Brian has constantly told me since it wasn't a very manly reaction, it was pure instinct). After a couple of seconds, I opened my eyes and turned round. I almost laughed!

Brian had one leg, one arm and half his head out the window. As our eyes met, his eyes almost popped out. Then I saw a horrible mark on his arm.

"Bri! What happened...?" I asked, confused, bumbling.

Suddenly he was shouting and it all kicked off.

"Help, Will! Pull me through, they're coming!"

As I stood up, someone charged into the room behind Brian. I grabbed onto his arm and heaved. At exactly the same time, the guy in the room pulled too. Brian screamed, we were cancelling each other out until Brian kicked hard into his face. The guy cried out, Brian pushed up and the momentum turned in our favour. He roared in pain, the window frame digging into him.

"Sorry!" I shouted.

"F*ck that! Pull!" he replied.

To my side the sound of the balcony doors being unlocked made me more scared than I'd ever been. It was the guy with bleached hair. I tugged at Brian with everything I had.

He moved quickly, his body popped out, I tried to catch him but there was too much force behind him and we hit the deck. I was still on the floor, hurting, but Brian was up. I'd been impressed with him at the Doctor's house, but the two of them hadn't been much of a threat. The three bikers waiting to burst onto the balcony weren't offering wine and nibbles. Brian didn't hesitate.

He picked up a garden chair, lifted it over his head and threw it inch perfectly as they came through the double doors. It hit.

Whatever gut instinct I had kicked in.

"Brian," I shouted, "This way!"

Scrabbling to my feet I jumped the gap like it wasn't there. Brian followed and we hammered down the fire escape. I was first and he was right behind me and obviously thinking about the next move as he saw where my car was, "Keys!" he shouted.

I grabbed them from my pocket and he took them from me as he pushed me onto the car roof.

223

Next thing I knew I was in the passenger seat and Brian was driving away.

Chapter 35

The following morning I was sat in Malcolm Malcolm's front room catching up on the football and telling him what had happened. We didn't want to get the hospitals involved, so Will had taken me to a nurse he knew who'd dressed my injuries. The pain was small enough now for me to enjoy my war-wounds and look back on a job well done. Apart from the fact Ryan Prince was probably after me now.

"So Kiki was at the crash, and Ryan Prince?" Mal asked.

"That's what Will heard Ryan say, before we f*cked over Ryan Prince and his men. Did I mention that?"

"Yes, Bri. But why is she with this guy? Stevie was a great player, how could she do that to him?" he said, angrily. I'd never heard him talk about Stevie like that before.

"I don't know, Mal. Women do funny things, don't they?"

"But not with a guy who killed the person you..."

"We don't know that. We know he was after Stevie, yes, and that he was there when Stevie crashed but Ryan said it wasn't him. He could have lied of course, but..."

"Whether he killed Stevie or not, look what he did to you! How can she go from someone like Stevie to him?"

"Mal, what's got into you?" I asked, "I mean she has a baby, Stevie's dead, the guy rescued her from the crash...I bet she was just after some help....."

"The tart!"

"Look, don't be down on Kiki," I told him, "She tried to stop them hurting me. You see, Will said he heard her tell them that I was alone. But I know I told her he was waiting outside....so she can't be all bad. If they'd known about Will, I could be dead because Ryan Prince is really hardcore....did I say how I f*cked three...actually four of them up?"

"Yeah, you've told me," Malcolm said, "And twice to Nev."

"Oh right."

The phone rang. Malcolm picked it up, pausing the football as he did so.

I started laughing because he'd paused it at the moment someone was falling down so it looked like the player was flying. When I was a kid I was always doing that when we first got a video – pausing players when they were in funny positions. It was really funny and if you were dead clever you could make it look like they were flying and Malcolm had done it without trying!

"Brian? I'll put him on."

"There's a car outside for you," said a woman's voice.

"On the road?" I asked, struggling to place her voice.

"Don't get smart with me..." she said.

"I wasn't," I said, because I wasn't.

"...just get in the car. I'm waiting for you."

Malcolm told me not to get into a car with an unknown woman. I told him it was something I'd done many times before and every time so far had led to me having a very happy ending. When I went outside I was faced with a white stretch limo.

Now, as someone who knows all about classy cars I bet you're wondering what I think about stretch limos now that they've become so common. Well, for me it comes down to the limo in question and whether it has what all classy limos have to have. It did.

A disco ball.

"Very nice, very classy," I said to the driver.

As I drove off not one part of me was worried. Will did ask me afterwards why not - 12 hours before I'd been locked in a room and tortured. So how could anyone get in a car a stranger had sent? Well, the truth was, last night's nastiness hadn't crossed my mind. I'd just helped myself to a coke from the mini-fridge and wondered who the woman on the phone was and what she could have been wearing.

The limo pulled up at a pretty sweet house just outside the city. I got out and the car drove away. It was an old farm and had that plant stuff climbing up the walls. Not in the way weeds grew on houses near Mal's. This was meant to be there because rich people think it looks good.

"Brian," came a woman's voice from a window above.

"Hello? Who...?"

"Dearie me, why've you gone back to your nasty little tracksuits again?"

"Ruby?" I asked, straining to see her.

"Who else did you think it was?"

"I didn't recognise your voice."

"Don't you think it's a bit stupid just getting in a car? From what I've heard you need to be more careful.

"What do you mean?" I said, "Look, can I come in?"

"Should I let you when you're dressed like a tramp?"

"You didn't send a limo to not let me in."

"Brian, are you using your brain again?"

"How did you find me?"

"That weird fan-club guy you live with. He's part of a lot of United fan sites; he's not hard to find if you know where to look."

"Oh," I nodded.

"So, tell me Brian, why did I send a limo?"

I racked my brain. This whole thing was a bit strange.

"S*x?"

"In the study! In the study," Ruby's voice said, waking me up, "I want you in the study."

"But we went in there," I mumbled, "We did it d*ggy style against the pinboard and I s*cked your ******* for at least ten minutes and then …"

"I know, but I'm not the type of woman to get someone over just to have s*x. Have you heard of v*brators…"

The door closed behind her. When I got out of bed I saw she'd left me another suit. It was a good one, but I didn't have my underpants. I had to make do with what I could find. What I found was something I'd worn before. Sometimes I'd even worn them during matches, but you probably already know about that seeing as Yvonne once told the press I'd done it so she could make herself her more famous.

"Ruby," I said as I went into the study, pushed on by my pride as an athlete, "I have used a v*brator before, and I can assure you when I'm in full training I can wiggle my c*ck faster than anything..."

"Brian," Ruby said with a smile, "Please meet, Sian."

"F*ck," I said, wide-eyed at the teenage girl sitting opposite Ruby at the desk. How had I not seen her? Sure, I was fighting for my s*x

227

reputation but Sian was blonde and tanned and really pretty. I should have seen her first thing. In my embarrassment I knocked an ash-tray onto the floor. I bent down to pick it up, relieved it hadn't broken on the wooden floor.

"Nice thong, Brian!" Ruby laughed.

"D*mmit!" I said, "That's not my fault you saw that. I'm thinner than Tony and I couldn't find a belt with a cool buckle so these trousers keep falling down!"

Sian laughed, "You're right, he does whine," she said to Ruby.

"Whine? I don't whine!"

"Brian, sit down, and try not to slice your b*lls on my underwear."

As I sat down, I wanted to take back some control, "Right, what's all this about then?"

"I think Tony might have been killed," Ruby said.

"I think I know who killed him," said Sian.

"What...?" I said, shaking my head, "You told me yourself it was suicide? This can't be...."

"I know what I said," Ruby told me leaning in, "but going through his things I found..."

My mobile rang, cutting her off.

"Hang on, this is Will, it could be an important update!" I told them.

"Brian, hang up, this is..." Ruby began.

"Will," I said, "How's it going?"

"F*cking hell, Brian!" Ruby said.

"F*cking hell, Brian!" said someone who wasn't Will on the phone.

"Yvonne?" I said.

"You need to stop whatever it is you're doing! Chesney and Baggio have been threatened."

I held the phone away from my ear because Yvonne had burst into loud crying.

Eventually Rico took over. He told me the whole story. They'd tracked Will down because they were desperate to get hold of me. It would take them twenty minutes to get back home and they wanted to see me there.

Ruby and Sian were far from happy. What they'd said about Tony was important, of course it was, but I had my priorities. Ruby lent me her driver and I promised her I'd come straight back.

It was nice to arrive at the house in a limo and wearing a suit. I wanted Rico and Yvonne to think I was doing ok. Even the thong cutting into my b*ttom couldn't stop me smiling as I arrived in style.

That didn't last long. It didn't feel good being shown into my own house. By Rico. My house! It was a horrible thing to happen. I knew that legally it was his now, but the fact was, it still felt like my place. I'd done a TV show once where they went round footballers' houses – I'd turned a room into an aquarium especially – and all the cool stuff I'd pointed out was still there. The proof about how far I'd come in life, from my mum and dad's council house, to a mansion. It was all gone now.

I didn't want to be nasty to Rico, but as soon as I saw his slicked back hair and silky shirts I wanted to hit him. I didn't hit him. I told him I wanted to instead, and said I didn't like his hair or shirt.

"Well, thanks Bri, you've always had a way with words...."

Happy I'd cussed him, it was time to get down business.

"What's going on?" I asked, "How are the lads? Yvonne?"

"Everything's been great, the lads are fine, Yvonne's at the studio a lot getting much better at presenting, I'm making loads of cash...but today hasn't been quite so...."

"Brian! What the f*ck have you been doing?" Yvonne shouted, running into the hallway.

She carried on swearing at me. For ages.

"Are they here, are the lads here?" I asked when she had to take a breath.

"No, and they're nothing to do with you."

"They're my kids!"

"Not your only kids though…"

Her shouting wasn't getting us anywhere, "Look, Yvonne….what were you talking about on the phone? What's happened?"

She made a big show of trying to stop crying and stuff. They led me into my study.

"Where've the game consoles gone?" I asked, "Where are my two calendars?"

"I use this room to work," Rico said, "I didn't think naked women or pictures of footballers with penises drawn on their heads was right."

I was about to argue when Yvonne held up a piece of paper and grabbed my attention completely. Then she held up another piece. And another.

Each piece of paper had words stuck on them - the letters must have been cut out of pages from a TV catalogue because there were lots of screens in the letters, not that I thought that mattered - '*Baggio gets it unless Parr stops*' and '*Chesney will get killed unless Dad forgets everything*'.

"F*cking' hell!" I said, "Where are they? Are they safe?"

"It's all your fault!" Yvonne shouted at me.

"Where the h*ll are they, you b*tch, answer me!" I shouted back, angry she was being so melodramatic – I was sure this wasn't my fault. Then I thought about Ryan Prince. Would he do something like this? Had he had the time? I had defeated him.

"They're fine, Bri," Rico said, "They're good actually. They're with Etienne. I took them to the new water-park recently and they love it. So Etienne takes them a couple of times a week now."

"Chesney loves the pool, how's his swimming? Is he doing enough football training?" I asked.

"That's not the f*cking point!" Yvonne screamed, silencing the room, "The point is that whatever you're doing you need to stop!"

"Look, Yvonne," I said.

"You have to stop, they'll get hurt! It'll be your fault!"

"They won't...have you told the police? We can get more guards, we can..."

"I've done all that," Rico said, "The police are looking into it. Security has been stepped up here. There's someone with Etienne now too. But Yvonne, and I, we thought we should talk face-to-face? And, well, obviously....we think you should stop this work of yours."

"What work?"

"All this pretending that you have to find Stevie's killer to prove it wasn't you!" Yvonne shouted.

"It wasn't!"

"What does it matter?" Yvonne cried, "You're free. Just leave it! Protect your boys, if it's the one thing you can do properly!"

"But don't you see, if they're doing this, it proves I'm getting close!" I said, "It means they don't like what I'm doing because I'll prove they're guilty."

"You can't! You can't! Stop and stop now before anyone else gets hurt!"

"No," I shouted back, "Someone killed Stevie, ruined me. I'm going to find out who and not be bullied..."

"Don't you love them?" she said, almost whispering.

"Course I do, they're my life...if you'd let me see them. But I can't give up...Rico says they're safe, keep them that way. I won't take long"

"Brian," Rico said, "Look, They are safe. But Yvonne's right, you're free, why don't you drop this? If I was your agent, I'd tell you to train, pick up a lower-league club in the close season, do your talking on the pitch and you could be back in the big time before you know it. Doesn't that sound better than running around upsetting people?"

They weren't going to change their minds and I knew that I was dealing with two people who were very good at getting what they wanted. I mean, they were in the house my blood, sweat and footballer's tears had bought, weren't they?

I figured the only way I could get what I wanted too was to lie, "Ok, ok, for the lads. I'll stop. I'll let the police do what they can."

"Really?" Rico said.

"I don't believe you," Yvonne said.

"Why not? The police are really helping me now anyway. They found the mobile in the dog's mouth!"

"What?" Yvonne said as though I was stupid.

"The mobile I found in the bedroom, that got snatched by the dog? Remember? I found it and they're doing tests on it right now. They're doing really good work to find the killer just like they said they would. So, if it means the lads will be safe, of course I'll stop. I was only trying to help them out...but now, for Chesney and Baggio, I'll leave them to it..."

They looked at each other, "Well, you better, Bri, or....or else," Yvonne said.

Chapter 36

For the first time, I was glad the lads were living in the house. If they'd been with me I couldn't have afforded proper protection. But, they weren't with me, Rico and Yvonne had them, which meant bodyguards would be with Etienne and the lads at all times. There was CCTV, there was the panic room if it came to that - and I knew how difficult it was to get to a member of my family in there!

There was no way anyone was going to get close to them. Not even Ryan Prince if it was him behind the threats. Or Blake, or Repinov, or whoever it was. Which is why, despite Yvonne being all girly about it, I didn't find the letters too worrying. I didn't like them, but on their own they weren't enough to stop me.

What did begin to worry me, as I drove back to Ruby's in the limo, was what might happen if the lads were too safe. I don't want to sound selfish and silly, but if the nasty people couldn't get the lads, surely they'd look for other methods to stop me. And who, at the moment, couldn't afford any protection? That's right, sooner or later surely they'd realise the easiest thing was going for me.

As soon as I got back to Ruby's house I asked her about what she'd meant about me 'needing to be more careful'.

"I've asked a few people who I know to let me know if your name comes up, anywhere, and last night it got out that Ryan Prince was asking where you were staying..." Ruby said.

"Oh, sh*t! Did he say why? Because I'd escaped him and beat his d*ck men up?"

"He'd hardly advertise that, would he?"

"Do you think people will tell him where I am?"

Ruby shrugged, I looked at Sian.

"Maybe," Sian said, "Though not that many people like him…"

I told them about the threats to the lads. They agreed it could be Ryan. They also said it could be someone else. Either way, we agreed I needed to look after myself. And stop getting into unknown cars even if it did lead to having s*x.

"F*ck! I need protection! But it's expensive."

"What about friends?"

I shrugged.

"What about when you were inside? From your tastes in bed I can tell you were protected in prison."

"What do you mean?"

"Well, when a man gets a*s-r*ped everyday it tends to get in the way of their s*x life once they get out. I don't get that from you, so I guess you were never…"

"Course I wasn't. Not once!"

"A pretty, young, famous thing like you, Bri?" Ruby said with a smile, "Not even interfered with once? Someone must have had your back, whether you knew it or not."

"The All Stars!" I said, as though I'd just won a trophy.

"Who?"

"These guys I played football with in jail. They looked after me."

"Can they fight?"

"They're all black."

"That doesn't mean a thing, Brian."

"No, you're right, but they can. They did, for me."

"So contact them, make sure that Ryan Prince doesn't get to you again, or anyone else."

"I will. I will, I'll do it now," I said getting up to go.

"Oh, no you won't. We want something from you."

"A threes-up?" I asked, "Well, ok, if it won't get into the papers…"

Ruby slapped me and then Sian did.

"Another time maybe?" I asked.

After they slapped me again they showed me a diary. Tony's diary. And then they got excited. As they both talked, I realised they must have sounded like I did when I was in prison. They were convinced what they were saying was right.

"Tony had never kept a diary before…he wasn't that kind of guy," Ruby told me, "After Stevie's death he started. Look!"

"Ok, but what does that prove?" I said, feeling all clever like Lyle, "I mean keeping a diary doesn't mean you're going to get murdered rather than commit suicide, does it? Or does it?"

They both looked at me. I think they were impressed.

"Shut up, Brian," Ruby said, "Look, Tony and I were separated so I didn't notice, but what I found at his office shows he changed after Stevie died. The diary, photos, loads of stuff on his Mac, it all shows two things. One that he was looking for Stevie's killer, and two that he thought he was being followed…especially in the weeks before he died."

"Ok, ok," I said, "But you told me he was hung, could someone else have done that?"

235

"Possibly," Ruby said, "I've asked the coroner to look at his death again."

"I don't understand who the coroner is, but that sounds like something Lyle would say, so ok," I nodded, "What about Tony's diary?"

"You can read for yourself," Ruby told me, "You can read can't you?"

"I had lessons in prison, but why not tell me!"

"Because Tony wasn't sure who might have killed Stevie he had a long list of suspects."

"That makes two of us with a list! Well, actually, if you add Will, and Mal and Nev it makes.... one, two, three...."

"Brian," Ruby said, "Did you learn to count in prison too?"

"Yes, a lovely lady called Miss Bewley taught me," I said, smiling.

"Do I detect a schoolboy... well, man...crush?"

"I messed it up, which is weird because I'm good with ladies....aren't I, Ruby?"

"Brian, focus. What were you saying?"

"Oh, right, well like Tony, we're at the stage of having a list suspects. We're narrowing them down. Then later, when we have a prime suspect, we'll get hard evidence and then nail them."

"Thanks for spelling out how a murder investigation works for us, did you learn that in prison?"

"No, Repinov told me that and so did Will. Which is why I feel ok that I don't know who it was yet....what did Tony know then?" I said to Ruby,

"At first he spent a lot of time thinking it must be to do with Stevie's contract situation with Blake."

"I think it could be Blake," I told her.

"Tony tried to find out how worried Blake was about Repinov sacking him if he found out about the big contracts..." Ruby said, "But there was also a fan, a mad one, who apparently loved Stevie..."

"Really? Not me...?"

"No. But when he found out about Stevie's problems, he started sending really nasty hate mail. This guy knew a lot more about Stevie than was in the papers too, which was why Tony took him seriously."

"Who was it?"

Ruby looked at the diary, "Greg Neal."

I couldn't believe it.

"What?" Ruby said, "Do you know him?"

I nodded, "But Greg told me I was his favourite player."

"Maybe you are, he certainly didn't like Stevie by the end....although seeing as you're in a lot of the photos and stories this guy has about Stevie, it would be unfair if he hated Stevie and liked you..."

Ruby showed me the letters Greg had sent - it really was bad. He said he'd loved Stevie more than any other player but that because Stevie was killing United, Greg was going to do anything to stop him. He even mentioned almost getting a tattoo for him!

Which meant Greg had lied to me?

Why? Or was that possible to obsess about two United players?

I remembered that Will had put Greg on the list of suspects too. I needed to speak to him again.

"There's someone else though," Sian said, "Which is why I'm here and I think he's the person who killed Stevie and Tony!"

"Who?" I said, standing up to get my head round all this new stuff.

"Shags," Ruby said.

"Shags!" I said.

Sian had been sleeping with Shags for months. She was going on about how she'd seen him really lose his temper at her and that she had no doubt he could kill someone. Shags being a d*ck to a hot chick was bad, but was she just another money-grabber out to make a story? Like all the ones who'd cashed in on me?

"Ok, ok," I said, interrupting her, "I get the fact you scr*wed. He's a footballer, you're fit. It's what happens. How does that mean he's mixed up with what happened?"

"He was with Tony and Stevie the night Stevie crashed," Sian said.

"Ok..."

"Tony left Stevie and Shags together. And in Tony's diary," Ruby continued, "He says Shags and Stevie were arguing. Stevie wanted some drugs and Shags didn't....so Shags was the last person to see Stevie alive...."

I shook my head. I told them what Dr Malone and Kiki had said. Sian looked annoyed at this new evidence.

"Well, ok, but that doesn't mean something didn't happen that night," Ruby argued, "In Tony's diary, it says that he found out that Shags had lied to the police about that night. That's why Shags left Tony and went to Rico," Ruby said.

"What do you mean lied?"

"Shags told the police that the night of the crash, after a few drinks with Stevie, he'd gone home," Ruby explained, "But Greg Neal sent Tony a photo showing Shags driving in a car behind Stevie and Kiki."

I looked at the picture of Shags in his SUV following the car Stevie and Kiki are in.

"Shags didn't come home that night like he told the police. This photo proves I'm not lying," Sian told me, worked up.

I nodded, then thought back to the questions I'd been asked in the

238

police station and the court. "What time did he get home in the end? Was he weird in the next few days?"

That was when I remembered Shags had acted weird the moment we'd found out about Stevie in the club-house. He'd taken sides against me.

"There's also this," Sian said, "I took it a couple of days after Stevie's death. Shags came home from what he said was charity work, but he stank of booze."

It was a photo. Shags in his front room, carrying a bag.

"What?" I asked.

Sian smiled and held out another photograph. It was a close-up shot of his bag and it showed a piece of paper with some names on. Mine, Stevie's, Tony's. Stevie was crossed out.

"I still don't think..." I said, not able to finish my sentence, "Why would Shags do it...? What's his...thingy?"

"Motive?" Sian asked.

I nodded.

"We're not sure," Ruby said.

"Well, I'm sure he lied to the police," Sian said, "Which is something that I want investigated or I'll take this story to the...."

"Sian!" Ruby said, silencing her, "Look, Brian, Shags has been cheating on Sian and she wants payback. I've asked her to not go to the papers until we've sorted out all this mess. And by that I mean we need to find out about Tony and Shags and all of this. And I want you to do it for me."

"What? Why?"

"You're doing it anyway. It's all linked to Stevie's death, it has to be and while you might not be the obvious choice, I think the fact you seem stupid kind of helps."

"Why should I? What's in it for me?"

Chapter 37

"What's that?" Mal asked, pointing at the envelope of cash I had in my hand when I got back to his.

"If I find out who killed Tony, if he was killed, I get 100 grand from his ex, Ruby. Until we know she's giving me money each week to carry on being clever and investigating. I've got a job!"

"Wow. Do you want to watch the DVD of the reserves play? Malcolm asked.

I'd half expected Mal to ask about Tony. Or why Ruby was so bothered about Tony now, even though she'd hated him when he was alive. I knew it was because she'd get more life insurance if he hadn't killed himself but Mal didn't know that and he didn't seem too bothered. He pressed play and, seeing as it had been a busy day, I sat back and enjoyed the match. It felt really great knowing I was being paid by Ruby while I was watching the match. Before then, when I was at Mal's watching football, I'd felt a bit bad and guilty that all I was doing was watching football when I had no money coming in. Now I didn't have to do that because I'd cleverly got myself a job.

It wasn't until a few hours of reserves football later when Nev came home that we began talking about the case again. Nev wasn't bothered about Ruby, he was more concerned about what Yvonne and Rico had said.

"So are you going to stop?" Nev asked.

"What do you think?" I said.

240

"Of course he's not," Malcolm said, "He's Brian Parr!"

"I know, Dad," Nev said, "But these people are serious. Look at his arm!"

"Nev, I know they're serious," I told him, "But I am Brian Parr! Whoever killed Stevie, whoever is threatening my lads, I'm not going to stop until I find them and get them."

"Brian," Nev said, "I would seriously consider..."

"And Nev, I've been hired as a spy too now. I'm getting paid! I'm like a superstar James Bond man!"

"He's Brian Parr, he's a superstar, with his fancy cars, scoring the best goals by far..." Mal started singing, "Sorry," he said, blushing, "I used to sing that from the stands all the time..."

Nev walked out. I realised I was stroking my plasters from where Ryan had hurt me. I needed to get protection.

Luckily Mal had this Facebook page for some fan sites and I used it to track down Chris and Ty on the Facebook thing.

I did this instant message thing and started chatting to them straightaway. It was nice to catch-up - they were the only ones out of the All Stars team so far - and it was exactly like having a face-to-face conversation with them without seeing them. Like a phone call I guess without the phone. It's hard to describe. It was good though, and Chris and Ty said for a bit of cash they'd try to find out if Ryan Prince was after me through some people they knew. As an afterthought, as I knew they had talked about drugs sometimes in prison, I told them to see if they could find out who Stevie's dealer had been.

Once the reserve matches had finished I cycled to Will's. He was really pleased about my cleverness asking Ty and Chris about the dealer, and he wanted to start listening to the Ruby conversation I'd taped on the Dictaphone immediately. This time I'd not taped the sh*gging!

"I'll stay here," I said, my eyes looking at his chair with wheels, "I won't get bored."

"No, Brian, I can't afford another lamp."

"I can, I've got 100 grand coming once I catch who killed Stevie."

"Well, no, Brian," Will reminded me, "Ruby said you have to find out about Tony not Stevie..."

"I know, but Tony's suspects are similar to ours, it's probably the same person so I'll get the cash!"

"Ok, but, it's not your money yet," Will replied.

"It's as good as, isn't it? Look, at United I got a bonus if I scored more than 20 goals in the season. I always spent the bonus money on a new car before the season had even kicked off!"

"Didn't that mean you just played for money, and wanted to score for money?"

"Well, no, but I suppose once I had to score four in the last two games or Rico said I'd have to send a Bentley back," I told him, "I fell out with a few players because I was taking all the free-kicks and hogging the ball... but it all worked out, I scored all four of United's goals in both matches."

"Your team-mates must have been really pleased," Will said.

"Course! It's a team game! Anyway, point is I've never missed a bonus. So of course I'll get this one, don't worry. No-one can say I'm not good with money! Will, can you lend my 85p for chips? I left my cash at Mal's."

When I came back from the chippy Will was looking serious. Like the Gaffer used to before a big game.

"What you said earlier, about being sure you'll get the bonus?"

"Yeah?" I said, starting to play keepy-uppy with the chip-paper.

"Do you really think you will?" he asked.

"Of course, every time I do spying we find something out."

"Yes," Will said, "But we haven't found anything big yet..."

"Look, with Ruby's cash I can keep doing this for a while, can't I? I'll be patient, like I'm playing a really boring defensive team. Pass the ball about, keep asking questions, tire them, keep probing, and as you go you learn each player, and as long as we use our heads eventually someone will make a mistake, or we'll see an opening and we'll be there to ball-sack it!"

I volleyed the chip-wrapper and shouted goal. Which made the sound of the lamp breaking seem less loud, which was good.

"Brian, I admire your determination," Will told him.

"That's exactly what Ruby told me when I was doing her, first we went to her study and I got out her..." I stopped, Will didn't want to know.

After that I left Will's so I wouldn't have to clean up the lamp. After an evening of watching the footie I was woken up the next day by Mal saying Will had come round.

While Mal gave Will a quick tour of the house I got ready to tell them my new cleverness.

"I've been thinking," I said, as I walked in on Mal telling Will about how embarrassed he was about the messy room he couldn't go into, "I need to find Etienne."

"Yes, you do," Will agreed.

"Why?" Nev said, appearing from the messy room, "How can he help?"

"We've never worked out who put the mobile in the bedroom for me to find. Etienne is in and out of the house all the time, Nev, so maybe he knows who put it there?"

Nev looked confused, or unsure, I'm not sure.

"So I need to speak to him, I need to find Etienne," I finished.

"What about Kiki?" Nev suggested, "Don't you still need to find out what she knows?"

"Ryan Prince could still be there," I said, remembering the pain of being burnt and deciding seeing a g*y man-nanny would be easier, "Etienne first."

"How do we find Etienne?" Will said.

I'd been thinking about this, "GSP!"

"What?" the three of them said.

"GSP?"

"Do you mean ESP?" Nev asked, "Has Dad got you watching those weird Sky psychic shows again? I know the two of you text in to find out football scores."

"I told you Nev, I've stopped doing that!" Mal said.

"Brian?" Will asked, "What are you talking about?"

"Because I had so many cars, the insurance man said we had to get the GSP things put in all of the cards which means you can find out where the car is by going onto a website. Rico set it up for me, but I never told Yvonne about it. I didn't want her checking up on me. "

"You mean GPS?" Will said.

"Do I?"

Will went onto his computer. It took a while to get to the right site because all I could remember was that it was in the colours of the United third strip from two seasons ago. Apparently you can't search for the colours of websites – and these IT geeks get called clever!

"Password?" Will asked

"Easy, my favourite formation."

"4-4-2," Malcolm said, smiling, "Bri, in the middle, with a defensive mid alongside him so Bri can roam forward."

"Actually, I prefer 4-3-1-2 with me in the hole. It gives me even more freedom and if you have good full-backs they can provide you with much-needed width."

Will, seeing that Malcolm might be about to cry, typed it in.

"Wow, you've got this on a lot of cars."

"I know. B*stard, Rico, they're all his now!"

"Which one will Etienne be driving?"

I weighed up the options.

Nev left to do his studying. Malcolm had some coaching on and I didn't think he'd be much use anyway; it was better he carried on spreading the word of the 'Parr Method'. Although at that point because people hated me so much apparently he was calling it the 'Mal Method' until I was liked again.

Will said he needed to write but I managed to persuade him to drive me to see Etienne. Sure, I was good on my bike and I could do wheelies, but even I couldn't keep up with a souped up SUV.

What was really cool was that Will brought his lap-top and so as he drove I had that on my lap and we could track Etienne's GPS signal. Very Hollywood.

Once we got onto the same road as Etienne we didn't need the lap-top anymore. Rico was obviously no better than me at stopping Yvonne from getting the cars painted whenever she wanted. We followed the ladybird-painted SUV until it parked up outside a big mall where the lads' favourite toy shop was.

One of the things I was good at with the lads, other than putting them through their paces during football practice, was buying them things. In the toy shop I knew exactly where they'd go first. The cuddly toy section. Easy. Excited, I hid between a couple of the massive teddy bears.

The problem was I started getting looks from people surprised to see a fully grown-man poking his head through the legs of a big green dragon, I guess I must have looked a bit strange.

Realising it was best if I didn't look weird, I decided to find a kid I could pretend was mine. Just as I was about to chase a little boy who had refused the chewing gum I'd offered I heard Baggio and Chesney. I dived down where I was.

It felt great to hear them and they were chanting some football songs like little hooligans which was cute: *"Town are sc*m, they all love b*m!"*

Behind them was Etienne. They were coming straight towards the crocodile I was lying next to. The crocodile's tongue felt tickly against my nose. It took all of my James Bond-ness not to giggle.

As the lads got closer, I knew I was meant to only be seeing Etienne, but I couldn't help moving towards them.

I felt hands grab me. A really hard grip on each arm. I was lifted up like I was nothing. Up and away.

It hurt like hell and I made a slight sound of pain – the lads hadn't notice me though. Etienne had.

He looked in time to see me being carried away by two very big and highly trained bodyguards. I tried to kick out, but they had me. I gave in and let them carry me away. I watched as the lads punched the some teddy bears in the face and Etienne stared at me with a confused look.

246

I ended up on my a*se by the bins at the back of the shopping centre.

I looked up at the two bodyguards.

"Stu, Kelvin!"

"Sorry, Bri, orders is orders," Kelvin said while Stu walked off with his walkie-talkie out.

"You looking after the lads?"

"Yup. But we're not meant to let you see Etienne either."

"Come on, mate, they're my kids."

"Bri, security hasn't been this tight since you did that Nazi salute in Italy when you just thought you were waving to the fans."

"I get it, I get it," I said as he helped me up, "You been going to the games?"

"Not really, they've been pretty sh*t without you anyway."

The two of them went back inside. I was on my way back to the car, gutted, when my mobile went.

It was a video call which sounded exciting, but it wasn't when I saw who it was.

"Rico! Yvonne!"

"You told us you were stopping this stupid f*cking search, Bri," Yvonne screamed, "And we've already caught you! That's quick to break a promise, even for you."

"Let me explain..."

"No. Let us explain. We asked you to stop putting your family in danger and you lied. We're calling the judge to say you've breached the custody laws..."

"The what?"

"...so you're going to be arrested again."

"You can't do that!"

"I'm going to. You signed all the papers, you knew the score..."

"I didn't. I signed because Rico told me!"

"Brian. I don't care. Now, do you want to go to jail?" Yvonne said.

Were they bluffing me? Rico knew I didn't understand law stuff. They might have been lying to me. But what if they weren't?

"Well, it's not murder, how long would I be in?"

Rico spoke up. He said it would be months, maybe more.

"So why are you telling me, Yvonne?" I was going to swear but stopped – as if she was a ref and I was already booked, "Why not just arrest me? Or are you just trying to scare me?"

"Oh, we could have you arrested in minutes. We just have a better idea, to help everyone."

"What's that?"

"Leave the country. If you do, and we don't have to get the police and press involved it's cleaner. That's why we're giving you this chance. We just want all this, and you, to go away."

"That's not fair!"

"What's not fair is putting your own children at risk!"

"What would I do if I'm not here?"

"Go to your Dad's in Spain, try to get a club there....Rico reckons you could."

"I don't want to, I live here!"

"It's your call. Do you want me to hang up and call the police?"

I had to think fast.

"Rico, Rico," I said trying to think what he would do.

"Yes, Brian."

My mind suddenly stuck on Ruby, and Tony, and the night when Rico had come back to Tony's agency with me and Shags.

248

"Please, I just need some more time," I pleaded, "I need to follow this through. You know how I like to follow through," I told her, thinking back to all of the moments we'd shared.

"No, Brian. We want you gone in an hour," Yvonne spat.

"Ok, Rico, how about if I mention Tony and his office and you and me and Shags and some others and then I mentioned the word photographs?"

"What?" Rico said.

In an instant their phone moved and it was filled with a close-up of Rico's face. I could hear Yvonne going mental in the background.

"You're lying!"

"I'm not. I saw Ruby the other day, Tony's wife. She'd rigged up the office to catch him cheating, and caught us too...ask her, she gave me copies..."

"Why?"

"I gave her something. Hang on, why are you sniffing the table like that, Rico? And who's wife is that? I don't understand these photos, maybe Yvonne can help me make sense of them? Or maybe I have to ask a journalist for help?"

"What do you want from me, Brian?" Rico snapped.

"Time."

"I can't, it's her call."

"F*ck that," I said, "I know she doesn't understand papers and stuff. You've always handled everything like that for her and me, which is why I signed the f*cking things in the first place! Tell her it takes some time, or else..."

"48 hours.... I can give you 48 hours."

"How long is that? In days."

"Two, Brian."

"Two? I need more! I can't finish this off by then."

"Brian, that's all I can give you. Two o'clock on Thursday."

Chapter 38

I'd told Brian that I thought his mission was exactly that: his. I didn't want to become a major part of the story, not because I was scared – although what had happened with Ryan Prince made me truly realise the level of danger we might be in – it was simply because I was his ghostwriter. Not his partner.

It changed with the time-limit. I felt I had to help him. It was outrageous that he'd been so exploited by Rico and Yvonne. They'd preyed on the fact he was scared and got him to sign over virtually everything. In my view he'd been robbed, so I took his copies of what he'd signed to a solicitor friend to see what his rights were. If there were any holes in what Rico had done, Brian had a chance.

If not, we had 48 hours.

Brian wanted to tackle things head on. Chris and Ty said they were making headway but didn't have any definite answers about Stevie's dealer. The one person who we knew had a lot of answers was Kiki. She'd been there the night of the crash. Why had they crashed? Because he was wasted? Or was he forced off the road? How had she got into the hands of Ryan Prince?

We drove to her flat; the 4x4 I'd seen Ryan and his guys pull up in was still outside.

"Sh*t!" Brian said, "I haven't got time to sit around and wait."

"She's our best hope. Let's give it a little bit of time."

"Who do we go to next, do you think? Got to be Blake hasn't it? Look into what Ruby told me?" he said.

I shrugged. After what he'd told me about the last time he'd tried to get close to Blake and Repinov I didn't fancy his chances.

We spent an uncomfortable hour and a half waiting. Brian spent most of it trying to work out how much of the 48 hours he had left before Yvonne blew the final whistle.

Just at the moment I thought Brian was about to explode, Ryan Prince came out of the building. He was on his own. He drove off.

"Let's go!" Brian said.

"Hang on," I warned, "What about the others?"

"They might have already left. Look, we don't have time to worry. Brian Parr likes action."

It was when he referred to himself in the third person that I remembered he was a footballer. "Kiki!" he said excitedly, getting out of the car as she appeared out of the front door.

Pushing a pram she headed away from us and towards a park at the end of the street. "Brian, no!" I shouted.

At the same moment the three other guys came out of the building.

Brian was running towards Kiki. At the last minute he saw them. He spun, incredibly quickly, but they saw him. In an instant they were chasing him. One of them pulling out his phone.

"Sh*t!" Brian shouted.

I was impressed by how fast he really was, but one of them was pretty quick too. I sat, frozen to the spot. What was I going to do? Could I help him? No, they were gone. I looked at the park Kiki had gone into. I didn't think twice.

I reached the park and was scanning the crowds for Kiki, when a car

251

screeched to a halt in the road behind me. Before I knew it Ryan Prince had jumped out and bustled past me.

"Sorry, mate" he said, jogging off into the park.

My heart was beating fast. He'd chased me down the fire escape but it was dark; he could have only seen my back. Before I could convince myself it was too dangerous to carry on I was following him. He would lead me to Kiki.

It didn't take him long to find her. I was about 20 metres away as he sat down next to her on a bench. At first she seemed annoyed to see him. He did some smiling, some defensive 'not-my-fault' hand gestures and eventually she allowed him a kiss. I had to get closer to them.

All the benches near them were full but behind them was a patch of grass. A couple who looked like students were lying on it and doing what I can only describe as dry-humping. I knew that it must have looked as though I had the whole of the park to choose from and I'd picked the one right next to the randy young couple. I had no choice.

Getting out my mobile to pretend I was reading an email or a text on it, I sauntered to a position behind the bench and then shuffled as close as to Kiki and Ryan as my nerves allowed. I turned away from them, but made sure I could hear what they were saying. Unfortunately this meant I was looking directly at the student couple.

I heard my phone go, a text from Brian: '**lost them c u b@k @ c@r**'.

He'd done it. Now it was my turn to step up.

"Look," Kiki said, "I just don't want to be surrounded by your gang for another minute…I'm fine here, just give me some space."

"This won't be forever," he said, "We just need this to die down, we just need to be careful."

"I get that. But he's not in this park is he? So being here is being careful!"

Ryan sighed. He got to his feet and got his mobile out.

"Talk to me," he said as he started walking away.

I glanced round, he was agitated, but talking immediately and when he was about five metres away I turned side-on to Kiki.

"Kiki!" I whispered, "Kiki!"

She didn't seem to hear me, which was when I saw the white of her ear-phones. She was listening to music. Ryan was circling, having a heated conversation, but I didn't have the b*lls to sit down next to her.

On the floor in front of me there were a couple of twigs, some pebbles. I threw a twig; it bounced back off the bench. I needed something heavier. Obviously I didn't want to hurt her, or even really hit her, but if I could loop a pebble over the bench and land it near her I'd get her attention.

As soon as I let go I knew I'd put far too much force behind it. It looped up, cleared the bench and plunged directly into the pram. Stevie Jr started wailing.

Kiki jumped to attention, ripping her earphones off. I was up on my feet before I even knew it, getting myself away before doubling back along on the path towards her.

"Oh," I said, looking concerned, "Someone's got a big pair of lungs?"

Kiki looked at me, harassed, but still smiled, "He's been hit by a stone. Who would do such a thing?"

"Really! That's horrible!" I agreed.

I looked at the baby and almost choked as I saw blood on the side of his head. Feeling like an utter b*stard I tried to help her look for who might have done it as she picked him up, "No, can't see any kids...I bet

253

they didn't mean it though?" I offered.

"Tell that to him if he grows up with a scar!"

"True," I said, wincing.

I looked around. Ryan was facing away from us for the moment.

"Kiki," I said, in a hurried whisper.

"What? How do you know my..."

"I'm a friend of Brian Parr's. I need to talk to you?"

"What?" she said, panicking, "Ryan's just there?"

"I know, but I need you to finish what you were saying the other night."

"I can't," she said, putting the baby back into his pram, ready to walk off.

"Please, for Brian," I said and then, surprising myself, "And for Stevie and his baby..."

She glanced over at Ryan. He was berating someone, "All he'll see is someone looking at a baby" I told her.

"What do you want to know?"

"After you left May, what happened?"

She still wasn't sure about talking. I put my hand on the pram, my eyes imploring her to speak.

"Was Stevie very drunk as he drove?"

"Yes," she said slowly, "But he'd taken the stuff the doctor gave him. That's not why we crashed."

"Why then?"

"After a couple of minutes we saw headlights behind us."

"What kind of car?"

"A big one?"

"Like Ryan's?"

She nodded, "But Ryan said that wasn't him, he'd come from town, not the house."

"Why was Ryan there though?"

She turned to him. He looked at us, she waved, my heart jumped into my throat but he carried on talking.

"Stevie owed them a lot of money. He'd missed a deadline, they'd seen us leave town that night and were waiting for him in a layby they knew he'd go past on the way to training. They were expecting it to be a lot later when suddenly we shot past as Stevie tried to escape the other car...so Ryan pulled out and followed us."

"So you were being chased by two cars?"

"Yes, and Stevie panicked and swerved...we crashed..."

"And...?"

"I can't, he'll come over..."

"Kiki, someone died, from what I can tell Ryan didn't kill Stevie, but he can't stop the truth getting out just because he doesn't want his business ruined."

I could tell this had hit home.

"Let's walk?" I suggested.

"Why?"

"We can say you were using the map to show me directions?"

She nodded. As we walked away from Ryan I felt I could press her again.

"What happened after the crash?"

"I thought Stevie was dead. I got out of the car, he wasn't moving..."

"It must have been horrible," I said.

"I could see a car at the side of the road. I ran to it, screaming he was dead."

"Whose car was it?"

"Ryan got out," she said, not enjoying remembering it, "I knew him from a few nights with Stevie."

"And...and what happened? How did you come to...get involved with him?"

"He asked if I was ok. He told me I should leave with them, before we got involved with the papers and police which would cause problems for Stevie seeing as I wasn't his wife. I was in shock. I just went along with it..."

I looked over my shoulder. Ryan had finished his call and was trying to find us.

"Did you see anything else?"

"We'd set off when another car appeared from nowhere, in front of us..."

"What kind of car?"

"I don't really know, a BMW? It was long, silver...that's why Ryan's so nervous, because someone saw his car and he doesn't know who."

"And the other car, the one behind you?"

"I didn't see it," she said, shaking her head.

"Who do you think it was?"

"It was from the house, so May?

"That makes sense but could it have been anyone else?"

"Stevie's dealers?" she suggested, "They'd been threatening Stevie more than Ryan"

"Who were his dealers?"

"I don't know."

"Does Ryan?"

"No, he hates drugs, he's just a money man...he thinks that the dealers were in the silver car but he's not sure...sh*t, he's coming..."

We'd reached the map. I put my finger on it. He was close. I needed to know one more thing. My heart was pounding so loud I could hear it in my head.

"What happened the next morning?"

"I couldn't believe it when the news said Stevie wasn't there. I presumed this meant he must be alive and was amazed!"

"That must have been a relief."

"It was, but it was so confusing. They said there was no blood found but I'd seen loads! And no-one had ever mentioned my hand-bag, but I'd left it in the passenger seat by accident. I thought that was strange, I thought it meant someone might have helped Stevie clear the mess up. I thought maybe even Brian had for a bit."

"Did you see Stevie again?"

She shook her head, "So, turn left out of here and it's on your left."

"Alright, babe, thought I'd lost you!" Ryan said with an edge.

"My fault," I said, "I needed some directions."

Thrilled by my success I jogged back to the car. Brian was nowhere to be seen. I got in and waited. We needed to find two cars. Someone with a 4x4 who was on the road between the crash and Stevie's house. And someone else with a silver saloon car who was there too.

Half an hour later Brian still wasn't answering his phone and he hadn't come back.

Chapter 39

By the time I'd lost them I was near Mal's so I texted Will to let him know I was ok and called in for a drink.

I was surprised to find someone else in the living room. A fat guy, bald, in a suit. He'd obviously interrupted Malcolm doing his sticker album because it was open on the United page with loads of packets of stickers on the floor.

What I liked about Malcolm's album was that he'd bought it at the beginning of the season, so it had stickers of Stevie and me. From the second edition onwards we'd been taken out and if you had a first edition you could swap them at the shops for the editions without us. Which many people did because kids got sad looking at Stevie, or angry when they saw stickers of me. Malcolm, though, because he was my fan, kept his. There was just one problem. As well as taking us out of the album, they stopped printing the stickers of us – both the England and United ones. Which meant the stickers of Stevie and me were rare, and they were the only ones Mal didn't yet have.

"Oh, it's you," the bald guy said as I walked in.

"Hi, Brian Parr," I said, offering to shake hands.

The guy shook his head and left.

"Who was that?"

"His son just got suspended from the police."

"Why?" I said sitting down.

"They say he's the one who messed with the evidence in your basement."

"What did his Dad want?"

"His son's been a friend of Nev's. They were at school."

"What? Why didn't Nev say he knew a policeman? Ever since I came out we've been trying to find out about what they've been trying to find out about!"

"Nev didn't know he was back working at the local station. He moved away for training a while back."

Mal was opening more packets of stickers. Desperate to find stickers of me. And Stevie. So far he'd had no luck. I'd suggested to Mal he went to a school and swap stickers with the kids there, but when he tried it the police were called.

"You want some help, Mal?"

He nodded, "Sorry, Bri, I would have thought about him being in the police earlier. I had no idea he was a fully qualified cop now....his Dad wanted to find out what we knew seeing as we've been helping you. His son says he's innocent."

I opened some packets of stickers. I stuck my fingers up at the players in the pictures - Mal did the same. As a man, an adult, there are people you don't like and you have to show them.

"Ok, but what we need to know," I said, thinking about the policeman and what Lyle had said in court, "... is why he moved the knife. Was it a mistake, or did someone pay him?"

"Bri, we can't be sure he did it. We've known this family forever, the boy's not like that. And his Dad says he swears he was on duty, but he never touched anything."

"And you believe him?"

"Even the police are saying it was carelessness actually, rather than a malicious act" came Nev's voice, from the hallway, "I just got off the phone with him. Hi, Brian."

Nev walked into the living room. I knew he didn't like his Dad spending so much money on stickers, "Dad, what are you...?"

"Not now, Nev, Bri needs our help."

"Hi, Nev, what do you mean carefulness and the other long word you mean."

"Care-less-ness," he said sitting down, "They're not alleging he tampered with evidence for any untoward reason, they're saying it was an accident: he knocked the belt and the knife fell out."

"Really?"

"The guy's always been clumsy…"

I did some thinking. Pulling my 'hang on a minute face'.

"Hang on a minute" I said, "but knocking it out of the belt doesn't say how it got into my 4x4!"

"I know, right?" Nev said, "Who knows with the police? Maybe they have some evidence that someone planted the weapon later?"

"So the police have got the wrong guy?"

"Maybe," Nev said, "I think they just want someone to blame so they can say they've cleared it up."

"I need to speak to him, can you arrange that?"

Nev said he'd try to fix it up as soon as possible.

"You up for watching a match, Bri?" Mal asked.

I wanted to but I told him I couldn't because of the deadline. I had 44 hours left. All I'd done was run away from some people. I needed results. As I was leaving I saw a letter on the table by the door addressed to me.

"What's that?" I asked Malcolm.

"Oh, just rubbish," Nev replied.

"Rubbish? It's got my name on?"

"It's from that nutter, Greg Neal," Mal said.

"Dad, don't…" Nev said.

"What are you talking about? Why don't I know about this?"

"Look, he came round a week or so ago," Mal told me.

"What!"

"It's nothing. He's crazy..." Mal pleaded, "Nev was with me, he agreed..."

"Agreed what?" I asked.

"That you shouldn't get involved with him."

"We don't want you back in jail," Nev told me, "If you mess around with Repinov again that's where you're going."

"But what if Greg's got something? I've got less than 48 hours, that's almost 2 days!"

Before they could talk me out of it I was getting the bike ready. The letter told me to get in touch – by text – if I wanted more info, so I did and straight away I got a text back telling me to meet him at an address not far away, to be careful and to look for his van on the street. It sounded cool, like in those spy movies and I was well up for it.

I was about to leave when I heard Mal screaming for joy. As though he'd just onion-sacked a great goal for United.

"Dad!" Nev said angrily when he saw me come in.

Malcolm hadn't seen me, he was jumping up and down! In his hand - a sticker!

"Is it me? Which one United or England?" I said happily.

The moment he heard me Mal, stopped jumping. He hugged the sticker to his chest.

"Which one is it, Mal?" I said, smiling, holding my hand out.

Slowly he handed me the sticker. It was Stevie. In his England kit.

"Stevie?" I asked, "Oh, great, I just thought, from the way you were...so happy...you must have found me?"

"It's just...I've spent so much...to get one of the four missing stickers. There's three left now, Bri..."

I nodded. I was pleased for him. Mal had got one of his stickers, it was obviously a great moment. Many times in my life I'd screamed and shouted over stickers. We all have, haven't we?

Chapter 40

When I got to the address Greg had given me I knew it was familiar, but couldn't work out why. I cycled over to his van and knocked on the door.

"Cool!" I said, as they hurried me inside.

The van was like in one of those films when the police have lots of cameras and screens inside. Tone smiled and went back to the computer that seemed to be controlling it all.

I knew I had to ask Greg about the threats he'd sent about Stevie, but first I wanted to know why he'd asked me to come. I told them about my time limit from Yvonne and got even more annoyed at Nev and Mal because Greg said he'd been trying to talk to me for over a week.

"I've never trusted that brat," Greg said, "I told you about how he followed me around when I first got with his Mum. Watching my every move to make sure I wasn't going to upset her."

"He's been good to me," I said, trying to protect Nev, "Apart from not passing on your message."

"I can see that," Greg said, "Actually once he started helping you out he left me alone. Anyway, you're here, I was about to go in, but you'll be much better at it."

"Hang on! I don't want to make a tw*t out of myself again."

"This time is different; do you want to know why?" Greg asked.

"I guess that's why I'm here."

"Check these photos out," Greg told me, "They're from the camera in Blake's office."

I flicked through the folder of photographs as Greg played commentator. All the time making sure I wasn't going to just go b*lls in first like last time. I was happy to give this lead a chance because of the time limit, but if it wasn't any good I was leaving or I'd be spending the rest of the 48 hours banged up.

Most of the photos Greg had were of Blake looking in a folder which he kept in a safe, behind one of his book-cases.

The photos had dates on which Greg said showed how often Blake was looking in the safe. The first time Blake had the folder was the day after the crash. Apparently he'd also looked at the same folder immediately after I'd been thrown out from Repinov's office.

"But it's still just a folder, isn't it? It's not the murderer, is it?" I said.

"But what's in it?" Greg asked.

"Writings?"

"That's where you're wrong," Greg smiled, "Tone has used some computer wizardy..."

"Wizard-whatty?"

Greg showed me another photo of Blake looking at the folder. Then he showed another one. It was like the movies. The second photo was the same, but part of it was much bigger.

"Have a look at what's on it."

I looked at the image, he was right, it was a photo.

"That's a car," I told them.

In quick succession he showed me pictures of Blake's folder. It was hard to be sure, but most were of cars, and if I had to guess some kind of 4x4. Stevie's? That's what I thought of straightaway. And I remembered the photo that Ruby had showed me that Greg had sent Tony – with Shags in his SUV following Stevie after he'd supposedly gone home.

I had to think. I didn't trust Greg. I didn't know if he was dodgy and out to get me, or if he was just obsessed with football and kept leaping to conclusions based on nothing. Some people did that.

"Is this it?" I asked, "Blake looking at pictures of cars?"

"We both know that to prove Repinov and Blake were behind Stevie's murder we need to know what happened that evening."

"What if it wasn't them behind the murder?" I asked him.

"What? Like who?"

"Like...I don't know? Someone who was threatening Stevie's life?"

"What do you mean, Brian?"

I slammed Greg against the side of the van. He struggled. He was no match for me. I'm a professional footballer.

"I've seen the death threats you sent to Stevie, and what you sent to Tony after Stevie had died. You know, the photo of Shags which proved he lied to the police. So you're threatening Stevie, snooping on Shags, filming the training ground, why should I trust you?"

"Brian, I have to protect United. Everything I did was for the club."

"By making threats? Spying on us, using death threats?"

"Look, I started with a fanzine, getting photos of United players, selling them to overseas fans..."

"I know all that. You've told me. I want to know about the threats!"

"The more I followed you, the more I saw of your lives, the more worried for United I got. Because of all your drinking and drugs..."

"I didn't touch drugs!"

"The moment any player does anything that could hurt United that's

264

when you overstep the mark. If Shags lies to the police, I warn him. If someone uses a doctor to cover up drugs, I try to stop him!"

Greg tried to get free, which was silly of him, so I pushed his shoulders back harder.

"Last time I helped you, I could have gone back to prison. Is that what you want?"

"No! I want to find out the truth! If I can do that, United can sign you again!"

I'd fallen for that idea before. I had to keep a clear head.

"How about this, Greg? You killed Stevie because, like you said in your death threats, he was f*cking up United and so was I, a bit, so you got me out of the way too? Out of everyone on my list of murder suspects, you're the one who followed us, who knew our lives!"

His eyes were bulging with fear. Did I have him?

"Come on, Greg, what have you got to say?"

"You're right," he struggled, "All of that's true. But I didn't use what I knew to kill anyone. I only wanted to stop Stevie hurting United and himself. Trust me."

"Trust you?"

"I've never lied to you, have I? I told you about the cameras..."

"You lied to me about the tattoo!" I said, "You told Stevie the same thing about the tattoo..."

Greg was sinking to his knees.

"Ok, ok," he sighed, "I said it to you so you'd like me when we first met. That was only so you'd help me get Repinov. I needed you because I was convinced we had him!"

"You made me think you really liked me!"

"I did, I do, I just...sometimes I have to think about United over its players. That's why I stepped up the letters against Stevie once he started using the doctor to hide his drugs."

"Why did you have to get involved? No-one had found out?"

"I had. And Blake had. If it got out United could have been stripped of the league, the cups, the Euros!" he finished, angrily.

"Hang on," I asked, shocked, "Did you say Blake knew about the....drugs?" I said, whispering the last word.

"About Stevie, sure!"

"How do you know?"

"I wasn't the only person who followed you lot, Blake did too."

"Why?"

"To look after you, as Stevie got worse I know Blake paid people to track Stevie sometimes. That's why I'm convinced the photos he's looking at are of the night of the crash..."

"But you don't know for sure?"

Greg shook his head, "How can I be until we get them!"

"Ok, let's do it! What's your plan?"

"Finally!" Greg said as I let him go, "Last night the Gaffer went into Blake's office to steal the photos."

"Steal these photos? Why?"

"I've no idea. We'll only know once we get them. We followed the Gaffer back home and they're still in there."

All of a sudden I realised where I was. Sometimes after nights out we'd come to the Gaffer's place to play tricks on him, like weeing in his garden.

"Is the house empty?" I asked.

"The Gaffer and his wife are in the garden but we can't afford to wait in case he moves them."

I looked into his eyes. I didn't feel like I was being set-up. But I wanted some advice. I made a call.

"Will! Will! How's it going?"

"Brian! Where are you??"

"I'm outside the Gaffer's house, I'm with Greg!"

"Brian! Be careful of Greg, you know what Ruby showed you he'd done."

I told him what Greg had said in his defence.

"Ok, ok, but they want you to try and break into the Gaffer's house, don't they?"

"They have a great plan for me to get in."

"So let *them* try! Look, I spoke to Kiki after you ran away."

"Will!" I said, talking over him, "Greg is short and fat and bald, Tone looks even worse. I'm a footballer, I'm the only one who can get inside."

"Brian, think about it, if these are photos of that night, why would Blake keep them?"

"Oh, I hadn't thought of that…it's just the photos, it looks like they're of cars, 4x4s…that's what Stevie was driving."

"4x4s?"

"Yeah, Tone did this zooming thing and made the photos big."

"Brian, what car does Blake drive?"

"Erm, off the top of my head, something silver….a saloon, a BMW, maybe a Merc. A good drive, but a bit old man for me. Why?"

He told me what Kiki had said about the silver Merc or BMW. Was Blake at the crash?

I hung-up and told Greg I was in. Tone told me his plan to get into the Gaffer's house. As I put on the uniform of a gas-man and listened to how to jimmy a window I felt good because Will was on his way over so I'd have a get-away car if things went wrong. I also felt good because Will had told me about Kiki's story about the night of the crash. I finally felt like we were making progress.

Chapter 41

"....you no good stinking bl*sdy tw*t, were you born a c*nting r*tard or did somebody f*ck all the sense out of your brain when you were young...?"

I'd been trapped under the Gaffer's desk for half an hour. Breaking in had been easy. I was in the study, trying to turn on his computer, when he came in, followed by his wife. They hadn't stopped arguing.

"...I mean of all the pig-headed, c*ck-munching, ferret-w*nking things to do, you have to go and do that!"

So far I hadn't heard the Gaffer say a word. Well, not a swear word, all he'd said was 'yes', 'no' and 'sorry'. I couldn't believe he let her speak to him like that! It must be where he got his ideas from!

"...I sat there listening to our a*shole neighbours all night without you, you sorry p*edo-r*mming d*ck, how dare you stand me up? And when you did get home, and I tried to get a f*ck, you couldn't even manage! I'm h*rny and I can't get c*ck from my own man!"

"Ok, darling, ok...I think you've got your message across," the Gaffer said softly, "But I do need to go. Mr Repinov is expecting me. My diary's open, book in the next night now and I won't miss it."

The Gaffer left. I managed to get a look at him and he didn't have any photos with him so I guessed they were still in the house and with any luck still in his study. I hoped his wife wouldn't stay in the room for too long. I was getting stiff. And not in the good way, you know, like before sh*gging.

"There, there dear," she said suddenly.

I froze. How did she know I was there?

"Have you come to see Mummy?"

'Mummy'? What would James Bond do if he'd been asked if he'd come to see his 'Mummy'.

I closed my eyes.

"Oh, we need to get you snipped soon or you'll be getting all the b*tches around here up the d*ff!"

I felt something licking my hand. I'd heard she was horny, but this was forward - was it time to get stiff in a good way? I hoped not, she was old but she was no Ruby. The licking got wetter as I slowly opened my eyes. It was a small dog. Not the Gaffer's wife. It licked my face and barked.

"What is it, darling?"

I had to shut it up. It licked me again, barked again. I felt it moving against my arm. It was sh*gging me! I put my hand down to move it away. It had a b*ner! It was really going for it now. Like a WAG on the dance-floor. It barked again.

"Right, that's enough…"

What would James Bond do if he had to save himself by w*nking off a dog? I'd never seen a movie with that happening – well, not a Bond movie – but I'd never seen him lose a mission either.

My fingers gripped its w*lly. It stopped barking, looking at me. I was about to pull on it when the phone rang in another room.

"Sh*t-sleeve!" the Gaffer's wife said, leaving the room.

I leapt up, the dog had gone out with her. I had to find the folder. I went to the desk. The Gaffer's diary was open. I had a clever thought. I went back to August - what had he been up to in the evenings before Stevie died?

The night of the crash it said he had some gala charity event thing. I took a photo of it on my phone. We could check his alibi later. There were always press at those events. I mean it's why you give money to charity, isn't it? Rico taught me that. One night I'd once given half a million and the next day I got a massive fashion deal for two million! Score! And Shags had gone even further and set up his own charity. It was called F.A.S and because I could never remember what it stood for I was always being clever when he said he was doing work for it– calling it 'Footballers A*s Sh*t' or 'Footballers A*s S*x'. Funny jokes like that.

From somewhere downstairs I heard the Gaffer's wife laugh. Then some doors shutting footsteps outside the house. Was she in the garden again?

I had to find the photos. I don't know how long it took me, but I got tired going through so many folders and books and seeing so many words. Just as I was beginning to wish I was doing something else like watching football, I felt something behind one of the drawers. I had to virtually break the desk to get to it. Had it fallen there or been put there on purpose?

I opened it up. I couldn't believe it.

I was speechless

Tone and Greg had got it right. It was the goal-sack! Lots of them were photos were of Stevie's car crash. Some were of Ryan Prince getting out his 4x4 like Will had said! Some weren't from that night and there were a few of some foreign looking guys and one even of Dr Malone. Suddenly I heard a bark behind me. The damn dog. It jumped onto the Gaffer's desk. It was barking. How long until the Gaffer's wife turned up? There was only one thing for it. I closed my eyes.

It was going ok, but just as I was about to finish I heard a footstep. Too late. I opened my eyes to see the door open. My fingers still moving. The dog kind of barked as the door opened. I felt the doggy j*zz hit the desk as the Gaffer's face seemed to scream in anger and surprise.

"Brian w*nking Parr, what the f*ck are you doing to my dog?"

"Gaffer? Why are you here?"

"It's my f*cking house! What in the name of your great-grandma's f*nbags are you doing? I'm calling the police."

Without thinking I charged and pushed him against the wall. Despite his age he was stronger than Greg, but I was still Brian Parr. Maybe this was what I needed to do? Go from suspect to suspect, pin them down and shout until they told the truth.

"What in the name of a sh*gging d*g's b*lls are you doing?" the Gaffer shouted.

"I want answers!" I shouted back, "How come you worked with Blake to kill Stevie!"

"What the c*nt are you talking about?"

"These photos, Gaffer!"

"I didn't have anything to do with Stevie or you..."

"You came to see me in disguise, you wanted to know if I knew it was you!"

"No, no! I came in disguise because someone had done you two in and I thought I might f*cking be next!"

"What do you mean?"

"Brian, think about it! Since Repinov and Blake came in, I'm made to play players I've never heard of and then my two biggest names get taken out....I'm threatened with the sack! I've built this team into champions and they want to throw me out?" he said, "I've been keeping an eye on Blake and the other day I saw his safe open and saw these so I took them!"

Something about the way the Gaffer was talking made me believe him. I let go of his collar.

"So you think they killed Stevie?" I said.

"Maybe, but whatever the h*ll they're up to, I don't like it."

Because the Gaffer had his suspicions, it was easy to explain to him why I thought Repinov and Blake were guilty. I didn't talk about Greg, but I did mention the contracts and the fact that I'd had s*x with Repinov's fiancé.

The Gaffer agreed both theories could be right, but said we'd only know once we understood that night. We got down to business and looked at the photographs together. It was like the old days when he'd take you aside and show you charts and tactics about the next match. He'd always been good at pointing and saying clever things.

"Well, this one...it's this lass Kiki, coming from Stevie's car and being approached by this Ryan Prince..."

"And this one, this is earlier, you can see Ryan and his guys have just pulled up, Stevie's bit on the side's still in the car and as she's said, there's another car too, hiding behind the corner...a big one."

"Toyota Prius, Gaffer," I'd said, "You can tell by the shape of the lights."

"For a sp*stic you do know your cars..."

The photos seemed to prove Kiki had told us the truth. Ryan Prince was a d*ck but he hadn't caused the crash. But who was in the Toyota and why did Blake have these pictures?

"These two are interesting," the Gaffer continued, "You see, they're taken from a different place and, and...Ryan Prince has left with Kiki but someone else is by Stevie's crashed car, and then in this photo there's two, actually three people...and further back someone with a torch; see that light?"

"What shall we do?" I asked, knowing I had to report back to Will and Greg.

"Well," the Gaffer said, "The only person who can explain these photos is Blake, and like him, I'm invited to Repinov's party tonight. He's celebrating his house being finished but there won't be a w*nking bouncy castle for you to jump on mind!"

Chapter 42

The Gaffer's wife blew her top when he told her I was now going to be his 'plus one' to the party. She was like a whole terrace full of Town fans calling me a c*nt in clever ways.

"Marriage!" was all the Gaffer said when we got into his car, "Here, Parr, this mask is yours."

"A cat?" I said, looking at it.

"Yes, a c*nting cat. Problems?"

I'd never really liked fancy dress parties or masked balls like this one, I hated people not being able to see my good looks - but this time I knew it would help because no-one would wonder who the handsome lad

273

was and realise it was me: Brian Parr, back from the clink.

Greg and Will watched us drive off. Will said he'd meet me outside Repinov's later while Greg was excited about getting ready to show the world everything Tone and him had found.

As we got nearer the houses got nicer and nicer. Thicker and stronger gates protecting the drive-ways. More and more CCTV watching the entrances. They were exactly the kind of places I'd once looked round. Inside the gates, it was obvious the house was massive. If you know anything about houses, that's the most important thing. The very front of it was the old mansion he'd bought. The sides, and what I presumed was behind, were all new extensions. Built out of metal and lots of glass. Cool.

As soon as we walked into the building, it was like we were in the biggest, coolest bar in the world and I was offered a glass of champagne immediately by a girl with br*asts I liked. The Gaffer showed his invitation. No-one as much as looked at me or my cat mask and we were in.

The reception room had the hugest chandelier I'd ever seen. Behind that was a massive picture of Repinov and Tammy. Tammy was in a similar position to how I'd last seen her in the VIP toilets - she was straddling him. It was all so class.

The place was heaving with people. All in masks. The lighting was dark, the music sounded really cool and there was that sound of people talking too. The Gaffer soon fell in with some people he knew, so I took my chance and started to look for Blake.

One guy I saw was in suit trousers but no top. He was ripped too and had a great sun-bed orange tan. I thought about taking my shirt off, but seeing as my eight-pack was so famous from all the modeling I was worried about getting found out.

That was when I noticed that a woman in a really glamorous small red dress which showed virtually all her big b*obs apart from her n*pples, had a mask with my face on. I couldn't believe it, I'd never seen myself with t*ts before, despite what some papers once printed.

To my left I heard laughter, and I knew it was Repinov under a big mask of a deer with those horn things, "It's like so OMG!" he was laughing, "Having it all finally done is such a total relief!"

Having gotten used to pinning up suspects against the wall, that's exactly what I wanted to do. It was tough to stop myself doing it to him, but Blake was my target.

When I turned I found myself face-to-face with myself.

"Well, hello," the hot girl in the red dress with my face said.

"Hi....er, Brian," I said, "How you doing?"

"I'm doing very well, P*ssy," she laughed, "You just arrived. Let me show you the house."

I'd never been called p*ssy before. Well, not without punching the person immediately afterwards. As I followed myself, checking out the great a*s she had in the hot dress, I realised that I recognised the girl's voice. It was Tammy. Repinov's fiancée.

"Tammy?" I said as soon as we got out onto the patio and were alone.

"How did you know?" she asked, taking off the mask.

There was no way I could take my mask off. People or CCTV would see me straightaway.

"It's me," I said.

"Who's me?" she laughed, reaching to take the cat mask off.

I stepped back, "Well, I'm....you!" I told her.

"What do you mean?" she asked.

"You...." I said, touching the mask, "...are me?

"OMG! You totally sound like a perfume advert or something!"

"And you totally sound like Repinov."

"OMG! Brian! What are you doing here? You've got to get out, now!"

"Now? Why?" I asked.

"He'll kill you if he knows you're here, he, like, totally hates you!"

"Me? Why?" I asked.

"Because of what we did!" she said.

"If he hates me, why are you wearing a mask of me?"

"He's p*ssed me off so I'm p*ssing him off," she said smiling, "Look leave now, he'll find you..."

"I'm fine, I've got this mask. I have to do something..."

She giggled, looking at me. A look I knew.

"Why don't we, like...make the most of it then?" she suggested.

Before, if I'd seen a guy turn down an offer like that I would have said he was g*y. But I had responsibilities now.

"I'd love to," I told her, "But I'm here to do something."

"Me?" she said smiling.

"No, it's about Stevie...and me...look, last time, that we...you know, I heard that Repinov found out. And that maybe he thought Stevie or me had you know, had s*x with you..."

"Yeah, he knows. His w*nker guards find everything out...." she smiled, ""Are you asking whether Serg could have like, sorted Stevie and you out because we f*cked?"

I nodded, impressed at how quick she was.

She looked at me, moving her arms round to her front and pushing up her t*ts. You could tell exactly why she'd was always in the Lad mags, she was a top bird, "F*ck me in the bathroom and I'll tell you."

Reader, I did. As I was zipping up she told me:

"Of course Serg, like, might have done something like that. I mean WTF I never said I did it with you or with Stevie, I just let him think what he wanted to and if that made him angry then he could have done it. Killed Stevie and set you up. Well, his guards would have done it. Good luck trying to prove it though!"

She left me in the bathroom wondering whether the person who'd come out of the garage with the body could have been one of his guards. Everyone had said the person did look a bit foreign, hadn't they? The guards weren't wearing masks. I decided to spend some time checking out them out.

"What the...?"

I knew the voice. Shags. He burst into the bathroom, a lion mask round his neck, unzipped and ready to p*e.

"I thought this was free I just saw Tammy leave..." Shags stopped himself, he knew the score.

He pushed past me and started to w*e.

"What the f*ck, Bri? You still doing this investigation b*llsh*t?"

"Mate, if you knew how often being like James Bond gets you laid, you wouldn't call it that."

"How many times?"

"Twice. In two days."

"That's nothing. I'm a footballer, remember?"

He was impressed when I told him about Ruby, though, and said he'd always fancied her. I saw his face go weird when I said Tony's name. Part of my wanted to pin him to the wall. I held off for the time being.

"Shags, mate, I have to ask you something. I know why you left Tony..."

277

"I left him because Rico was better, that's why you were with him."

"No, you left because he knew you'd lied to the police."

"What? F*ck off, Bri, all this trying to think has sent you mental!"

"Why did you lie?" I said, blocking his way, "Why did you follow Stevie that night?"

He tried to push me to the side. He was strong as always, but I dug in.

.

"I didn't follow him, I left him…"

"I've seen a photo!" I told him, knowing I had to ask him about the list Sian saw too.

"F*ck that, I went straight home!" he shouted.

There was a knock at the door, "Excuse me! There's shouting, what is the matter?"

Saved by the bodyguard, Shags shook his head at me opened the door and disappeared into the crowd of people who were in the ballroom waiting for the live music to start.

Chapter 43

"Brian," the Gaffer said, sneaking up on me as I was secretly, and really carefully, looking at the guards, "Why are you pressed against the bl*ody wall. People are staring at you!"

"They're not!"

I looked and they were.

"I just heard Blake leave to do a conference call in the study," the Gaffer carried on. "Come on!"

We spent ages trying to find our way and we had to be careful, but thankfully some of the rooms had signs on and eventually we found it. My hand was sticky with sweat as I turned the handle, the Gaffer behind me, checking no-one was coming down the corridor. We crept into what was like a huge library. There were bookshelves everywhere with what I reckoned were books on them. In the middle of the room was a really long table. On one wall was a big poster, signed, of Angela Lansbury. At the opposite end of the room to us was a door which looked like it led out to a balcony.

Then, a door opened. It was a door in the bookshelves!

We had no time to hide. My only choice was to use the surprise we had. A big guy, wearing an eagle mask came out, on the phone. I sped across the room, jumped onto the table, over a chair and back onto the floor. I was on him. Pinning him against the wall.

"Wait! No!" the Gaffer said.

"Blake!" I shouted, "It's me!"

I ripped Blake's mask off.

It wasn't Blake. Whose mask had I ripped off?

Something smelt. I could hear a trickle. Not-Blake was w*tting himself! Luckily, the Gaffer knew him. Martin Bull a club investor. He was angry at what I'd done, but more embarrassed about what he'd done to himself. He agreed he wouldn't tell anyone what had happened as long as we didn't tell anyone that he'd weed himself. Which I never did.

As soon as Martin had left the study, the balcony door opened. This time it was Blake. I knew because he wasn't wearing a mask. Unless it was somebody wearing a Blake mask. But Blake wasn't handsome like me so why would anyone wear his face not a Brian Parr mask? Blake was looking at his mobile and didn't see me jump onto the table.

He only heard me. He screamed, but I got my hand over his mouth as my arms locked around his throat.

The strength he'd shown in Repinov's office was still there, but I wasn't letting the advantage I had go this time. I kneed the back of his knees, dug my chin into his shoulder and forced him onto chair until he stopped struggling.

"Look, Blake, Brian wants to ask you some questions, ok? He'll let you go if you help...." the Gaffer said, "And this isn't his loony theories anymore; we've got the photos from your safe."

As soon as the Gaffer told him that, I felt Blake relax in my arms. Was he not going to fight anymore because we had him? I hoped so.

"I just want to talk," I told him.

"So why did you attack me?"

"I...I..." I didn't know what to say.

"Blake, you're the one who needs to talk," the Gaffer said, "We've both seen the photos."

"Yeah, tell us what you did to Stevie! You and Repinov!" I shouted.

"We didn't do anything!"

"It's not what the photos show, is it?" I shouted. "Come on, I've got evidence now, not signed shirts! What were you doing there and what did you do to Stevie?"

I felt like I was winning! I was excited but this time, I also felt like I had the facts to back myself up. I was about to find out the secret behind Stevie's death!

Blake sat there, scowling, "Look, I have no intention of trying to cover myself. The photographs say it all."

"What do they say?"

He looked at me. Everything about him made me irritated – his stupid

280

big white hair and bushy eyebrows, his old, ugly face.

"Brian," he said looking at me, "I know you've got it in your head it was us who did this, but it wasn't. You have to drop this."

"Never."

"Even if you hurt me, like you want to, I won't say anything different; it's the truth."

"The truth? I know you have to make the club profitable and you hated the fact you'd given Stevie and me such big contracts! You got him killed and stuffed me, and Repinov didn't mind because I did Tammy!"

"Shut up!" he screamed, bursting, "Look at the photographs, I took them all. Did you see me doing anything wrong in them?"

"Well, no, but why did you take them?" I asked

"To f*cking save him!"

"Don't give me that. You wanted him out, and he wouldn't leave so you killed him!"

"Killed him? He was worth a huge amount to the club...as were you."

"But you still had him killed."

"Why would I kill someone we could make 20 million from?"

I looked at the Gaffer, he was as deep in thought as I'd ever seen him.

"Of course I had to justify Stevie's contract," Blake continued, "which is why I was trying to help. I found out about Stevie's life off the field and knew we couldn't afford someone on such huge money ruining themselves. It's not the early 90s! I wanted him off the booze and drugs and gambling!"

"Why not just talk to the Gaffer, talk to me?"

"I had to keep it quiet, so I decided to do it myself – one false word and it would have been be all over the press."

"How was taking photos helping him?"

"I took them so I could blackmail everyone on his case and get them to leave him alone. Then I could use them to force him to sort himself out too. I even booked him into rehab."

"And, Bri, if he was doing something wrong why would he take photos and keep them?" the Gaffer said with a shrug.

I nodded, remembering Will had said the same thing. Was Blake really innocent?

"The night he crashed, I took a call from a bar saying he was drinking. I decided I had to act. The rehab place was ready to take him whenever I got him there. You can check my emails," he said, nodding to his mobile, "It's all in there…"

The Gaffer picked it up and started looking.

"Seeing we had another keeper as cover, I thought it was time to get Stevie into rehab - tell the fans he was injured. That night, it didn't take long to see he was being followed. At first I didn't know if they were the dealers or the people he was in debt to…

"Ryan Prince?" I asked.

"Yeah," Blake said, "A nasty b*stard. With photos I thought I could either go to the police or call them off."

"What then?"

"I followed Ryan towards Stevie's house. Before we got there, they stopped in a layby, I drove past and doubled back. I presumed Stevie was sleeping it off and was about to head home when his car came off the road in front of me. I got out and I took the photos …."

"What about the last photos?" the Gaffer asked.

"I hadn't called 999 because I thought he was dead from the girl's reaction and thought getting involved wouldn't help. But on my way home, I couldn't get it out my head that he might be alive, so I went

282

back. As I got near I saw people by the car. I stopped and took some photographs."

"But you don't know who they were?"

"No, I reckon they must have been the ones in the Prius."

"That's what I thought," I said, "And were you surprised about the news the next day?"

"Of course I was....I mean I knew he'd crashed, but no body, no blood?"

"I heard you talking to Repinov."

"I know, and to him I had to pretend I knew nothing about it."

"Why?"

"In my past I was...well, I made some bad decisions, and when I managed to get on the board of United, I vowed I'd never get caught up in anything like that again. I love United, you know?"

"So do I!" I said.

"Me too..." the Gaffer agreed.

"Problem was, looking after Stevie meant I had to go back to a few old ways, and I knew Repinov would get rid of me if he found out."

"Why? He's as dodgy as they come, isn't he?" I said.

"Because he's foreign and rich?" Blake replied.

"That's what oligarchs do! I mean you don't look like he does, and have all the money and bodyguards he does, without being dodgy, do you?"

"Sergei's done everything by the book. He's terrified of being called corrupt, he's had enough of that back home."

"So he is corrupt back home?"

"Look, this guy's really just a playboy. He hardly has anything to do with the club unless it's unveiling a new signing. All he does is spend

money on Tammy and partying…and the bodyguards?   They're
because he's f*cked so many wives and daughters he's worried
someone's going to hurt him. You saw how he was about the shirts.
That's all he cares about, his reputation. He wouldn't risk getting
involved with murder…"

"What if he knew, or thought, Stevie or I had s*x with Tammy?"

"Well," Blake thought, "He cheats but he wouldn't like anyone having
s*x with her."

 "I did. Twice," I boasted, without thinking, "And just now. From
b*hind."

"Brian!" the Gaffer said.

Blake look shocked but he said, "But killing you for that? No way, it
wouldn't be worth it."

Blake meant what he was saying. I could see that but it went against
everything I'd been thinking!

I didn't know what to say, "I don't know if I can believe you."

"Do you want to catch whoever killed Stevie?"

"Yes!"

"Then you can't waste any more time investigating me. Yes, I'm
guilty of not reporting a car crash, and fleeing the scene of a
crime….and if you do tell anyone I'll lose my job, but I wasn't behind
Stevie's killing."

"What about me?" I asked, "Someone set me up!"

"Why would I set you up?"

"My contract."

"Your contract? We paid you that because you're worth it…I'd have
paid you more if you'd have had a better agent…"

"F*cking Rico," I said instinctively.

"Think about it, I didn't have a replacement for you lined up, not like for Stevie. And not having you has been a huge reason we're doing so badly."

"We're still fourth..." the Gaffer protested.

"Which isn't good enough, is it Brian?"

"No, but if I was important, why did you leave me in prison?"

"The sponsors made it clear we had to...and at the time I thought you might be guilty..."

"But you knew I wasn't at the crash!"

"He was in your basement, how was I to know you didn't get him from the car and take him there?"

I racked my brain to think what kind of questions Will would ask, or Nev, or Lyle, "Ok, so what did you and Repinov do in between the crash and when I found him? How do I know you weren't out there, setting me up and getting Stevie killed?"

Blake went into a long story about where they were, which the Gaffer backed up because he was there. Everything he said made sense and suddenly I was facing the prospect of relegating one of my top suspects from the list. And if Repinov was off the list too, with so little time left, where did that leave me?

"So what should I do?" I asked Blake, "Who did kill him? Who did set me up?"

"Because you're not going to stop, and because you now know what I was trying to hide, I'll help all I can," he agreed, after thinking for a while, "You need to find out who these people are, the ones who went to the car last," he said holding up a photo, "...they must be the one's moving Stevie."

Chapter 44

It was a relief to see the two of them come through the gates. Even though it had only been an hour or so I'd been worried the whole time. I presumed they hadn't been able to get anything done in that time and were coming out with their tails between their legs.

"So, you're Parr's writer are you" Hooper said as he got into the back seat, "It's a wonder to me the d*ft w*nker can speak sometimes, let alone hold a f*cking pen so I guess you're needed."

The two of them set about telling me what had happened. Far from them accomplishing nothing, what they'd found out from Blake was by far the biggest leap in the investigation so far.

"Are you sure he wasn't lying? Are we certain about this?" I asked.

"As far as I can tell, and I've seen that guy lie more than most, he was telling the truth," Hooper said, "The photos back it up."

"What are we going to do?" Brian said, "Where next? Who next?"

"I...well..." I stuttered, trying to plan the next move.

"We've got to find out who did it! This isn't fair! I've gone through loads of the suspects on your list thing and no-one's guilty! They've all got proof that it wasn't them! This is so, so hard! It's like playing against a team who have 22 players!"

"Shut-up, Parr, stop whining like a little girl who's just seen exactly what type of lollipop her uncle's talking about," Hooper began, making me wince.

As the Gaffer was telling me off, I forced myself to think. There was no-one who could get me focused like the Gaffer could. Not even a really hot girl with big b*obs. That's why he'd been the manager I'd played my best football for.

I thought back through everything I'd seen and been involved in. It was like the highlights they showed at the end of the season. Except what I was watching was things like finding Stevie dead. And the photographs of the basement with the knife missing. And what I was looking out for wasn't footage of fans celebrating amazing things I'd done, it was for things I'd missed and people we needed to talk to who I could see quickly.

The mobile.

I needed to speak to Etienne but he was protected by Rico's guards.

Were there any other ways to find out who left that mobile in my room?

There had to be.

It felt like I was just getting somewhere when Will's phone rang. I was going to speak but I felt the Gaffer's hand grip my neck, "Focus, Parr, focus, you can do it. Use your photographic memory, use it!"

Then his phone rang too. Two, ringing at once. Just as I realised the Gaffer had been nice to me rather than been swearing at me, I realised I had a plan.

In the bedroom, with Yvonne trapped inside in the closet, there'd been two phones ringing too. I'd picked Yvonne's up and seen a picture of a foreign guy. I fast-forwarded my memory to the film of the foreign guy coming out of my garage earlier the same night.

"Yvonne. We have to see Yvonne."

It was about ten by the time we got to Brian's old house. No-one was answering and I'd never seen him so impatient. I suppose it was to be

287

expected.

Hooper had left us outside Repinov's house. He'd said he wanted to help Brian but didn't think it was wise for him to be seen ripping around the city accusing people of murder.

Eventually Brian gave up waiting by the gates and called on Roy. The neighbor who used to film him. If Roy still kept an eye on what happened in Brian's house, perhaps he'd know if Yvonne was in? Or where she might be?

I waited with instructions to stop Yvonne if I saw her. Thankfully, Brian came back five minutes later. With a smile on his face.

"There's only Etienne and the lads in the house. The bodyguards, Kelvin and Stu have knocked off for the night," he said checking his watch. "It's past bedtime so Etienne must be staying late to babysit. "What do you want to do?"

He got out his phone, "You call Etienne and then go in and ask him about how the phone got in the bedroom? I'll wait here."

"What?"

"You call Etienne and then go in and ask him about how the phone got in the bedroom? I'll wait here."

"I know what you said, but how am I meant to do that? He's not just going to let me in."

"Well, he certainly won't let me in, will he?" Brain stated, "He'd lose his job. Come on, the clock's ticking, stop time-wasting."

"Time-wasting? Come off it Brian. Don't be a d*ck! I'm here to help but I can't do the impossible."

As his face turned angry, I shrank a little.

My fear was misguided, "Sorry, mate," he said.

He thought a minute, his mouth making all kinds of contortions. Then he said, "Look, we're always having people round to the house to sort things out. You could call Etienne and say Rico gave you his number and you're here to check the panic room security or something."

Brian's plan worked immediately. Etienne asked a few questions, looked at me on the camera and buzzed me in.

When Brian spoke of how nice his house had been he sometimes got misty-eyed. I could see why. It was tacky in places, but everything was so expensive it almost didn't matter. Apart from one too many Siberian tiger pictures, rugs and life-sized models. While Etienne put the boys to sleep, I was let into the master bedroom. As I pretended to check the panic room, I built up my courage. Eventually he came in and asked me, "Everything ok?"

"Look, Etienne," I said, a frog in my throat, "I lied... Brian sent me."

"What? Then you've got to leave!"

"Please, just one question, that's all, Brian needs you."

"I can't, you must go..."

"Etienne..."

"Don't make me call the police."

I nodded, but as I knew I had to say it anyway, "What Brian wants to know..."

"My daddy's called Brian..." came a voice from the landing.

"Baggio, go to bed..." Etienne told him.

"...is did you put a mobile phone in their bedroom on the night he found Stevie?" I continued.

"I did that!" Baggio shouted.

"And if so who asked you do it?" I finished.

"Mummy's friend asked me to," Baggio shouted again, "I got ten quid."

"Baggio!" Etienne said.

"Hang on," I told him, "Did you hear him?"

"He's just messing around."

"I'll show you where I put it," Baggio smiled, "For another tenner?"

He marched into the room and, after I'd paid him, he pointed to exactly where Brian said he'd found it.

"He said it would help Daddy but not to tell anyone. Ever. But he only gave me ten, not twenty, or fifty, so now you've paid up it's definitely ok to tell you now."

"Who was it? What does he look like?"

"I can't remember. But he was foreign, like some of the men in Daddy's football team."

"When was it?"

"The day Daddy got in trouble."

Chapter 45

As Will drove he shouted instructions at me to help me get the lap-top on and boot up the internet thing. I couldn't believe it had been Baggio who'd put the phone there for me. Little legend.

But I didn't like the sound of 'mummy's friend. Sounded like she'd been b*ning some d*ck behind my back. Then again, he'd left the mobile for me hadn't he? Maybe he was alright? Whoever he was I had to find him. Yvonne was our link to him, so we were hoping the GPS tracker would tell us where she was.

By the time we got to town I still hadn't managed to get the laptop turned on. Or open. Will had to pull over and do it himself. While he was doing it I got a text from Rico: *Coming back from London, Etienne told me a friend of yours came round. STAY AWAY! I can't stop Yvonne calling the police!*

I wondered if Yvonne was with him. I hoped not. I had to talk to her as soon as I could. It was more and more obvious that Yvonne was mixed up in what had happened to Stevie.

"If she's in the car you think she is, she's close," Will told me, "Do you know this address?"

I nodded when I saw the details, "The TV studio. Where she did the poker show."

Since Rico had become her agent I'd heard Yvonne had been getting better presenter gigs - but she still did the late night show she'd done when I was with her. As we got near to the building I told Will to park round the side. A couple of times in the past, I'd surprised Yvonne by getting into her changing room by climbing up the side of the building. The fact I could do it always turned her on and so I got to s*x her in any position I wanted to. Will was a bit worried I wouldn't make the climb. But I'd made it up when I wanted s*x and this was at least, of not even more, important.

"You stay here," I told Will.

"I was going to. There's something I need to do."

"What?

"I'll tell you when you come back," he said, already typing something into the GPS website.

Half-way up the drain-pipe I remembered that every time I'd done it before I'd been really drunk and really h*rny. A combination which has always made me act without thinking.

This time was different. I began to worry if I could make it. I looked down. Bad choice. What was I doing so high up? I still had a few

291

metres to go and the skin of my fingers was scraping off against the brickwork. I gritted my teeth. Imagining some fans cheering me on. Yes, that was it! I had to pretend I was playing football, and the whole crowd wanted me to win. All I had to do was shimmy up the drain-pipe, use the toilet window to as a stepping stone and then slip into the dressing-room. Goal sack!

It hurt, but I got high enough up. Taking a deep breath I hung my foot off the wall and stretched for the window sill. The rest of my body clinging for my life. In one motion I pushed off the wall. My hands in the air. Gripping for a new hold.

I clamped down. I got it.

I pushed myself through the window and down onto the safety of the floor. I grinned. I was sweating, I was bleeding, and I'd taught the wall exactly what being Brian Parr was all about.

The dressing room was empty. It hadn't changed apart from the framed photo of me was now of Rico. Presuming Yvonne was in the studio I sat down to get my breath back. Knickers and bras were all over the place and I thought about getting involved but didn't want to get caught. I decided to read a mag instead.

I reached out and picked one up off the side-table. It must have been the studio's because it was about TV equipment whereas Yvonne only read about diets and celebrities. Still, if it was like those car magasines I figured it might have some bikini girls draped over some wide-screens.

As I flicked through, I noticed a few pages had bits cut out. There was a big 'B' cut out of a TV screen; an 'A' cut out of another. I smiled because it reminded me of the day Miss Bewley had made me do that to help me learn the alphabet.

I stopped smiling when I remembered where else I'd seen letters cut out of TVs.

The threats to the lads. The reason Yvonne was going to call the police on me and stop me doing what I had to do.

My heart was hammering, my fists clenched. Now I really had to see her. I knew she had a diary by the mirror which would tell me what show she was on and what time she'd finish.

I found the diary. It was the United one I'd given her at the start of the season before all this awfulness had happened. I found the date. She wasn't meant to be working! I turned on the TV screen and flicked to the show. She wasn't presenting. She wasn't in the building!

She must have left one of the cars in the car park after her last shift! And the GPS had tricked us! I swore. A lot. At her.

One of my feet was out the window when I had a thought. I went back to the diary. I looked at the dates around Stevie's disappearance. The night before I'd found Stevie Yvonne hadn't had a show.

I swore again. You see, that was the night I'd been home alone when Dr Malone had come round. And I was home alone because she'd told me she was doing a show.

I went as quickly as possible down the wall and into the car. I was furious, excited, and ready to tell Will everything when he stopped me in my tracks.

"Do you want to know where Yvonne was the night before you found Stevie?" he asked.

"How do you know about that? I only just found out! I haven't said it to you! Can you mind read?"

"Brian, what are you talking about?" he asked, "Listen, this GPS website has all the history on it. I should have thought about it before.

293

Anyway, I've been looking at where Yvonne was the night Stevie crashed and the nights after."

"And?"

"The night she said she was working, she drove to an address about five minutes from here."

"Let's go there."

"Brian, that's not all I found out from the GPS," he said, and I knew he was serious now, "I typed in the night Stevie crashed."

"And?"

"At the time of the crash, one of your cars, the Range Rover, drove to the crash site from your house and back, via Stevie's house..."

"Do you think...?" I said, finding it hard to complete my sentence, "Do you think she ...did it?"

Will took out one of Blake's photos with the three people by the car, "If one of these is Yvonne, then who could the two others be?"

"Stevie and May?" I wondered.

"Could be," Will replied, "It really could be."

There was excitement in his voice which I felt too. I also felt sick. I wanted to find out the truth, but even though Yvonne had f*cked me over, I didn't want her to be the killer. That felt wrong for some reason. Like cheering on a team you hate because you need them to beat a team you hate even more.

Will and I were both thinking so much as we drove to the next place that we hardly said a word. As we got closer I recognised something, "Will, pull over, this is the exact spot Stevie used to stop at when he wanted to score drugs."

"Where did he meet the dealers?"

"He'd go round that corner, to the left."

"Which is where we're headed," Will said.

As soon as I saw the building I realised it was where Edi lived; hadn't Mum said he had problems with the people in the penthouse?

"This has to be the dealer's place," I told Will, "But what's Yvonne got to do with them?"

"Does she do drugs?"

"Never..." I said, before remembering the guy in the phone, "That foreign guy though, 'mummy's friend' as Baggio called him. He's foreign, he could be a dealer! And he could be the guy outside my garage with the body!"

I couldn't think straight as more possibilities clicked into place in my brain.

"What do you want to do?" Will asked. I think he was a bit scared. I was too; this was it.

Chapter 46

The plan was, well, we didn't really have a plan except try to find out who these dealers Stevie and maybe Yvonne were mixed up with.

"How about we check the mailboxes? That might have someone's name you recognise," Will had said, but to do that we needed to get inside the building so we hid behind a car and waited for someone to turn up.

After ten minutes of day-dreaming about what it was going to be like playing for United again Will gave me a nudge. I snapped away from celebrating a hat-trick and saw a woman approaching.

Rocking up from my squatting position, I waited until she was completely in the building before rushing to the door and grabbing the handle before it shut. I turned to Will and held the door open for him. But before he got there, two guys in hoodies got out of a car. Like they'd been waiting for us to show. I sensed them looking at me. Was this a trap? They were coming towards us.

"Brian!" one shouted.

"Run!" I said, grabbing Will by the collar.

He was slow to react. I pulled at his collar, he stumbled. The two men were on us. Will was struggling to get up. I was going to have to fight them off. I couldn't get caught!

"Bri!" they shouted, "Bri! Calm down! It's us!"

I took a breath. Relaxed. As the guys pulled down their hoods I saw it was Chris and Ty. I hadn't seen them since prison.

"What are you doing here?" I said.

"What you asked us to do," Chris said.

"Stevie's dealer?"

"Of course! You got our message right?" Ty asked.

"What message?"

"You weren't answering your mobile so we told that boy, Neville, to let you know we'd found them."

I checked my phone. It had been on silent in the Gaffer's house and now I had lots of missed calls, presumably from Nev and the boys, "I haven't spoken to him."

"How did you get here, then?" Chris said puzzled.

"It's a long story," I replied, "So what's the plan?"

"A few guys we know from our estate, they deal for this guy. He's a top dog, and we've got an interview..."

"An interview?"

"We've been vouched for, but he wants to meet us before we start selling for him. We thought we'd see who he is for sure then let you know."

"Have you got any idea who he might be?" Will said.

"We've been watching the place a while, we think it's this guy."

Chris showed me a photo on his phone. I couldn't believe it, but considering what I'd just found out it made sense.

Yvonne's dad.

"I want to go in," I told them.

"Brian, no," Will said, "If Yvonne's lying about the threats to your boys, and May's involved too, their Dad isn't going to just give you a hug and shake your hand is he? We should go to the police."

"With what? I need proof."

"Drug dealing?" Will wondered.

"They wouldn't listen to me with no proof and I don't have time to waste. I'm going in," I told them, "Help me with a plan."

They did. And when we were ready, Ty said, "Ok, you ready?"

"Brian?" Will pleaded, "Is this the best way? Really?"

"Let's do it," I nodded.

We made sure all of our mobiles were on and working. Then I got hold of Ty round the neck and Will got Chris. They'd given us their knives and we held them to their necks and approached the flats.

This was it.

Would I do the same again now? Maybe not, but I wasn't thinking straight. I thought going in with weapons would scare them and make them confess. But they were gangsters, so why would they?

As soon as I hammered on the door the handle moved. Time for action. Chris and Ty started screaming. The door was opened by a big skin-head. He looked hard-as-nails but the sight of us surprised him. I kicked hard, knocking the door and him backwards.

"Help us, man, help us!" Chris was shouting.

"They f*cking mean business, they f*cking mean business," Ty was screaming.

Just as I did on the football pitch when the ball was passed to me, I scanned the room and worked out where the danger might come from. It was a big, open-plan penthouse, all white, very stylish. To my left some guys were cutting up drugs at the table in the kitchen. To my right, in the far corner, people were watching TV.

One was May. Next to her was her Dad. Mr Lewis. He had straggly long hair and was wearing lots of jewelry and as he turned away from the TV to look at me I could tell from his eyes he'd been sampling the drugs. But his face changed when he saw me. From nice old jolly ex-hippy, to an angry, nasty thug.

He stood up. As did most of the guys in the kitchen and two by the TV. They were slow though, probably because of the drugs and because they weren't ready. They hadn't expected Brian Parr to burst in.

Behind me Will shut the door and locked it. Together we edged into the centre of the room.

"What do you think you're doing?" Mr Lewis shouted

"Shut the f*ck up," I told him, "I'll be asking the questions. Try anything and I'll f*ck up one of your people."

Ty screamed and started pleading.

"You haven't got the b*lls," Mr Lewis said, "Sotis, your gun."

I couldn't back-out. Like going in for a 50-50 tackle. If you flinch and only put in 40% you're more likely to get hurt than win the tackle. If I wanted to walk out of the situation I had to give 110%. That was maths.

"B*lls? I'll give you b*lls," I shouted at him, losing it, my face going red, "I've lost everything. My club, my England captaincy, my boot deals, Stevie, my lads, my house, all my mates - and I think you're the reason for all of it."

Mr Lewis started laughing.

The man he'd called Sotis, a guy with long hair and a Mediterranean tan, passed him a gun. I know I'm handsome as James Bond and as good at s*xing women as he is too. At that moment though, all I wished was that I was as good at carrying a gun as Bond.

"Now, seeing as you're as thick as my d*ck," Mr Lewis, said, which was a line I would have thought was funny if I wasn't so scared, "I'm impressed you've got this far seeing as we've been watching you f*nny around like a r*tard since you got out."

"F*ck you," I shouted.

"What's going on?" came a voice from the mezzanine floor, Yvonne's voice, "Brian? Dad, you said he'd never find out"

"Find out what?" I screamed, unable to help myself, "That you killed Stevie and ruined my life?"

Yvonne ran down the stairs, glaring at me as she came.

On the sofa, May had started chanting some of her spiritual b*llsh*t, "And you can shut that sh*t up as well, you lying b*tch!" I shouted at May.

I froze. Mr Lewis had cocked the gun. I didn't exactly know what that did, but I'd seen enough films to know that it was bad to hear that sound.

"Now, now, Parr, not treating my daughters properly got you into this

299

mess in the first place. You and that drug addict cheating piece of sc*m. He's dead, I think it's time you were."

He aimed. I squealed. So did Ty.

"He won't," Will stated, nervous as h*ll but deadly serious, "The gun has no silencer. Remember what your Mum told you?" Will carried on, "Edi gets kept awake from noise from the penthouse? If he fires, the police will be here in seconds. Keep going Brian, keep going..."

I nodded.

"So you admit it?" I asked, "You admit killing Stevie, and setting me up?"

"Admit it? You think I can just sit back and watch my daughters, both my daughters, be treated like pieces of meat? Course not. So you two c*nts got your lesson, you deserved it."

"Yes!" I said, wanting to jump for joy.

We had him! We had it! His confession. All four of us, Will, Chris, Ty and me, had our mobile phone microphones recording and we had Will's Dictaphone too. Which meant we now had the proof we needed. Will glared at me. His eyes intense.

"Shit!" I said, realising I couldn't act too pleased because the recording had to be secret, "Right, f*ck you Mr Lewis, I'm going to get you now."

"F*ck me?" he smiled, "Your friend is right, I can't shoot, but I do have more people than you."

"Come any closer, I'll cut his throat."

Ty screamed again.

"No, you won't. You've done what you always did on the pitch. Run into dead-ends."

"I never!"

"You've got in here, you've asked your question but do you have an exit plan? Killing this guy? I don't care, I don't even know who he f*cking is!"

"I....I....will, I'll kill him..."

"You know what? When you first came in, I thought you might. A former superstar who looks like a homeless b*m. Beaten and bruised, with f*ck-all left, I thought you might have lost it. But, no, you still have some hope don't you? You're not desperate enough to be a killer..."

Ty yelped, as I dug the knife into his neck.

I was trying my best to con him, like I'd occasionally pretended to a ref I'd been hurt by a tackle. But as Mr Lewis looked at me, and I wondered how he was so clever when his daughters were both pretty stupid, we both knew he was right.

"So, now you know you won't harm him, me and my guys are just going to walk together all at once and we're going to f*cking get you."

I stepped back towards the door. The only hope we had was to get out. Now.

Mr Lewis and his men were closing in. Like zombies in a film. Here and there I could see a knife. I glanced left. Six guys from the kitchen were approaching too.

Six? There'd been seven before. I spun round. One of the dealers was trying to go past Will and I on the wing to block the door. Will saw what was happening the same time I did. We both ran.

"Get them!" screamed Mr Lewis, "F*cking stop them!"

My heart jumped like it did when I was free and one-on-one with the keeper. Then something, which wasn't a defender's nasty tackle, smashed into me. Someone had thrown a chair. I screamed in pain as I slammed against the floor and into the wall.

Chapter 47

Will and I were tied up and forced to our knees. We protested, we begged. They just laughed at us. They took our mobiles and Will's Dictaphone. When they saw we'd been recording them they smashed them.

After Mr Lewis had had a huge argument with Yvonne – she was angry that he'd let me get so far in the investigation – he ordered the guy called Sotis to take us to a bedroom. We were shoved onto the floor and tied to a big, four-poster bed. I looked around. My heart sank when I saw the windows were all locked. Mr Lewis was obviously much more of a professional than Ryan Prince.

Will and I were both nervous. We kept wheeling between feeling positive and thinking we were f*cked. The scariest thing was thinking how could they ever let us go now we knew they'd killed Stevie? Even if we had no evidence, the police would have to investigate and find out about the drugs if nothing else. So how could they let us go?

On the other hand we'd told them people knew where we were and that if anything happened to us, they'd tell the police. We thought that might stop them doing anything too bad to us? Maybe. Maybe not. The fact was we had no idea.

As time passed, the only thing that stopped me from going crazy was how Mr Lewis was treating Chris and Ty. They'd been congratulated like heroes for stopping me which meant for the time being their two recordings of the confessions were safe. And the icing on the evidence

302

cake was that after Will and I had been tied up Ty went to the toilet. On his way back, he nodded to me, carefully, and smiled. Which I took to mean his recording was ok. I wanted to shout in delight and put my shirt over my head. I just about managed to not do that.

Knowing we had the proof calmed me down. In a way it felt like it was the end of the season. After a long journey, I'd arrived at where I wanted to be. I'd found the killer. It felt great to know the answer even though I didn't know about Yvonne and May yet. How much had they been involved? Because May was driving behind Stevie and Kiki and because the GPS told us Yvonne had driven to the crash, it seemed obvious that the three people in Blake's photograph were Stevie and the two of them.

Will said the GPS showed Yvonne had then driven back to our house, via May's – what then? Had Stevie been in our basement the whole time? Was he alive, or dead?

Not knowing how long we'd be in the room I tried to sleep. The belts they'd tied me up with dug into my skin every time I moved which was incredibly painful. Even for me. As morning light came through the blinds I started trying to work out how many hours I had left before Yvonne could call the police. I realised that maybe that was their plan - wait until I was arrested and then say I was only accusing them because I was angry.

Then things got worse.

I needed a p*o and it felt like a runny one.

"What should I do?" I asked Will, scared.

You see ever since I became an adult I've hated p*oing my pants.

"Can't you hold it in?"

"No!" I screamed, "Help me! What would James Bond do?"

303

"James Bond?" Will smiled. "Like in 'Diarrhea is Forever'?"

"Is that a joke?"

"The Man with the Golden B*m'?"

Will, who looked ill after no sleep, was laughing now. He couldn't stop. I would have hit him but I had my hands on my b*m so nothing would come out. I started shouting. After I don't know how long and with the runny p*o almost out, the Sotis guy opened the door. Looking hungover.

"What the f*ck!" he shouted.

"I need to go p*o!"

"So what? We can't move you, Mr Lewis' rules..." he said, turning away.

"It's a runny p*o," I screamed as if my life depended on it, "It's a runny p*o g*dd*mit!"

He stopped and looked back at me.

"Yvonne hates it when me or the kids messed the carpets up with p*o!" I argued, "I bet Mr Lewis is the same! Come on, before I p*o everywhere."

He shouted something to people in the living room.

"Do you need to go as well?" he asked Will "This will be your only chance..."

"Until when?" I asked. "What are you going to do with us?"

He looked at me, "You can sh*t, that's it," he said, "Don't take your eyes off them," he ordered.

Four guys came in, they all looked as tired as Sotis, hungover and annoyed we'd woken them. I couldn't believe our luck when I realised two of them were Ty and Chris. Sotis sat down with another foreign guy and lit a cigarette.

We were led to a bathroom just off the living room. It w

with the six of us in there, it was really cramped

"I want to go first," I told them.

Ty and Chris were holding Will. As the two guys holding me

me, I felt my p*o ready to go. While they were bent over, I looke

Chris and Ty. They were already undoing Will's belts. This was it, I

realised. Our escape.

First though, I needed my p*o. When they were done I sat down and

everything streamed out.

 "F*cking hell," one of the guys said.

The smell was bad. The noises coming from my b*ttom were even

worse. The moment it seemed like I'd done, the two guys who weren't

on my side relaxed. Having been holding their breath, they relaxed

and tried to get some fresh air. A big mistake.

At exactly the same moment, I let rip with even more runny p*o and

Ty and Chris started fighting. In an instant one of the guys was in the

bath and Chris had stamped on him twice and Ty had wrestled the

other into the shower. Ty slammed the shower door shut, Will threw

him the metal toilet cleaner and Ty shoved it through the handle so he

couldn't get out.

In the living room Sotis and the guy with him were slow to react. I

jumped up from the toilet and followed Ty and Chris out the bathroom.

Will was slower. He was last out.

Sotis was on his feet but Ty had momentum and smashed him out of

the way. Chris opened the front door of the flat and the four of us were

out! We sprinted towards the fire exit stairs. Going as fast as we could.

"Brian, pull your trousers up," Will shouted from behind me.

As a kid one of my favourite tricks to play on people was to do a

te because it was so clever and as I did it a

away from angry people with my pants

d come in useful a few times once I'd

to doing WAGS. So while I knew that

'p, I was able to carry on running down

ull stay ahead of the voices behind us.

u open the fire exit.

"Our car!" Chris shouted.

Now we were out on the street I took a second and pulled up my trousers. There was still some runniness in my pants but I had to think of more important things than wiping my b*m.

When we were almost at the car, Sotis and the other guy burst out onto the street.

Will slipped. He screamed in pain, Chris and Ty were getting in the car.

I couldn't get to both. I had to choose.

Chapter 48

By the time I'd got to Will, Sotis and the other guy were about 10 metres away. The car was a little bit closer with the engine running. I pulled Will up. I could see blood through his trousers.

"Leave me," Will shouted, "Ty and Chris have to get away!"

He was right. They'd helped us, their cover was blown.

Sotis was 5 metres away. Will was f*cked. I still had a chance to escape but I wasn't going to make the car!

"Go, go!" I shouted to them.

306

They screeched off down the street.

I ran for it. Behind me Sotis picked up Will. It was hard leaving him but I couldn't get caught and be forced to wait until Yvonne made sure I was arrested.

I sprinted for my life. The guy following me was quick too. Ahead were streets of houses. There was nowhere to turn and he was too close for me to duck down and hide.

My only choice was to keep running.

The fact the street was uphill made it more difficult. I was going so fast it wasn't long before my lungs were burning. I took the chance to glance back. He hadn't gained, he hadn't got further away. I was impressed.

I had to choose left or right. I went right.

Which was wrong. I was in a cul-de-sac. I was going to have to fight.

I turned around and raised my fists as he stopped next to me.

"I know you," I said, without thinking.

The night before, Sotis had tied us up, not this guy. Now I was closer to him, something about him was weirdly familiar.

"You don't!" he replied; his voice made me think harder.

"I do, who are you?"

He had a short, dark beard and black, curly hair. He definitely looked foreign.

A switch flicked in my head.

"You're the one..."

He came at me, throwing a punch. I dodged easily, stepping back.

"Hey," I said, "Hey, why...?"

This time he kicked at me. I caught his foot. More luck than anything, but once I had his foot I wasn't letting go. I twisted it. He cried out in

307

pain. I let go, he stumbled, I moved in; blocking a jab, grabbing his neck and pushing him hard against the wall.

"I saw your photo on Yvonne's phone! You're her friend!"

"I'm not!" he pleaded, shaking his head frantically.

Now I'd heard him speak I was certain I knew his voice, "You gave Baggio that phone! You warned me."

"No, no...."

"Which means you're the one who stole Roy's film - you got me out!"

"I didn't, I didn't do that!" he said, his eyes wide.

He kicked back against the wall, using the momentum to push into me, almost getting free but I held him tight and to calm him down I got a punch into his stomach.

Once he'd got his breath back, we found a wall to sit on. He was younger than I'd thought, his beard covering up for a baby's face.

"How come you helped me?"

"I can't say."

"Why not?"

"I work for him. I'd lose my job, maybe worse...."

"But he's already confessed."

"He didn't," he said, "Listen to the recordings your friends must have. He never says it."

"What? What do you mean?"

"Just listen."

I frowned. At that moment I couldn't focus on that.

"So you work for Yvonne's Dad? For how long?"

"Three years, since I came to this country..."

"What do you do? Deal drugs? Chase people?"

"Ok, it's not a great job, not like yours, but it pays well."

I thought for a second, despite how tired I was; what did I need to ask him to get evidence?

"I've been locked up all night" I began, "And all the time, one of the people keeping me locked up is the person who got me out of jail. Why did you help?"

"I can't say," he looked straight at me, not giving anything away.

"You saved me from jail, you must care..."

"I didn't save you from jail!" he shouted, standing up.

"I know you did! Baggio told me you gave him the phone!"

"I paid him to keep quiet."

"Don't blame him, maybe if you'd given him a bit more? 50 maybe, 100? No good son would lie to their Dad for a tenner!" I told him, "Look, please, how did you get me out of jail?"

"That wasn't me!"

"Ok, ok," I said, seizing on the one thing he had admitted like the tabloid guys would, "Why were you going to help me?"

"I love United," he said, finally.

"Me too," I told him, "What's your name?"

"Nicos."

"Nicos, talk to me, if not I'll call the police."

"You can't..."

"Your boss kidnapped me, he's got my mate, he said he killed Stevie, course I'll call them."

He lit a cigarette.

"The day after the crash I heard Mr Lewis telling Sotis, my younger brother..."

"Your brother?"

He nodded, "...he's younger, but he does anything Mr Lewis tells him, so he's the favourite…"

"What a s*ck-a*s."

"Mr Lewis was angry, he said he was finally going to get Stevie and you for treating his girls so badly."

"Did he say how?"

"Not to me," he didn't, "I didn't know that we'd been selling Stevie drugs either…and Stevie didn't know it was Mr Lewis he was buying them from. Only Sotis ever sold to him."

"Really?"

Nicos nodded, "Sotis and me drove to your house. I knew Mr Lewis was your girlfriend's dad but I'd never seen her because I thought there was a big family problem? But that morning, when we said we were from her Dad, she was really pleased we were there. She was really nice and flirty…"

"Yeah," I said, irritated, "That sounds like Yvonne."

Nicos smoked hard on his cigarette, his hand was shaking. It seemed like he'd wanted to talk for a long time but was also finding it hard telling the truth about Mr Lewis and his brother.

"Sotis told me to wait in the kitchen, and left with her…"

"Where did they go? To my basement? To see Stevie?" I guessed excitedly.

"All I know," he shrugged, "is that I knew something was happening that was going to hurt you, and I wanted, as a United fan, to help. I may work for Mr Lewis, but that doesn't mean I like how he always goes about his business. That's when I saw your boy and realised I had a few mobiles on me we used for the drugs. I thought I might be able to help you…and, well, you know the deal we made…"

"So why did you call me? What happened? And why did you call

Yvonne – she even had you photo on her mobile!"

I was getting worked up, but I knew I had to keep control. I didn't want Nicos to stop talking.

"As we were leaving, Sotis said we had to both swap numbers with her in case she needed any help any time. She took my photo then."

"Then what?"

"I went to the match, I saw you score those goals…"

"Did you think it was a red card?"

"No way!"

I offered him a high-five, then realised it wasn't quite the right moment.

"Then Sotis called, knowing I was at the match, and told me to follow you. I watched you go into the night club and when I told them they said I had to steal your car…"

"That was you?" I said, before checking my temper.

"I'm sorry…"

"What did you do with it?"

"I was told was to check your glove-box and make sure there was a camera in there. There was. Then I drove it to one of our garages."

"The camera?" I asked, before it dawned on me, "Oh, that was one May and I…had used…"

"I don't know," Nicos said, "I gave it to Mr Lewis who said he was setting you up for a big fall."

"Which is why you called?"

"Yes, yes," he said, "I didn't know what they wanted the camera for but I wanted to warn you about it. I called a few times but didn't get through. So I called Yvonne's number, it was a risk but I thought she might be with you…."

I thought back to that night, "How come you told me to call you in an hour? Leaving the house got me in a lot of trouble."

"As soon as you said Stevie was dead, it all changed! I thought the whole thing was about s*x photos and then it was murder?"

"They were hot s*x photos!"

"I had to have time to see if I could help, but after an hour, all I'd found out was that Stevie had been in one of our units that day. By then you were caught... I was with you by then, I was in the field."

"Not my best moment."

"No, but luckily for me, I saw the dog take the mobile. I knew Mr Lewis and Sotis would recognise the make if it was found and they knew I'd been at your house and you were talking about a phone. So I had to leave you and find the dog..."

"It was you who killed it?"

"Did I? I shot at it, but in the dark I never found it."

"I found it! You shot it in the head."

He shrugged.

"And then you tried to help me?" I continued, "And you found out about the film from my neighbour and sent it in to help me win the case?"

Nicos stood up, "That wasn't me!"

His phone went. "It's my brother."

I wanted him to carry on talking. Then I remembered Will.

"Answer it," I told him, "Try to find out where my friend is, I need to help him."

Chapter 49

I'd tried to fight back, but I was no match for Sotis —my knee was hurting too. I watched as Chris and Ty escaped and Bri ran off with one of the dealers chasing him.

Sotis effortlessly dragged me through the door and inside. As he shut the door I tried to get control. I was one-on-one with the guy. Surely it was worth trying to escape before we were back upstairs?

As the lift pinged open, I hoped that his concentration might drop for a second. Long enough for me to break free. I bent my knees, biting away the pain, and tried with all the strength I had to burst away.

I shouldn't have bothered. His hand on my neck gripped harder. He turned and with his free arm punched me. Twice. Hard. I felt I was going to be sick the entire time we were in the lift.

The moment the door to the penthouse was opened I could tell the whole place was in disarray.

"Sotis, where the f*ck is he?"

"Nicos went for him."

"What use is the writer?"

"Someone to barter with is always useful."

"'Someone to barter with is always useful'," Mr Lewis said in a wicked voice, "You f*ck-up! Call your brother. Now."

"What did he want?" I asked, "What did he say when you told him you'd lost me?"

Nicos looked at me, I could tell he was finding it hard – being pulled in two directions and wanting to be loyal to both, "To come back. Now."

"What are they doing?"

"Leaving."

"Leaving, where?"

He shook his head.

"Please," I said, "I need to know where they are. I can't let them get away with it or hurt my friend."

Nicos looked around, his tongue running over his teeth as he weighed things up. I got the sense that he was going to tell me – to do the right thing.

His punch took me completely by surprise. I doubled up and hit the floor instantly. It was a sharp pain. I'd done ribs before and I knew he'd just broken at least one.

Nicos was already out of sight. I laid my head on the floor, trying to get my breath back. My eyes closed, I needed sleep.

But I couldn't let myself. I stood up.

I kind of recognised the area I was in. I staggered forwards.

"Brian?" came a lovely lady voice, was I in a dream?

"Brian?"

I spun round, Miss Bewley was standing in her dressing gown, in a doorway, holding some milk.

"Are you an angel, sent to help me, and give me milk?"

"No," she said, "I live here. You haven't come to try it on again have you?"

My mind tried to work out if she was coming on to me. Sadly, I felt so tired and beaten my radar was broken.

Seeing her again, even though I felt bad, brought back lots of the romantic thoughts I'd had about her inside. How many times had I pretended she was a p*rn-star (not a slutty one) not a teacher? And then the last time I'd spoken to her I'd made a mess of things and felt awful for a few minutes about it. All of that came flooding back and it

314

felt like I'd been head-butted.

It's been claimed I began to cry, but it also started raining a little bit at the same time so no-one can be sure.

"My god, she said, "you look awful! What's happened?"

I stood there and told her exactly what had happened to me in the last 12 hours. When I'd finished, she invited me inside.

"Oi! Parr!" I turned round, a guy in a white van was driving by, "Looking good you arrogant c*ck!"

"C*nt!" I shouted as he rode away.

"Brian!" she said, shocked.

"Sorry, Miss Bewley."

"Don't call me that!"

"Sorry, Miss Bewley."

Sotis threw me on the sofa as he went to call his brother. Mr Lewis sat down, playing with the gun he'd held on Brian the day before. He was angry. Deep in thought. Everyone else was trying to look busy – like they weren't at fault for letting Brian escape and for Chris and Ty duping them all.

When Sotis came back he sat down and whispered to Mr Lewis. They talked for a while.

"Get them ready," Mr Lewis said finally, "We leave in ten minutes."

I felt that any minute they could turn on me but as things panned out I didn't appear to be a number one priority. Sotis disappeared and came back with two leather bags. If they were leaving, what about me? I was squirming in my seat, feeling flushed and sweaty.

*"I don't want to f*cking go," Yvonne shouted.*

"Hey, Sis" said May, "This is the way it's meant to be, my cards

said..."

"Stop talking f*cking crap," Yvonne told May, "I have to meet Rico! He's lined an audition up, I've..." Yvonne started to tell her Dad.

"No way," he said, "We have to go now!"

"We don't have to go at all! Brian's going to be arrested in a couple of hours, why worry?"

"You know why, he's going to be saying we killed Stevie!"

"And!" Yvonne shouted, "Even if people do believe him, which I doubt, you said there's no evidence!"

"I know, but look around!" he said, gesturing to the flat, "With my record, if anyone starts looking I'm f*cked. If we go to Spain things will blow over!"

"The audition's at 12, it'll take half an hour max!" Yvonne pleaded, "Daddy, I want this so much."

"Yvonne," May piped up, "I've told you before, you're not meant to be a presenter."

"Oh, f*ck off, May! This is my chance to be on a TV show I like for once!"

"F*ck yourself, you stupid b*tch," May screamed, dropping all the airs of her spiritual persona, "You're right it's not the bl*ody cards that say you won't make it, it's you being cr*p!"

"Oi, you two!" Mr Lewis raged, "Shut it! We're leaving!"

That did the trick. Yvonne, shrugged, picked up her bag and sat down, waiting. I felt Mr Lewis' eyes fall on me. After what seemed like forever, he spoke, "Sotis, I was too harsh, earlier. Bring the writer."

This time Sotis tied a gag round my mouth. We took the elevator down and were joined by two heavies. Wherever we were heading I didn't have much choice in the matter. The only hope I had was that Brian had got away from the guy chasing him so he could bring help.

The elevator got us down to the car park. Sotis barked some orders and people spread out to get to their cars. Behind me a suitcase was dropped.

It was Yvonne's, she was struggling with it, but no-one seemed to notice or offer her help. Sotis unlocked a saloon car and put me in the back seat as everyone got into the car.

"Hang on..." Mr Lewis said.

"Where's Yvonne?" May asked.

"F*cking b*tch!" Sotis screamed, he opened the door of the car and at the same time I heard a screech of rubber tires and turned around just in time to see a tartan Porsche speed out of the car park. It had to be Yvonne.

"How did this happen?" Mr Lewis shouted, "How did this happen! First him, now her! You bunch of f*cking idiots! I told you we all had to go. All of us..." he shouted again, punching the seat in front of him.

Miss Bewley's house wasn't flashy like mine or pokey like Malcolm's and I felt comfortable in it instantly. Everywhere was painted white, all the floors were wooden and there were big paintings of naked people; you could see t*ts and everything.

"Can I get you something to eat?" she asked once I'd spent a while in the toilet dealing with my runny p*o.

"Do you have any mini-pizzas?"

She laughed at me, "Brian, it's just gone 8...oh, I forgot, it's not breakfast for you!"

"I do have them for breakfast, the pepperoni ones are nice for waking up. It's the spice I suppose. Do you have any?"

"No, I can make you a cheese sandwich?"

"Well, it seems to me," she said, as I ate what she'd made me, "You need to call the police..."

"I don't know. I thought I had him, and it felt great, but after what Nicos said about the recording I need to listen to it."

"Who else could have killed him?"

As I was working through our list of suspects, she stopped me.

"Hang on," she said, "This Dr Malone...tell me about him."

"Oh, well he's not called that really. He's called...Dan."

"Webb....? I know him...he's the prison doctor."

"Oh yeah, well, it turned out he was innocent..."

"Wait, Brian, he *was* the prison doctor. He just got suspended."

"Suspended? Why?"

"He was doing illegal work on the side."

"Do they know about the drugs Stevie was taking?" I said, worried about United and my medals.

"No, what I've heard is that people, well, gangsters, were using him if people got injured but they didn't want the police to find out. They have him on CCTV going into the hospital and stealing supplies."

"Do you think you would be able to check when he was doing this?" I stood up, thinking about Stevie, and how he'd been injured in the crash.

"I don't know," she said, "I can ask."

This got me worked up again. I felt tired but I had to keep moving. For all I knew the police were going to be after me in a few hours time.

We checked into a standard airport hotel where we had to wait for a few hours until it was time for the flight. In my head I kept playing out

318

scenarios of what they'd do to me.

They couldn't get me through customs without me breaking their cover. In any case I didn't have my passport. I reckoned the most likely thing they'd do, and thankfully it was relatively painless, was leave me locked up the hotel room once they left. By the time I was found they'd already be out of the country.

Once in the room May started laying out her Tarot cards, Mr Lewis started drinking the mini-bar, Sotis and the other two watched TV. I was gagged and tied up and laid on a bed and my mind began going crazy. Hoping Brian would burst through the door any moment. Working out how to use the recordings that Chris and Ty had. And the next moment thinking about how the book was going to end.

We'd only been in the room for about ten minutes – long enough for Mr Lewis to have two whiskies – when his mobile went.

"Yvonne!" he snapped, "Where the f*ck are you?"

He stood up and started pacing.

"We're on the 4 o clock flight. If you have to do your f*cking audition, do it and then get here!"

He listened for a bit and then punched the wall!

"Yes, tell Rico to sort out the lads and bring them over tomorrow, we didn't get them tickets. And of course do that, call them now, tell the police he's broken his agreements and get him banged up as soon as possible....why? Why do you have to wait for f*cking Rico to do that? Do it yourself, do it now, we need him out of the picture...the writer? Yes, he's here...well, what do you think?"

After he'd hung up, I spent the next three hours torturing myself, going over every possible question Yvonne could have asked about me that could get the response, 'well, what do you think?'

319

Chapter 50

Miss Bewley dropped me off at Mal's house saying she was going to find out about Dr Webb and his suspension. As soon as I opened the door, I heard Chris and Ty talking and rushed to the kitchen.

"Brian!" Mal said, "You're here! You're safe!"

"You solved it, Brian!" Nev told me, "They played us the recording. Congratulations!"

"I need to hear it again."

Once we had, everyone congratulated me again, but I knew it wasn't enough.

"No, no! He never admits it, he lets me say it all. Come on Nev," I said, "You do law, you know about this stuff, he never says it. He just says what I want to hear!"

"I see what you're saying," Nev agreed, "And in court you'd need more evidence than just this, but it's obviously him."

"He never says it, Nev!"

"Why else would he let you think it was him?"

"Because he wants to look hard?" I said. "I used to do that all the time, about girls, or fights. You let people think stuff sometimes, don't you? And he's a gangster, he needs to look hard."

"Not if it gets the police on him," Nev argued.

"Or..." I said, my mind racing, "he's protecting someone, like May and Yvonne – he wants us to think it's him, not them."

"Brian," Nev said, "They're involved, but he's a gangster and he's telling you he did it! You've done so well! You should be happy."

Of course I wanted to be happy. But I couldn't be certain. It was like I'd beaten the keeper, but hit the cross bar; the ball was heading down and time had frozen before we knew whether it would bounce over the line or not.

"Nev, we don't know what happened after they took him from the crash..."

"Well, who else could it be?" Nev said, getting annoyed at me.

"Well, think!" I said, pacing the kitchen, "There are still loads of people who might have done it! Shags is lying, Blake could be b*llsh*tting us! I mean I think it was Mr Lewis, but I don't know for sure and I'm running out of time!"

Everyone it could be came into my head and I couldn't stop talking about them, one by one, going over all the evidence again and again and then the doubts and the questions we had no answers to. I was panicking because I didn't have long and because Will was with Mr Lewis.

"Brian, Brian..." Ty said, "Sit down mate, we get you, we get you."

I had a glass of pop to calm me down. Chris and Ty went into the living room for a cigarette and Mal passed me the house phone.

"This morning..." Mal said, "Lyle left a message."

"What the h*ll are you playing at?" the message began, "The police have just called, not that I know why they still think I'm your lawyer, and they say they're looking to pick you up for breaching your custody arrangements. They're not going to be busting down doors for a couple of hours yet, so if for once you'll listen to me...get the h*ll out of there!"

As soon as he'd mentioned the police, my mind was in a blur. How could I find out the truth when so many people were involved? There was only one thing for it.

"Mal, can I have a mini pizza?"

I was half way through when I had a plan. It popped into my head like the ball bouncing up nice and sweet from a deflection and all you need to do is smash it into the back of the net.

"Mal, I know what we have to do!"

"What?" he asked.

"I need to get everyone in a room together and I need to ask them what happened. That's what my parents used to do when us kids had been bad. Pretty soon one of us would tell on the other and it'd all come out. It's how they do it in courts as well, get the suspects and watch them accuse each other."

"That's not how they do it in courts," Nev said. "Brian, you've been in court, you know that."

"Well it's what they should do!"

"How are you going to get everyone in the same place?" Nev asked, "...it's impossible."

"Nev, have you ever heard of a one-two?" I asked him.

He shook his head, "It's the best move in football because it's the simplest. Thus, to get people in the same place, I'll just tell them to meet me there."

"What are you talking about? Why would Yvonne's Dad meet you?"

"I'll say I'm giving myself up to swap for Will."

"Oh," Nev said, I think surprised at my cleverness, "Ok, What about Repinov?"

"I'll tell him I have...information about Blake, or Tammy. For Blake, I'll say I have information on Repinov, for Rico I'll say I'm giving myself up and he can have the press access for the story, for Ryan

322

Prince I'll tell him...I'll just tell him I want to talk to him about Stevie's baby and he'll come to try and beat me up."

I stopped, I felt like when I'd done a really great dribble.

"That's brilliant, Bri!" Mal said, "Isn't it Nev?"

Nev shrugged. I didn't care. I'd get everyone in the same place and with Chris and Ty acting as bouncers I'd make sure no-one left until we'd found the killer.

"Wow!" I heard Chris shout from upstairs, stopping my train of thought, "This is mental!"

"What?" I heard Ty say as he came in from outside and then pounded up the stairs.

"What's going on?" Mal asked, worried, "Nev?"

"I thought I locked it!" Nev said.

"But...no....!" Mal said, sounding like he was going to cry.

"What guys?" I asked, "What?"

I started heading up the stairs.

"Oh....Brian!" I heard Mal say, sounding like a girl who knows I'm leaving and not coming back.

Ty and Chris were standing in the room I'd never been in because Mal said it was full of rubbish. I went in, Mal, trying to stop me. I walked in to a room of heartbreak.

I stood, speechless in the middle. If I'd walked into my girlfriend's house and seen her seeing to all of my other team-mates at the same time (which had happened once when I was at Town) I wouldn't have felt more betrayed.

It was a shrine to Stevie.

The shrine to me Mal had in his living room (a giant sized photo of me, a photo of me and him at that competition he'd won) looked like a goal scored in training compared to the Cup Final hat-trick of a shrine that he'd done for Stevie. There were hundreds of photos, headlines and adverts with Stevie in.

I did the only thing a self-respecting pro-footballer could do: I fainted.

Chapter 51

"Do you really love me, Mal?"

"Course I do," Mal said, "Think about what I've done for you!"

"But would you have done even more for Stevie?"

He nodded, "He may well have got my bedroom and I'd have taken Nev's," he told me.

At least he was being honest. I can't say it didn't hurt but I had to play the bigger man. I was prepared to accept that some people would pick the wrong guy to be their hero.

After I managed to stop crying we worked on my plan.

"Where do you want to meet?" Chris asked.

I thought long and hard about this. I wanted it to be somewhere that meant something. A place where Will could write a great ending.

"How about Wembley?" I said to all the faces leaning in.

"Say what?" Ty asked.

Everyone was looking at me blankly.

"Brian," Chris told me, "You want to meet in an hour. Even we couldn't get to Wembley by then and we already know about it, let alone everyone else."

"Oh."

"We've got to make it easy for them to get there," Ty said.

I thought about where would be the best place for me to finally sort out things for Stevie. I couldn't believe my luck when I named the place and Chris said his sister had keys to it because she worked there. It was like fate or even destiny.

Whichever is better.

With that sorted, I gave a pep talk like I'd heard the Gaffer do so many times. A lot of it focused on how we were going to get people to stay once they got there. We had to make sure that the murderer, whoever it was, couldn't just walk out once they realised we'd set a trap. Once I'd inspired them, I sent them off, feeling I'd done a really great job.

"What the f*ck is he talking about?" Ty asked Chris as they left. "Sometimes, he is one stupid son of a gun. I love the guy, and somehow he always lucks through, but j*sus, what do we have to do?"

"I think," Chris said, "He wants us bring along some of our guys, to make sure people don't try to bail."

"Yeah, that makes sense," Ty nodded, "I can kind of see how he tried to say that. But what was all that about corners? That shit's got nothing to do with what we're up to!"

Pleased they'd got my message I got to work with Nev. I wanted to look great for my big moment and Nev had agreed to help style me.

"We really have to go," Mal said, half an hour later "we might be late!"

"Calm down, Dad," Nev replied "I'll take Brian on my scooter? Is that ok, Bri? It'll only take five more minutes."

"But there's only room for two on the scooter," Mal shouted back.

"You get a taxi," Nev said, "We'll meet you there."

Once I was happy with my hair, I put on Tony's suit, borrowed a shirt from Malcolm, and joined Nev who had got the scooter ready. On my way out I noticed Nev had forgotten all the photos and documents I'd gathered that we needed!

"Nev, you forgot this!"

"Shit, sorry," he said, "It's the rush."

Nev sped off. We had five minutes. Chris and Ty had texted saying that they had secured the place and everything was good. Which was great to know. I knew I really had to get those guys trials with some good clubs in the close season to say thanks.

Thinking of agents, I remembered Rico. Getting my phone out with Nev going so fast wasn't easy, but I managed. No answer. Checking the streets to see where I was, I couldn't believe what I saw!

"Nev! This is the wrong way!"

"What?" Nev said?

"Pull over! I screamed, "Pull over."

We'd been going for five minutes in the wrong direction! What was he doing?

"I'm sorry, Bri," he said, "I'm sorry!"

Nev had thought a place near the United ground was where I had meant! I couldn't believe it.

Late for my own…well, I didn't know what you called it, but I was late for it all the same!

Nev span around started zipping through the streets. We were making good progress now. Almost there. We turned a corner and I could see the place. Outside I saw Blake's silver car, what had to be Repinov's SUV with the number-plate said REP 1, Lyle's Jaguar and even Miss Bewley's nice little Golf.

"Shit!" Nev shouted.

Nev pulled a sharp left and darted off the road down a side-street.

"What the sh*t are you doing?" I shouted.

326

"Police!" he screamed, as he carried on pressing the accelerator hard, "they saw us!"

I couldn't believe it!

I didn't want to get arrested, but having been so close I didn't want to speed away either! I tried to turn around to see if we were being followed.

"Nev!" I shouted, "Nev, we have to stop. We can't go too far," I shouted over the engine.

"There!" he shouted, pointing at the mirror, "They're after us!"

He turned a quick right, then left. Desperately turning to see who was following us I almost fell off the scooter. My heart was thumping and my brain was going crazy!

My phone started ringing as we pulled out onto a main carriageway. It was Rico!

"Nev," I shouted, "Nev, if we've lost them, pull over!"

Chapter 52

"Rico!" I said.

"Brian," he said, sounding irritated, "Where are you?"

"I'm outside the City Hotel! On my way to..."

"I'm inside the City Hotel," he interrupted, "Yvonne's about to finish her audition...."

He mentioned a big TV show but I wasn't listening. If Yvonne was there, where were Will, May and Mr Lewis? Were they at the meeting I'd set-up?

Checking my watch I knew I was now really late. We'd lost the police, well I couldn't see any, and I knew I had to get to the meeting. We were about five minutes away but I also needed Yvonne there because I knew she was involved.

"Rico come outside. Now!"

"I've got to wait for her!"

"This is important, mate," I told him, "It'll take a minute. Max."

The moment he came out onto the street I started telling him everything I knew about Yvonne.

"Brian, you're lying," he said, though his voice wavered, "You're just trying to stop us calling the police."

"No," I told him, "Nev show him."

From his lawyer's briefcase we got out some of Blake's photos and the GPS records.

"It's her," Rico said, shocked, examining the photo closely, "And May, with Stevie, and what about these cars? And what's this light?"

He was pointing at a small light behind the 4x4. We didn't have time to explain everything. I just needed his help with Yvonne and I told him about the meeting.

"Rico, I'm already late, I can't have it falling apart because I'm not there."

"I get it, Bri, you can count on me. Remember that, if this all works out."

I nodded, knowing that if Rico was trying to smooth-talk me it was because he thought I was going to win and that soon I'd be playing football. It felt great.

What was also great was that in hardly any time at all, Rico had Yvonne in his car and he'd agreed to follow me.

Rico pulled out of the City Hotel car park and we followed them to the meeting place. When they pulled up I could see Yvonne having a go at Rico. Asking why he'd stopped. Then she saw me. She freaked.

"Brian, what the f*ck is going on?" Yvonne shouted, "I need to be with my Dad!"

"Your Dad's in there," I told her.

"In where?"

"In the…" I never got to finish my sentence.

I heard Rico shout my name. I spun. I was hit. The punch knocked me into Rico's car, but not to the floor, which was a blessing.

If I'd gone down I would have had no chance. Using the car I pushed myself up and towards my attacker, smothering his second punch. It still a hurt, a blow to my already broken rib, but it didn't finish me. I'm Brian Parr. I screamed and pushed back against him.

Gaining some distance. I recognised him. One of Ryan Prince's men. Ryan was behind him. "What sort of f*ck up is late for something he arranged himself?" Ryan spat.

"I'm being fashionable," I told him.

The other guy lunged at me, I parried and moved away. Looking around I could see four of them. Even if Nev and Rico had stepped in I didn't fancy my chances. Rico would never put his pristine face in danger and Nev couldn't harm a fly. Not because he was g*y but because he was weak and scrawny because he'd never played football.

They had me surrounded and started pressing in on me. I found myself trapped against Nev's bike, with nowhere to turn. Ryan pushed through his goons. I could hear Nev, breathing hard behind me. I didn't know how to signal 'start your engine and use your scooter as a deadly weapon' so I just waved my hand a lot trying to get him to understand what I wanted. As I did I felt the spare helmet.

Just as Ryan was about to throw a punch he looked at Nev, "You...?"

It was all the hesitation I needed. I grabbed the helmet by the bit that goes round the cheek and swung it as hard as I could into the side of Ryan's head.

He went down. I went mental. Smashing away with the helmet. Screaming and shouting as I hit everything I could. They got a couple of kicks in, which hurt, but I'll say it again: I'm Brian Parr. And the most important meeting of my life was happening metres away and I was late.

"Brian," Nev said, when they were all on the floor.

I went over to Ryan and dragged him up.

Rico came over to help. I had to get inside, with Ryan, but I couldn't just leave his guys.

"Rico, we need to get these d*cks somewhere safe, somewhere they won't try and punch me again."

"Like where?" he asked.

I looked over to the car Yvonne was in.

Fuming at me because she was locked inside.

Chapter 53

I hadn't heard what was said when Brian called Mr Lewis, all I knew was Brian wanted to do a deal. Him for me. I knew instantly that there was no way that that was what Brian was planning on doing. So did Mr Lewis, but he was obviously someone who didn't like being beaten. I could tell as soon as he finished chatting to Brian on the phone that he couldn't resist the chance to get his revenge rather than fly away to the safety of Spain.

Sotis and Nicos were in the car with us as we bombed back into town.

"Do you think the police are there?" May asked.

"I doubt it. He thinks the police are out to arrest him," her Dad replied.

"You sure?" May asked.

"Parr's planning something, but he's not going to the fuzz. Sotis, call the guy you told to wait outside the place Parr told us to meet. See what's going on."

As Sotis weaved through the city traffic and talked in Greek on the phone I realized I had to be ready to seize the moment if Brian was planning something to get me. I tried to loosen the belt around my wrists and shake away my tiredness.

"He says there's nothing weird at the moment," Sotis said, "Just after he arrived a woman came in and opened the place, apart from that...nothing."

We pulled up in a square. Across the road was a garish sign, 'Dazzlers'. A nightclub that looked worn and sad in the daylight. And probably at night too. The guy on the door came over. From what I could tell, since he'd spoken to Sotis on the phone, a couple of people had gone inside. It sounded very much like Miss Bewley and Dr Malone.

What was Brian up to?

Sotis went through the double-doors first, then May, then Nicos and me, with Mr Lewis at the back. As the door shut I heard Nicos c*ck his gun. Sweat was pouring off my forehead.

There was a smell of stale beer and it had carpets - never a good sign for a nightclub. But the building itself was actually quite ornate and as

331

we walked the darkened corridor I realised Dazzlers had once been a theatre I used to love; mostly because it was in the round. The corridor we were in came out into the auditorium, on the same level as the stage. Despite the apparent sh*tness of the venue, Brian had been very clever.

The old stage - now the dance-floor - was surrounded by tiers of seating which meant as we emerged from the tunnel it was like walking into a coliseum. We were flanked by walls but no longer under a ceiling: the perfect place to be ambushed from above.

Sotis turned round just before it happened. Like a trapped animal he must have realised how vulnerable we were. In a flash we were surrounded and our way was blocked.

Our attackers swept down the aisle. Sotis tried to fight but was overwhelmed in an instant. Before Mr Lewis had raised his gun, he had three aimed at him.

"Do what they say," Mr Lewis told Sotis and Nicos who were still struggling.

One of the guys, who I later found out was Ty, came up and led me away. Nicos, Sotis and Mr Lewis had their hands tied and were made to sit on the front row. Miss Bewley was sat opposite them, looking nervous. Dr Malone was next to her.

I was given a drink and some food. There was still about twenty minutes left before the agreed time. Chris got everyone back in position. Apparently they'd been let in the back entrance, which was why Sotis' guy had missed them, and they had that covered as well. The only way anyone could come in was the same way we had. Brian and these guys seemed to have everything covered.

As I finally made it onto the dance-floor of Dazzlers, a place I'd had my fair share of WAG-tastic success in the past, I looked around at all the faces watching me. It was perfect. I'd seen films where this happened and the main person got to be amazing and walk around and tell people who'd not done it and why and who had done it and why and then everyone thought they were amazing.

"Oh, finally, d*ck-f*ck Parr's here," the Gaffer said, the first person to see me.

"What is this, Parr? Being late for your own meeting, you must be sh*tting me or something," Repinov said.

Everyone seemed annoyed. Or so I thought until I saw Miss Bewley who gave me a nice smile and Will who looked tired but ok. Etienne was next to them. He waved, but when he saw Ryan Prince behind me his face changed completely.

"I know, Etienne," I said, "Bleached hair can look really bad sometimes, can't it?"

Chris and Ty came and took Ryan off me. Yvonne went over to Mr Lewis who was looking at me as if I was a piece of sh*t.

"Why are we here, Bri?" Shags asked, "Why did you choose Dazzlers? The sh*ttest club in town?"

"Well, mate, apart from the fact it was the safest place to get a lot of people together who might not like me, this was the place where..." I said, remembering, "...over a few beers, Stevie persuaded me to join United...so it's right that we..."

"That was f*cking me!" Shags interrupted, "I persuaded you. Stevie thought you should stay with your home-town club... "

"No way," I said, "It was Stevie and me. That's why we're here....surely..."

333

Shags shook his head. Repinov coughed. I felt stupid and everyone was looking at me.

"So," I said, "What's been going on?"

"We've been doing what you wanted us to do, you f*cking idiot!" Mr Lewis shouted angrily. "Although how you managed to get us all here, when we all have working brains and you don't, I'll never know!"

"It's about being a star in a great team," I replied, "Isn't it, Shags?"

"F*ck off, Brian," he agreed.

"Thanks Chris and Ty, you've been like really good full-backs, even wingers today! And thanks to all your mates too," I paused, clocking what Mr Lewis had said, "What do you mean you've been doing what I got you here to do?" I asked.

"You wanted us here to sort out who the killer is," Mr Lewis said, "So we've f*cking done it."

"What?" I said.

"You what?" shouted Yvonne even louder, "You f*cking told us it was..."

"...me?" Mr Lewis finished, "Yeah, I said that. But that was because you wanted to hear it."

"What the f*ck?" Yvonne screamed, "You've used that to get me and May to trust you!"

"What the f*ck?" I shouted even louder, "What do you mean you've sorted it out! How? I wanted to work it out!"

I stamped my feet. Miss Bewley winced.

"Brian, Brian," Repinov said trying to calm me down, "I know you want to be like Angela Lansbury, it's natural. But the thing is, we are all totally bored and shit of you ruining our lives and parties so we thought we'd sort it out for you!"

My mind was racing, "What? You mean you know the murderer?"

Repinov nodded, "We all totally got what you were doing and could, see that your friends weren't going to let us leave, so we decided to get this shit together. One by one I got people to say what they knew and well, like, we totally worked out who it was."

"Is the person in here?"

He nodded again.

"Are you sure? Because this is a murder, people will lie about it you know? A few times I've left people thinking they were innocent and then," I was talking quickly, trying to get out all my thinking at once, "...when I got home and told Mal, Nev and Will, I realised they were lying. Like Shags! Shags, you lied to me!"

"What? I f*cking didn't!" he protested, getting to his feet.

"You did, the night Stevie left, you did follow him. I've seen the photo but you told me you hadn't! And I've seen a list of yours which had Tony, Stevie and me on it...and think about it, two of them are dead and I went to jail! So maybe it was you, Shags? I know you've got more bonus money with me and Stevie not around, is that why you did it? And then maybe you killed Tony once he wasn't your agent anymore, or because he knew?"

Was Ruby here? I'd asked Chris to let her know. I spun round; "Ruby, see, it might be Shags! Can I have my money now?"

"No, Brian," she said, "Shags came to see Sian and I after you accused him. He wasn't trying to harm Stevie or Tony or you. He was trying to save you."

"Save?" I asked, "What the..."

"Tony, committed suicide," Shags said, "The coroner verified it. I was trying to save him, and Stevie."

"What the f*ck are you talking about?"

"F.A.S. Brian," Shags said to me.

"Footballers A*s Shagging?" I said, looking around for people to laugh with.

"No, 'Footballers Against Suicide'. My charity."

"What are you talking about?"

"Bri, I set up a charity after my cousin killed himself when he got released by City? Remember? You're one of the f*cking patrons!" Shags said, "It's what I do in my spare time. I try and help people in football who are thinking of hurting themselves. Back in August Stevie was displaying all the signs, as was Tony because of his money problems, so I had them on my list to help."

"So why am I on that list?"

"I put you on when you get arrested. A lot of remand prisoners try to kill themselves. And with you being famous, I knew it was going to be tough. When you got really low inside, we made sure you were on a proper suicide watch."

"Ok, so why didn't you tell me I was on your list? Why didn't you tell Tony and Stevie about it?"

"I did tell them! But they didn't listen and how could I tell you? United had banned me from contacting you directly while you were inside!"

I looked around, trying to work it out. Everyone else seemed to believe him. But as I've said before, I wouldn't have been a good footballer if I couldn't deal with messing up in front of loads and loads of people. I mean some of the most childish and stupid things I've ever done have been on the pitch with millions of people watching so of course I could mess up in front of about thirty people and carry on, "So why did you lie to me, mate, once I was out?"

"I didn't want to get drawn into your madness and jeopardize anything before the World Cup. I thought if I just kept telling you to f*ck off you'd finally give up. It's what you used to do."

A few people agreed with him. I wasn't having that!

"Ok, ok, so Shags lied to me, not about how much he killed people, but about how nice he is, but....but how do you know everyone else is telling the truth? If the murderer is here, he'd lie..."

"Excuse me, Brian," May said, "The murderer could be a woman you know; that's s*xist of you."

Now one of the things I once liked about May was how classy she was with all her fairness for women stuff. Right then though, all she did was annoy me. So I turned my attention to her.

"Well, was it you or Yvonne? We have photos of you two leading Stevie away from the car crash! Did you take him back to mine and kill him?"

"No, they didn't," Mr Lewis said.

"He's right," the Gaffer agreed.

"Wasn't them," Blake nodded.

Mal was shaking his head.

"What!" I said, bursting my top, "What is this! Why do you all know?" It felt like when I was injured and United were doing really well and winning without me, "This is my thing! My moment! Will's writing a book about this! How's the ending going to look if I don't solve it and everyone else does? I'm going to look f*cking stupid!"

"Look, Brian," Blake said, "Face up to it, we've sorted it...we know who did it."

"You know, or you think you know? Because if you were sure, wouldn't you have called the police? Chris and Ty would let you do that if you had found the killer..."

"The fuzz? That's not something all of us would want, actually, Brian," Mr Lewis said, "Look, I'm not sitting around here all f*cking day, let's just tell him."

"No! I want to work it out!" I pleaded.

"But..." someone started.

"Let me do it...come on it won't take long/ I know most of it anyway!"

"Brian," Shags said, "I've got a kit launch, followed by dinner..."

Lots of other people started making excuses.

"F*cking shut-up! I don't have plans!! I lost everything! The least you can do is give me a bit of time to try and work it out!"

Chapter 54

Everyone was watching. I took a breath. It felt like I was about to take a penalty.

"Ok," I said, turning to Repinov, "So in your murder shows, if I was like James Bond, I'd walk around being clever in front of you for a while, wouldn't I?"

"Hurry up, d*ck," someone said, though I didn't catch who.

Repinov nodded, then gestured for me to begin.

I put my hands behind my back because I thought that would look good and I began to walk, slowly but intelligently, in a circle. Looking at all the faces. One of them was the murderer!

"So, we know that a lot of people were on the scene after Stevie left his house. May who'd chased him, Ryan Prince who wanted to jump him and Blake who was taking photos...but after the crash, we know

338

that Yvonne and May left with Stevie. Right?"

"Right," said almost everybody – it felt like school, with the voices sounding just as bored as I always had in class.

"Now, we know from the GPS that Yvonne then drove home. But she went via May's house. So May must have driven her car back, to get it away from the crash site, and then, maybe she got in the car with Yvonne, maybe she didn't...?"

I looked at the seats, Blake was about to speak, as was Yvonne. I put my finger up to stop them. This was my moment. How could I find out? It had been 7 in the morning. Yvonne drove home. What happened at my house at about 7.30?

"Etienne, did you see Yvonne arrive that morning?"

"I did," he said.

"Get in!" I said before remembering I had to look clever, "Yeeeeesssssss! Was May with her?"

"She was."

"Ok, and did you see Stevie in the car? Who may have been hung-over and a bit injured?"

"I didn't."

"You sure, where did you see them from?"

"I was washing up the breakfast bowls."

"So you were looking out of the kitchen window and Yvonne would have parked outside the front door even though she knew not to."

"F*ck off, Brian, that was always a stupid rule."

"Cars do not like to be left out in the daylight for too long, Yvonne, bird sh*t is a nightmare!" I shouted at her, "Ok, ok, let's focus. So what that means is that they must have dropped Stevie off somewhere."

I spun round and looked at Mr Lewis. He rolled his eyes and I saw

339

him call me a c*nt to Sotis.

"Now, obviously, that was probably with Mr Lewis, being a notorious drug-dealer and kidnapping-man. Seeing as one of his daughters has only just said she thought he had killed Stevie, perhaps it's safe to say that he then took over looking after Stevie?"

"'Safe to say'? You sound like a prize kn*b, mate," Shags said.

"Mr Lewis said he only admitted killing Stevie for his rep, so what we need to know is what happened next!"

"We already f*cking know!" Mr Lewis shouted, "I met them on the road in between May's and Yvonne's house and took him before...."

"Let him speak!" Mr Repinov shouted, "This man was your country's captain and it all got stolen and shit from him, so OMG give him a chance..."

I couldn't believe Repinov had been so nice to me. Again.

"Ok," I said, "Well, Stevie was injured, so..." I looked at Miss Bewley, "Miss Bewley, did you have any luck finding out whether Dr Malone was naughty in the hospital?"

"'Naughty in the hospital'. F*cking hell," said the Gaffer.

"I didn't find anything about that night, sorry Brian," she told me.

I looked at the Doctor. He looked shifty. Was he involved? Miss Bewley couldn't prove it, but could I? What else could I remember from the night Will and I had burst into his house? I thought loads. Going back his living room.

"The car-park fob!" I shouted happily at him, "The f*cking car-park fob! You work for Mr Lewis! And the night after the crash you went to help Stevie at Mr Lewis' flat!" I said as I turned round to Mr Lewis.

"You're right," Mr Lewis agreed, "But what's this sh*t about a car-park fob?"

"When I was the Doctor's house I saw a car-park fob on his key ring when I was looking for a weapon. But when I followed him at work he parked outside, and at his house he parked outside, and at the apartment he did his drug stuff from he parked outside too. So what does he need a car-park fob for? Well, you've got an underground car park at your place! You see?"

I was really, really happy with that. Mal looked pleased for me, so did Will.

"Ok, so Doctor, you helped Stevie after the crash?"

He nodded.

"But what did you do then?"

I thought through the rest of what I knew. Nicos had said he'd gone to my house with Sotis. The only other thing that came to mind was the camera and the fact he'd had to take it to a garage unit.

"Ok, ok," I said, "So, you didn't want anyone to know about Stevie, did you Mr Lewis? So you took him to one of your garage-units."

"How d'you...?"

"And....and....you'd told people that you were going to bring Stevie and me down..." then I realised what his plan had been, "...but you weren't going to kill us, you were going to expose us in the press. Which was why you needed the camera from my car! Because it had pictures of May and me on...and you knew about Stevie's drugs!"

"How do you know that?" he shouted.

"Nicos told me," I shrugged, before I realised how bad that might be for him.

"No!" Nicos shouted.

"What the f*ck?" Sotis screamed, launching himself at Nicos.

While Ty and Chris stopped the fighting, I was thinking.

Everything pointed to Mr Lewis having Stevie. Everything led back to him.

I knew from the GPS that Yvonne had gone to Mr Lewis' penthouse during that evening, at the same time I was at home with Dr Malone. I knew that the next night, after the match, Nicos had stolen my car because Mr Lewis had made him. And he'd left the phone for me because he knew Mr Lewis had a plan.

Everyone else, like the Gaffer and Blake had alibis. It all pointed to Mr Lewis, so why did everyone in the room think it wasn't him? What was I missing?

"Brian?" Shags said, "Are you ok? You look like you're trying to push a sh*t out."

"I'm thinking."

I kept on thinking. Hard. People were laughing at me, but I was thinking too hard to care. But I could tell that Will, Mal, Miss Bewley and Ruby were backing me up.

Eventually, I'd thought so hard that I couldn't think of anything else.

"Look, it has to be Mr Lewis!" I said, "He had Stevie, he's nasty and everyone else had alibis!"

"So have I," Mr Lewis said.

"What?"

"I thought you didn't want me to tell you, Brian," he taunted.

I didn't. But I had to know. I nodded.

"We had Stevie. He was safe and not too badly hurt, as Dr Malone will testify," Mr Lewis began, "When we got him, he was angry, he was going on about you and May and this Kiki....so I decided to ruin the both of you, gut your careers, get you to pay for what you were doing to my girls."

342

"How?"

"The new United regime had gone public on not allowing players to act like footballers. If I could show the world what you and Stevie were up to, they'd have to get rid of you."

"You bl*ody tw*t."

"The publicity of Stevie being missing was playing into our hands. I decided to keep him for a day and then I could expose him as being on a drugs binge in front of the whole world. Once Nicos had the pictures of you from your car everything was ready, then disaster struck. Someone took Stevie from the garage."

"B*llocks!" I shouted.

"It's true."

"Who says?"

"Sotis, the Dr..."

"They're just lying to protect you!" I said, appealing to people, "Who else is your alibi? Anyone who doesn't work for you?

"Well, yes, Greg."

I turned to Greg.

"I didn't know Mr Lewis knew about me and what I was doing," Greg began, "...but after Stevie had been taken, he got that guy there," he said pointing to Sotis, "to bring me in. I spent all evening with them, going over tapes I'd made and my CCTV to work out where Stevie might be and who might have taken him. We did it at Tone's place, in the Fan Attic, he was there all night."

"So you see, Parr, it wasn't me," Mr Lewis said with a horrible smile.

I was back in the centre of the dance-floor. I slowly turned around. All of these faces, who'd taken up my time for so long when all I'd wanted to be doing was banging goals in the ball sack! And still no answer!

"Go on, then, who is it?"

"Brian," Repinov said, "It's coolio, relax. In a way you solved it by bringing us all together."

"Who...was...it?" I asked.

"Ryan Prince," he said.

"What the..." shouted Ryan, still nursing his head.

"You were there at the crash. Stevie owed you thousands," Mr Lewis said, "You must have waited, and followed Stevie back to mine."

"I saw you drive off," Blake added, "But not how far."

"I didn't...it wasn't..." Ryan protested.

"If Stevie was taken from Mr Lewis," I said wanting to get in on the act, and turning on Ryan, "I can't think of anyone else who could have done it. You've got guys working for you, getting into a garage would have been easy!"

"No!" Ryan said.

"And then you must have done it in my house for an alibi!" I shouted, "You b*stard!"

"But how the f*ck did I get in?" he asked, "And anyway, I do have an alibi! This is a f*cking stitch-up, you w*nkers!"

"WTF who's your alibi?" Repinov asked him.

"Kiki. I spent the day with her!"

"Kiki?" I shouted, expecting her to answer.

I looked around the seats. I'd forgotten her!

"Sh*t," I said, "My bad."

"Ok, ok," Repinov said, "Who can, like, contact her?"

Ruby said she could because they were in talks about the flat.

"If you're lying," Mr Lewis told Ryan, "It's you..."

It took about ten minutes for Ruby to get back to us. His alibi checked out.

Chapter 55

"You all got it wrong!" I said, trying not to sound pleased.

"We didn't," Blake said.

"You must have done!" I said.

"Ask your writer friend," he replied, "he agreed with us. Stevie wasn't killed by anyone in here when we talked it through."

"Will?" I asked.

"Brian, we went over things, it all made sense," Will told me, "We didn't miss anything on anyone, the only person it could have been was Ryan."

"So what now?" I asked.

"It must have been one of you who arrived late!" Shags said.

"Not Yvonne," Mr Lewis said, "She's vouched for."

"And Rico was with me," the Gaffer said.

"Oh yeah, then I suppose it's Nev," I said, nearly laughing at how ridiculous it sounded, "Nev who hates football and rides around on his scooter, who doesn't know any of you..."

Behind me I heard what sounded like someone falling down but I didn't turn around as I thought it was someone laughing at my joke.

"No, Neville!" Malcolm shouted.

I turned. Nev had got a gun from one of Ty's mates. He was staggering backwards.

"Nev! Do you know who it is?" I asked, "We don't need to kill them, you should know that from your law work, we just need to get them."

"F*cking h*ll," Nev said, "You're so stupid. At least my Dad chose the right player to like the most."

"What?" I said, not getting it.

He turned to Lyle, pointed the gun at him, "Sorry you won't get any money from going to court again and I guess this means I won't be getting that contract?"

"What are you talking about?" Lyle said, all worked up.

Then, just like that, Nev fired the gun. At me.

Yvonne and May screamed! People started running.

The gun-shot was ringing in my ears.

But, as you can tell from the fact I'm telling you this – or telling Will to type about me telling you this – he missed. I mean he always wanted to be a lawyer, so when had he ever shot a gun before?

In the middle of all the panic I got myself to my feet and saw Nev and Lyle running up the stairs.

I ran after them, sprinting with all my might. The hits I'd taken from Ryan's men were still sore but I wasn't letting him get away. Behind me I could hear Mal spluttering for breath and I could hear someone else following too, muttering "OMG!" as they ran. Repinov!

So much was going through my head. Not in any particular order, just thoughts and ideas mounting up as the case against Nev gathered momentum.

That night by the crash scene. The light that no-one had identified in the photographs: Nev's scooter.

The big shrine to Stevie, the heartbreakingly smaller one to me. When had Nev ever been shown that amount of love by Mal?

Mal's driving ban. Recently spent more time together than ever before. Nev had finally got a true taste of what United had stolen from him – a Dad he really got along with, as long as football wasn't around.

The cost of following United. The piles of match tickets from all over Europe weren't going to help Nev. He'd saved nothing to help Nev study to be a lawyer.

Football had taken away his Dad, split up his family and it looked like it was going to stop him living his dream. Which is why we think, now that we have most of the facts, that Nev started to plan how he might get his payback on the people who were living the dream at his expense.

We think Nev had been planning things for about six months.

When Nev was living with Greg he started to follow his step-dad's work and began to learn Stevie's habits. He knew Stevie was heading for a fall. He decided to use it to his advantage

When we'd walked onto the dance-floor in Dazzlers, Etienne hadn't been looking at Ryan Prince like I'd thought. He wasn't shocked by Ryan's bad hair, in fact he'd recognised Nev. The two of them had met in a bar the summer before and spent a night together. After which one of the sets of keys to our house had gone missing. Which meant now Nev had a way to get at me too.

In Nev's room we also found keys to Stevie and May's house and the flat Stevie shared with Kiki – we don't know how he got them.

When Ryan had recognised Nev outside Dazzlers, it was because one night Nev had played in a poker game with Stevie. Stevie was hammered and Nev kept on telling him his luck would change and he should keep playing. Ryan said it was that night which pushed Stevie's credit over the limit and after that he never got out of debt.

347

The night of Stevie's crash, with so many people watching Stevie because his life was so out-of-control, it seems that Nev hung back. He followed the injured Stevie as he was passed from Yvonne and May to Sotis and Mr Lewis. He watched as they put Stevie in the garage and took his chance.

Dr Malone and Nicos have both said that as they pulled up to the garage they saw a scooter parked nearby. When Stevie was locked up, but alone, Nev took his chance. Did he tell Stevie he was rescuing him? And that my house was the safest place to go so Mr Lewis couldn't find him? We don't know.

Dressed as someone foreign (as we saw on Roy's video) he got Stevie down into the basement and then...well, we know what happened then. He'd got rid of the player he hated the most and ruined the player he hated the second most.

There was no way that Nev knew I would become friends with Mal and we'd rope him into helping me. But it probably worked in his favour. He got to keep an eye on me and try to lead me away from the truth. Which, up until the very last moment, had worked; but even trying to get me lost on the way to the meeting hadn't saved him.

As I chased after Nev and Lyle that day I obviously didn't know everything. Some was filled in later, with help from Lyle, Greg and Mal.

"Nev!" I shouted, as I burst out of the fire exit about 10 metres behind them.

Nev was holding Lyle by the arm but Lyle was moving pretty quickly – even though he's been telling people he only tried to escape because Nev forced him.

He turned. Unlike me, Nev wasn't used to running at speed and doing something else at the same time. I could dribble a football, wave at fans, trip someone up, and swear at someone all at the same time as I was sprinting. As he span round he lost his footing on a pothole. He stumbled. I charged on. He got round the corner, down a back alley. He was still struggling to stay up straight. By that time I was virtually upon him.

"Nooo!" he shouted, as I jumped like a rugby player and tackled him to the ground.

He hit the ground with a scream. I got up, we were between two bins. Repinov, who'd kept a good pace for someone small and podgy, steamed in and made sure Lyle couldn't get away. Mal was right behind him.

"Nev! What are you doing?" Mal screamed, looking horrified, "You almost killed Brian."

"It was him" Lyle said, "All him!"

Nev backed against the wall. He seemed to remember he had a gun and aimed it at us, forcing us back.

"Nev, relax, we can work this out!"

"Not now you know it was me!"

"OMG, it really was him!" Repinov said, shocked.

"No!" Mal shouted, "Nev! You couldn't have hurt Stevie! Not Stevie!"

"I did. I did, Dad because of you. "

Mal rushed him, "You stupid, nasty, f*cking…boy!"

Mal was drowned out by a gunshot. This time Nev hit. Mal was thrown back against the wall.

"WTF! OMG!"

"Nev!" I shouted, "What have you done?"

"It's his fault!" he panted, straightening his glasses, "I took it out on

Stevie and you. Thinking you'd conned him, but it's his fault really!"

Repinov pushed Lyle against the wall to stop him running and went over to Mal.

"He's alive, just..." Repinov said, getting out his phone and calling 999.

"Nev, give me the gun," I said,

"F*ck you! F*ck you! I can't believe you've beaten me. You're f*cking stupid! I was so close, I got you off, I made Lyle loads of money, I was finally going to get what I wanted and start working and then he..." Nev screamed, rocking up on his feet, tears running down his face, "...he had to keep supporting you? Instead of me! All my life it's been the stupid men kicking that f*cking ball who he's cared about, not me!"

"You can't blame him for liking football! Football's brilliant!"

"It ruined everything! He put everything into United and Stevie..."

"And me!" I protested.

"...and I got nothing. That's why I have nothing. No family, no prospects, no..."

"Nev, please, calm down. Look, that's not true, you have all that..."

"Brian," he said, pointing the gun at me, "You know how you felt when you went to jail? Well, imagine being there but knowing you had done the murder and everyone knew?"

"That would be bad."

"Well, that's the only thing I've got to look forward too."

"Nev, come on..."

He leant back against the wall.

"Look, like, you seriously did all this?" Repinov said, from where he was holding Mal, "you killed one of my players, ruined another and shot your own Dad, because you were ignored as a kid?"

"Shut-up! Shut-up!" Nev sobbed.

He was crying now. I wanted to get the gun from him as soon as possible.

"We were close," Nev turned to Lyle.

"We! I don't know what you're talking about!"

"Don't lie," Nev said, getting angry again, wiping away his tears.

That was my moment. Nev was looking directly at Lyle. He didn't hear me plant my left foot down before I smashed my right foot into his jaw like I was about to score a World Cup winning penalty.

He flew back against the wall, hitting his head again. The gun hit the floor. I grabbed it. I checked he was ok. He was out cold.

I looked at Lyle, who squirmed under my stare, "Right, you f*cking lawyer tw*t," I shouted, standing over him, "You better tell me what Nev was on about."

I let him get his breath back. He argued a bit more and I had to use a bit of force to get him to talk. I won't go into any more details because even though he's in jail now, he's suing me for hurting him.

"Ok, ok, I interviewed him for a job."

"What job? A murderer's job?"

"No, Brian. That's not a type of job. As a trainee."

"And let me guess, to get the job he had to kill an England international?"

"Brian, this is hurting," he asked, "I've said I'll tell you, just let me speak you f*cking idiot!"

"Ok," I said.

He screamed, "What was that for?" he asked.

I'd twisted his ear really hard for being mean.

351

"Ok, well even though he was the best candidate there were other people with more....credibility behind them. You know, sons and daughters of friends and colleagues..."

"Oh, it's like that is it, the law world?"

"What do you mean?"

"I don't know, I was just...saying, carry on," I told him with another pull of his ear.

"Arrgh, ok, well one night soon after I saw him in a club, I think he'd followed me..."

"A g*y club!"

Lyle nodded, "...and well, he came up to me and said that even though we'd turned him down, he wasn't going to give up. He asked that if he could help us make a huge amount of money and raise our reputation, would we take him on and pay for all his training? Naturally I said 'yes'. Thinking nothing of it."

"When did you next hear from him?"

"The day after Stevie's crash. He was excited, a bit crazy..."

"Well, obviously he was a bit crazy, he killed Stevie!" I said.

"He didn't tell me that. All he said was that he had a way for my company to make a lot of money out of it and for him to become a lawyer."

"How?"

"He said that you were going to be framed for the murder and that I had to get the job of defending you. He said we'd win but wouldn't say how. I went along with it, but as the case went on I began to think I'd made a massive mistake. It looked like we were going to lose right up until he got that tape in my hand during the case. It was only when we were playing the tape in court that I realised it was him on camera with

352

the body, but no-one else noticed. After that I had to go along with what he wanted, if I'd told the police I would have been ruined, so would the firm."

Later, Will and I realised that Nev must have known all about Roy's camera and how he filmed my house. He disguised himself as East European because he knew Repinov and Mr Lewis both had guys from there working for them. He went out onto the drive-way with Stevie's body at the same time he knew I was playing for United. That way he'd have the proof Lyle needed to get me off.

As a back-up, he'd also paid his friend in the police to tamper with evidence so that Lyle would have something to fight about during the trial. In the end, that play hadn't worked, but it didn't matter. The video was enough. Having helped Lyle to such a famous victory, Nev got the job he'd wanted and got Stevie and me out the way.

Standing over Lyle, I heard sirens. It sounded like a lot of police were coming.

Finding out who'd killed Stevie didn't feel very satisfying.

I felt sad more than anything. Nev had obviously done a terrible thing, but he hadn't done it for any cool reasons like being Russian or being a dealer. Or even for any glamorous reasons like because he was jealous of Stevie's new girl, or jealous that Stevie was a really good footballer. He'd done it because he was sad about his chances in life.

Chapter 56

Still, Repinov didn't let me be sad for long. By the time the reporters had arrived he'd offered me a new deal. The ribs are fixed now. I spent the World Cup being annoyed I wasn't there but training hard and now it's pre-season time and I'm enjoying playing with Shags again. And being sworn at by the Gaffer again.

And I'm enjoying being Brian Parr again. Who wouldn't?

Afterword by ghost-writer Will J Robson

That ending is how Brian wanted the book to finish. As a footballer he's been bred to put everything into a match while it's happening. Then once it's over, it's his job to forget about it so he can start focusing on the next match. The fact he still tells me that he should never have been sent off on the night he found Stevie shows it doesn't always work. But as far as this book and the case goes, he feels the final whistle has blown.

Once Nev was arrested, his contract with United was signed and the papers announced he really wasn't guilty, Brian told me that I had the story and he didn't want to do anymore sitting down on my wheeled chair and talking to me when he could be playing football or buying cars. I've lost count of the times I've told Brian how helpful a follow-up interview with him would be. Every time we book it in he either cancels or just doesn't show and now Rico is hassling me to get it finished so Brian can receive his share of the royalties.

As a writer, though, I can't just leave the story immediately after Nev's arrest. I've always been someone who enjoys a good round-up of what happened to characters in a film once the credits roll. Which is why I've done my best to chat to the people involved to piece together what's happened since Brian called them all to the 'Dazzlers'.

I'll start with the people who were arrested that day. Nev and Lyle are awaiting trial for their roles in Stevie's death. Nev for murder, while the charge against Lyle seems to keep changing. The problem is he knows what he's talking about and while the police don't want to let him off with an easy charge they're finding it hard to prove how involved he really was.

Yvonne and May were investigated for withholding evidence but no charges were brought against them. I'm told that is because Brian did a deal with them over custody of the kids and so he didn't press charges but it's all a bit murky.

Mr Lewis and Sotis didn't get so lucky. Last month they both pled guilty to drug-dealing and are in prison for that while awaiting trial for kidnapping. Brian still talks about that escape with a twinkle in his eye, remembering himself as a 'hero'. I'm really hoping that doesn't prejudice his testimony but who can say with Brian. I'll be telling the court what I've written in this book and it should be enough.

Away from the courts and over to United, Repinov and Blake still run the club and to help keep the fans happy they've created a fans forum which includes Mal and Greg. Apparently they go to meetings with the board once a month to talk about football. Mal tells me he enjoys it and from my occasional glances at the back-pages it seems that United are doing better this season, the Gaffer is still in charge and Brian is playing well.

Shags retired from football after the World Cup. He's now running his charities, trying to get Rico to get him work on TV and is also dating Miss Bewley, Brian's prison teacher. Why is she with Shags and not the hero of our tale? Well, to celebrate his new contract, Brian invited her out on a date. If this book was a rom-com they might have ended *up together. Instead Brian apparently started talking about his 'f*ingering' technique after about half an hour and she walked out - ignoring his pleas that his f*ngering chat normally worked. She hasn't spoken to him since, but having volunteered to help FAS, she met Shags and according to the tabloids they've had a few r*mps and things are going well.*

On the home front, I saw Etienne the other day - we play squash - and he says that Brian sees the boys a lot. He's also trying to become part of Carly's life too. When I said that it sounded like Brian has grown up as a father Etienne winced - it seems that the only time Brian really sees the boys, and Carly, is too take them on training sessions.

A few footballers he knows have kids who are already on the books of some clubs and he's desperate to get all three signed up as soon as possible. The kids come back to Etienne absolutely knackered and normally in tears, but Brian says it's the only way to get to the top. He ignores Etienne's pleas to stop using United's first team training program on a three, five and six year old.

As for Brian, I get texts from him now and again. Not about this book, but about ideas for his next one. So far they've ranged from me writing a book about a footballing wizard called Brian Parr-ter to me following his journey into the 'spy system' once he's retired (he's already applied to MI5 and says he watches Spooks and 24 on repeat as preparation for the interview).

He's playing for United, he's been called up for the England squad and tells me he's enjoying being single and d*ting lots of girls.

Has he changed from the experience? No. Have I? Yes. I still hate football, but I don't hate all footballers.

The End

15778203R00200

Printed in Great Britain
by Amazon